Penguin Twentieth-Century Classics

TYPHOON AND OTHER STORIES

Joseph Conrad (originally Józef Teodor Konrad Nałęcz Korzeniowski) was born in the Ukraine in 1857 and grew up under Tsarist autocracy. His parents, ardent Polish patriots, died when he was a child, following their exile for anti-Russian activities, and he came under the protection of his tradition-conscious uncle, Thaddeus Bobrowski, who watched over him for the next twenty-five years. In 1874 Bobrowski gave in to his nephew's passionate desire to go to sea, and Conrad travelled to Marseilles, where he served in French merchant vessels before joining a British ship in 1878 as an apprentice. In 1886 he obtained British nationality and his Master's certificate in the British Merchant Service. Eight years later he left the sea to devote himself to writing, publishing his first novel, *Almayer's Folly*, in 1895. The following year he married Jessie George and eventually settled in Kent, where he produced within fifteen years such modern classics as *Youth*, *Heart of Darkness*, *Lord Jim*, *Typhoon*, *Nostromo*, *The Secret Agent* and *Under Western Eyes*. He continued to write until his death in 1924. Today Conrad is generally regarded as one of the greatest writers of fiction in English – his third language. He once described himself as being concerned 'with the ideal value of things, events and people'; in the Preface to *The Nigger of the 'Narcissus'* he defined his task as 'by the power of the written word . . . before all, to make you *see*.'

Paul Kirschner was born and grew up in New York City. He was educated at Cornell University, City College of New York and Yale Drama School, before taking his M.A. and Ph.D. at the University of London. He is at present a Lecturer in English at Queen Mary & Westfield College, University of London, having taught previously at the University of Geneva and City University of New York. A Vice-Chairman of the Joseph Conrad Society (UK), Dr Kirschner is the author of *Conrad: the Psychologist as Artist* and many articles on Conrad.

JOSEPH CONRAD

TYPHOON

AND OTHER STORIES

EDITED, WITH AN INTRODUCTION, NOTES AND
APPENDIX (*ONE DAY MORE*) BY

PAUL KIRSCHNER

PENGUIN BOOKS

PENGUIN BOOKS

Published by the Penguin Group
27 Wrights Lane, London W8 5TZ, England
Viking Penguin Inc., 40 West 23rd Street, New York, New York 10010, USA
Penguin Books Australia Ltd, Ringwood, Victoria, Australia
Penguin Books Canada Ltd, 2801 John Street, Markham, Ontario, Canada L3R 1B4
Penguin Books (NZ) Ltd, 182–190 Wairau Road, Auckland 10, New Zealand

Penguin Books Ltd, Registered Offices: Harmondsworth, Middlesex, England

First published by William Heinemann 1903
Published in Penguin Books 1990
1 3 5 7 9 10 8 6 4 2

Made and printed in Great Britain by
Richard Clay Ltd, Bungay, Suffolk
Filmset in 9/11 pt Monophoto Photina

CONTENTS

ACKNOWLEDGEMENTS AND EDITORIAL NOTES

I am indebted to Hofstra University's Axinn Library for providing me with a microfilm of the first edition of *Typhoon and Other Stories* containing Conrad's corrections, and the page proofs of the corresponding volume of the Heinemann Collected Edition. I also thank the Beinecke Rare Book and Manuscript Library of Yale University for allowing me to quote from the manuscripts of 'Falk' and 'Amy Foster', Cornell University Library for providing a copy of the manuscript in Ford Madox Ford's hand of part of a dramatization of 'To-morrow', and the Berg Collection, New York Public Library, for a microfilm of the holograph manuscript of 'The Son' ('To-morrow'). I am grateful to the Joseph Conrad Estate for permission to obtain a copy of the last-named manuscript. The Joseph Conrad Society (UK) and the Polish Library in London (POSK) have been consistently helpful.

My particular thanks go to Donald Rude and John Stape for their help in locating manuscripts and for providing me with copies of Conrad's letters to Eugene Saxton and Louise Burleigh, respectively. David Leon Higdon and Owen Knowles have been extremely generous with their time, and Neil Entwistle and Anne Brice of Queen Mary & Westfield College Library have met with alacrity and equanimity my insatiable requests for inter-library loans. Lastly, I owe a special debt to Sam and Helga Harrison and Eliane Tomarkin for their advice and logistical support.

In my text a row of three or four single-spaced dots (...) indicates an editorial deletion. Double-spaced dots (. . .) indicate suspension points in the original text. (Four dots include a full stop.) In keeping with Penguin house style, outer quotation marks are single, not double.

ABBREVIATIONS

I have used the following abbreviations in my text (see Select Bibliography for full details):

Baines: Jocelyn Baines: *Joseph Conrad: A Critical Biography*
BL: Ashley Collection, British Library (London)
CEW: Norman Sherry: *Conrad's Eastern World*
CH: ——: *Conrad: The Critical Heritage*
CLJC: Frederick R. Karl and Laurence Davies, eds.: *The Collected Letters of Joseph Conrad*, Vols. 2 and 3
JCKH: Jessie Conrad: *Joseph Conrad as I Knew Him*
JCLCG: C. T. Watts, ed.: *Joseph Conrad's Letters to Cunninghame Graham*
LBM: William Blackburn, ed.: *Joseph Conrad: Letters to William Blackwood and David S. Meldrum*
LL: G. Jean-Aubry: *Joseph Conrad: Life and Letters*, 2 vols.
Najder: Zdzisław Najder: *Joseph Conrad: A Chronicle*

INTRODUCTION

A few months before his death, Conrad affirmed that each of his short-story volumes had a 'unity of outlook': an 'inner consistency' springing 'from sources profounder than the logic of a deliberate theory'.[1] As far as I know, no critic has tried to define the 'inner consistency' of *Typhoon and Other Stories* and thereby explore the literary interval between the completion of *Lord Jim* in 1900 and the commencement of *Nostromo* in 1902.

For Conrad that interval marked the end of a lingering farewell to his simpler life as a seaman. In October 1898 he had written to Mrs Bontine that his new residence, Pent Farm, was 'near the sea, though not absolutely in sight of it', adding that as soon as he had finished *Lord Jim* he would 'use and abuse everybody's good will, influence, friendship to get back on blue water. I am by no means happy on shore' (*CLJC*, 2, p. 105). But three weeks later he told her son, Cunninghame Graham, that it was already too late: 'This confounded literature has ruined me entirely' (*CLJC*, 2, p. 116); and in February 1899 he jokingly dismissed approaches to Glasgow shipowners on his behalf: 'They will never give a ship to a "chiel" that can write prose – or who is even suspected of such criminal practices' (*CLJC*, 2, p. 155).

The self-deprecation sounds a bit complacent: Conrad speaks of being ruined by literature in the way W. C. Fields might have deplored the harmful effects of alcohol. But the nostalgia was real. In November 1901 he wrote wistfully to his publisher, William Blackwood: 'I can't forget the days when "climate" did not exist for me as long as there was enough air to breathe and not too much wind to keep my feet' (*CLJC*, 2, p. 301). And a year later Olive Garnett wrote in her diary after visiting Pent Farm: 'Conrad spoke very despondingly about his work, said he often had a mind to return to the sea ... but he had gout in the foot and it wd. not be honourable to engage.'[2]

Such feelings must have been sharpened by growing material anxieties: in his letters Conrad speaks constantly not only of agonizing slowness in writing, but of ailments, thoughts of early death and, above all, intricate schemes involving his newly-acquired agent, J. B. Pinker, to pay his ever-mounting debts.[3] While finishing 'To-morrow' he wrote to Pinker that he was 'nearly going mad with worry' (*CLJC*, 2, p. 365), and to David Meldrum, 'I am inutterably [*sic*] weary of all this' (*CLJC*, 2, p. 369). Bound to produce a certain number of words each day or suffer anguish as his family's breadwinner, he must have looked back on his sea life as the very essence of freedom. But despair alternated with optimism. According to Meldrum, Conrad was 'in great spirits'[4] when he arrived in Blackwood's office on 14 July 1900 with the ending of *Lord Jim*, and his mood was still sanguine in September, when he announced, 'I must make a fresh start without further delay' (*CLJC*, 2, p. 289). The 'fresh start' was 'Typhoon', the first story of a volume promised to William Heinemann.

Unity was a prime consideration. 'Falk', Conrad told George Blackwood, was 'specifically intended for Mr. H[einemann]'s book; designed to go with the other [*sic*] of that group' (*CLJC*, 2, p. 375). And in a note for the collector Thomas Wise he emphasized that the separate publication of 'Typhoon' in 1902 'spoiled the set of the 4 stories'.[5]

The 'set', published in 1903, presents a chiaroscuro of sea and land life in an alternating rhythm of hope and despair. 'Typhoon' and 'Falk' both deal with sea life, affirming deep convictions by the moral vindication of the protagonists and ending on a relatively optimistic note, although each with a dose of wryness. The alternating shorter stories, 'Amy Foster' and 'To-morrow', are set firmly on land, not far from where Conrad was living; and their central figure either perishes in despair or is condemned to domestic slavery, mocked by the 'hopeful madness' of a fixed idea. The stories are not printed in the order of their writing (in which I shall discuss them); but their order in the first – and this – edition perhaps better reflects the see-saw mental struggle of a man pining for lost freedom while doggedly mooring himself to an existence that must often have seemed to combine hopeless slavery and hopeful madness.

So much for biographical correlatives of the volume's 'inner consistency'. For the literary figures in the carpet we must look at the individual stories in detail.

Although immediately hailed as a descriptive *tour de force*, 'Typhoon' has generally been read as a simple story, posing only one problem: how could a man so stolidly heroic as MacWhirr in resisting elemental fury be so stupid as to sail his ship into it in the first place? Or, more precisely, how should we finally regard such a man? Recently, two critics have richly harvested the comic elements in the story, but it is not sure whether they have thereby answered or begged the question.[6] It is true that Conrad referred to 'Typhoon' as 'my first attempt to treat a subject jocularly, so to speak' (*CLJC*, 2, p. 304); but the comedy remains the means to an end; to an implied statement of belief which the comic conventions serve to make effective.

'Whom you laugh at,' wrote Turgenev, 'you forgive, and come near loving';[7] and the comic portrayal of MacWhirr helps to win affection for him. On his very first appearance he has to be gently assisted with his unrolled umbrella, which he immediately calls by the Dickensian character-name for troublesome umbrellas – 'the blessed gamp' – thus endearing himself by fallibility while privately saluting the master of comic endearment. (A deconstructionist before his time, Conrad often alludes covertly to his own literary method.) With similar artistic frankness, the very first sentence of the story repudiates Jukes's superficial verdict at the end. Mac-Whirr's face – 'the exact counterpart of his mind' – presents 'no marked characteristics of firmness or stupidity'. Unlike Captain Allistoun in *The Nigger of the 'Narcissus'*, MacWhirr has no ambition to arrive at his destination faster than expected (even delay, when justified, does not disturb him); above all, he has no wish, like Allistoun, to end his days out of sight of the sea; for he is in his element, doing the work he loves. It is his mysterious love of the sea that links this 'perfectly satisfactory son of a petty grocer in Belfast' with the Rodinesque image of 'an immense, potent and invisible hand thrust into the ant-heap of the earth, laying hold of shoulders, knocking heads together, and setting the unconscious faces of the multitude towards inconceivable goals and in undreamt-of directions'. The narrator adds, with ironic bathos, 'His father never relly forgave him for this undutiful stupidity.' (The

5

term 'stupidity' thereby loses all meaning and value, dwindling to a petty grocer's label for a force of nature – one later to be pitted against other natural forces.)

MacWhirr is not only a source of comedy: he is defined and vindicated by it. The celebrated Siamese-flag incident is no isolated comic anecdote but a recurrent motif. To Jukes the flag is a mobile sign, symbolizing all un-English things he distrusts. Mobility in interpreting signs characterizes intelligence: a single unvarying response, like that governing MacWhirr's literal interpretation of Jukes's epithet 'queer', denotes instinct. Later, Jukes again evokes the flag in his fear that the coolies, once recovered, will 'fly at our throats' because the *Nan-Shan* 'isn't a British ship now.... The damn'd Siamese flag.' MacWhirr's remark, 'We are on board, all the same,' lacks jingoistic stridency: it simply states that what matters is not a flag but the men who sail under it.[8] Finally, Jukes's words are echoed by the malicious second mate, whining about maltreatment by MacWhirr to his new-found sycophantic friend: 'I would talk and raise trouble if it wasn't for the damned Siamese flag.' The nationalistic meaning of the flag, apparently invoked to illustrate MacWhirr's obtuseness, is later seen as an alibi for xenophobic jitters, then for downright baseness. MacWhirr's instinctual 'stupidity' is steadily revalued in moral terms.

Jukes's defence of the second engineer, whom MacWhirr threatens to fire for profanity, leads to another seeming display of dense-mindedness, as MacWhirr expostulates 'against the use of images in speech'. But his real provocation is the 'filthy bad temper' he detects behind the words of the second engineer, whom he calls 'a very violent man'. The fact that he himself proceeds to swear comically absolves him of prudery; it does not invalidate the aversion to violence that makes every ship he sails in a 'floating abode of harmony and peace' (with that very camaraderie of which Jukes boasts when writing to his chum). In the event, Jukes is proved right about the second engineer, who, still swearing, is undaunted by the typhoon: the aim is not to demonstrate the infallibility of the captain but rather to dramatize, without pomposity, what MacWhirr personally stands for. He swears against swearing much as he later has to give the second mate who attacks him 'a push'. His resistance to violence includes violence done to language: the improper use of words, or in a current jargon that would no doubt mystify him, the irresponsibility of signifier to signified.[9]

Jukes and MacWhirr change sides over the boatswain, whom MacWhirr regards as a 'first-rate petty officer' but whom Jukes dislikes because 'the men did what they liked with him and he had not an ounce of initiative in his character, which was easy-going and talkative'. It seems paradoxical that MacWhirr should value a garrulous man; but once again the issue lies deeper than words. The boatswain – the immediate overseer of the crew – has 'none of the classical attributes of his rating' and does not impose a sergeant-major's discipline. He is liked by the men, and MacWhirr prefers that kind of authority, even when lax. It is no accident that it is the boatswain who reports the fighting to MacWhirr and later takes the lead in breaking it up, nor that he is characterized in simian terms.[10] Like the captain, he has an unsympathetic wife (who keeps a grocer's shop); and he guesses she would call him a fool (as MacWhirr's grocer father called him an ass) for going to sea. The two men, far apart in rank, are linked by their instinctual nature.

The decisive clash between Jukes and MacWhirr (the story is structured on their contrast) comes when Jukes suggests altering the ship's course on the pretext that he is 'thinking of our passengers'. MacWhirr's amazement at hearing 'a lot of coolies spoken of as passengers' has caused some democratic unease, but what MacWhirr objects to once again is an abuse of language, and – even more – a perversion of function. The coolies may be 'passengers' in the sense of being conveyed, but they have not paid to travel on a passenger ship: they are being shipped home in a cargo vessel and therefore, professionally speaking, they are cargo.[11] MacWhirr regards the word 'passengers' applied to the coolies much as he does the word 'queer' applied to the flag. Moreover, his rebuke to Jukes – 'Why don't you speak plainly? Couldn't tell what you meant' – is morally justified because Jukes is clothing his fears for the ship (and, inevitably, himself) in spurious sympathy for human beings he normally would not think twice about – to whom, indeed, he later refers as 'a cargo of Chinamen' and even 'brutes'. He is not condemned for this very human subterfuge, but neither does MacWhirr seem a racist for resisting moral blackmail and refusing to tack his steamer, whose functions he respects, as if she were a sailing-ship 'to make the Chinamen comfortable'. His obtuseness about what lies behind Jukes's humanitarian excuse is quaintly funny, but behind his own attitude lies a genuine 'confession of faith', delivered 'with the utmost simplicity of manner and tone' and producing on Jukes's face a 'mixture of vexation and astonished respect'. 'A gale is a gale, Mr. Jukes,' MacWhirr tells his mate, 'and a full-powered steamship has got to face it. There's just so much dirty weather knocking about the world, and the proper thing is to go through it with none of what old Captain Wilson of the *Melita* calls "storm strategy".' Insofar as dodging the 'winds of heaven' offends his idea of 'the proper thing', MacWhirr seems moved by something akin to a sentiment of honour.[12]

That sentiment may be unconsciously at work just before the renewal of the storm, when MacWhirr asks, 'You left them pretty safe?' 'Are you thinking of the coolies, sir?' asks Jukes ('coolies' now, not 'passengers'), and tells how he rigged life-lines, adding that 'it may not matter in the end'. But MacWhirr insists:

> 'Had to do what's fair, for all – they are only Chinamen. Give them the same chance with ourselves – hang it all. She isn't lost yet. Bad enough to be shut up below in a gale —'
>
> 'That's what I thought when you gave me the job, sir,' interjected Jukes moodily.
>
> '— without being battered to pieces,' pursued Captain MacWhirr with rising vehemence. 'Couldn't let that go on in my ship if I knew she hadn't five minutes to live. Couldn't bear it, Mr. Jukes.'

It is obvious who is thinking of the Chinamen here (and who of himself). Moreover, Conrad firmly establishes MacWhirr as the only man on board who does think of them. We are told the crew's view: 'What the devil did the coolies matter to anybody?' The boatswain, having delivered his message, gives 'no more thought to the coolies'. Even MacWhirr's wise counterpart, Solomon Rout, on being told the coolies are fighting, answers brusquely, 'It don't matter much what they do.'

MacWhirr, however, needs Jukes, who is even more 'ordinary' than himself, being 'as ready a man as any half-dozen young mates that may be caught by casting a net upon the waters'. He is as ordinary in his assumption of racial superiority as in his lack of talent for foreign languages, mangling 'the very pidgin English cruelly' when he speaks to the Chinamen. He may even be typical, at a time of England's greatest imperial expansion, in his faith in his own imagination, which here proves a handicap: '... [he] had never doubted his ability to imagine the worst; but this was so much beyond his powers of fancy that it appeared incompatible with the existence of any ship whatever.' It is precisely because Jukes has these 'powers of fancy' that he is dismayed when they are exceeded. Yet MacWhirr himself is not as devoid of imagination as he has been painted. While Jukes's inmost feeling is that 'The men on board did not count, and the ship could not last', MacWhirr is shouting 'Rout . . . good man' and 'builders . . . good men'. Jukes can 'perfectly imagine' the appalling scene in the 'tween-deck, but only to characterize it as a 'disaster': MacWhirr thinks of others and even puts himself in their place, because in him imagination serves 'a humane intention and a vague sense of the fitness of things', rather than concern for personal survival or the need of self-affirmation.

Conrad nevertheless takes good care to dissociate Jukes from his homologue, 'Lord' Jim on the *Patna*.[13] Jukes is 'daunted; not abjectly, but only so far as a decent man may, without becoming loathsome to himself.' For if he needs MacWhirr to steady him and tell him what needs doing, MacWhirr needs a ready, quick-thinking, self-respecting mate to remedy what is wrong, never mind how. The symbolic potential of the story is nowhere higher than when Jukes, giving way to despair, feels an arm thrown over his shoulders and responds 'with great intelligence by catching hold of his captain round the waist' – the evolutionary joke being that he is responding not with intelligence but by instinct. The ensuing image of the two men 'clasped thus in the blind night, bracing each other against the wind, cheek to cheek and lip to ear, in the manner of two hulks lashed stem to stern together' is like a brief symbolic vision of instinct and intelligence holding fast against a universe of manifest entropy. But the allegorical vision immediately dissolves into lifelike complexities of character and situation. Jukes is no emblem of intelligence: aggrieved at not receiving enough praise for rigging life-lines, he forgets that the idea first came from the carpenter, who 'showed the greater intelligence' and without a word fetched the chain and rope for the job. On the other hand Jukes deserves credit for having the helmsman relieved (the boatswain being unable to command the necessary authority). And MacWhirr at last grudgingly pays heed to 'the books', which say 'the worst is not over yet' – although he quickly adds, apropos of the Chinamen: 'You don't find everything in books' (thereby showing imagination of a kind scholars might envy).

Whether MacWhirr does 'a very stupid thing' by taking the *Nan-Shan* 'straight through the typhoon'[14] begins to seem beside the point. What we are invited to contemplate is the impenetrable barrier dividing the operative modes of intelligence and instinct, each dominant in a different character, with intelligence in every way second in command and, we are forced to feel, rightly so. This is not only unflattering (since we deem ourselves intelligent) but also disturbing, because in our century instinct has got a bad name. We discount, or disbelieve in, the existence of a positive species-instinct rooted in resistance to, not identification with, nature: an instinct that, true to its root, may take us into trouble, but can also take us through it, 'plain and straight'. Its power to inspire is clearly demonstrated:

> 'Don't you be put out by anything,' the Captain continued, mumbling rather fast. 'Keep her facing it. They may say what they like, but the heaviest seas run with the wind. Facing it – always facing it – that's the way to get through. You are a young sailor. Face it. That's enough for any man. Keep a cool head.'
>
> For some reason Jukes experienced an access of confidence, a sensation that came from outside like a warm breath, and made him feel equal to every demand. The distant muttering of the darkness stole into his ears. He noted it unmoved, out of that sudden belief in himself, as a man safe in a shirt of mail would watch a point.

The very simplicity and modesty of MacWhirr's mumbled words give them their human potential. Of course, it is also the 'tyranny of training and command' that enables them to take effect. The main concern here, however, is not with the justification of authority *per se* as the means to survival, as in *The Nigger of the 'Narcissus'*, but rather with its use for purposes *in excess* of survival. The incident that manifests this concern is the one that inspired the story's first title: 'Equitable Division' (*CLJC*, 2, p. 169).

Jukes, of course, is concerned only to keep the coolies locked up until the *Nan-Shan* meets some 'man-of-war': he places his faith in the freemasonry of European imperialism, 'for surely any skipper of a man-of-war – English, French, or Dutch – would see white men through as far as row on board goes.' Afterwards he would hand the coolies over to their own corrupt overlords. He is even prepared to throw the dollars down to them and let them 'fight it out amongst themselves'.

But MacWhirr, a man of peace, insists on keeping 'the matter quiet' for the sake of 'all concerned' and being 'fair to all parties'. And when Jukes starts passing out rifles to the crew because MacWhirr has let the coolies out on deck, the captain reprimands him and orders the men disarmed before someone gets hurt, swearing humorously (and therefore unsententiously): 'Damme, if this ship isn't worse than Bedlam!' Instead of washing his hands of the coolies, he goes out of his way to do 'the fair thing by them as near as possible', in sharp contrast to Jukes's callous words to his chum: 'They had had a doing that would have shaken the soul out of a white man. But then they say a Chinaman has no soul.' Astonishingly, it is MacWhirr who has been charged with embodying the 'racism of British imperialism',[15] while Jukes's blatantly racist words have gone unnoticed. There is basically nothing wrong with Jukes's character: he is generous and frank in his defence of the second engineer and rejection of the second mate. But his callowness makes him vulnerable to the ideology of his day. MacWhirr thinks things out for himself.

And yet Jukes desires a share in his captain's achievement, to the extent of proudly quoting (and partly plagiarizing) MacWhirr's words in his letter ('This certainly is coming as near as can be to keeping the thing quiet for the benefit of all concerned....The skipper remarked to me the other day, "There are things you find nothing about in books"'.) In an indirect tribute to MacWhirr's moral ascendancy, Jukes is even forced to admit the advantages of the Siamese flag: 'Had we been an English ship ... there would have been no end of inquiries and bother, claims for damages and so on.'

The precise value of MacWhirr's action, however, remains incommunicable. When he writes to his wife, implicitly asking her sanction, she is only briefly alarmed by a hint that her husband, whom she regards as no more than a passport to respectability and good shopping, may be coming home again. Solomon Rout's wife,

11

by contrast, misses her husband and takes deep interest in his life, but her curiosity about the 'rather clever' thing his captain has done is baffled because Solomon doubts her ability to 'understand how much there was in it', and remains silent. One man opens his heart to a selfish woman who skims over his words; another – the only man on the ship wise enough to appreciate MacWhirr's conduct[16] – disappoints a wife hungry for details. And Jukes, 'unable to generalize', is too self-centred to grasp significances at all. But this ironic comedy of missed connections underlines the fact that the real value here is moral, not material, having no existence apart from the concrete circumstances that produce it: unlike the money, it is indivisible and cannot be shared.

This points to one aspect of Conrad's 'fresh start'. As in *The Nigger*, inner and outer disruption are verbally linked,[17] but the hierarchy of command is not threatened, and internal disorder is provoked not by a dying seaman's flaunted mortality but by something more mundane and banal: a self-destructive scramble for loose money. In the New York *Critic* version, the boatswain, seeing the cause of the riot, looks at a silver dollar 'as one would recognize a familiar object in the improbabilities of a nightmare'.[18] Although Conrad deleted the simile, the boatswain's words – 'Blamed money skipping all over the place, and they are tumbling after it head over heels – tearing and biting like anything. A regular little hell in there' – point to Marlow's alternative night-mare in 'Heart of Darkness': those blind and violent forces whose social and political evolution Conrad was soon to describe in *Nostromo* under the philosophical term 'Material Interest'.

The artistic method too is a fresh start, with sobriety as its keynote. The frame narrator is replaced, as it were, by a trio of letter-writers unable or unwilling to communicate inner truth: the epistemological impasse is dramatized, not rhapsodized. Metaphors are renounced for similes or labelled as figures of speech ('he nearly, as the saying is, jumped out of his skin'). As Leavis remarked long ago, 'the significance is not adjectival';[19] it is given by what Conrad called 'the picture-producing power of arranged words' (*CLJC*, 2, p. 435). The ship's struggles are anthropomorphized while the Chinamen are dehumanized into a compact, struggling mass, so that disorder becomes a growing common factor of human and non-human worlds alike. Against it is pitted the 'irresistible precision' of the imperturbable engine-room machinery, its ponderous movements enacted by arranged words to make us see the heart of that 'full-powered steamship', which MacWhirr instinctively recognizes has been evolved to resist, not evade, 'dirty weather'. The deepest feelings and highest tributes are quietly or drily understated, with a minimum of authorial commentary.[20] Despite, or because of, his distaste for talk, Mac-Whirr speaks some of Conrad's strongest lines of dialogue, whether inspiring Jukes, uttering his short soliloquy ('I wouldn't like to lose her') or ending a chapter with the ringing cry 'Yes!' (twenty years before the same life-affirming word was found to end *Ulysses*). The manner may have changed, but the grand theme is the same as it was, treated more sombrely, in *The Nigger of the 'Narcissus'*, 'Heart of Darkness' and *Lord Jim*: the nature of mankind and the problematics of its survival.

Unlike *The Nigger*, however, 'Typhoon' does not invite social allegory. In a key statement published just after the completion of 'Typhoon' and 'Falk', Conrad gave a measure of his artistic ambition:

> Egoism, which is the moving force of the world, and altruism, which is its morality, these two contradictory instincts of which one is so plain and the other so mysterious, cannot serve us unless in the incomprehensible alliance of their irreconcilable antagonism. Each alone would be fatal to our ambition. For, in the hour of undivided triumph, one would make our inheritance too arid to be worth having and the other too sorrowful to own.[21]

And so Jukes is last heard belittling MacWhirr while echoing his words. Jukes must believe in his own mental superiority to his captain, just as the engine-room crew must believe, for their own morale, that they are more important to the ship than those silly 'deck people'. In its delicate and complex 'equitable divisions' – between egocentric intelligence and species-instinct, imagination and intuition, order and justice – 'Typhoon', far from being a simple story, is both the incarnation of a moral and philosophical vision and an artistic feat of the highest order.

When Conrad began to write 'Typhoon' in October 1900 he already had 'Falk' in mind (*CLJC*, 2, 295). He later described its theme: 'Contrast of common sentimentalism with the frank stand-point of a more or less primitive man (Falk himself) who regards the preservation of life as the supreme moral law' (*CLJC*, 2, 399; my translation). As I once observed, Falk virtually personifies Schopenhauer's 'will to live', an unconscious striving in man and nature to exist and increase, which, being unappeasable, eternally engenders suffering.[22] Falk suffers doubly: first, because an enforced, extreme assertion of his will to live has deeply scarred his idea of himself as a civilized man (the 'idea', for Schopenhauer, was the world's redeeming aspect), and secondly because self-preservation includes his senses, and thus his desire for Hermann's heroically constructed niece, whose 'girlish form must have shouted aloud of life to that man':

> He wanted that girl, and the utmost that can be said for him was that he wanted that particular girl alone. I think I saw then the obscure beginning, the seed germinating in the soil of an unconscious need, the first shoot of that tree bearing now for a mature mankind the flower and the fruit, the infinite gradation in shades and in flavour of our discriminating love.... He was hungry for the girl, terribly hungry, as he had been terribly hungry for food.
>
> Don't be shocked if I declare that in my belief it was the same need, the same pain, the same torture.

Schopenhauer would not have been shocked. But he is philo-sophically only half the story: the 'contrast of common senti-mentalism' implies a flirtation with Nietzsche. The narrator sees Falk as a 'man of seven-foot six, living in a world of dwarfs', a superman mirrored in the heavens above the *Diana*: 'The multitude of stars gathered into clusters, in rows, in lines, in masses, in groups, shone all together, unanimously – and the few isolated ones, blazing by themselves in the midst of dark patches, seemed to be of a superior kind and of an inextinguishable nature.' Nietzschean overtones accompany the presentation of Falk from the start. He is described as extracting 'his pound and a half of flesh from each of us merchant-skippers' hard upon the only mention of his full name: 'Christian Falk' ('Falke' is German for 'hawk'). If Falk seems more voracious by half than Shylock, we may reflect on the incongruity between Christianity and a frank and el-emental nature.[23] The irony would have pleased Nietzsche, who saw 'attained unanimity in sympathetic regard' not as progress but 'only another, later constitution, one which is weaker, frailer, more easily hurt, and which necessarily generates a morality rich in consideration'.[24] The squeamish Hermann thus shrieks the word 'Beast!' at Falk's disclosure, but the narrator uses the same word to explain Falk's sexual attractiveness: 'He was a strange beast. But maybe women liked it.... I suppose every woman at the bottom of her heart considers herself a tamer of strange beasts.' (The narrator himself admires Falk's 'hard straight masculinity that would conceivably kill but would not condescend to cheat'; when he is lifted off his feet by Falk he exclaims, 'What a man!')

Of the two world-views implicit in 'Falk', Conrad may have been more interested in Nietzsche's: 'Hermann and his wife are the people I wanted to *do*,' he told Meldrum, 'the story of Falk being more or less of a foil to the main purpose' (*CLJC*, 2, p. 441). Whereas the lively Jukes served as a foil for the pedestrian yet heroic MacWhirr, here Captain Hermann, simple and un-imaginative like Captain MacWhirr, progressively loses, by his pettiness and calculating self-interest, whatever endearing traits he at first seemed to possess. His feelings are determined by 'the opinion generally received'; and his hypocritical respectability is ridiculed in one of Conrad's funniest oxymorons: 'He wouldn't like it to get about that he had been intimate with an eater of men – a common cannibal.' The narrator, when asked his opinion, shows a fine sense of Hermann's financial need to be mollified: '"In all these tales," I observed, "there is always a good deal of exaggeration."'

There are, after all, cannibals and cannibals. Falk's revelation spotlights those suspect qualities in the Hermanns already present in the narrator's description of their 'saintly retreat' and the Hermann children's devotion to their 'horrid' rag-doll – 'exercising and developing their racial sentimentalism by means of that dummy'. Apart from the niece, Falk's only kindred spirit on the *Diana* is the baby Nicholas, 'the least sentimental person in the family', who gnaws ropes or rains blows on whoever touches him – a miniature edition of the will to live. Sentimentalism is subtly linked to self-interest when the narrator describes Hermann as also 'racially thrifty',[25] hence anxious to marry off his niece and avoid paying her passage home now that her usefulness as child-

15

minder and wife-companion is at an end. His hypocritical mean-
ness is set against the honest egoism which prompts Falk to
disclose his past:

> 'I should want my wife to feel for me,' he said. 'It has made me
> unhappy.' And how could he keep the knowledge of it to himself –
> he asked us – perhaps through years and years of companionship?
> What sort of companionship would that be? A wife must know.

Like MacWhirr, Falk thinks things out: egoism, like altruism,
arrives by mysterious ways at just conclusions.[26] Here too it is a
matter of facing things, and of depth of feeling which latter-day
sentimentalists like the Hermanns totally lack ('Those good people
did not seem to be able to retain an impression for a whole twelve
hours'). It is the amount of the narrator's loss through theft that
makes the deepest impression on Hermann apart from Falk's confession of having eaten man, to which he reacts with a comic
blindfold of materialistic pragmatism: 'What for?'

The situation is morally complicated, however, because admira-
tion of elemental honesty implicitly endorses monopolistic ruthlessness in a world of economic cannibalism. In fact, the whole
fabric of the narrative on which the cannibal motifs are printed is
woven of financial relations. The narrator, looking for a river-pilot,
witnesses a slapstick version of them in the tipsy, *déclassé* Johnson,
holding a banana and tossing dollars through the air to the native
woman who lives with him (like a parody of Jukes's simple proposal
for dealing with the coolies). Johnson can afford to play the
disinterested gentleman because he has already received money
from Falk. The narrator is then threatened with a lawsuit and
having to borrow money at exorbitant interest from the local
sharks, who have backed Falk financially from the start in return
for good towing facilities. Meanwhile Hermann fumes over unpaid
damages, and the narrator suffers from his predecessor's shady
dealings and conversion of money into sex. (It is in fact the theft of
his own money that brings the narrator into relationship with
Hermann and Falk.) Even Falk has money worries, owing to
Schomberg's slander that, being too cheap to marry, he trifled
with the affections of Miss Vanlo, causing her brother to run up
debts (which in fact Falk himself paid). The narrator's relation to
Falk, at once less intimate and more familiar than Marlow's to

Kurtz, is that contingent, 'absurd' relation which insinuates itself everywhere between people in our world: the cash nexus, or, in Conrad's more pregnant phrase, Material Interest.

Such contingency, and the need to prepare for Falk's confession, stimulates interesting stylistic experiment. The proleptic overture at a river hostelry, with its evocation of primitive feasts, German ships and so on, is followed by permeation of the entire narrative with references to food and eating, down to Schomberg's indigestible chops (a faint foreshadowing of Joyce's technique in the Lestrygonian chapter of *Ulysses*). In keeping with Falk's bizarre revelation, diction and imagery are characterized not by referential precision, as in 'Typhoon', but by burlesque exaggeration. Thus the Hermanns' drying laundry evokes 'obese and invisible bodies', while Falk is described as a 'bloated monopolist', baby Nicholas as a 'bald-headed ruffian' and the niece, in Schomberg's lip-smacking phrase, as a 'fine lump of a girl'. The similes ('He bounced in his chair as if I had run a pin into him') slightly caricature reality to help the reader digest Falk's disclosure.

The narrator also observes himself with detachment: he may 'lie with a glibness and effrontery that amazed even me at the time', giggle 'with the sheer nervousness of escaped danger', mutter to himself ('Let us be calm') or mock his own vanity ('How proud I am of my presence of mind!'). This self-alienation distances the reader from Falk's experience – like using the passive voice and a matter-of-fact tone to describe the fate of the carpenter ('He was eaten, of course').

Whether 'Falk' achieves Conrad's declared aim is debatable. The narrator's 'Ah!' of enlightenment, coinciding with the reader's, refers to all Falk's peculiarities (vegetarianism, reclusive life, habitual shudder), so that the retrospective illumination is of Falk, not the Hermanns: the details of the narrator's own troubles seem at times to have been introduced merely to delay it, as in a shaggy-dog story with a gruesome point. Baffled by the story's failure to be serialized, Conrad feared he had not sufficiently established Falk's personality: 'I wanted to make Falk stand for so much that I neglected, in a manner, to set him on his feet. This is one of my weaknesses ...' (*CLJC*, 2, p. 441).[27]

But there are more inherent difficulties: we need to be told, for instance, that Falk is 'a witness to the mighty truth of an unerring and eternal principle', whereas MacWhirr's conduct speaks for itself. Furthermore, sympathizing with Falk and the girl's compassion is one thing; admiring the 'principle' Falk represents would take most readers further than they are prepared to go, especially after the totalitarian abuse of Nietzsche's philosophy. The Hermanns and Schomberg are not the only bourgeois in the story: when Falk hints at an 'accident' in his past the narrator exclaims, 'Then in heaven's name say nothing about it', anticipating Hermann, who reacts to the confession disqualifying Falk as a suitor with something like unconscious Yiddish humour: 'Who was asking him?' Falk himself insists on his 'desire of respectability, of being like everybody else', and there is a curious ambiguity in the narrator's remark that Falk 'might have been a member of a herd, not of a society', for is not society traditionally compared to a herd? Such contradictions, artistically right in 'Typhoon', here reflect the difficulties of playing off one form of egoism against another. The calculated springing of a secret like Falk's in order to show up petty-bourgeois hypocritical squeamishness may be a case of artistic overkill, and it is hard to share the narrator's uplift at the end, despite the mythological machinery (Falk as centaur or Hercules; the girl as Diana, nymph of chastity and the hunt). In keeping with the 'jocular' treatment in 'Typhoon' the story may be read – up to a point – as philosophical black comedy; but the magazine editors cannot be blamed for rejecting it. For better or worse there is more Hermann than Falk in most of us.[28]

The narrator in 'Falk' is merely delayed getting out to sea, but the characters in 'Amy Foster' are landlocked for good. Kennedy, the secondary narrator, has left an adventurous life as 'the companion of a famous traveller' for the narrow round of an English country doctor; the eponymous figure is a dull-witted, kind-hearted daughter of the soil, and the protagonist – a Carpathian mountaineer – has been shipwrecked on the Kentish coast while emigrating to America. Critics have tended to expound the story biographically, and indeed Conrad's working titles, 'A Husband' and 'A Castaway', each suggest an autobiographical impulse. Jessie Conrad may well have told her Polish husband how he frightened her during their honeymoon in Brittany when he became delirious with malarial fever and began muttering in 'a strange tongue',[29] thereby providing the climax for the emotional logic of the story. But to this well-known source must be added another: Conrad's lasting mental association of the castaway with his own traumatic separation from the sea. In 1916 he wrote humorously to Clement Shorter, one of the first editors to publish his work:

> Thus you have been for me a friend of the early days ... when I first emerged from the sea – so to speak. Pray don't imagine I am trying to establish a comparison with the Divine Aphrodite. It was nothing so dazzling as that. The greater my gratitude then to the small band that, from the first, discerned my shrinking humanity and encouraged it with friendly signs from the shore.[30]

Conrad no doubt also drew on his own feelings of cultural isolation living among Kentish farmers; and there may be other autobiographical echoes.[31] Literary sources include an anecdote in Ford Madox Ford's *The Cinque Ports*, Flaubert's 'Un Coeur Simple'[32] and the nineteenth-century Polish emigrant-tale.[33]

All this, however, is peripheral to the theme, defined by Conrad as the 'essential difference of races' (*CLJC*, 2, p. 399; my translation) and by the narrator as 'that fear of the Incomprehensible that hangs over all our heads'. The two ideas are related in literature. Describing *Seraphina* [*Romance*], on which he was then collaborating with Ford, Conrad argued that romantic feeling 'lies principally in the glamour memory throws over the past and arises from contact with a different race and a different temperament' (*CLJC*, 2, p. 339). In this sense 'Amy Foster' shows romantic feeling turned inside out to reveal its horrifying hidden face, in a tradition that goes back to *The Sufferings of Young Werther*[34] and acquires special force here by its avatar in the outwardly least romantic of beings.

Contact with another race does kindle in Amy Foster's dull brain a spark of romantic imagination (perhaps hereditary: her father caused a scandal by running off with his own father's cook). But its ephemerality is forecast by Amy's failure of nerve when the 'outlandish' parrot to which she is devoted is attacked by the cat and shrieks for help 'in human accents' – a prolepsis later echoed in two references to Yanko as 'outlandish'. Technically this recalls the training-ship episode in *Lord Jim*, but 'Amy Foster' is far more pessimistic, since romantic imagination here is seen in relation not to professional conduct in an emergency but to the normal demands of a fundamental human bond. If the romantic feeling that inspires the bond can turn to terror at the first simple test, the implications for human life are bleak indeed. Moreover, Amy's desertion of her sick husband is as instinctive as MacWhirr's concern to stop the fighting on his ship. Intelligence by definition corrects itself: instinct is final.

But MacWhirr's instinct, after all, led him to the sea, whereas Amy's is land-bound; it is no accident that each time Kennedy mentions unreasoning fear the land is evoked (at first in contrast with the sea) so as to suggest something more sinister than Hardyesque indifference:

> ... the rim of the sun, all red in a speckless sky, touched familiarly the smooth top of a ploughed rise near the road as I had seen it times innumerable touch the distant horizon of the sea. The uniform brownness of the harrowed fields glowed with a rose tinge, as though the powdered clods had sweated out in minute pearls of blood the toil of uncounted ploughmen.

A waggon rolls by, and

> the clumsy figure of the man plodding at the head of the leading horse projected itself on the background of the Infinite with a heroic uncouthness. The end of his carter's whip quivered high up in the blue.

After Kennedy's next reference to 'unaccountable terror' the penal overtones of 'harrowed' fields, blood, sweat, toil and upraised whip are deepened: 'The men we met walked past, slow, unsmiling, with downcast eyes, as if the melancholy of an overburdened earth had weighted their feet, bowed their shoulders, borne down their glances.' The children of agriculture, 'uncouth in body and as leaden of gait as if their very hearts were loaded with chains', are like convicts.[35]

By contrast, Yanko is described as 'the most innocent of adventurers ever cast out by the sea'. With his springy step, 'skimming' stride (a word that refers to sailing in 'Typhoon'), natural grace and far-reaching eyes (which significantly lose their power only 'before the immensity of the sea') he offends the inmates of this earthbound world by every trait suggesting lightness, grace, poetry or feeling – leaping stiles, lying in the grass to look at the sky, singing and dancing, and above all, excitability.[36]

The most characteristic feature of the castaway's new world is materialism: the bedrock of social differences and even the forms of religion, manifested for Yanko in the 'little steel cross' worn by Miss Swaffer at her belt. There are no 'images of the Redeemer' by the roadside: existence seems 'overshadowed by the everyday material appearance, as if by the visions of a nightmare' (anticipating, like the cancelled simile in 'Typhoon', the nightmare of Material Interest that grips Mrs Gould in *Nostromo*).

Yanko's natural religious feeling embarrasses the 'young ladies from the Rectory' in their attempt to prepare him for conversion: they cannot 'break him of the habit of crossing himself' (so vulgar compared with *wearing* a cross), for their religious observance is as superficial as their cultural self-improvement through struggles with Goethe and Dante. Yanko cannot understand the impoverished aspect of the churches 'among so much wealth'; his puzzlement at weekday church closure is at once touchingly realistic and wickedly satirical: 'Was it to keep people from praying too often?'

Even Yanko's benefactor, Swaffer – himself regarded as eccentric for sitting up late to read books, but respected because he can write a cheque for £200 without thinking twice – exploits the foreigner as a kind of household serf until Yanko saves his grandchild's life; only then does he pay him regular wages and let him eat from the kitchen table. Yet it takes Swaffer, the nearest thing to lord of the manor in this community, to silence all xenophobic objections to the courting of Amy by making Yanko a householder with a brick cottage and an acre of land.

But one way or another materialism is fatal to the spirit: as soon as Yanko becomes a property-owner he begins to seem less inwardly free (foreshadowing the embourgeoisement of the characters at the end of *Nostromo*). In Amy the change works differently: her spark of romantic attraction is snuffed out by maternity, leaving the darkness of the far side of romance: terror of, rather than attraction to, the unfamiliar and incomprehensible, particularly when manifested in language (as in the human-sounding shrieks of the parrot). The scene in which Amy responds to the sick man's request for water in his own tongue by snatching her baby and running as from an earthquake is one of Conrad's most convincing statements of human isolation, compressing two primitive terrors into one: that of the Incomprehensible and that – less noticed but equally potent – of suddenly becoming unintelligible to those closest to oneself.

The indictment of social intolerance and materialist ethos, and the exposure of the roots of language in non-rational feeling, are rendered all the more telling by an anti-sentimental narrator who, with his corrosive scientific intelligence, is the antithesis of Marlow in 'Youth' and supplies no glamour of memory. As in 'Heart of Darkness', however, frame and secondary narrators merge in the last line to produce a characteristic Conradian reverberation, while economy of style avoids what, by 1902, Conrad had come to fear: 'the superfluous word' (*CLJC*, 2, p. 460). More modest in scale than 'Heart of Darkness', the story achieves a comparable sense of devastating truth about human nature, harder to shrug off because closer to home.

If 'Falk' was meant as a companion-piece for 'Typhoon', the kinship of 'Amy Foster' and 'To-morrow' is more obvious. Both stories are set in the same part of Kent and focus initially on a character who is not the protagonist. This time, the victim is not an 'outlandish' man from outside the community but an ordinary member of it, described by Conrad eighteen years later as 'absolutely the first conscious woman-creation in the whole body of my work'.[37] She is tragic, moreover, as a woman; trapped by male propensity to erect a one-sided view of life into a rigid principle or idea. (It is surprising that literary feminists have not used her as ammunition.) Her pallid, 'unrefreshed' face and 'full figure' portray a sexuality entombed by a monstrously obese, widowed father stricken with blindness 'in the full flush of business' (business presumably replacing youth in this village, shut off from the sea by a wall). Carvil, the simplest of materialists, bases all his self-esteem on having 'made enough money to have ham and eggs every morning'. This unhealthy diet has not improved his temper: he avenges himself on his daughter as if she had personally devised his infirmity, making himself 'helpless beyond his affliction to enslave her better'. She submits passively, but when her 'only friend' (her landlord) reflects on her father's extravagance she expresses in a low key a bitter consciousness of her generic fate:

'Of course it isn't as if he had a son to provide for,' Captain Hagberd went on a little vacantly. 'Girls, of course, don't require so much – h'm – h'm. They don't run away from home, my dear.'

'No,' said Miss Bessie, quietly.

Unlike Carvil, Hagberd skimps on his material needs to such an extent that Bessie wonders what he lives on. But his miserliness is not materialistic; it serves the idea of his son's return, fixed in the never-never land of that proverbially indefinite word, 'to-morrow'. Harry's future 'home' is in fact Hagberd's present one: a mental status quo that must not be disturbed either by doubt of Harry's eventual return or *by the return itself*, for 'every mental state, even madness, has its equilibrium based upon self-esteem.' (Hagberd's rests on his shrewd appreciation of the comforts of dry land.) Conrad deconstructively explains that Hagberd's 'disease of hope' blinds him 'to truth and probability, just as the other old man in the other cottage has been made blind, by another disease, to the light and beauty of the world.' Idealist and materialist are each appropriately afflicted.

Bessie shuttles between them, filially chained to her father and humouring her landlord, with whom she carries on a parody of flirtation, blushing at his winks (Conrad deleted a manuscript reference to her not being in her first youth). Moreover, she complements Hagberd, whose 'hopeful craze' serves to 'mock her own want of hope', for she 'does not seem to be able to see any change or any end to her life' (an undeconstructed variant on the theme of blindness). She even becomes Hagberd's accomplice, protecting him from recognizing his own madness in the townspeople's grins. (In an interesting manuscript passage Conrad suggested that the community sea-port might itself be mad, awaiting the return of its former prosperity on no firmer grounds than Hagberd's expectation of his son.)

Harry's arrival destabilizes this trinity of domestic tyranny, madness and despair. He threatens the safety of Hagberd's idea by materializing it, and he infects Bessie with hope, not only through his seducer's instinct but by his incarnation of a wandering life that excites both her pity for his homelessness and her envy of his freedom. For a moment she almost believes that Harry, in whom she sees the 'very spit' of her symbolic lover, may be drawn – along with his potential of freedom – into her own feminine gravitational field: an irrational hope, since that freedom depends precisely on his remaining outside it. Her hope is smothered at birth by Harry's loathing of physical enclosure. When Hagberd, obsessed by domesticity, spills the beans about intending her for his future daughter-in-law, he ironically turns the key on her domestic prison and bars her time-honoured feminine way to self-assertion. Harry's violent embrace only drives home her perception of her fate. The imaginative pattern of 'Amy Foster' is reversed: the outlandish 'wild animal under a net' is a woman outwardly domestic and submissive, and the seafaring adventurer (who hums an 'outlandish' tune) departs a free man.

This airtight pessimistic design has been found too stark, and Conrad himself resented having to adapt the story 'down to the needs of a magazine' (*CLJC*, 2, p. 225). It is true that the absence of focus on Bessie at the start robs her plight of deeper pathos, while the use of the barber for exposition seems forced, since the community is not at issue, as in 'Amy Foster'. Yet the story is haunting, with startling insight into delusional mental processes and a scenic development that led Sidney Colvin to suggest a stage adaptation (see Appendix). The crossfire in which Bessie is caught is like a disguised sketch of the twin nightmares of materialism and idealism which Conrad had evoked in 'Heart of Darkness' and was about to explore in depth from 1902 to 1909 in *Nostromo*, *The Secret Agent* and *Under Western Eyes*.

In their order of writing, the stories in *Typhoon* show the shadow of the land, with its insularity, materialism and 'hopeful madness' falling inexorably over characters and mood. MacWhirr may have been 'disdained by destiny and by the sea', but when the test comes he shows his mettle; Hermann, equally disdained, shrinks from truth; his ship is not a 'floating abode of harmony and peace' like MacWhirr's, but an ostrich's refuge, ludicrously resembling a country cottage (as he himself resembles a 'sedentary grocer'). In 'Amy Foster' and 'To-morrow' the ship-into-cottage metamorphosis is complete: in one such cottage a castaway breathes his last; in another a domestic slave gives her blind father tea; in a third a 'captain' who has never strayed from the coast dottily accumulates furniture for a seafaring son who appears only to illuminate madness and despair. Like the narrator in 'Falk', Bessie is literally lifted off her feet by a man from the sea who seems to exist outside any society; and the link between the sea and freedom clinches the inner design of the volume, which begins with a father calling his son an ass for going to sea and ends with a son scorning to live in the house of a father who feels towards the sea 'a profound and emotional animosity'.[38]

Even tiny details reappear in altered form throughout the book: the helmsman's striped shirt in 'Typhoon' becomes the striped old cotton shirt given to Yanko for work in the garden.[39] Harry tells Bessie, 'The whole world ain't a bit too big for me to spread my elbows in,' whereas MacWhirr was content to spread his on the bridge-rail and Bessie can spread hers only on the fence of her back garden. And the breathtaking glimpse in 'Typhoon' of 'the starless night of the immensities beyond the created universe, revealed in its appalling stillness through a low fissure in the glittering sphere of which the earth is the kernel' shrinks into Hagberd's 'expression of horror and incredulity as though he had seen a crack open out in the firmament'.

This denaturing process acts like a hinge,[40] binding the exploration of romantic imagination in the early Marlow stories to the insidious theme of material interest, whether expressed in the loose dollars rolling in the 'tween-deck, the rolling silver dollar pursued by Mrs Johnson in 'Falk' or the half-sovereign Harry extracts from Bessie. MacWhirr's imperturbable command, 'Pick up all the money,' issued on a possibly foundering ship, might pass for a transmutation by Conrad of the rueful sense of his own life: on 10 June 1902 he wrote to Galsworthy, 'All my art has become artfulness in exploiting agents and publishers' (CLJC, 2, p. 424). But in his art, money never finally prevails. Facing ruin, the captain in 'Falk' is pressed into service of an elemental instinct that puts money in perspective, as MacWhirr's opposite instinct does in 'Typhoon'. By contrast, Yanko's accession to property leads only to death in despair. Even Harry rises briefly above his shabby exploitation of Bessie: 'You can't buy me in, . . . and you can't buy yourself out.' The real tension informing the sea/land dichotomy is between the subtle corrupting processes of material interest and the integrity of human personality. The decks are being cleared for Nostromo.

Typhoon also marks a self-conscious expansion of Conrad's stylistic palette. Consider the playful mythopoesis at the end of 'Falk':

But the two, standing before each other in sunlight with clasped hands, had heard nothing, had seen nothing and no one. Three feet away from them in the shade a seaman sat on a spar, very busy splicing a strop and dipping his fingers into a tar-pot, as if utterly unaware of their existence.

For an instant Falk and the girl step out of this world like reincarnations of the Flying Dutchman and Senta,[41] while in the oblivious seaman Conrad anticipates by over three decades Auden's insight from the Old Masters that marvellous events are invariably ignored by eye-witnesses who go on peacefully about their business.[42] Yet the legendary allusion is no sooner evoked than discarded: the story ends with plain Mr and Mrs Falk having left town, perhaps chased by a hotel-keeper's gossip. The Wagnerian effect was a mere stylistic gambol – and indeed the whole story may be read as an invitation to compose our own motifs (as in the 'open work' expounded sixty years later by Umberto Eco[43]).

Conrad's growing artistic self-confidence stands out in his declaration to Blackwood a year after he finished 'Falk': 'I am *modern*, and I would rather recall Wagner the musician and Rodin the Sculptor ... and Whistler the painter who made Ruskin the critic foam at the mouth[44].... They had to suffer for being "new"' (*CLJC*, 2, p. 418). Rodin and Wagner left their mark on *Typhoon*, and the interdisciplinary consciousness of being 'new' puts Conrad in the forefront of 'modernism'. He sensed that romance was being squeezed out in a new era of power-worship and economic cannibalism on an unprecedented scale. In the manuscript of 'Falk' a wistful passage recalls in Marlovian manner the vanished era of sailing ships: 'Ah! That was a generation. A generation that came nearest to the hearts of men in the swift rush of evolution hurrying towards these monsters of form or size that are either inhuman or gigantic aping the ways of hotels or else of warehouses. Well, never mind.'[45] In the story the passage itself has vanished; there is only the captain's admission: 'I never realised so well before that this is an age of steam. The exclusive possession of a marine boiler had given Falk the whip hand of us all.' The expunging of the first passage signals final acceptance of a changed world. In February 1902, just after finishing 'To-morrow', Conrad wrote to Wells: 'The future is of our own making – and (for me) the most striking characteristic of the century is just that development, that maturing of our consciousness which should open our eyes to that truth – or that illusion. Anything that would help our intelligences towards a clearer view of the consequences of our social action is of the very greatest value' (*CLJC*, 2, pp. 386–7).

About to embark on a long literary voyage to explore, from West to East, the moral consequences of social action, Conrad knew that his 'fresh start' in *Typhoon* had marked his departure from the late nineteenth century and his landfall in our own.

NOTES TO THE INTRODUCTION

1. 'Preface to "The Shorter Tales of Joseph Conrad"', *Last Essays* (London: Dent, 1925), pp. 207–9.
2. Thomas C. Moser, 'From Olive Garnett's Diary: Impressions of Ford Madox Ford and His Friends, 1890–1906', *Texas Studies in Literature and Language* 16 (1974), pp. 524–5.
3. After taking out two life-insurance policies, Conrad used them as security for a loan from the Standard Life Insurance Company, with John Galsworthy and William Blackwood as sureties. He then assigned one policy to Pinker till paid up, in return for Pinker's paying off his total indebtedness to the Company; the premiums on the assigned policy plus repayment with interest to Pinker to be deducted from his future earnings, with Pinker as his sole agent.
4. *LBM*, p. 104.
5. Note for Mr T. J. Wise in *Typhoon*, New York & London: G. P. Putnam's Sons (1902), British Library. The set has most recently been broken in the World's Classics edition entitled *Typhoon and Other Tales* (Oxford University Press, 1986), which replaces 'To-morrow' by 'The Secret Sharer', written some eight years later.
6. See Charles Schuster, 'Comedy and the Limits of Language in Conrad's "Typhoon"', *Conradiana*, 16 (1984), pp. 55–71, and Ian Watt, 'Comedy and Humour in "Typhoon"', *The Ugo Mursia Memorial Lectures*, ed. Mario Curreli (Milan: Mursia International, 1988), pp. 39–67. According to Watt, Jukes presumably learns what Conrad must have learned about his superiors: that 'their very lack of interest or skill in conversation and books ... may even have left them freer to do in a more single-minded way the one thing that they have trained themselves to do' (p. 55). The story, he concludes, is about 'the corrections which experience administers to ideas' – 'a classic theme of intellectual comedy' consistent with Conrad's fiction, which 'normally exhibits a fairly critical attitude to theory as opposed to

practice' (p. 54). The trouble with this view is that MacWhirr never 'trained himself' to deal with the unprecedented situation on the *Nan-Shan*, that he nearly loses his ship precisely by preferring practice to theory, and that Jukes still regards him as 'stupid' at the end.

7. 'Hamlet and Don Quixote', *Fortnightly Review*, London, Chapman & Hall, CCCXXXII (1 August 1894), p. 194. For a discussion of this essay in relation to Conrad, see Paul Kirschner, *Conrad: the Psychologist as Artist* (Edinburgh: Oliver & Boyd, 1968), pp. 241–3.

8. It is Jukes who stresses the word 'we' in his letter to his chum, adding obtusely, 'There are feelings that this man simply hasn't got.'

9. This preference for objects of perception over words or ideas is decisive. During his inspection tour of the *Nan-Shan* MacWhirr ignores the hyperbole of the firm's partners and instead draws attention to a defective lock, which he seizes and rattles: 'A brand new lock and it won't act at all. See? See?' The junior partner is disgusted; significantly it is the senior man who reprimands the joiner about the lock: 'The Captain could see directly he set eye on it.' It is the same eye on which MacWhirr depends during the storm: 'He was trying to see, with that watchful manner of a seaman who stares into the wind's eye as if into the eye of an adversary, to penetrate the hidden intention and guess the aim and force of the thrust.' Charles Schuster argues that MacWhirr cannot have a passion to know the truth about the world because he is not self-reflective enough; that his concern is with 'world', not abstract 'truth' (Schuster, *op. cit.*, p. 71, n. 25). But there is nothing abstract in MacWhirr's truth, which is reached not by logic or imagination but by intuitively coming to grips with things. This unreflecting passion for the speech of 'every-day, eloquent facts' leads MacWhirr to live on the bridge of his ship, closer to wind and wave; and it is crucial, for it lies at the heart of his question to his exasperated mate: 'How can you tell what a gale is made of till you get it?'

10. The primate-like hirsuteness of the boatswain provides a link with MacWhirr, who is first presented clutching his umbrella in a 'powerful, hairy fist'. (The evil second mate has 'no hair on his face'.)

11. One of the original titles for the story was, in fact, 'A Skittish Cargo' (*CLJC*, 2, p. 237).

12. Honour was a key concept for Conrad, as it was for Alfred de Vigny, whose philosophy Conrad's father extolled (Baines, p. 7). In his peroration to *Servitude et Grandeur Militaires* (1835), Vigny, observing the decline of religious belief, asked, 'What is left to us that is sacred?' and found it was Honour, which he defined as 'manly decency' (*la pudeur virile*) and 'a male religion' without images, dogmas or written laws: 'Man, in the name of Honour, feels stirring within him something like a part of himself, and that tremor awakens all the forces of his pride and primitive energy.' Seven

months after finishing 'Typhoon' Conrad told Blackwood: 'A wrestle with wind and weather has a moral value like the primitive acts of faith on which may be built a doctrine of salvation and a way of life' (*CLJC*, 2, p. 354).

13. Dwight H. Purdy has shown how, when revising the New York *Critic* text of the story, Conrad carefully avoided the resemblance ('Conrad at Work: The Two Serial Texts of *Typhoon*', *Conradiana*, 19 (1987), pp. 112–15).

14. Baines, p. 257.

15. Daniel R. Schwarz, *Almayer's Folly to Under Western Eyes*, London, Macmillan (1980), p. 116. Schwarz claims, without evidence, that Mac-Whirr's commitment to the Chinese is based 'simply on his conception of the White Man's Burden' (p. 117).

16. Solomon Rout's forename doubtless suggests proverbial wisdom, an engine-room counterpart of MacWhirr's 'silence of enlightened comprehension dwelling alone up there with a storm'. But critics who proceed to link MacWhirr's 'equitable division' with the Judgement of Solomon seem too ingenious. Solomon's judgement was a test of motherhood based on the *indivisibility* of the child. An apter biblical correlative would be King Solomon's proverb: 'A false balance is an abomination to the Lord/But a just weight is his delight.'

17. In *The Nigger of the 'Narcissus'* Wait's cough tosses him 'like a hurricane' (Penguin Classics, 1988, p. 17). In 'Typhoon', the boatswain opens the 'tween-deck door 'as though he had opened the door to the sounds of the tempest'.

18. Quoted in Purdy, *op. cit.*, p. 118, n. 6.

19. F. R. Leavis, *The Great Tradition* (London: Chatto and Windus, 1948) p. 175.

20. Conrad carefully eliminated authorial commentary and inside views of the characters in revising the *Critic* text (Purdy, *op. cit.*, pp. 111–12).

21. *The New York Times*, 24 August 1901 (*CLJC*, 2, p. 348).

22. See Kirschner, *op. cit.*, pp. 266–9. Tony Tanner echoes my remarks in '"Gnawed Bones and Artless Tales"', *Joseph Conrad: A Commemoration*, Norman Sherry, ed. (London: Macmillan, 1976), p. 22.

23. The incongruity is stressed in the image of Falk's 'anchorite's bony head fitted with a Capuchin beard and adjusted to a herculean body' and later 'his mighty trunk ... and that incongruous, anchorite head'.

24. Walter Kaufmann, ed., *The Portable Nietzsche* (New York: Viking Press, 1954), p. 522.

25. Replying to a charge that he was too lenient towards the English, Conrad protested that his aim was to point out not the 'inferiority of races' but the '*difference* of races', adding, 'Hermann is a German, but so is Stein' (*CLJC*, 3, p. 93; my translation).

26. He avoided it in 'Typhoon', which originally opened with MacWhirr confronting 'a barometer he had no reason to distrust'. (See H. T. Webster, 'Conrad's Changes in Narrative Conception in the Manuscripts of *Typhoon and Other Stories* and *Victory*', *PMLA*, 64 (1948), p. 953.) Conrad later added a preliminary sketch to set MacWhirr 'on his feet'.

27. In September 1903 Conrad wrote to Wells: 'An *enlightened* egoism is as valid as an *enlightened* altruism – neither more nor less' (*CLJC*, 3, p. 63).

28. Jessie Conrad recalled being 'quite physically sick when I typed those pages' (*JCKH*, p. 118).

29. Ibid., p. 35.

30. Letter dated 31 December 1916, BL.

31. Juliet McLauchlan sees an echo of Conrad's childhood in Yanko's travel impressions: 'The tremendous sense of vast distances and totally strange surroundings may well have grown out of the small child Conrad's own impressions of his enforced and doubtless incomprehensible journeys across a continent' ('"Amy Foster" – Echoes from Conrad's Own Experience?', *Polish Review*, XXVIII, No. 3 (1978), p. 8.

32. For both these sources see Richard Herndon, 'The Genesis of Conrad's "Amy Foster"', *Studies in Philology*, LVII (1960), pp. 549–66. Ford's anecdote concerned a shipwrecked German sailor in Kent who was ill-used by the local people and finally sought refuge in a pigsty, where he was found by the police. Ford claimed that Conrad had taken the story from him and rewritten it. According to Jessie Conrad, Ford's only ground for the claim was having pointed out to Conrad the grave of one or two foreign seamen in Winchelsea churchyard: 'This fact and a story – a mere fragment heard during a meal in a country inn – gave Conrad the material he needed. The actual character, Amy Foster, was for many years in our service, and it was her animal-like capacity for sheer uncomplaining endurance that inspired Conrad' (*JCKH*, p. 118). The anecdote's relation to the story is that of grit to the pearl.

33. See Andrzej Busza, 'Conrad's Polish Literary Background and Some Illustrations of the Influence of Polish Literature on His Work', *Antemurale*, X (Rome, Institutum Historicum Polonicum, 1966), pp. 224–30.

34. See my 'Conrad, Goethe and Stein: the Romantic Fate in *Lord Jim*', *Ariel*, 10, 1 (January 1979), pp. 72–4.

35. See p. 298, note 24.

36. Excitability was a well-documented trait in Conrad (see Baines, p. 444; Najder, pp. 230, 335, 452).

37. Letter to Pinker, 17 August 1919, *LL*, II, p. 225.

38. Paternal blindness and oppression is an obsessive theme in Conrad's fiction, nowhere more so than in 'To-morrow'. On one hand, Bessie's widowed father enslaves and abuses her; on the other, the widowed

Hagberd first kindles, then smothers Bessie's hope (partly through his past abuse of his own son). For a biographical source of this theme see Kirschner, *op. cit.*, pp. 259–60.

39. Although he retains his 'national brown cloth trousers', on Sundays he is put into a 'slop-made pepper-and-salt suit' – a sartorial smothering of personality anticipating that self-inflicted by Nostromo, who, in the new Sulaco, sheds his distinctive finery for 'the vulgarity of a brown tweed suit' (*Nostromo*, Dent Collected Edition, p. 527).

40. Over sixty years ago Jessie Conrad called *Typhoon* 'a transition book' (*JCKH*, p. 50).

41. After evoking the fable Conrad describes Falk as 'that dark navigator'. This, and the ending ('Those two met in sunshine') evoke Wagner's opera, where the Dutchman is traditionally dressed in black, and, after the vessel sinks, is seen with Senta transfigured in the rising sun. (But see p. 301, note 47.

42. Cf. W. H. Auden, 'Musée des Beaux Arts', *Collected Shorter Poems: 1927–1957* (London: Faber & Faber, 1966), p. 123.

43. Umberto Eco, *The Open Work*, trans. Anna Cancogni (Cambridge, Mass.: Harvard University Press, 1989): a translation of *Opera Aperta* (Milan: Bompiani, 1962).

44. When the American painter James A. McNeill Whistler (1834–1903) exhibited his proto-abstract painting *Nocturne in Black and Gold: The Falling Rocket* in London in 1877, Ruskin wrote: 'I have seen, and heard, much of Cockney impudence before now, but never expected to hear a coxcomb ask two hundred guineas for flinging a pot of paint in the public's face.' Whistler sued for libel, and at the trial explained that the title of the painting expressed his interest in art for art's sake: 'It is an arrangement of line, form and colour first, and I make use of any incident of it which shall bring about a symmetrical result.' British justice vindicated the painter: he was awarded a farthing in symbolic damages and ruined by the legal costs he had incurred. (See *American Painting: From its Beginnings to the Armory Show* by Jules David Prown (London: Macmillan, 1980), pp. 111 and 117.) Whistler's belief (following the ideas of Théophile Gautier and Baudelaire) that the art object should be judged solely by its own internal aesthetic laws, independently of any outside interest, was evidently congenial to Conrad.

45. Falk, MS, p. 12.

SELECT BIBLIOGRAPHY

LETTERS

G. Jean-Aubry: *Joseph Conrad: Life and Letters* (two volumes, London: Heinemann, 1927; Garden City, New York: Doubleday Page, 1927)

Edward Garnett, ed.: *Letters from Conrad, 1895–1924* (London: The Nonesuch Press, 1928)

William Blackburn, ed.: *Letters to William Blackwood and David S. Meldrum* (Durham: Duke University Press, 1958)

Zdzisław Najder, ed.: *Conrad's Polish Background: Letters to and From Polish Friends* (London: Oxford University Press, 1964)

C. T. Watts, ed.: *Joseph Conrad's Letters to Cunninghame Graham* (London: Cambridge University Press, 1969)

Frederick R. Karl and Laurence Davies, eds.: *The Collected Letters of Joseph Conrad* (Cambridge: Cambridge University Press, 1983 onwards)

BIOGRAPHIES

Jocelyn Baines: *Joseph Conrad: A Critical Biography* (London: Weidenfeld and Nicolson, 1960)

Frederick R. Karl: *Joseph Conrad: The Three Lives* (New York: Farrar, Straus and Giroux; London: Faber and Faber; 1979)

Zdzisław Najder: *Joseph Conrad: A Chronicle* (London: Cambridge University Press, 1983; New Brunswick, N.J.: Rutgers University Press, 1983)

BACKGROUND AND SOURCES

Jessie Conrad: *Joseph Conrad as I Knew Him* (London: Heinemann, 1926)

John D. Gordan: *Joseph Conrad: the Making of a Novelist* (Cambridge, Mass.: Harvard University Press, 1940)

Norman Sherry: *Conrad's Eastern World* (Cambridge: Cambridge University Press, 1966)

— — : *Conrad's Western World* (Cambridge: Cambridge University Press, 1971)

Zdzisław Najder: *Conrad Under Familial Eyes* (Cambridge: Cambridge University Press, 1984)

CRITICISM

F. R. Leavis: *The Great Tradition* (London: Chatto and Windus, 1948)

Douglas Hewitt: *Conrad: a Reassessment* (Cambridge: Bowes and Bowes, 1952)

Paul Wiley: *Conrad's Measure of Man* (Madison, Wisconsin: University of Wisconsin Press, 1954)

Thomas Moser: *Joseph Conrad: Achievement and Decline* (Cambridge, Mass.: Harvard University Press, 1957)

Albert Guerard: *Conrad the Novelist* (Cambridge, Mass.: Harvard University Press, 1958)

R. W. Stallman, ed.: *The Art of Joseph Conrad: A Critical Symposium* (East Lansing: Michigan State University Press, 1960)

Eloise Knapp Hay: *The Political Novels of Joseph Conrad* (Chicago and London: Chicago University Press, 1963)

J. Hillis Miller: *Poets of Reality* (Cambridge, Mass.: Harvard University Press, 1966). [Contains a chapter on Conrad]

Avrom Fleishman: *Conrad's Politics* (Baltimore: Johns Hopkins Press, 1967)

Paul Kirschner: *Conrad: the Psychologist as Artist* (Edinburgh: Oliver and Boyd, 1968)

Lawrence Graver: *Conrad's Short Fiction* (Berkeley and Los Angeles: University of California Press, 1969)

Bruce Johnson: *Conrad's Models of Mind* (Minneapolis: University of Minnesota Press, 1971)

Norman Sherry, ed.: *Conrad: The Critical Heritage* (London and Boston: Routledge and Kegan Paul, 1973)

Jacques Berthoud: *Joseph Conrad: The Major Phase* (London: Cambridge University Press, 1978)

Jeremy Hawthorn: *Language and Fictional Self-Consciousness* (London: Edward Arnold, 1979)

Ian Watt: *Conrad in the Nineteenth Century* (Berkeley: University of California Press, 1979; London: Chatto and Windus, 1980)

Daniel R. Schwarz: *Conrad: Almayer's Folly to Under Western Eyes* (London and Basingstoke: Macmillan, 1980)

Cedric Watts: *A Preface to Conrad* (London and New York: Longman, 1982)

RECENT BIBLIOGRAPHIES

David Leon Higdon: 'Conrad in the Eighties: A Bibliography and Some Observations', *Conradiana*, 17 (1985), pp. 214–49

— — : 'Current Conrad Bibliography (1984–86)', *Conradiana*, 19, (1987), pp. 215–29

Martin Ray: 'Joseph Conrad and His Contemporaries: An Annotated Bibliography of Interviews and Recollections' (London: Joseph Conrad Society (UK), 1988)

ARTICLES, INTRODUCTIONS, ETC.

On 'Typhoon'

Douglas Brown: 'Introductory Essay', *Three Tales from Conrad* (London: Hutchinson, 1960)

Charles I. Schuster: 'Comedy and the Limits of Language in Conrad's "Typhoon"', *Conradiana*, 16 (1984), pp. 55–71

Cedric Watts: Introduction to *'Typhoon' and Other Tales* (Oxford: Oxford University Press, 1986)

Dwight H. Purdy: 'Conrad at Work: The Two Serial Texts of *Typhoon*', *Conradiana*, 19 (1987), pp. 99–119

Ian Watt: 'Comedy and Humour in *Typhoon*', *The Ugo Mursia Memorial Lectures* [Papers from the International Conrad Conference, University of Pisa, 7–11 September 1983], ed. Mario Curreli (Milan: Mursia International, 1988)

On 'Amy Foster'

Richard Herndon: 'The Genesis of Conrad's "Amy Foster"', *Studies in Philology* 57 (1960), pp. 549–66

Robert Andreach: 'The Two Narrators of "Amy Foster"', *Studies in Short Fiction* 2 (1965), pp. 262–9

Andrzej Busza: 'Amy Foster', in 'Conrad's Polish Literary Background and Some Illustrations of the Influence of Polish Literature on His Work', *Antemurale* X (Rome: Institutum Historicum Polonicum, 1966), pp. 224–30

Juliet McLauchlan: '"Amy Foster" – Echoes from Conrad's Own Experience?', *Polish Review*, Vol. XXIII, No. 3 (1978), pp. 3–8

On 'Falk'

Bruce Johnson: 'Conrad's "Falk": Manuscript and Meaning', *Modern Language Quarterly* 26 (1965), pp. 267–84

Tony Tanner: '"Gnawed Bones" and "Artless Tales" – Eating and Narrative in Conrad', *Joseph Conrad: A Commemoration* [Papers from the 1974 International Conference on Conrad], ed. Norman Sherry (London: Macmillan, 1976), pp. 17–36

Phillipe Jaudel: 'Silent Communication in "Falk": Stares, Glares and Gestures', *L'Epoque Conradienne* (1985), pp. 47–59

Mario Curreli and Fausto Ciompi: 'A Socio-Semiotic Reading of Conrad's "Falk"', *L'Epoque Conradienne 1988*, ed. John Stape, (Limoges: Société Conradienne Française, 1988), pp. 35–45

On 'To-morrow'

Jean Durin: 'Procrastination and Petrification in Joseph Conrad's "To-morrow"' [in French], *L'Epoque Conradienne* (1985), pp. 137–53

On One Day More

Max Beerbohm, 'Mr. Conrad's Play', *Around Theatres* (London: Rupert Hart-Davis, 1953), pp. 384–7

Note on the Text

> ... perhaps my very anxiety as to the proper use of a language of which I feel myself painfully ignorant produces the effect of laboured construction; whereas as a matter of striving my aim is simplicity and ease. *Conrad to Hugh Clifford, 2 December 1902.*

> Of course: Gambusino. I ought to have corrected my proofs carefully. *Conrad to Cunninghame Graham, 21 May 1903.*

According to its description by the Houghton Library at Harvard, Conrad completed the manuscript of 'Typhoon' at midnight, 10–11 January 1901. (The manuscript, and a revised typescript, were withdrawn from the library in 1974 by the depositor, whose address is unknown.) In 1902 the story appeared in *Pall Mall Magazine* from January to March, and in the New York *Critic* from February to May. Conrad specified that the *Pall Mall* text (with minor stylistic changes) should be used for setting the story in book form, namely *Typhoon and Other Stories*, published by Heinemann in 1903. He reluctantly allowed the separate publication of 'Typhoon' in New York by Putnam's in 1902, but complained afterwards that he had not seen the proofs and that the text had been set up 'from an uncorrected MS' (*CLJC*, 2, p. 466).

'Falk' was completed in May 1901; on 7 June Conrad returned two corrected typescripts to Pinker, asking to see proofs. However, the story was never serialized; it was first published in the Heinemann volume in 1903 and in New York the same year by McClure, Phillips & Co., together with 'Amy Foster' and 'To-morrow'. In 1915 the three stories were reissued by Doubleday, in an edition which, as Conrad told Doubleday's editor, contained many misprints.

Conrad finished 'Amy Foster' in June 1901 and 'To-morrow'

early the following January; they appeared, respectively, in the *Illustrated London News* in December 1901 and the *Pall Mall Magazine* in August 1902.

Conrad's handwritten corrections in a disbound copy of the British first edition (now in the Hofstra library) suggest it was used to prepare the text of the 1920 and 1921 American and British collected editions. Conrad also asked that first-edition spelling should be followed in the collected edition of *The Nigger of the 'Narcissus'* (*LL*, II, p. 248). I have therefore taken the British first edition as my copy text. But I was not asked to produce a critical edition, and indeed in this case textual 'authority' is something of a will o' the wisp. The disbound copy contains a grand total of three autograph corrections; the collected edition page proofs in the Hofstra library none at all. Legend has it that Conrad was a meticulous corrector and proof-reader, but he did not devote the same care to every volume; and except for the title story he seems to have devoted very little to *Typhoon*. Some of the variants between the manuscript, serial and first-edition versions of the stories may be compositor's errors or editorial emendations overlooked by Conrad; certainly many misprints and slips in grammar, idiom, spelling and punctuation in the first edition survive in the collected ones. And although reading Conrad is like rediscovering one's own language, it must be remembered that English was Conrad's third language (after Polish and French), and that he aspired to write it clearly and idiomatically. I have therefore aimed at removing distracting or confusing mistakes while remaining faithful to Conrad's conceptual and stylistic intentions (and stylistic idiosyncrasies). To that end I have consulted autograph manuscript (AMS) versions of 'Amy Foster', 'Falk' and 'To-morrow', the serial versions of 'Typhoon', 'Amy Foster' and 'To-morrow', the 1921 Heinemann Collected Edition (HC) and the Dent Collected (DC) edition, which descends via a duplicate set of plates from the 1920 Doubleday (Sun-Dial) edition.

The only substantive changes I have made in 'Typhoon', apart from Conrad's own correction of 'queerly' to 'quaintly' (p. 64) are from HC, which supplies the missing 'as' in 'as though' (p. 96) and the correct tense 'has' for 'had' (p. 79). In 'Amy Foster' I have adopted the AMS insertion of 'brick', instead of 'black', to describe Amy's cottage (p. 136), presumably to designate a dwelling worthy of an acre of land. (I have seen many brick cottages, but none I could confidently call 'black'.) I have also emended 'wicker-gate' to 'wicket-gate' (p. 161), correcting an error that Conrad pointed out to Doubleday's editor in 1915 and then himself overlooked when preparing the collected editions. I have corrected 'should' to 'would' (p. 155) and 'mirage or' to 'mirage of' (p. 144) as in HC and DC, and I have followed Watts (1986) in emending 'used to see' to 'used to seeing' (p. 155).

'Falk' presents the least satisfactory text, perhaps because there was no serial version to revise. Apart from Conrad's corrections – 'trombone' for 'trump' and 'my' for 'any' (p. 173) – I have adopted the AMS reading 'All her hands forward' (p. 166) instead of 'All her hands were forward', since we immediately learn that one of the hands is in fact aft. I have supplied the verb 'is' in 'All I can say his name' (p. 172), leaving the relative pronoun omitted. I have emended 'inspired courage into' to 'inspired courage in' (p. 227), and 'set about to make' to 'set about making' (p. 193), but retained the possibly Gallic word-order of 'when I got first the command' (p. 166) and the AMS and first-edition 'unwell rather' (p. 233) in preference to 'rather unwell' in HC and 'unwell' in DC. I have preferred the lesser evil of a comma to the anacoluthon in the long sentence beginning 'For half an hour longer' (p. 181).

In 'To-morrow' I have preferred the idiomatic serial reading 'looking about uneasily' (p. 249) to 'looking uneasily', although it may have been a magazine editor's emendation (the manuscript reads 'looking uneasily as though'). On the other hand, I have adopted the AMS reading of the first and last lines of Harry's song, as more suggestive of a song being sung.

Without following any rigid policy, I have emended punctuation to clarify authorial intentions. For instance, the manuscript of 'Amy Foster' shows Conrad hesitating between 'passed' and 'passes' and between 'was' and 'is' (p. 138) and in both cases choosing the present, presumably because it seemed illogical to him to relegate Amy's stammer and kind heart to the past simply to comply with the tense sequence of Kennedy's narrative. All editors have adopted Conrad's choice in the first instance and disregarded it in the second. I have followed them, but I have clarified the first choice by placing a colon after 'utterance' (p. 138) to indicate that Kennedy is interrupting his narrative to describe Amy's speech habit in the present tense.

As regards spelling, I have regularized the abbreviation 'boss'n' because it is the one used most often in the first edition and may represent a remembered pronunciation. (When I asked a friend of Northern Irish extraction to pronounce the written word 'boatswain' he did so in a way best rendered phonetically by 'boss'n'.) I have also regularized 'tugboat', 'steamship', 'donkey-man', 'wheel-house' and 'stateroom' (the last two spellings appearing in the AMS of 'Falk'). I have modernized some spellings and used hyphens to prevent confusion; but I have left unchanged those spellings that suggest authorial preference or a period flavour (e.g., 'East-end', 'neck-tie', 'brandy and soda').

Punctuation that clearly does not belong to a quotation is placed outside the quotation marks, a practice generally followed by Conrad himself in his manuscripts. Conrad's documentary device of punctuating reported speech as if it were direct is also handled more logically in the manuscripts than in the printed versions, and I have followed the former where possible. I have italicized non-naturalized foreign words and phrases, except where phoneticized (e.g., 'Gottferdam'); but I have not italicized English words (e.g., 'suite' and 'fracas'), preferring quotation marks for intended ironic effect. (I have also removed quotation marks from the names of public houses, where no irony is intended.)

I have preferred the DC text to that of HC for the 'Author's Note', but I have not tried to improve the questionable syntax and tense use in the first paragraph or untangle the meaning of 'returning coolies' in the second.

Space does not permit a rationale for each emendation: a complete list (except for corrections of obvious misprints and the above-mentioned italicizations and placing of punctuation outside quotation marks) is given below, followed in square brackets by corroborative instances, e.g., [AMS = autograph manuscript; C = Conrad's authority; S = serial version; DC = Dent Collected Edition; HC = Heinemann Collected Edition]. (The first-edition reading follows in parentheses.) No corroboration is given for corrections of obvious spelling mistakes.

Page 51, line 24:   'Falk' (Falk)

51, 25:	*Tales of Unrest* [HC]; ('Tales of Unrest')
55, 27:	sir' [DC] ('sir,')
56, 26:	son, too! [DC] (son too!)
59, 37:	MacWhirr, [DC] (MacWhirr)
61, 8:	boss'n (bo'ss'en)
63, 17:	words (words,)
64, 4:	quaintly [C; DC; HC] (queerly)
64, 5:	children (children,)
64, 13 *et passim*:	stateroom (state-room)
64, 35:	nature'' ', (nature';'')
65, 35:	long run [HC] (long-run)
66, 16:	too, [DC; HC] (too)
69, 22:	worn out, [HC] (worn out)
73, 1:	pipe-fashion (pipe fashion)
73, 31:	Jukes' [DC; HC] (Jukes's)
79, 30:	has [HC] (had)
81, 18 *et passim*:	wheel-house (wheelhouse)
84, 10:	bridge, [DC] (bridge)
92, 3:	tween- [DC] (tween)
95, 20:	see; (see,)
96, 32:	as though [HC] (though)
100, 27:	yellow face [HC] (yellow-face)
101, 18:	bag, (bag)
101, 19:	off (off,)
101, 23:	striped [DC; HC] (stripped)
102, 2:	compass card (compass-card)
102, 19:	bulkhead [HC] (bulk-head)
103, 3 *et passim*:	steering-gear [DC; HC] (steering gear); stopped, (stopped)
107, 3 *et passim*:	donkey-man (donkeyman)
109, 16:	. . .' (. . .,')
112, 17:	waist-deep (waist deep)
119, 25:	boss'n's (boss'en's)
120, 36:	half-way [HC] (half way)
129, 38:	boss'n (boss'en)
130, 17 *et passim*:	Hong Kong (Hong-Kong)
135, 14:	Ship Inn [AMS; S; HC] ('Ship Inn')
135, 15:	by, [DC] (by)

136, 21:	brick [AMS] (black)
137, 8:	shepherd, [HC] (shepherd;)
138, 3:	utterance: (utterance,)
139, 22:	overburdened [AMS] (over-burdened)
139, 37:	startled – (startled, –)
140, 6:	blur (blurr)
141, 31:	emigrant ship [DC; HC] (emigrant-ship)
144, 6–7:	overfull (over full)
144, 17:	mirage of [AMS; S; DC] mirage or
145, 1:	countryside [AMS; HC] (country-side)
146, 12:	back door (back-door)
146, 26:	has admitted [DC] (had admitted)
147, 22:	emigrant ship [AMS] (emigrant-ship)
148, 28:	Ship Inn [S; HC] ('Ship Inn')
153, 15:	overshadowed [AMS; S] (over-shadowed)
153, 32:	grandchild [AMS; HC] (grand-child)
153, 39:	horse-pond (horsepond)
155, 4:	seeing (see)
155, 17:	would [AMS; S; DC; HC] (should)
155, 22:	devil' [AMS] (devil,")
155, last:	expostulate; (expostulate:); forcibly; (forcibly:)
156, 14:	heart, [AMS] (heart;)
158, 30–1:	Coach and Horses, [AMS] ('Coach and Horses,')
159, 32:	half-dressed (half dressed)
161, 17:	those [HC] (these)
161, 21:	wicket [AMS; C] (wicker)
165, 8:	salt water [HC] (salt-water)
165, 15:	decrepit (decrepid)
165, 29:	changes; (changes,); works, (works)
165, 30:	men, (men)
166, 2:	Plate (Platte)
166, 15:	short [AMS] (short,)
166, 16:	forward were [AMS] (were forward)
166, 26:	fifty [AMS] (fifty,)
168, 7:	garments that, (garments that)
168, 24:	well-behaved (well behaved)
169, 12:	pleasant; (pleasant)
169, 16:	niece, [DC; HC] (niece)
170, 20:	a- (a)

41

171, 6:	shirt-sleeves [DC; HC] (shirt sleeves)
171, 25–6:	opened hopefully, (opened, hopefully)
172, 12:	say is (say)
172, 15:	it, [DC] (it)
172, 36:	suite [AMS] (*suite*)
173, 1:	'suite' [AMS] ('*suite*')
173, 17:	trombone [C; DC; HC] (trump)
173, 21:	my [C; DC; HC] (any)
173, 28:	world-proof (world proof)
174, 28:	ironwork, (ironwork)
176, 30:	unseeing, [AMS; DC] (unseeing)
176, 35–6:	battleship [HC] (battle-ship)
177, 20 *et passim*:	tugboat (tug-boat)
177, 33:	one especially, (one, especially)
178, 3:	sun [AMS] (sun,); out, (out); reach, (reach)
179, 14:	'*Wie geht's?*' ('Wie geht's,')
180, 10:	you, too, [DC] (you too)
180, 16:	paddle-wheels, (paddle-wheels)
181, 14:	Falk, (Falk); us, (us)
181, 15:	up and, (up, and)
181, 17:	), said () he said)
181, 25:	odd, [HC] (odd)
182, 18:	travelling, [AMS; HC] (travelling)
182, 25:	money, (money); that, [AMS] (that)
183, 6:	hairbrushes [AMS] (hair-brushes)
183, 12:	which, (which)
183, 13:	look-out [DC] (look out)
183, 21:	words, [AMS] (words)
184, 31:	hairbrush [AMS] (hair-brush)
185, 9:	sun-rays (sun rays)
185, 27:	*table d'hôte* (table-d'hôte)
185, 31:	'Mistake, [HC] ('Mistake)
186, 9:	young [AMS] (young man)
186, 37:	dear, [DC] (dear)
189, 27:	waterside [AMS; HC] (water side)
190, 26:	married, [DC] (married)
190, 33:	remarked that 'it [AMS] (remarked, 'that it
190, 37:	half-open [DC; HC] (half open)
191, 27:	night-shirt [HC] (night shirt)

192, 9:	Hermann, [DC] (Hermann)
192, 29:	Schomberg, [DC; HC] (Schomberg)
193, 12:	making, (to make)
194, 20:	were' he [AMS] (were,' he)
194, 21:	word, 'trash!' [AMS] (word – 'trash.'); reiterated, [HC] (reiterated)
195, 37:	iron-grey [AMS] (iron grey)
195, last:	a uniform [HC] (an uniform)
196, 34:	lived, (lived)
197, 11:	thoroughfare, [AMS, HC] (thoroughfare)
197, 16:	ankle-deep (ankle deep)
198, 29:	hussars (Hussars)
199, 21:	jerk; (jerk,); driver, (driver); down, (down)
202, 27:	'fracas' [AMS] (*fracas*)
202, 28:	'Fracas' [AMS] (*Fracas*)
203, 15:	'fracas' [AMS] ('*fracas*')
205, 14:	he 'didn't [AMS] ('he didn't)
205, 16:	this, (this)
205, 36:	voice; (voice,)
206, 29:	is, (is); mind, (mind)
207, 3:	courting [AMS] (courting,)
209, 15:	sailor, [DC] (sailor)
210, 5:	Well, [DC; HC] ('Well,)
210, 6:	ago. [DC; HC] (ago.')
211, 3:	step-dance (step dance)
211, 20:	red- (red)
214, 1:	'*Ach so!*' [AMS] ('*Ach So!*')
214, 25:	time, too [DC] (time too)
215, 8:	hand (hand,)
215, 9:	called, (called)
215, 14:	seven-foot (seven foot)
216, 30:	long-drawn [DC] (long drawn)
218, 35:	course, (course)
219, 14:	staterooms [AMS] (state-rooms)
220, 16:	quarter-deck [DC; HC] (quarter deck)
225, 4:	'Break-down,' ('Break down,')
225, 8:	sink, (sink)
226, 4:	as [AMS] (as,); call [AMS] (call,)
226, 9:	everyone (AMS; DC) (every one)

227, 2:	in (into)
227, 7:	chief engineer (chief-engineer)
227, 11:	waifs: (waifs,)
228, 35:	reasserted (re-asserted)
229, last:	after- [DC] (after)
230, 11:	on Falk, [HC] (on, Falk)
230, 23:	fresh-water pump [DC; HC] (fresh water-pump)
231, 3:	brass-framed [DC] (brass framed)
231, 20:	second- (second)
231, 37:	after-deck [DC] (after deck)
232, 9:	I, too, [DC] (I too)
234, 3:	Yes! [AMS; DC; HC] ('Yes!)
234, 5:	went . . . [DC; HC] (went . . .')
239, 26:	clothes-line (clothes line)
240, 5:	being' (being,')
240, 11:	answered (answered,)
240, 12:	think' (think,')
240, 21:	maker. High [AMS] (maker; high)
240, 22:	Colebrook; (Colebrook,)
241, 1:	gusto (gusto,)
241, 33:	Strange [AMS] (Strange,); confess [AMS] (confess,)
242, 18:	evasive (evasive,)
242, 19:	forgotten [HC] (forgotten,)
242, 20:	forgotten, [S; HC] (forgotten)
243, 9:	nose [DC] (nose,)
244, 11:	land' (land,')
244, 13:	undersized (under-sized)
244, 14:	grass-plot (grass plot)
244, 35:	vertical, (vertical); columns; (columns,)
245, 20:	cunningly, 'the (cunningly: 'the)
245, 39:	mahogany-coloured [HC] (mahogany coloured)
246, 24:	tenant (tenant,)
247, 14:	slow, [S] (slow)
248, 7:	you, (you)
248, 11:	daylight [AMS; DC; HC] (day-light)
249, 5:	looking about [S] (looking)
249, 19:	sheet iron [AMS] (sheet-iron)
250, 15:	another (another,)
252, 17:	crazy? (crazy.) [AMS: Is he quite crazy?]

44

253, 14:	murmured: (murmured.)
252, 2:	grinning [AMS] (grinning,)
256, 6:	bitterly. 'From [AMS] (bitterly: from)
257, 1:	hair, (hair)
257, 29–30:	sea-wall [AMS; DC] (sea wall)
258, 1:	oh, ho! Rio ! . . . [AMS] (ho, ho Rio!)
258, 4:	Rio . . . Grande. [AMS] (Rio Grande.)
258, 37:	mountain-top [HC] (mountain top)
258, 37 *et passim*:	Gambusinos [C] (Gambucinos)
259, 21:	Mazatlán (Mazatlan)
260, 2 *et passim*:	*Gambusino* [C] (*Gambucino*)

Typhoon
And Other Stories

By

Joseph Conrad

Author of

"The Nigger of the 'Narcissus,'" &c.

Far as the mariner on highest mast
Can see all around upon the calmed vast.
So wide was Neptune's hall . . .
KEATS[1]

London
William Heinemann
1903

To R. B. Cunninghame Graham[2]

AUTHOR'S NOTE[3]

THE main characteristic of this volume consists in this, that all the stories composing it belong not only to the same period but have been written one after another in the order in which they appear in the book.[4]

The period is that which follows on my connection with *Blackwood's Magazine*.[5] I had just finished writing 'The End of the Tether'[6] and was casting about for some subject which could be developed in a shorter form than the tales in the volume of 'Youth' when the instance of a steamship full of returning coolies from Singapore to some port in northern China occurred to my recollection. Years before I had heard it being talked about in the East as a recent occurrence. It was for us merely one subject of conversation amongst many others of the kind. Men earning their bread in any very specialized occupation will talk shop, not only because it is the most vital interest of their lives, but also because they have not much knowledge of other subjects. They have never had the time to get acquainted with them. Life, for most of us, is not so much a hard as an exacting taskmaster.

I never met anybody personally concerned in this affair, the interest of which for us was, of course, not the bad weather but the extraordinary complication brought into the ship's life at a moment of exceptional stress by the human element below her deck. Neither was the story itself ever enlarged upon in my hearing. In that company each of us could imagine easily what the whole thing was like. The financial difficulty of it, presenting also a human problem, was solved by a mind much too simple to be perplexed by anything in the world except men's idle talk for which it was not adapted.

From the first the mere anecdote, the mere statement I might say, that such a thing had happened on the high seas, appeared to me a sufficient subject for meditation. Yet it was but a bit of a sea yarn after all. I felt that to bring out its deeper significance which

49

was quite apparent to me, something other, something more was required; a leading motive that would harmonize all these violent noises, and a point of view that would put all that elemental fury into its proper place.

What was needed of course was Captain MacWhirr.[7] Directly I perceived him I could see that he was the man for the situation. I don't mean to say that I ever saw Captain MacWhirr in the flesh, or had ever come in contact with his literal mind and his dauntless temperament. MacWhirr is not an acquaintance of a few hours, or a few weeks, or a few months. He is the product of twenty years of life. My own life. Conscious invention had little to do with him. If it is true that Captain MacWhirr never walked and breathed on this earth (which I find for my part extremely difficult to believe), I can also assure my readers that he is perfectly authentic. I may venture to assert the same of every aspect of the story, while I confess that the particular typhoon of the tale was not a typhoon of my actual experience.

At its first appearance 'Typhoon', the story, was classed by some critics as a deliberately intended storm-piece.[8] Others picked out MacWhirr, in whom they perceived a definite symbolic intention. Neither was exclusively my intention. Both the typhoon and Captain MacWhirr presented themselves to me as the necessities of the deep conviction with which I approached the subject of the story. It was their opportunity. It was also my opportunity; and it would be vain to discourse about what I made of it in a handful of pages, since the pages themselves are here, between the covers of this volume, to speak for themselves.

This is a belated reflection. If it had occurred to me before it would have perhaps done away with the existence of this Author's Note; for, indeed, the same remark applies to every story in this volume. None of them are stories of experience in the absolute sense of the word. Experience in them is but the canvas of the attempted picture. Each of them has its more than one intention. With each the question is what the writer has done with his opportunity; and each answers the question for itself in words which, if I may say so without undue solemnity, were written with a conscientious regard for the truth of my own sensations. And each of those stories, to mean something, must justify itself in its own way to the conscience of each successive reader.

'Falk' – the second story in the volume – offended the delicacy of one critic at least by certain peculiarities of its subject. But what is the subject of 'Falk'? I personally do not feel so very certain about it. He who reads must find out for himself. My intention in writing 'Falk' was not to shock anybody. As in most of my writings I insist not on the events but on their effect upon the persons in the tale. But in everything I have written there is always one invariable intention, and that is to capture the reader's attention, by securing his interest and enlisting his sympathies for the matter in hand, whatever it may be, within the limits of the visible world and within the boundaries of human emotions.

I may safely say that Falk is absolutely true to my experience of certain straightforward characters combining a perfectly natural ruthlessness with a certain amount of moral delicacy. Falk obeys the law of self-preservation without the slightest misgivings as to his right, but at a crucial turn of that ruthlessly preserved life he will not condescend to dodge the truth. As he is presented as sensitive enough to be affected permanently by a certain unusual experience, that experience had to be set by me before the reader vividly; but it is not the subject of the tale. If we go by mere facts then the subject is Falk's attempt to get married; in which the narrator of the tale finds himself unexpectedly involved both on its ruthless and its delicate side.

'Falk' shares with one other of my stories ('The Return' in the *Tales of Unrest* volume) the distinction of never having been serialized. I think the copy was shown to the editor of some magazine who rejected it indignantly on the sole ground that 'the girl never says anything'. This is perfectly true. From first to last Hermann's niece utters no word in the tale – and it is not because she is dumb, but for the simple reason that whenever she happens to come under the observation of the narrator she has either no occasion or is too profoundly moved to speak.[9] The editor, who obviously had read the story, might have perceived that for himself. Apparently he did not, and I refrained from pointing out the impossibility to him because, since he did not venture to say that 'the girl' did not live, I felt no concern at his indignation.

All the other stories were serialized. 'Typhoon' appeared in the early numbers of the *Pall Mall Magazine*, then under the direction of the late Mr. Halkett. It was on that occasion, too, that I saw for the first time my conceptions rendered by an artist in another medium. Mr. Maurice Greiffenhagen knew how to combine in his illustrations the effect of his own most distinguished personal vision with an absolute fidelity to the inspiration of the writer. 'Amy Foster' was published in *The Illustrated London News*, with a fine drawing of Amy on her day out giving tea to the children at her home, in a hat with a big feather. 'To-morrow' appeared first in the *Pall Mall Magazine*. Of that story I will only say that it struck many people by its adaptability to the stage, and that I was induced to dramatize it under the title of 'One Day More'; up to the present my only effort in that direction. I may also add that each of the four stories on their appearance in book form was picked out on various grounds as the 'best of the lot' by different critics, who reviewed the volume with a warmth of appreciation and under-standing, a sympathetic insight and a friendliness of expression for which I cannot be sufficiently grateful.

1919   J. C.

TYPHOON

TYPHOON

I

CAPTAIN MACWHIRR, of the steamer *Nan-Shan*,[10] had a physiognomy that, in the order of material appearances, was the exact counterpart of his mind: it presented no marked characteristics of firmness or stupidity; it had no pronounced characteristics whatever; it was simply ordinary, irresponsive, and unruffled.

The only thing his aspect might have been said to suggest, at times, was bashfulness; because he would sit, in business offices ashore, sunburnt and smiling faintly, with downcast eyes. When he raised them, they were perceived to be direct in their glance and of blue colour. His hair was fair and extremely fine, clasping from temple to temple the bald dome of his skull in a clamp as of fluffy silk. The hair of his face, on the contrary, carroty and flaming, resembled a growth of copper wire clipped short to the line of the lip; while, no matter how close he shaved, fiery metallic gleams passed, when he moved his head, over the surface of his cheeks. He was rather below the medium height, a bit round-shouldered, and so sturdy of limb that his clothes always looked a shade too tight for his arms and legs. As if unable to grasp what is due to the difference of latitudes, he wore a brown bowler hat, a complete suit of a brownish hue, and clumsy black boots. These harbour togs gave to his thick figure an air of stiff and uncouth smartness. A thin silver watch-chain looped his waistcoat, and he never left his ship for the shore without clutching in his powerful, hairy fist an elegant umbrella of the very best quality, but generally unrolled. Young Jukes, the chief mate, attending his commander to the gangway, would sometimes venture to say, with the greatest gentleness, 'Allow me, sir' – and possessing himself of the umbrella deferentially, would elevate the ferule, shake the folds, twirl a neat furl in a jiffy, and hand it back; going through the performance with a face of such portentous gravity, that Mr..Solomon Rout, the chief engineer, smoking his morning cigar over the skylight, would turn away his head in order to hide a smile. 'Oh! aye! The blessed gamp[11] .... Thank 'ee, Jukes, thank 'ee,' would mutter Captain MacWhirr heartily, without looking up.

Having just enough imagination to carry him through each successive day, and no more, he was tranquilly sure of himself; and from the very same cause he was not in the least conceited. It is your imaginative superior who is touchy, overbearing, and difficult to please; but every ship Captain MacWhirr commanded was the floating abode of harmony and peace. It was, in truth, as impossible for him to take a flight of fancy as it would be for a watchmaker to put together a chronometer with nothing except a two-pound hammer and a whip-saw in the way of tools. Yet the uninteresting lives of men so entirely given to the actuality of the bare existence have their mysterious side. It was impossible in Captain MacWhirr's case, for instance, to understand what under heaven could have induced that perfectly satisfactory son of a petty grocer in Belfast to run away to sea. And yet he had done that very thing at the age of fifteen. It was enough, when you thought it over, to give you the idea of an immense, potent, and invisible hand thrust into the ant-heap of the earth, laying hold of shoulders, knocking heads together, and setting the unconscious faces of the multitude towards inconceivable goals and in undreamt-of directions.

His father never really forgave him for this undutiful stupidity. 'We could have got on without him,' he used to say later on, 'but there's the business. And he an only son, too!' His mother wept very much after his disappearance. As it had never occurred to him to leave word behind, he was mourned over for dead till, after eight months, his first letter arrived from Talcahuano. It was short, and contained the statement: 'We had very fine weather on our passage out.' But evidently, in the writer's mind, the only important intelligence was to the effect that his captain had, on the very day of writing, entered him regularly on the ship's articles as Ordinary Seaman. 'Because I can do the work,' he explained. The mother again wept copiously, while the remark, 'Tom's an ass,' expressed the emotions of the father. He was a corpulent man, with a gift for sly chaffing, which to the end of his life he exercised in his intercourse with his son, a little pityingly, as if upon a half-witted person.

MacWhirr's visits to his home were necessarily rare, and in the course of years he despatched other letters to his parents, informing them of his successive promotions and of his movements upon the vast earth. In these missives could be found sentences like this: 'The heat here is very great.' Or: 'On Christmas day at 4 P.M. we fell in with some icebergs.' The old people ultimately became acquainted with a good many names of ships, and with the names of the skippers who commanded them – with the names of Scots and English shipowners – with the names of seas, oceans, straits, promontories – with outlandish names of lumber-ports, of rice-ports, of cotton-ports – with the names of islands – with the name of their son's young woman. She was called Lucy. It did not suggest itself to him to mention whether he thought the name pretty. And then they died.

The great day of MacWhirr's marriage came in due course, following shortly upon the great day when he got his first command.

All these events had taken place many years before the morning when, in the chart-room of the steamer *Nan-Shan*, he stood confronted by the fall of a barometer he had no reason to distrust. The fall – taking into account the excellence of the instrument, the time of the year, and the ship's position on the terrestrial globe – was of a nature ominously prophetic; but the red face of the man betrayed no sort of inward disturbance. Omens were as nothing to him, and he was unable to discover the message of a prophecy till the fulfilment had brought it home to his very door. 'That's a fall, and no mistake,' he thought. 'There must be some uncommonly dirty weather knocking about.'

The *Nan-Shan* was on her way from the southward to the treaty port of Fu-chau, with some cargo in her lower holds, and two hundred Chinese coolies returning to their village homes in the province of Fo-kien, after a few years of work in various tropical colonies. The morning was fine, the oily sea heaved without a sparkle, and there was a queer white misty patch in the sky like a halo of the sun. The fore-deck, packed with Chinamen, was full of sombre clothing, yellow faces, and pigtails, sprinkled over with a good many naked shoulders, for there was no wind, and the heat was close. The coolies lounged, talked, smoked, or stared over the rail; some, drawing water over the side, sluiced each other; a few slept on hatches, while several small parties of six sat on their heels surrounding iron trays with plates of rice and tiny teacups; and every single Celestial of them was carrying with him all he had in the world – a wooden chest with a ringing lock and brass on the corners, containing the savings of his labours: some clothes of ceremony, sticks of incense, a little opium maybe, bits of nameless rubbish of conventional value, and a small hoard of silver dollars, toiled for in coal lighters, won in gambling-houses or in petty trading, grubbed out of earth, sweated out in mines, on railway lines, in deadly jungle, under heavy burdens – amassed patiently, guarded with care, cherished fiercely.

A cross swell had set in from the direction of Formosa Channel about ten o'clock, without disturbing these passengers much, because the *Nan-Shan*, with her flat bottom, rolling chocks on bilges, and great breadth of beam, had the reputation of an exceptionally steady ship in a sea-way. Mr. Jukes, in moments of expansion on shore, would proclaim loudly that the 'old girl was as good as she was pretty'. It would never have occurred to Captain MacWhirr to express his favourable opinion so loud or in terms so fanciful.

She was a good ship, undoubtedly, and not old either. She had been built in Dumbarton less than three years before, to the order of a firm of merchants in Siam – Messrs. Sigg[12] and Son. When she lay afloat, finished in every detail and ready to take up the work of her life, the builders contemplated her with pride.

'Sigg has asked us for a reliable skipper to take her out,' remarked one of the partners; and the other, after reflecting for a while, said: 'I think MacWhirr is ashore just at present.' 'Is he? Then wire him at once. He's the very man,' declared the senior, without a moment's hesitation.

Next morning MacWhirr stood before them unperturbed, having travelled from London by the midnight express after a sudden but undemonstrative parting with his wife. She was the daughter of a superior couple who had seen better days.

'We had better be going together over the ship, Captain,' said the senior partner; and the three men started to view the perfections of the *Nan-Shan* from stem to stern, and from her keelson to the trucks of her two stumpy pole-masts.

Captain MacWhirr had begun by taking off his coat, which he

hung on the end of a steam windlass embodying all the latest improvements.

'My uncle wrote of you favourably by yesterday's mail to our good friends – Messrs. Sigg, you know – and doubtless they'll continue you out there in command,' said the junior partner. 'You'll be able to boast of being in charge of the handiest boat of her size on the coast of China, Captain,' he added.

'Have you? Thank 'ee,' mumbled vaguely MacWhirr, to whom the view of a distant eventuality could appeal no more than the beauty of a wide landscape to a purblind tourist; and his eyes happening at the moment to be at rest upon the lock of the cabin door, he walked up to it, full of purpose, and began to rattle the handle vigorously, while he observed, in his low, earnest voice, 'You can't trust the workmen nowadays. A brand-new lock, and it won't act at all. Stuck fast. See? See?'

As soon as they found themselves alone in their office across the yard: 'You praised that fellow up to Sigg. What is it you see in him?' asked the nephew, with faint contempt.

'I admit he has nothing of your fancy skipper about him, if that's what you mean,' said the elder man curtly. 'Is the foreman of the joiners on the *Nan-Shan* outside? . . . Come in, Bates. How is it that you let Tait's people put us off with a defective lock on the cabin door? The Captain could see directly he set eye on it. Have it replaced at once. The little straws, Bates . . . the little straws. . . .'[13]

The lock was replaced accordingly, and a few days afterwards the *Nan-Shan* steamed out to the East, without MacWhirr having offered any further remark as to her fittings, or having been heard to utter a single word hinting at pride in his ship, gratitude for his appointment, or satisfaction at his prospects.

With a temperament neither loquacious nor taciturn, he found very little occasion to talk. There were matters of duty, of course – directions, orders, and so on; but the past being to his mind done with, and the future not there yet, the more general actualities of the day required no comment – because facts can speak for themselves with overwhelming precision.

Old Mr. Sigg liked a man of few words, and one that 'you could be sure would not try to improve upon his instructions'. MacWhirr, satisfying these requirements, was continued in command of the *Nan-Shan*, and applied himself to the careful navigation of his ship in the China seas. She had come out on a British register, but after some time Messrs. Sigg judged it expedient to transfer her to the Siamese flag.[14]

At the news of the contemplated transfer Jukes grew restless, as if under a sense of personal affront. He went about grumbling to himself, and uttering short scornful laughs. 'Fancy having a ridiculous Noah's Ark elephant in the ensign of one's ship,' he said once at the engine-room door. 'Dash me if I can stand it: I'll throw up the billet. Don't it make *you* sick, Mr. Rout?' The chief engineer only cleared his throat with the air of a man who knows the value of a good billet.

The first morning the new flag floated over the stern of the *Nan-Shan* Jukes stood looking at it bitterly from the bridge. He struggled with his feelings for a while, and then remarked, 'Queer flag for a man to sail under, sir.'

'What's the matter with the flag?' inquired Captain MacWhirr. 'Seems all right to me.' And he walked across to the end of the bridge to have a good look.

'Well, it looks queer to me,' burst out Jukes, greatly exasperated, and flung off the bridge.

Captain MacWhirr was amazed at these manners. After a while he stepped quietly into the chart-room, and opened his International Signal Code-book at the plate where the flags of all the nations are correctly figured in gaudy rows. He ran his finger over them, and when he came to Siam he contemplated with great attention the red field and the white elephant. Nothing could be more simple; but to make sure he brought the book out on the bridge for the purpose of comparing the coloured drawing with the real thing at the flagstaff astern. When next Jukes, who was carrying on the duty that day with a sort of suppressed fierceness, happened on the bridge, his commander observed:

'There's nothing amiss with that flag.'

'Isn't there?' mumbled Jukes, falling on his knees before a deck-locker and jerking therefrom viciously a spare lead-line.

'No. I looked up the book. Length twice the breadth and the elephant exactly in the middle. I thought the people ashore would know how to make the local flag. Stands to reason. You were wrong, Jukes. . . .'

60

'Well, sir,' began Jukes, getting up excitedly, 'all I can say —' He fumbled for the end of the coil of line with trembling hands.

'That's all right.' Captain MacWhirr soothed him, sitting heavily on a little canvas folding-stool he greatly affected. 'All you have to do is to take care they don't hoist the elephant upside-down before they get quite used to it.'

Jukes flung the new lead-line over on the fore-deck with a loud 'Here you are, boss'n – don't forget to wet it thoroughly,' and turned with immense resolution towards his commander; but Captain MacWhirr spread his elbows on the bridge-rail comfortably.

'Because it would be, I suppose, understood as a signal of distress,' he went on. 'What do you think? That elephant there, I take it, stands for something in the nature of the Union Jack in the flag. . . .'

'Does it!' yelled Jukes, so that every head on the *Nan-Shan*'s decks looked towards the bridge. Then he sighed, and with sudden resignation: 'It would certainly be a dam' distressful sight,' he said meekly.

Later in the day he accosted the chief engineer with a confidential 'Here, let me tell you the old man's latest.'

Mr. Solomon Rout (frequently alluded to as Long Sol, Old Sol, or Father Rout), from finding himself almost invariably the tallest man on board every ship he joined, had acquired the habit of a stooping, leisurely condescension. His hair was scant and sandy, his flat cheeks were pale, his bony wrists and long scholarly hands were pale too, as though he had lived all his life in the shade.

He smiled from on high at Jukes, and went on smoking and glancing about quietly, in the manner of a kind uncle lending an ear to the tale of an excited schoolboy. Then, greatly amused but impassive, he asked:

'And did you throw up the billet?'

'No,' cried Jukes, raising a weary, discouraged voice above the harsh buzz of the *Nan-Shan*'s friction winches. All of them were hard at work, snatching slings of cargo, high up, to the end of long derricks, only, as it seemed, to let them rip down recklessly by the run. The cargo chains groaned in the gins, clinked on coamings, rattled over the side; and the whole ship quivered, with her long grey flanks smoking in wreaths of steam. 'No,' cried Jukes, 'I didn't. What's the good? I might just as well fling my resignation at this bulkhead. I don't believe you can make a man like that understand anything. He simply knocks me over.'

At that moment Captain MacWhirr, back from the shore, crossed the deck, umbrella in hand, escorted by a mournful, self-possessed Chinaman, walking behind in paper-soled silk shoes, and who also carried an umbrella.

The master of the *Nan-Shan*, speaking just audibly and gazing at his boots as his manner was, remarked that it would be necessary to call at Fu-chau this trip, and desired Mr. Rout to have steam up to-morrow afternoon at one o'clock sharp. He pushed back his hat to wipe his forehead, observing at the same time that he hated going ashore anyhow; while overtopping him Mr. Rout, without deigning a word, smoked austerely, nursing his right elbow in the palm of his left hand. Then Jukes was directed in the same subdued voice to keep the forward 'tween-deck clear of cargo. Two hundred coolies were going to be put down there. The Bun Hin Company were sending that lot home. Twenty-five bags of rice would be coming off in a sampan directly, for stores. All seven-years'-men they were, said Captain MacWhirr, with a camphor-wood chest to every man. The carpenter should be set to work nailing three-inch battens along the deck below, fore and aft, to keep these boxes from shifting in a sea-way. Jukes had better look to it at once. 'D'ye hear, Jukes?' This Chinaman here was coming with the ship as far as Fu-chau, – a sort of interpreter he would be. Bun Hin's clerk he was, and wanted to have a look at the space. Jukes had better take him forward. 'D'ye hear, Jukes?'

Jukes took care to punctuate these instructions in proper places with the obligatory 'Yes, sir', ejaculated without enthusiasm. His brusque 'Come along, John; make look see' set the Chinaman in motion at his heels.

'Wanchee look see, all same look see can do,' said Jukes, who having no talent for foreign languages mangled the very pidgin-English cruelly. He pointed at the open hatch. 'Catchee number one piecie place to sleep in. Eh?'

He was gruff, as became his racial superiority, but not unfriendly. The Chinaman, gazing sad and speechless into the darkness of the hatchway, seemed to stand at the head of a yawning grave.

'No catchee rain down there – savee?' pointed out Jukes. 'Sup-

pose all'ee same fine weather, one piecie coolie-man come topside,'
he pursued, warming up imaginatively. 'Make so – Phooooo!' He
expanded his chest and blew out his cheeks. 'Savee, John? Breathe
– fresh air. Good. Eh? Washee him piecie pants, chow-chow top-side
– see, John?'

With his mouth and hands he made exuberant motions of
eating rice and washing clothes; and the Chinaman, who concealed
his distrust of this pantomime under a collected demeanour tinged
by a gentle and refined melancholy, glanced out of his almond
eyes from Jukes to the hatch and back again. 'Velly good,' he
murmured, in a disconsolate undertone, and hastened smoothly
along the decks, dodging obstacles in his course. He disappeared,
ducking low under a sling of ten dirty gunny-bags full of some
costly merchandise and exhaling a repulsive smell.

Captain MacWhirr meantime had gone on the bridge, and into
the chart-room, where a letter, commenced two days before,
awaited termination. These long letters began with the words 'My
darling wife', and the steward, between the scrubbing of the floors
and the dusting of chronometer-boxes, snatched at every opportunity to read them. They interested him much more than they
possibly could the woman for whose eye they were intended; and
this for the reason that they related in minute detail each successive
trip of the Nan-Shan.

Her master, faithful to facts, which alone his consciousness
reflected, would set them down with painstaking care upon many
pages. The house in a northern suburb to which these pages were
addressed had a bit of garden before the bow-windows, a deep
porch of good appearance, coloured glass with imitation lead
frame in the front door. He paid five-and-forty pounds a year for it,
and did not think the rent too high, because Mrs. MacWhirr (a
pretentious person with a scraggy neck and a disdainful manner)
was admittedly ladylike, and in the neighbourhood considered as
'quite superior'. The only secret of her life was her abject terror of
the time when her husband would come home to stay for good.
Under the same roof there dwelt also a daughter called Lydia and a
son, Tom. These two were but slightly acquainted with their
father. Mainly, they knew him as a rare but privileged visitor, who
of an evening smoked his pipe in the dining-room and slept in the
house. The lanky girl, upon the whole, was rather ashamed of

him; the boy was frankly and utterly indifferent in a straight-forward, delightful, unaffected way manly boys have.

And Captain MacWhirr wrote home from the coast of China twelve times every year, desiring quaintly to be 'remembered to the children' and subscribing himself 'your loving husband,' as calmly as if the words so long used by so many men were, apart from their shape, worn-out things, and of a faded meaning.

The China seas north and south are narrow seas. They are seas full of every-day, eloquent facts, such as islands, sand-banks, reefs, swift and changeable currents – tangled facts that nevertheless speak to a seaman in clear and definite language. Their speech appealed to Captain MacWhirr's sense of realities so forcibly that he had given up his stateroom below and practically lived all his days on the bridge of his ship, often having his meals sent up, and sleeping at night in the chart-room. And he indited there his home letters. Each of them, without exception, contained the phrase, 'The weather has been very fine this trip', or some other form of a statement to that effect. And this statement, too, in its wonderful persistence, was of the same perfect accuracy as all the others they contained.

Mr. Rout likewise wrote letters; only no one on board knew how chatty he could be pen in hand, because the chief engineer had enough imagination to keep his desk locked. His wife relished his style greatly. They were a childless couple, and Mrs. Rout, a big, high-bosomed, jolly woman of forty, shared with Mr. Rout's tooth-less and venerable mother a little cottage near Teddington. She would run over her correspondence, at breakfast, with lively eyes, and scream out interesting passages in a joyous voice at the deaf old lady, prefacing each extract by the warning shout, 'Solomon says!' She had the trick of firing off Solomon's utterances also upon strangers, astonishing them easily by the unfamiliar text and the unexpectedly jocular vein of these quotations. On the day the new curate called for the first time at the cottage, she found occasion to remark, 'As Solomon says: "the engineers that go down to the sea in ships behold the wonders of sailor nature"', when a change in the visitor's countenance made her stop and stare.

'Solomon . . . Oh! . . . Mrs. Rout,' stuttered the young man, very red in the face, 'I must say . . . I don't . . .'

'He's my husband,' she announced in a great shout, throwing

herself back in the chair. Perceiving the joke, she laughed immoderately with a handkerchief to her eyes, while he sat wearing a forced smile, and, from his inexperience of jolly women, fully persuaded that she must be deplorably insane. They were excellent friends afterwards; for, absolving her from irreverent intention, he came to think she was a very worthy person indeed; and he learned in time to receive without flinching other scraps of Solomon's wisdom.

'For my part,' Solomon was reported by his wife to have said once, 'give me the dullest ass for a skipper before a rogue. There is a way to take a fool; but a rogue is smart and slippery.' This was an airy generalisation drawn from the particular case of Captain MacWhirr's honesty, which, in itself, had the heavy obviousness of a lump of clay. On the other hand, Mr. Jukes, unable to generalize, unmarried, and unengaged, was in the habit of opening his heart after another fashion to an old chum and former shipmate, actually serving as second officer on board an Atlantic liner.

First of all he would insist upon the advantages of the Eastern trade, hinting at its superiority to the Western ocean service. He extolled the sky, the seas, the ships, and the easy life of the Far East. The *Nan-Shan*, he affirmed, was second to none as a sea-boat.

'We have no brass-bound uniforms, but then we are like brothers here,' he wrote. 'We all mess together and live like fighting-cocks. . . . All the chaps of the black-squad are as decent as they make that kind, and old Sol, the Chief, is a dry stick. We are good friends. As to our old man, you could not find a quieter skipper. Sometimes you would think he hadn't sense enough to see anything wrong. And yet it isn't that. Can't be. He has been in command for a good few years now. He doesn't do anything actually foolish, and gets his ship along all right without worrying anybody. I believe he hasn't brains enough to enjoy kicking up a row. I don't take advantage of him. I would scorn it. Outside the routine of duty he doesn't seem to understand more than half of what you tell him. We get a laugh out of this at times; but it is dull, too, to be with a man like this – in the long run. Old Sol says he hasn't much conversation. Conversation! O Lord! He never talks. The other day I had been yarning under the bridge with one of the engineers, and he must have heard us. When I came up to take my watch, he steps out of the chart-room and has a good look all round, peeps over at the sidelights, glances at the compass, squints upwards at the stars. That's his regular performance. By-and-by he says: "Was that you talking just now in the port alleyway?" "Yes, sir." "With the third engineer?" "Yes, sir." He walks off to starboard, and sits under the dodger on a little campstool of his, and for half an hour perhaps he makes no sound, except that I heard him sneeze once. Then after a while I hear him getting up over there, and he strolls across to port, where I was. "I can't understand what you can find to talk about," says he. "Two solid hours. I am not blaming you. I see people ashore at it all day long, and then in the evening they sit down and keep at it over the drinks. Must be saying the same things over and over again. I can't understand."

'Did you ever hear anything like that? And he was so patient about it. It made me quite sorry for him. But he is exasperating too, sometimes. Of course one would not do anything to vex him even if it were worth while. But it isn't. He's so jolly innocent that if you were to put your thumb to your nose and wave your fingers at him he would only wonder gravely to himself what got into you. He told me once quite simply that he found it very difficult to make out what made people always act so queerly. He's too dense to trouble about, and that's the truth.'

Thus wrote Mr. Jukes to his chum in the Western ocean trade, out of the fulness of his heart and the liveliness of his fancy.

He had expressed his honest opinion. It was not worth while trying to impress a man of that sort. If the world had been full of such men, life would have probably appeared to Jukes an unentertaining and unprofitable business. He was not alone in his opinion. The sea itself, as if sharing Mr. Jukes' good-natured forbearance, had never put itself out to startle the silent man, who seldom looked up, and wandered innocently over the waters with the only visible purpose of getting food, raiment, and house-room for three people ashore. Dirty weather he had known, of course. He had been made wet, uncomfortable, tired in the usual way, felt at the time and presently forgotten. So that upon the whole he had been justified in reporting fine weather at home. But he had never been given a glimpse of immeasurable strength and of immoderate wrath, the wrath that passes exhausted but never appeased – the wrath and fury of the passionate sea. He knew it existed, as we know that crime and abominations exist; he had heard of it as a peaceable citizen in a town hears of battles, famines, and floods, and yet knows nothing of what these things mean – though, indeed, he may have been mixed up in a street row, have gone without his dinner once, or been soaked to the skin in a shower. Captain MacWhirr had sailed over the surface of the oceans as some men go skimming over the years of existence to sink gently into a placid grave, ignorant of life to the last, without ever having been made to see all it may contain of perfidy, of violence, and of terror. There are on sea and land such men thus fortunate – or thus disdained by destiny or by the sea.

II

OBSERVING the steady fall of the barometer, Captain MacWhirr thought, 'There's some dirty weather knocking about.' This is precisely what he thought. He had had an experience of moderately dirty weather – the term dirty as applied to the weather implying only moderate discomfort to the seaman. Had he been informed by an indisputable authority that the end of the world was to be finally accomplished by a catastrophic disturbance of the atmosphere, he would have assimilated the information under the simple idea of dirty weather, and no other, because he had no experience of cataclysms, and belief does not necessarily imply comprehension. The wisdom of his country had pronounced by means of an Act of Parliament that before he could be considered as fit to take charge of a ship he should be able to answer certain simple questions on the subject of circular storms such as hurricanes, cyclones, typhoons; and apparently he had answered them, since he was now in command of the *Nan-Shan* in the China seas during the season of typhoons.[15] But if he had answered he remembered nothing of it. He was, however, conscious of being made uncomfortable by the clammy heat. He came out on the bridge, and found no relief to this oppression. The air seemed thick. He gasped like a fish, and began to believe himself greatly out of sorts.

The *Nan-Shan* was ploughing a vanishing furrow upon the circle of the sea that had the surface and the shimmer of an undulating piece of grey silk. The sun, pale and without rays, poured down leaden heat in a strangely indecisive light, and the Chinamen were lying prostrate about the decks. Their bloodless, pinched, yellow faces were like the faces of bilious invalids. Captain MacWhirr noticed two of them especially, stretched out on their backs below the bridge. As soon as they had closed their eyes they seemed dead. Three others, however, were quarrelling barbarously away forward; and one big fellow, half naked, with herculean shoulders, was hanging limply over a winch; another, sitting on the deck, his knees up and his head drooping sideways in a girlish attitude, was plaiting his pigtail with infinite languor depicted in his whole person and in the very movement of his fingers. The smoke struggled with difficulty out of the funnel, and instead of streaming away spread itself out like an infernal sort of cloud, smelling of sulphur and raining soot all over the decks.

'What the devil are you doing there, Mr. Jukes?' asked Captain MacWhirr.

This unusual form of address, though mumbled rather than spoken, caused the body of Mr. Jukes to start as though it had been prodded under the fifth rib. He had had a low bench brought on the bridge, and sitting on it, with a length of rope curled about his feet and a piece of canvas stretched over his knees, was pushing a sail-needle vigorously. He looked up, and his surprise gave to his eyes an expression of innocence and candour.

'I am only roping some of that new set of bags we made last trip for whipping up coals,' he remonstrated gently. 'We shall want them for the next coaling, sir.'

'What became of the others?'

'Why, worn out, of course, sir.'

Captain MacWhirr, after glaring down irresolutely at his chief mate, disclosed the gloomy and cynical conviction that more than half of them had been lost overboard, 'if only the truth was known', and retired to the other end of the bridge. Jukes, exasperated by this unprovoked attack, broke the needle at the second stitch, and dropping his work got up and cursed the heat in a violent undertone.

The propeller thumped, the three Chinamen forward had given up squabbling very suddenly, and the one who had been plaiting his tail clasped his legs and stared dejectedly over his knees. The lurid sunshine cast faint and sickly shadows. The swell ran higher and swifter every moment, and the ship lurched heavily in the smooth, deep hollows of the sea.

'I wonder where that beastly swell comes from,' said Jukes aloud, recovering himself after a stagger.

'North-east,' grunted the literal MacWhirr, from his side of the bridge. 'There's some dirty weather knocking about. Go and look at the glass.'

When Jukes came out of the chart-room, the cast of his countenance had changed to thoughtfulness and concern. He caught hold of the bridge-rail and stared ahead.

The temperature in the engine-room had gone up to a hundred and seventeen degrees. Irritated voices were ascending through the skylight and through the fiddle of the stokehold in a harsh and resonant uproar, mingled with angry clangs and scrapes of metal, as if men with limbs of iron and throats of bronze had been quarrelling down there. The second engineer was falling foul of the stokers for letting the steam go down. He was a man with arms like a blacksmith, and generally feared; but that afternoon the stokers were answering him back recklessly, and slammed the furnace doors with the fury of despair. Then the noise ceased suddenly, and the second engineer appeared, emerging out of the stokehold streaked with grime and soaking wet like a chimney-sweep coming out of a well. As soon as his head was clear of the fiddle he began to scold Jukes for not trimming properly the stokehold ventilators; and in answer Jukes made with his hands deprecatory soothing signs meaning: No wind – can't be helped – you can see for yourself. But the other wouldn't hear reason. His teeth flashed angrily in his dirty face. He didn't mind, he said, the trouble of punching their blanked[16] heads down there, blank his soul, but did the condemned sailors think you could keep steam up in the God-forsaken boilers simply by knocking the blanked stokers about? No, by George! You had to get some draught too – may he be everlastingly blanked for a swab-headed deck-hand if you didn't! And the chief, too, rampaging before the steam-gauge and carrying on like a lunatic up and down the engine-room ever since noon. What did Jukes think he was stuck up there for, if he couldn't get one of his decayed, good-for-nothing deck-cripples to turn the ventilators to the wind?

The relations of the 'engine-room' and the 'deck' of the *Nan-Shan* were, as is known, of a brotherly nature; therefore Jukes leaned over and begged the other in a restrained tone not to make a disgusting ass of himself; the skipper was on the other side of the bridge. But the second declared mutinously that he didn't care a rap who was on the other side of the bridge, and Jukes, passing in a flash from lofty disapproval into a state of exaltation, invited him in unflattering terms to come up and twist the beastly things to please himself, and catch such wind as a donkey of his sort could find. The second rushed up to the fray. He flung himself at the port ventilator as though he meant to tear it out bodily and toss it overboard. All he did was to move the cowl round a few inches, with an enormous expenditure of force, and seemed spent in the effort. He leaned against the back of the wheel-house, and Jukes walked up to him.

'Oh, Heavens!' ejaculated the engineer in a feeble voice. He lifted his eyes to the sky, and then let his glassy stare descend to meet the horizon that, tilting up to an angle of forty degrees, seemed to hang on a slant for a while and settled down slowly. 'Heavens! Phew! What's up, anyhow?'

Jukes, straddling his long legs like a pair of compasses, put on an air of superiority. 'We're going to catch it this time,' he said. 'The barometer is tumbling down like anything, Harry. And you trying to kick up that silly row . . .'

The word 'barometer' seemed to revive the second engineer's mad animosity. Collecting afresh all his energies, he directed Jukes in a low and brutal tone to shove the unmentionable instrument down his gory throat. Who cared for his crimson barometer? It was the steam – the steam – that was going down; and what between the firemen going faint and the chief going silly, it was worse than a dog's life for him; he didn't care a tinker's curse how soon the whole show was blown out of the water. He seemed on the point of having a cry, but after regaining his breath he muttered darkly, 'I'll faint[17] them', and dashed off. He stopped upon the fiddle long enough to shake his fist at the unnatural daylight, and dropped into the dark hole with a whoop.

When Jukes turned, his eyes fell upon the rounded back and the big ears of Captain MacWhirr, who had come across. He did not look at his chief officer, but said at once, 'That's a very violent man, that second engineer.'

'Jolly good second, anyhow,' grunted Jukes. 'They can't keep up steam,' he added rapidly, and made a grab at the rail against the coming lurch.

Captain MacWhirr, unprepared, took a run and brought himself up with a jerk by an awning stanchion.

'A profane man,' he said obstinately. 'If this goes on, I'll have to get rid of him the first chance.'

'It's the heat,' said Jukes. 'The weather's awful. It would make a saint swear. Even up here I feel exactly as if I had my head tied up in a woollen blanket.'

Captain MacWhirr looked up. 'D'ye mean to say, Mr. Jukes, you ever had your head tied up in a blanket? What was that for?'

'It's a manner of speaking, sir,' said Jukes stolidly.

'Some of you fellows do go on! What's that about saints swearing? I wish you wouldn't talk so wild. What sort of saint would that be that would swear? No more saint than yourself, I expect. And what's a blanket got to do with it – or the weather either . . . The heat does not make me swear – does it? It's filthy bad temper. That's what it is. And what's the good of your talking like this?'

Thus Captain MacWhirr expostulated against the use of images in speech, and at the end electrified Jukes by a contemptuous snort, followed by words of passion and resentment: 'Damme! I'll fire him out of the ship if he don't look out.'

And Jukes, incorrigible, thought: 'Goodness me! Somebody's put a new inside to my old man. Here's temper, if you like. Of course it's the weather; what else? It would make an angel quarrelsome – let alone a saint.'

All the Chinamen on deck appeared at their last gasp.

At its setting the sun had a diminished diameter and an expiring brown, rayless glow, as if millions of centuries elapsing since the morning had brought it near its end. A dense bank of cloud became visible to the northward; it had a sinister dark olive tint, and lay low and motionless upon the sea, resembling a solid obstacle in the path of the ship. She went floundering towards it like an exhausted creature driven to its death. The coppery twilight retired slowly, and the darkness brought out overhead a swarm of unsteady, big stars, that, as if blown upon, flickered exceedingly and seemed to hang very near the earth. At eight o'clock Jukes went into the chart-room to write up the ship's log.

He copied neatly out of the rough-book the number of miles, the course of the ship, and in the column for 'wind' scrawled the word 'calm' from top to bottom of the eight hours since noon. He was exasperated by the continuous, monotonous rolling of the ship. The heavy inkstand would slide away in a manner that suggested perverse intelligence in dodging the pen. Having written in the large space under the head of 'Remarks' 'Heat very oppressive', he stuck the end of the penholder in his teeth, pipe-fashion, and mopped his face carefully.

'Ship rolling heavily in a high cross swell,' he began again, and commented to himself, 'Heavily is no word for it.' Then he wrote: 'Sunset threatening, with a low bank of clouds to N. and E. Sky clear overhead.'

Sprawling over the table with arrested pen, he glanced out of the door, and in that frame of his vision he saw all the stars flying upwards between the teakwood jambs on a black sky. The whole lot took flight together and disappeared, leaving only a blackness flecked with white flashes, for the sea was as black as the sky and speckled with foam afar. The stars that had flown to the roll came back on the return swing of the ship, rushing downwards in their glittering multitude, not of fiery points, but enlarged to tiny discs brilliant with a clear wet sheen.

Jukes watched the flying big stars for a moment, and then wrote: '8 P.M. Swell increasing. Ship labouring and taking water on her decks. Battened down the coolies for the night. Barometer still falling.' He paused, and thought to himself, 'Perhaps nothing whatever'll come of it.' And then he closed resolutely his entries: 'Every appearance of a typhoon coming on.'

On going out he had to stand aside, and Captain MacWhirr strode over the doorstep without saying a word or making a sign.

'Shut the door, Mr. Jukes, will you?' he cried from within.

Jukes turned back to do so, muttering ironically: 'Afraid to catch cold, I suppose.' It was his watch below, but he yearned for communion with his kind; and he remarked cheerily to the second mate: 'Doesn't look so bad, after all – does it?'

The second mate was marching to and fro on the bridge, tripping down with small steps one moment, and the next climbing with difficulty the shifting slope of the deck. At the sound of Jukes' voice he stood still, facing forward, but made no reply.

'Hallo! That's a heavy one,' said Jukes, swaying to meet the long roll till his lowered hand touched the planks. This time the second mate made in his throat a noise of an unfriendly nature.

He was an oldish, shabby little fellow, with bad teeth and no hair on his face. He had been shipped in a hurry in Shanghai, that trip when the second officer brought from home had delayed the ship three hours in port by contriving (in some manner Captain

MacWhirr could never understand) to fall overboard into an empty coal-lighter lying alongside, and had to be sent ashore to the hospital with concussion of the brain and a broken limb or two.

Jukes was not discouraged by the unsympathetic sound. 'The Chinamen must be having a lovely time of it down there,' he said. 'It's lucky for them the old girl has the easiest roll of any ship I've ever been in. There now! This one wasn't so bad.'

'You wait,' snarled the second mate.

With his sharp nose, red at the tip, and his thin pinched lips, he always looked as though he were raging inwardly;[18] and he was concise in his speech to the point of rudeness. All his time off duty he spent in his cabin with the door shut, keeping so still in there that he was supposed to fall asleep as soon as he had disappeared; but the man who came in to wake him for his watch on deck would invariably find him with his eyes wide open, flat on his back in the bunk, and glaring irritably from a soiled pillow. He never wrote any letters, did not seem to hope for news from anywhere; and though he had been heard once to mention West Hartlepool, it was with extreme bitterness, and only in connection with the extortionate charges of a boarding-house. He was one of those men who are picked up at need in the ports of the world. They are competent enough, appear hopelessly hard up, show no evidence of any sort of vice, and carry about them all the signs of manifest failure. They come aboard on an emergency, care for no ship afloat, live in their own atmosphere of casual connection amongst their shipmates who know nothing of them, and make up their minds to leave at inconvenient times. They clear out with no words of leave-taking in some God-forsaken port other men would fear to be stranded in, and go ashore in company of a shabby sea-chest, corded like a treasure-box, and with an air of shaking the ship's dust off their feet.

'You wait,' he repeated, balanced in great swings with his back to Jukes, motionless and implacable.

'Do you mean to say we are going to catch it hot?' asked Jukes with boyish interest.

'Say? . . . I say nothing. You don't catch me,' snapped the little second mate, with a mixture of pride, scorn, and cunning, as if Jukes' question had been a trap cleverly detected. 'Oh no! None of you here shall make a fool of me if I know it,' he mumbled to himself.

Jukes reflected rapidly that this second mate was a mean little beast, and in his heart he wished poor Jack Allen had never smashed himself up in the coal-lighter. The far-off blackness ahead of the ship was like another night seen through the starry night of the earth – the starless night of the immensities beyond the created universe, revealed in its appalling stillness through a low fissure in the glittering sphere of which the earth is the kernel.

'Whatever there might be about,' said Jukes, 'we are steaming straight into it.'

'*You've* said it,' caught up the second mate, always with his back to Jukes. 'You've said it, mind – not I.'

'Oh, go to Jericho!' said Jukes frankly; and the other emitted a triumphant little chuckle.

'You've said it,' he repeated.

'And what of that?'

'I've known some real good men get into trouble with their skippers for saying a dam' sight less,' answered the second mate feverishly. 'Oh no! You don't catch me.'

'You seem deucedly anxious not to give yourself away,' said Jukes, completely soured by such absurdity. 'I wouldn't be afraid to say what I think.'

'Aye, to me! That's no great trick. I am nobody, and well I know it.'

The ship, after a pause of comparative steadiness, started upon a series of rolls, one worse than the other, and for a time Jukes, preserving his equilibrium, was too busy to open his mouth. As soon as the violent swinging had quieted down somewhat, he said: 'This is a bit too much of a good thing. Whether anything is coming or not, I think she ought to be put head on to that swell. The old man is just gone in to lie down. Hang me if I don't speak to him.'

But when he opened the door of the chart-room he saw his captain reading a book. Captain MacWhirr was not lying down: he was standing up with one hand grasping the edge of the bookshelf and the other holding open before his face a thick volume. The lamp wriggled in the gimbals, the loosened books toppled from side to side on the shelf, the long barometer swung in jerky circles, the table altered its slant every moment. In the midst of all this stir and movement Captain MacWhirr, holding on, showed his eyes above the upper edge, and asked, 'What's the matter?'

'Swell getting worse, sir.'

'Noticed that in here,' muttered Captain MacWhirr. 'Anything wrong?'

Jukes, inwardly disconcerted by the seriousness of the eyes looking at him over the top of the book, produced an embarrassed grin.

'Rolling like old boots,' he said sheepishly.

'Aye! Very heavy – very heavy. What do you want?'

At this Jukes lost his footing and began to flounder.

'I was thinking of our passengers,' he said, in the manner of a man clutching at a straw.

'Passengers?' wondered the Captain gravely. 'What passengers?'

'Why, the Chinamen, sir,' explained Jukes, very sick of this conversation.

'The Chinamen! Why don't you speak plainly? Couldn't tell what you meant. Never heard a lot of coolies spoken of as passengers before. Passengers, indeed! What's come to you?'

Captain MacWhirr, closing the book on his forefinger, lowered his arm and looked completely mystified. 'Why are you thinking of the Chinamen, Mr. Jukes?' he inquired.

Jukes took a plunge, like a man driven to it. 'She's rolling her decks full of water, sir. Thought you might put her head on perhaps – for a while. Till this goes down a bit – very soon, I dare say. Head to the eastward. I never knew a ship roll like this.'

He held on in the doorway, and Captain MacWhirr, feeling his grip on the shelf inadequate, made up his mind to let go in a hurry, and fell heavily on the couch.

'Head to the eastward?' he said, struggling to sit up. 'That's more than four points off her course.'

'Yes, sir. Fifty degrees . . . Would just bring her head far enough round to meet this . . .'

Captain MacWhirr was now sitting up. He had not dropped the book, and he had not lost his place.

'To the eastward?' he repeated, with dawning astonishment. 'To the . . . Where do you think we are bound to? You want me to haul a full-powered steamship four points off her course to make the Chinamen comfortable! Now, I've heard more than enough of mad things done in the world – but this . . . If I didn't know you, Jukes, I would think you were in liquor. Steer four points off . . .

And what afterwards? Steer four points over the other way, I suppose, to make the course good. What put it into your head that I would start to tack a steamer as if she were a sailing-ship?'

'Jolly good thing she isn't,' threw in Jukes, with bitter readiness. 'She would have rolled every blessed stick out of her this afternoon.'

'Aye! And you just would have had to stand and see them go,' said Captain MacWhirr, showing a certain animation. 'It's a dead calm, isn't it?'

'It is, sir. But there's something out of the common coming, for sure.'

'Maybe. I suppose you have a notion I should be getting out of the way of that dirt,' said Captain MacWhirr, speaking with the utmost simplicity of manner and tone, and fixing the oilcloth on the floor with a heavy stare. Thus he noticed neither Jukes' discomfiture nor the mixture of vexation and astonished respect on his face.

'Now, here's this book,' he continued with deliberation, slapping his thigh with the closed volume. 'I've been reading the chapter on the storms there.'

This was true. He had been reading the chapter on the storms.[19] When he had entered the chart-room, it was with the intention of taking the book down. Some influence in the air – the same influence, probably, that caused the steward to bring without orders the Captain's sea-boots and oilskin coat up to the chart-room – had as it were guided his hand to the shelf; and without taking the time to sit down he had waded with a conscious effort into the terminology of the subject. He lost himself amongst advancing semi-circles, left- and right-hand quadrants, the curves of the tracks, the probable bearing of the centre, the shifts of wind and the readings of barometer. He tried to bring all these things into a definite relation to himself, and ended by becoming contemptuously angry with such a lot of words and with so much advice, all head-work and supposition, without a glimmer of certitude.

'It's the damnedest thing, Jukes,' he said. 'If a fellow was to believe all that's in there, he would be running most of his time all over the sea trying to get behind the weather.'

Again he slapped his leg with the book; and Jukes opened his mouth, but said nothing.

'Running to get behind the weather! Do you understand that, Mr. Jukes? It's the maddest thing!' ejaculated Captain MacWhirr, with pauses, gazing at the floor profoundly. 'You would think an old woman had been writing this. It passes me. If that thing means anything useful, then it means that I should at once alter the course away, away to the devil somewhere, and come booming down on Fu-chau from the northward at the tail of this dirty weather that's supposed to be knocking about in our way. From the north! Do you understand, Mr. Jukes? Three hundred extra miles to the distance, and a pretty coal bill to show. I couldn't bring myself to do that if every word in there was gospel truth, Mr. Jukes. Don't you expect me . . .'

And Jukes, silent, marvelled at this display of feeling and loquacity.

'But the truth is that you don't know if the fellow is right anyhow. How can you tell what a gale is made of till you get it? He isn't aboard here, is he? Very well. Here he says that the centre of them things bears eight points off the wind;[20] but we haven't got any wind, for all the barometer falling. Where's his centre now?'

'We will get the wind presently,' mumbled Jukes.

'Let it come, then,' said Captain MacWhirr, with dignified indignation. 'It's only to let you see, Mr. Jukes, that you don't find everything in books. All these rules for dodging breezes and circumventing the winds of heaven, Mr. Jukes, seem to me the maddest thing, when you come to look at it sensibly.'

He raised his eyes, saw Jukes gazing at him dubiously, and tried to illustrate his meaning.

'About as queer as your extraordinary notion of dodging the ship head to sea, for I don't know how long, to make the Chinamen comfortable; whereas all we've got to do is to take them to Fu-chau, being timed to get there before noon on Friday. If the weather delays me – very well. There's your log-book to talk straight about the weather. But suppose I went swinging off my course and came in two days late, and they asked me: "Where have you been all that time, Captain?" What could I say to that? "Went around to dodge the bad weather," I would say. "It must've been dam' bad," they would say. "Don't know," I would have to say; "I've dodged clear of it." See that, Jukes? I have been thinking it all out this afternoon.'

He looked up again in his unseeing, unimaginative way. No one had ever heard him say so much at one time. Jukes, with his arms open in the doorway, was like a man invited to behold a miracle. Unbounded wonder was the intellectual meaning of his eye, while incredulity was seated in his whole countenance.

'A gale is a gale, Mr. Jukes,' resumed the Captain, 'and a full-powered steam-ship has got to face it. There's just so much dirty weather knocking about the world, and the proper thing is to go through it with none of what old Captain Wilson of the *Melita*²¹ calls "storm strategy". The other day ashore I heard him hold forth about it to a lot of shipmasters who came in and sat at a table next to mine. It seemed to me the greatest nonsense. He was telling them how he – out-manœuvred, I think he said, a terrific gale, so that it never came nearer than fifty miles to him. A neat piece of head-work he called it. How he knew there was a terrific gale fifty miles off beats me altogether. It was like listening to a crazy man. I would have thought Captain Wilson was old enough to know better.'

Captain MacWhirr ceased for a moment, then said, 'It's your watch below, Mr. Jukes?'

Jukes came to himself with a start. 'Yes, sir.'

'Leave orders to call me at the slightest change,' said the Captain. He reached up to put the book away, and tucked his legs upon the couch. 'Shut the door so that it don't fly open, will you? I can't stand a door banging. They've put a lot of rubbishy locks into this ship, I must say.'

Captain MacWhirr closed his eyes.

He did so to rest himself. He was tired, and he experienced that state of mental vacuity which comes at the end of an exhaustive discussion that has liberated some belief matured in the course of meditative years. He had indeed been making his confession of faith, had he only known it; and its effect was to make Jukes, on the other side of the door, stand scratching his head for a good while.

Captain MacWhirr opened his eyes.

He thought he must have been asleep. What was that loud noise? Wind? Why had he not been called? The lamp wriggled in its gimbals, the barometer swung in circles, the table altered its slant every moment; a pair of limp seaboots with collapsed tops went sliding past the couch. He put out his hand instantly, and captured one.

Jukes' face appeared in a crack of the door: only his face, very red, with staring eyes. The flame of the lamp leaped, a piece of paper flew up, a rush of air enveloped Captain MacWhirr. Beginning to draw on the boot, he directed an expectant gaze at Jukes' swollen, excited features.

'Came on like this,' shouted Jukes, 'five minutes ago . . . all of a sudden.'

The head disappeared with a bang, and a heavy splash and patter of drops swept past the closed door as if a pailful of melted lead had been flung against the house. A whistling could be heard now upon the deep vibrating noise outside. The stuffy chart-room seemed as full of draughts as a shed. Captain MacWhirr collared the other sea-boot on its violent passage along the floor. He was not flustered, but he could not find at once the opening for inserting his foot. The shoes he had flung off were scurrying from end to end of the cabin, gambolling playfully over each other like puppies. As soon as he stood up he kicked at them viciously, but without effect.

He threw himself into the attitude of a lunging fencer, to reach after his oilskin coat; and afterwards he staggered all over the confined space while he jerked himself into it. Very grave, straddling his legs far apart, and stretching his neck, he started to tie deliberately the strings of his sou'-wester under his chin, with thick fingers that trembled slightly. He went through all the movements of a woman putting on her bonnet before a glass, with a strained, listening attention, as though he had expected every moment to hear the shout of his name in the confused clamour that had suddenly beset his ship. Its increase filled his ears while he was getting ready to go out and confront whatever it might mean. It was tumultuous and very loud – made up of the rush of the wind, the crashes of the sea, with that prolonged deep vibration of the air, like the roll of an immense and remote drum beating the charge of the gale.

He stood for a moment in the light of the lamp, thick, clumsy, shapeless in his panoply of combat, vigilant and red-faced.

'There's a lot of weight in this,' he muttered.

As soon as he attempted to open the door the wind caught it.

Clinging to the handle, he was dragged out over the doorstep, and at once found himself engaged with the wind in a sort of personal scuffle whose object was the shutting of that door. At the last moment a tongue of air scurried in and licked out the flame of the lamp.

Ahead of the ship he perceived a great darkness lying upon a multitude of white flashes; on the starboard beam a few amazing stars drooped, dim and fitful, above an immense waste of broken seas, as if seen through a mad drift of smoke.

On the bridge a knot of men, indistinct and toiling, were making great efforts in the light of the wheel-house windows that shone mistily on their heads and backs. Suddenly darkness closed upon one pane, then on another. The voices of the lost group reached him after the manner of men's voices in a gale, in shreds and fragments of forlorn shouting snatched past the ear. All at once Jukes appeared at his side, yelling, with his head down.

'Watch – put in – wheel-house shutters – glass – afraid – blow in.'

Jukes heard his commander upbraiding.

'This – come – anything – warning – call me.'

He tried to explain, with the uproar pressing on his lips.

'Light air – remained – bridge – sudden – north-east – could turn – thought – you – sure – hear.'

They had gained the shelter of the weather-cloth, and could converse with raised voices, as people quarrel.

'I got the hands along to cover up all the ventilators. Good job I had remained on deck. I didn't think you would be asleep, and so . . . What did you say, sir? What?'

'Nothing,' cried Captain MacWhirr. 'I said – all right.'

'By all the powers! We've got it this time,' observed Jukes in a howl.

'You haven't altered her course?' inquired Captain MacWhirr, straining his voice.

'No, sir. Certainly not. Wind came out right ahead. And here comes the head sea.'

A plunge of the ship ended in a shock as if she had landed her forefoot upon something solid. After a moment of stillness a lofty flight of sprays drove hard with the wind upon their faces.

'Keep her at it as long as we can,' shouted Captain MacWhirr.

Before Jukes had squeezed the salt water out of his eyes all the stars had disappeared.

III

JUKES was as ready a man as any half-dozen young mates that may be caught by casting a net upon the waters; and though he had been somewhat taken aback by the startling viciousness of the first squall, he had pulled himself together on the instant, had called out the hands and had rushed them along to secure such openings about the deck as had not been already battened down earlier in the evening. Shouting in his fresh, stentorian voice, 'Jump, boys, and bear a hand!' he led in the work, telling himself the while that he had 'just expected this'.

But at the same time he was growing aware that this was rather more than he had expected. From the first stir of the air felt on his cheek the gale seemed to take upon itself the accumulated impetus of an avalanche. Heavy sprays enveloped the *Nan-Shan* from stem to stern, and instantly in the midst of her regular rolling she began to jerk and plunge as though she had gone mad with fright.

Jukes thought, 'This is no joke.' While he was exchanging explanatory yells with his captain, a sudden lowering of the darkness came upon the night, falling before their vision like something palpable. It was as if the masked lights of the world had been turned down. Jukes was uncritically glad to have his captain at hand. It relieved him as though that man had, by simply coming on deck, taken most of the gale's weight upon his shoulders. Such is the prestige, the privilege, and the burden of command.

Captain MacWhirr could expect no relief of that sort from any one on earth. Such is the loneliness of command. He was trying to see, with that watchful manner of a seaman who stares into the wind's eye as if into the eye of an adversary, to penetrate the hidden intention and guess the aim and force of the thrust. The strong wind swept at him out of a vast obscurity; he felt under his feet the uneasiness of his ship, and he could not even discern the shadow of her shape. He wished it were not so; and very still he waited, feeling stricken by a blind man's helplessness.

To be silent was natural to him, dark or shine. Jukes, at his elbow, made himself heard yelling cheerily in the gusts, 'We must have got the worst of it at once, sir.' A faint burst of lightning quivered all round, as if flashed into a cavern – into a black and secret chamber of the sea, with a floor of foaming crests.

It unveiled for a sinister, fluttering moment a ragged mass of clouds hanging low, the lurch of the long outlines of the ship, the black figures of men caught on the bridge, heads forward, as if petrified in the act of butting. The darkness palpitated down upon all this, and then the real thing came at last.

It was something formidable and swift, like the sudden smashing of a vial of wrath. It seemed to explode all round the ship with an overpowering concussion and rush of great waters, as if an immense dam had been blown up to windward. In an instant the men lost touch of each other. This is the disintegrating power of a great wind: it isolates one from one's kind. An earthquake, a landslip, an avalanche, overtake a man incidentally, as it were – without passion. A furious gale attacks him like a personal enemy, tries to grasp his limbs, fastens upon his mind, seeks to rout his very spirit out of him.

Jukes was driven away from his commander. He fancied himself whirled a great distance through the air. Everything disappeared – even, for a moment, his power of thinking; but his hand had found one of the rail-stanchions. His distress was by no means alleviated by an inclination to disbelieve the reality of this experience. Though young, he had seen some bad weather, and had never doubted his ability to imagine the worst; but this was so much beyond his powers of fancy that it appeared incompatible with the existence of any ship whatever. He would have been incredulous about himself in the same way, perhaps, had he not been so harassed by the necessity of exerting a wrestling effort against a force trying to tear him away from his hold. Moreover, the conviction of not being utterly destroyed returned to him through the sensations of being half-drowned, bestially shaken, and partly choked.

It seemed to him he remained there precariously alone with the stanchion for a long, long time. The rain poured on him, flowed, drove in sheets. He breathed in gasps; and sometimes the water he swallowed was fresh and sometimes it was salt. For the most part he kept his eyes shut tight, as if suspecting his sight might be destroyed in the immense flurry of the elements. When he ventured to blink hastily, he derived some moral support from the green gleam of the starboard light shining feebly upon the flight of rain and sprays. He was actually looking at it when its ray fell upon the uprearing sea which put it out. He saw the head of the wave topple over, adding the mite of its crash to the tremendous uproar raging around him, and almost at the same instant the stanchion was wrenched away from his embracing arms. After a crushing thump on his back he found himself suddenly afloat and borne upwards. His first irresistible notion was that the whole China Sea had climbed on the bridge. Then, more sanely, he concluded himself gone overboard. All the time he was being tossed, flung, and rolled in great volumes of water, he kept on repeating mentally, with the utmost precipitation, the words: 'My God! My God! My God! My God!'

All at once, in a revolt of misery and despair, he formed the crazy resolution to get out of that. And he began to thresh about with his arms and legs. But as soon as he commenced his wretched struggles he discovered that he had become somehow mixed up with a face, an oilskin coat, somebody's boots. He clawed ferociously all these things in turn, lost them, found them again, lost them once more, and finally was himself caught in the firm clasp of a pair of stout arms. He returned the embrace closely round a thick solid body. He had found his captain.

They tumbled over and over, tightening their hug. Suddenly the water let them down with a brutal bang; and, stranded against the side of the wheel-house, out of breath and bruised, they were left to stagger up in the wind and hold on where they could.

Jukes came out of it rather horrified, as though he had escaped some unparalleled outrage directed at his feelings. It weakened his faith in himself. He started shouting aimlessly to the man he could feel near him in that fiendish blackness, 'Is it you, sir? Is it you, sir?' till his temples seemed ready to burst. And he heard in answer a voice, as if crying far away, as if screaming to him fretfully from a very great distance, the one word 'Yes!' Other seas swept again over the bridge. He received them defencelessly right over his bare head, with both his hands engaged in holding.

The motion of the ship was extravagant. Her lurches had an appalling helplessness: she pitched as if taking a header into a void, and seemed to find a wall to hit every time. When she rolled she fell on her side headlong, and she would be righted back by such a demolishing blow that Jukes felt her reeling as a clubbed man reels before he collapses. The gale howled and scuffled about gigantically in the darkness, as though the entire world were one black gully. At certain moments the air streamed against the ship as if sucked through a tunnel with a concentrated solid force of impact that seemed to lift her clean out of the water and keep her up for an instant with only a quiver running through her from end to end. And then she would begin her tumbling again as if dropped back into a boiling cauldron. Jukes tried hard to compose his mind and judge things coolly.

The sea, flattened down in the heavier gusts, would uprise and overwhelm both ends of the *Nan-Shan* in snowy rushes of foam, expanding wide, beyond both rails, into the night. And on this dazzling sheet, spread under the blackness of the clouds and emitting a bluish glow, Captain MacWhirr could catch a desolate glimpse of a few tiny specks black as ebony, the tops of the hatches, the battened companions, the heads of the covered winches, the foot of a mast. This was all he could see of his ship. Her middle structure, covered by the bridge which bore him, his mate, the closed wheel-house where a man was steering shut up with the fear of being swept overboard together with the whole thing in one great crash – her middle structure was like a half-tide rock awash upon a coast. It was like an outlying rock with the water boiling up, streaming over, pouring off, beating round – like a rock in the surf to which shipwrecked people cling before they let go – only it rose, it sank, it rolled continuously, without respite and rest, like a rock that should have miraculously struck adrift from a coast and gone wallowing upon the sea.

The *Nan-Shan* was being looted by the storm with a senseless, destructive fury: trysails torn out of the extra gaskets, double-lashed awnings blown away, bridge swept clean, weather-cloths burst, rails twisted, light-screens smashed – and two of the boats had gone already. They had gone unheard and unseen, melting, as it were, in the shock and smother of the wave. It was only later, when upon the white flash of another high sea hurling itself amidships, Jukes had a vision of two pairs of davits leaping black and empty out of the solid blackness, with one overhauled fall flying and an iron-bound block capering in the air, that he became aware of what had happened within about three yards of his back.

He poked his head forward, groping for the ear of his commander. His lips touched it – big, fleshy, very wet. He cried in an agitated tone, 'Our boats are going now, sir.'

And again he heard that voice, forced and ringing feebly, but with a penetrating effect of quietness in the enormous discord of noises, as if sent out from some remote spot of peace beyond the black wastes of the gale; again he heard a man's voice – the frail and indomitable sound that can be made to carry an infinity of thought, resolution and purpose, that shall be pronouncing confident words on the last day, when heavens fall, and justice is done – again he heard it, and it was crying to him, as if from very, very far – 'All right.'

He thought he had not managed to make himself understood. 'Our boats – I say boats – the boats, sir! Two gone!'

The same voice, within a foot of him and yet so remote, yelled sensibly, 'Can't be helped.'

Captain MacWhirr had never turned his face, but Jukes caught some more words on the wind.

'What can – expect – when hammering through – such — Bound to leave – something behind – stands to reason.'

Watchfully Jukes listened for more. No more came. This was all Captain MacWhirr had to say; and Jukes could picture to himself rather than see the broad squat back before him. An impenetrable obscurity pressed down upon the ghostly glimmers of the sea. A dull conviction seized upon Jukes that there was nothing to be done.

If the steering-gear did not give way, if the immense volumes of water did not burst the deck in or smash one of the hatches, if the engines did not give up, if way could be kept on the ship against this terrific wind, and she did not bury herself in one of those awful seas, of whose white crests alone, topping high above her bows, he could now and then get a sickening glimpse – then there was a chance of her coming out of it. Something within him seemed to turn over, bringing uppermost the feeling that the *Nan-Shan* was lost.

'She's done for,' he said to himself, with a surprising mental agitation, as though he had discovered an unexpected meaning in this thought. One of these things was bound to happen. Nothing could be prevented now, and nothing could be remedied. The men on board did not count, and the ship could not last. This weather was too impossible.

Jukes felt an arm thrown heavily over his shoulders; and to this overture he responded with great intelligence by catching hold of his captain round the waist.

They stood clasped thus in the blind night, bracing each other against the wind, cheek to cheek and lip to ear, in the manner of two hulks lashed stem to stern together.

And Jukes heard the voice of his commander hardly any louder than before, but nearer, as though, starting to march athwart the prodigious rush of the hurricane, it had approached him, bearing that strange effect of quietness like the serene glow of a halo.

'D'ye know where the hands got to?' it asked, vigorous and evanescent at the same time, overcoming the strength of the wind, and swept away from Jukes instantly.

Jukes didn't know. They were all on the bridge when the real force of the hurricane struck the ship. He had no idea where they had crawled to. Under the circumstances they were nowhere, for all the use that could be made of them. Somehow the Captain's wish to know distressed Jukes.

'Want the hands, sir?' he cried apprehensively.

'Ought to know,' asserted Captain MacWhirr. 'Hold hard.'

They held hard. An outburst of unchained fury, a vicious rush of the wind absolutely steadied the ship; she rocked only, quick and light like a child's cradle, for a terrific moment of suspense, while the whole atmosphere, as it seemed, streamed furiously past her, roaring away from the tenebrous earth.

It suffocated them, and with eyes shut they tightened their grasp. What from the magnitude of the shock might have been a column of water running upright in the dark, butted against the ship, broke short, and fell on her bridge, crushingly, from on high, with a dead burying weight.

A flying fragment of that collapse, a mere splash, enveloped them in one swirl from their feet over their heads, filling violently their ears, mouths and nostrils with salt water. It knocked out their legs, wrenched in haste at their arms, seethed away swiftly under their chins; and opening their eyes, they saw the piled-up masses of foam dashing to and fro amongst what looked like the fragments of a ship. She had given way as if driven straight in. Their panting hearts yielded too before the tremendous blow; and all at once she sprang up again to her desperate plunging, as if trying to scramble out from under the ruins.

The seas in the dark seemed to rush from all sides to keep her back where she might perish. There was hate in the way she was handled, and a ferocity in the blows that fell. She was like a living creature thrown to the rage of a mob: hustled terribly, struck at, borne up, flung down, leaped upon. Captain MacWhirr and Jukes kept hold of each other, deafened by the noise, gagged by the wind; and the great physical tumult beating about their bodies, brought, like an unbridled display of passion, a profound trouble to their souls. One of these wild and appalling shrieks that are heard at times passing mysteriously overhead in the steady roar of a hurricane, swooped, as if borne on wings, upon the ship, and Jukes tried to outscream it.

'Will she live through this?'

The cry was wrenched out of his breast. It was as unintentional as the birth of a thought in the head, and he heard nothing of it himself. It all became extinct at once – thought, intention, effort – and of his cry the inaudible vibration added to the tempest waves of the air.

He expected nothing from it. Nothing at all. For indeed what answer could be made? But after a while he heard with amazement the frail and resisting voice in his ear, the dwarf sound, un-conquered in the giant tumult.

'She may!'

It was a dull yell, more difficult to seize than a whisper. And presently the voice returned again, half submerged in the vast crashes, like a ship battling against the waves of an ocean.

'Let's hope so!' it cried – small, lonely and unmoved, a stranger to the visions of hope or fear; and it flickered into disconnected words: 'Ship . . . This . . . Never – Anyhow . . . for the best.' Jukes gave it up.

Then, as if it had come suddenly upon the one thing fit to withstand the power of a storm, it seemed to gain force and firmness for the last broken shouts:

'Keep on hammering . . . builders . . . good men . . . And chance it . . . engines . . . Rout . . . good man.'

Captain MacWhirr removed his arm from Jukes' shoulders, and thereby ceased to exist for his mate, so dark it was; Jukes, after a tense stiffening of every muscle, would let himself go limp all over. The gnawing of profound discomfort existed side by side with an incredible disposition to somnolence, as though he had been buffeted and worried into drowsiness. The wind would get hold of his head and try to shake it off his shoulders; his clothes, full of water, were as heavy as lead, cold and dripping like an armour of melting ice: he shivered – it lasted a long time; and with his hands closed hard on his hold, he was letting himself sink slowly into the depths of bodily misery. His mind became concentrated upon himself in an aimless, idle way, and when something pushed lightly at the back of his knees he nearly, as the saying is, jumped out of his skin.

In the start forward he bumped the back of Captain MacWhirr, who didn't move; and then a hand gripped his thigh. A lull had come, a menacing lull of the wind, the holding of a stormy breath – and he felt himself pawed all over. It was the boatswain. Jukes recognised these hands, so thick and enormous that they seemed to belong to some new species of man.

The boatswain had arrived on the bridge, crawling on all fours against the wind, and had found the chief mate's legs with the top of his head. Immediately he crouched and began to explore Jukes' person upwards, with prudent, apologetic touches, as became an inferior.

He was an ill-favoured, undersized, gruff sailor of fifty, coarsely hairy, short-legged, long-armed, resembling an elderly ape. His strength was immense; and in his great lumpy paws, bulging like brown boxing-gloves on the end of furry forearms, the heaviest objects were handled like playthings. Apart from the grizzled pelt on his chest, the menacing demeanour and the hoarse voice, he had none of the classical attributes of his rating. His good nature almost amounted to imbecility; the men did what they liked with him, and he had not an ounce of initiative in his character, which was easy-going and talkative. For these reasons Jukes disliked him; but Captain MacWhirr, to Jukes' scornful disgust, seemed to regard him as a first-rate petty officer.

He pulled himself up by Jukes' coat, taking that liberty with the greatest moderation, and only so far as it was forced upon him by the hurricane.

'What is it, boss'n, what is it?' yelled Jukes, impatiently. What could that fraud of a boss'n want on the bridge? The typhoon had got on Jukes' nerves. The husky bellowings of the other, though unintelligible, seemed to suggest a state of lively satisfaction. There could be no mistake. The old fool was pleased with something.

The boatswain's other hand had found some other body, for in a changed tone he began to inquire: 'Is it you, sir? Is it you, sir?' The wind strangled his howls.

'Yes!' cried Captain MacWhirr.

IV

ALL that the boatswain, out of a superabundance of yells could make clear to Captain MacWhirr was the bizarre intelligence that 'All them Chinamen in the fore 'tween-deck have fetched away, sir.'

Jukes to leeward could hear these two shouting within six inches of his face, as you may hear on a still night half a mile away two men conversing across a field. He heard Captain MacWhirr's exasperated 'What? What?' and the strained pitch of the other's hoarseness. 'In a lump . . . seen them myself . . . Awful sight, sir . . . thought . . . tell you.'

Jukes remained indifferent, as if rendered irresponsible by the force of the hurricane, which made the very thought of action utterly vain. Besides, being very young, he had found the occupation of keeping his heart completely steeled against the worst so engrossing that he had come to feel an overpowering dislike towards any other form of activity whatever. He was not scared; he knew this because, firmly believing he would never see another sunrise, he remained calm in that belief.

These are the moments of do-nothing heroics to which even good men surrender at times. Many officers of ships can no doubt recall a case in their experience when just such a trance of confounded stoicism would come all at once over a whole ship's company. Jukes, however, had no wide experience of men or storms. He conceived himself to be calm – inexorably calm; but as a matter of fact he was daunted; not abjectly, but only so far as a decent man may, without becoming loathsome to himself.

It was rather like a forced-on numbness of spirit. The long, long stress of a gale does it; the suspense of the interminably culminating catastrophe; and there is a bodily fatigue in the mere holding on to existence within the excessive tumult; a searching and insidious fatigue that penetrates deep into a man's breast to cast down and sadden his heart, which is incorrigible, and of all the gifts of the earth – even before life itself – aspires to peace.

Jukes was benumbed much more than he supposed. He held on – very wet, very cold, stiff in every limb; and in a momentary hallucination of swift visions (it is said that a drowning man thus reviews all his life) he beheld all sorts of memories altogether unconnected with his present situation. He remembered his father, for instance: a worthy business man, who at an unfortunate crisis in his affairs went quietly to bed and died forthwith in a state of resignation. Jukes did not recall these circumstances, of course, but remaining otherwise unconcerned he seemed to see distinctly the poor man's face; a certain game of nap played when quite a boy in Table Bay on board a ship, since lost with all hands; the thick eyebrows of his first skipper; and without any emotion, as he might years ago have walked listlessly into her room and found her sitting there with a book, he remembered his mother – dead, too, now – the resolute woman, left badly off, who had been very firm in his bringing up.

It could not have lasted more than a second, perhaps not so much. A heavy arm had fallen about his shoulders; Captain Mac-Whirr's voice was speaking his name into his ear.

'Jukes! Jukes!'

He detected the tone of deep concern. The wind had thrown its weight on the ship, trying to pin her down amongst the seas. They made a clean breach over her, as over a deep-swimming log; and the gathered weight of crashes menaced monstrously from afar. The breakers flung out of the night with a ghostly light on their crests – the light of sea-foam that in a ferocious, boiling-up pale flash showed upon the slender body of the ship the toppling rush, the downfall, and the seething mad scurry of each wave. Never for a moment could she shake herself clear of the water; Jukes, rigid, perceived in her motion the ominous sign of haphazard floundering. She was no longer struggling intelligently. It was the beginning of the end; and the note of busy concern in Captain MacWhirr's voice sickened him like an exhibition of blind and pernicious folly.

The spell of the storm had fallen upon Jukes. He was penetrated by it, absorbed by it; he was rooted in it with a rigour of dumb attention. Captain MacWhirr persisted in his cries, but the wind got between them like a solid wedge. He hung round Jukes' neck as heavy as a millstone, and suddenly the sides of their heads knocked together.

'Jukes! Mr. Jukes, I say!'

He had to answer that voice that would not be silenced. He answered in the customary manner: '. . . Yes, sir.'

And directly, his heart, corrupted by the storm that breeds a craving for peace, rebelled against the tyranny of training and command.

Captain MacWhirr had his mate's head fixed firm in the crook of his elbow, and pressed it to his yelling lips mysteriously. Sometimes Jukes would break in, admonishing hastily: 'Look out, sir!' or Captain MacWhirr would bawl an earnest exhortation to 'Hold hard, there!' and the whole black universe seemed to reel together with the ship. They paused. She floated yet. And Captain MacWhirr would resume his shouts. '. . . Says . . . whole lot . . . fetched away . . . Ought to see . . . what's the matter.'

Directly the full force of the hurricane had struck the ship, every part of her deck became untenable; and the sailors, dazed and dismayed, took shelter in the port alleyway under the bridge. It had a door aft, which they shut; it was very black, cold, and dismal. At each heavy fling of the ship they would groan all together in the dark, and tons of water could be heard scuttling about as if trying to get at them from above. The boatswain had been keeping up a gruff talk, but a more unreasonable lot of men, he said afterwards, he had never been with. They were snug enough there, out of harm's way, and not wanted to do anything, either; and yet they did nothing but grumble and complain peevishly like so many sick kids. Finally, one of them said that if there had been at least some light to see each other's noses by, it wouldn't be so bad. It was making him crazy, he declared, to lie there in the dark waiting for the blamed hooker to sink.

'Why don't you step outside, then, and be done with it at once?' the boatswain turned on him.

This called up a shout of execration. The boatswain found himself overwhelmed with reproaches of all sorts. They seemed to take it ill that a lamp was not instantly created for them out of nothing. They would whine after a light to get drowned by – anyhow! And though the unreason of their revilings was patent –

since no one could hope to reach the lamp-room, which was forward – he became greatly distressed. He did not think it was decent of them to be nagging at him like this. He told them so, and was met by general contumely. He sought refuge, therefore, in an embittered silence. At the same time their grumbling and sighing and muttering worried him greatly, but by-and-by it occurred to him that there were six globe lamps hung in the 'tween-deck, and that there could be no harm in depriving the coolies of one of them.

The *Nan-Shan* had an athwartship coal-bunker, which, being at times used as cargo space, communicated by an iron door with the fore 'tween-deck. It was empty then, and its manhole was the foremost one in the alleyway. The boatswain could get in, therefore, without coming out on deck at all; but to his great surprise he found he could induce no one to help him in taking off the manhole cover. He groped for it all the same, but one of the crew lying in his way refused to budge.

'Why, I only want to get you that blamed light you are crying for,' he expostulated, almost pitifully.

Somebody told him to go and put his head in a bag. He regretted he could not recognise the voice, and that it was too dark to see; otherwise, as he said, he would have put a head on *that* son of a sea-cook, anyway, sink or swim. Nevertheless, he had made up his mind to show them he could get a light, if he were to die for it.

Through the violence of the ship's rolling, every movement was dangerous. To be lying down seemed labour enough. He nearly broke his neck dropping into the bunker. He fell on his back, and was sent shooting helplessly from side to side in the dangerous company of a heavy iron bar – a coal-trimmer's slice probably – left down there by somebody. This thing made him as nervous as though it had been a wild beast. He could not see it, the inside of the bunker coated with coal-dust being perfectly and impenetrably black; but he heard it sliding and clattering, and striking here and there, always in the neighbourhood of his head. It seemed to make an extraordinary noise, too – to give heavy thumps as though it had been as big as a bridge girder. This was remarkable enough for him to notice while he was flung from port to starboard and back again, and clawing desperately the smooth sides of the bunker in the endeavour to stop himself. The door into the 'tween-deck not fitting quite true, he saw a thread of dim light at the bottom.

Being a sailor, and a still active man, he did not want much of a chance to regain his feet; and as luck would have it, in scrambling up he put his hand on the iron slice, picking it up as he rose. Otherwise he would have been afraid of the thing breaking his legs, or at least knocking him down again. At first he stood still. He felt unsafe in this darkness that seemed to make the ship's motion unfamiliar, unforeseen, and difficult to counteract. He felt so much shaken for a moment that he dared not move for fear of 'taking charge again'. He had no mind to get battered to pieces in that bunker.

He had struck his head twice; he was dazed a little. He seemed to hear yet so plainly the clatter and bangs of the iron slice flying about his ears that he tightened his grip to prove to himself he had it there safely in his hand. He was vaguely amazed at the plainness with which down there he could hear the gale raging. Its howls and shrieks seemed to take on, in the emptiness of the bunker, something of the human character, of human rage and pain – being not vast but infinitely poignant. And there were, with every roll, thumps too – profound, ponderous thumps, as if a bulky object of five-ton weight or so had got play in the hold. But there was no such thing in the cargo. Something on deck? Impossible. Or alongside? Couldn't be.

He thought all this quickly, clearly, competently, like a seaman, and in the end remained puzzled. This noise, though, came deadened from outside, together with the washing and pouring of water on deck above his head. Was it the wind? Must be. It made down there a row like the shouting of a big lot of crazed men. And he discovered in himself a desire for a light too – if only to get drowned by – and a nervous anxiety to get out of that bunker as quickly as possible.

He pulled back the bolt: the heavy iron plate turned on its hinges; and it was as though he had opened the door to the sounds of the tempest. A gust of hoarse yelling met him: the air was still; and the rushing of water overhead was covered by a tumult of strangled, throaty shrieks that produced an effect of desperate confusion. He straddled his legs the whole width of the doorway and stretched his neck. And at first he perceived only what he had come to seek: six small yellow flames swinging violently on the great body of the dusk.

It was stayed like the gallery of a mine, with a row of stanchions in the middle, and cross-beams overhead, penetrating into the gloom ahead – indefinitely. And to port there loomed, like the caving in of one of the sides, a bulky mass with a slanting outline. The whole place, with the shadows and the shapes, moved all the time. The boatswain glared: the ship lurched to starboard, and a great howl came from that mass that had the slant of fallen earth.

Pieces of wood whizzed past. Planks, he thought, inexpressibly startled, and flinging back his head. At his feet a man went sliding over, open-eyed, on his back, straining with uplifted arms for nothing: and another came bounding like a detached stone with his head between his legs and his hands clenched. His pigtail whipped in the air; he made a grab at the boatswain's legs, and from his opened hand a bright white disc rolled against the boat-swain's foot. He recognised a silver dollar, and yelled at it with astonishment. With a precipitated sound of trampling and shuffling of bare feet, and with guttural cries, the mound of writhing bodies piled up to port detached itself from the ship's side and shifted to starboard, sliding, inert and struggling, to a dull, brutal thump. The cries ceased. The boatswain heard a long moan through the roar and whistling of the wind; he saw an inextricable confusion of heads and shoulders, naked soles kicking upwards, fists raised, tumbling backs, legs, pigtails, faces.

'Good Lord!' he cried, horrified, and banged-to the iron door upon this vision.

This was what he had come on the bridge to tell. He could not keep it to himself; and on board ship there is only one man to whom it is worth while to unburden yourself. On his passage back the hands in the alleyway swore at him for a fool. Why didn't he bring that lamp? What the devil did the coolies matter to anybody? And when he came out, the extremity of the ship made what went on inside of her appear of little moment.

At first he thought he had left the alleyway in the very moment of her sinking. The bridge ladders had been washed away, but an enormous sea filling the after-deck floated him up. After that he had to lie on his stomach for some time, holding to a ring-bolt, getting his breath now and then, and swallowing salt water. He struggled farther on his hands and knees, too frightened and distracted to turn back. In this way he reached the after-part of the wheel-house. In that comparatively sheltered spot he found the second mate. The boatswain was pleasantly surprised – his impression being that everybody on deck must have been washed away a long time ago. He asked eagerly where the captain was.

The second mate was lying low, like a malignant little animal under a hedge.

'Captain? Gone overboard, after getting us into this mess.' The mate, too, for all he knew or cared. Another fool. Didn't matter. Everybody was going by-and-by.

The boatswain crawled out again into the strength of the wind; not because he much expected to find anybody, he said, but just to get away from 'that man'. He crawled out as outcasts go to face an inclement world. Hence his great joy at finding Jukes and the Captain. But what was going on in the 'tween-deck was to him a minor matter by that time. Besides, it was difficult to make yourself heard. But he managed to convey the idea that the Chinamen had broken adrift together with their boxes, and that he had come up on purpose to report this. As to the hands, they were all right. Then, appeased, he subsided on the deck in a sitting posture, hugging with his arms and legs the stand of the engine-room telegraph – an iron casting as thick as a post. When that went, why, he expected he would go too. He gave no more thought to the coolies.

Captain MacWhirr had made Jukes understand that he wanted him to go down below – to see.

'What am I to do then, sir?' And the trembling of his whole wet body caused Jukes' voice to sound like bleating.

'See first . . . Boss'n . . . says . . . adrift.'

'That boss'n is a confounded fool,' howled Jukes shakily.

The absurdity of the demand made upon him revolted Jukes. He was as unwilling to go as if the moment he had left the deck the ship were sure to sink.

'I must know . . . can't leave . . .'

'They'll settle, sir.'

'Fight . . . boss'n says they fight. . . . Why? Can't have . . . fighting . . . board ship. . . . Much rather keep you here . . . case . . . I should . . . washed overboard myself. . . . Stop it . . . some way. You see and tell me . . . through engine-room tube. Don't want you . . . come up here . . . too often. Dangerous . . . moving about . . . deck.'

Jukes, held with his head in chancery, had to listen to what seemed horrible suggestions.

'Don't want . . . you get lost . . . so long . . . ship isn't. . . . Rout . . . Good man . . . Ship . . . may . . . through this . . . all right yet.'

All at once Jukes understood he would have to go.

'Do you think she may?' he screamed.

But the wind devoured the reply, out of which Jukes heard only the one word, pronounced with great energy '. . . Always . . .'

Captain MacWhirr released Jukes, and bending over the boat-swain, yelled 'Get back with the mate.' Jukes only knew that the arm was gone off his shoulders. He was dismissed with his orders – to do what? He was exasperated into letting go his hold carelessly, and on the instant was blown away. It seemed to him that nothing could stop him from being blown right over the stern. He flung himself down hastily. and the boatswain, who was following, fell on him.

'Don't you get up yet, sir,' cried the boatswain. 'No hurry!'

A sea swept over. Jukes understood the boatswain to splutter that the bridge ladders were gone. 'I'll lower you down, sir, by your hands,' he screamed. He shouted also something about the smoke-stack being as likely to go overboard as not. Jukes thought it very possible, and imagined the fires out, the ship helpless. . . . The boatswain by his side kept on yelling. 'What? What is it?' Jukes cried distressfully; and the other repeated, 'What would my old woman say if she saw me now?'

In the alleyway, where a lot of water had got in and splashed in the dark, the men were still as death, till Jukes stumbled against one of them and cursed him savagely for being in the way. Two or three voices then asked, eager and weak, 'Any chance for us, sir?'

'What's the matter with you fools?' he said brutally. He felt as though he could throw himself down amongst them and never move any more. But they seemed cheered; and in the midst of obsequious warnings, 'Look out! Mind that manhole lid, sir', they lowered him into the bunker. The boatswain tumbled down after him, and as soon as he had picked himself up he remarked, 'She would say, "Serve you right, you old fool, for going to sea."'

The boatswain had some means, and made a point of alluding to them frequently. His wife – a fat woman – and two grown-up daughters kept a greengrocer's shop in the East-end of London.

In the dark, Jukes, unsteady on his legs, listened to a faint thunderous patter. A deadened screaming went on steadily at his elbow, as it were; and from above the louder tumult of the storm descended upon these near sounds. His head swam. To him, too, in that bunker, the motion of the ship seemed novel and menacing, sapping his resolution as though he had never been afloat before.

He had half a mind to scramble out again; but the remembrance of Captain MacWhirr's voice made this impossible. His orders were to go and see. What was the good of it, he wanted to know. Enraged, he told himself he would see – of course. But the boatswain, staggering clumsily, warned him to be careful how he opened that door; there was a blamed fight going on. And Jukes, as if in great bodily pain, desired irritably to know what the devil they were fighting for.

'Dollars! Dollars, sir. All their rotten chests got burst open. Blamed money skipping all over the place, and they are tumbling after it head over heels – tearing and biting like anything. A regular little hell in there.'

Jukes convulsively opened the door. The short boatswain peered under his arm.

One of the lamps had gone out, broken perhaps. Rancorous, guttural cries burst out loudly on their ears, and a strange panting sound, the working of all these straining breasts. A hard blow hit the side of the ship: water fell above with a stunning shock, and in the forefront of the gloom, where the air was reddish and thick, Jukes saw a head bang the deck violently, two thick calves waving on high, muscular arms twined round a naked body, a yellow face, open-mouthed and with a set wild stare, look up and slide away. An empty chest clattered turning over; a man fell head first with a jump, as if lifted by a kick; and farther off, indistinct, others streamed like a mass of rolling stones down a bank, thumping the deck with their feet and flourishing their arms wildly. The hatch-way ladder was loaded with coolies swarming on it like bees on a branch. They hung on the steps in a crawling, stirring cluster, beating madly with their fists the underside of the battened hatch, and the headlong rush of the water above was heard in the intervals of their yelling. The ship heeled over more, and they began to drop off: first one, then two, then all the rest went away together, falling straight off with a great cry.

Jukes was confounded. The boatswain, with gruff anxiety, begged him, 'Don't you go in there, sir.'

The whole place seemed to twist upon itself, jumping incessantly the while; and when the ship rose to a sea Jukes fancied that all these men would be shot upon him in a body. He backed out, swung the door to, and with trembling hands pushed at the bolt. . . .

As soon as his mate had gone Captain MacWhirr, left alone on the bridge, sidled and staggered as far as the wheel-house. Its door being hinged forward, he had to fight the gale for admittance, and when at last he managed to enter, it was with an instantaneous clatter and a bang, as though he had been fired through the wood. He stood within, holding on to the handle.

The steering-gear leaked steam, and in the confined space the glass of the binnacle made a shiny oval of light in a thin white fog. The wind howled, hummed, whistled, with sudden booming gusts that rattled the doors and shutters in the vicious patter of sprays. Two coils of lead-line and a small canvas bag, hung on a long lanyard, swung wide off and came back clinging to the bulkheads. The gratings underfoot were nearly afloat; with every sweeping blow of a sea, water squirted violently through the cracks all round the door, and the man at the helm had flung down his cap, his coat, and stood propped against the gear-casing in a striped cotton shirt open on his breast. The little brass wheel in his hands had the appearance of a bright and fragile toy. The cords of his neck stood hard and lean, a dark patch lay in the hollow of his throat, and his face was still and sunken as in death.

Captain MacWhirr wiped his eyes. The sea that had nearly taken him overboard had, to his great annoyance, washed his sou'-wester hat off his bald head. The fluffy, fair hair, soaked and darkened, resembled a mean skein of cotton threads festooned round his bare skull. His face, glistening with sea-water, had been made crimson with the wind, with the sting of sprays. He looked as though he had come off sweating from before a furnace.

'You here?' he muttered heavily.

The second mate had found his way into the wheel-house some time before. He had fixed himself in a corner with his knees up, a fist pressed against each temple; and this attitude suggested rage, sorrow, resignation, surrender, with a sort of concentrated unforgiveness. He said mournfully and defiantly, 'Well, it's my watch below now: ain't it?'

The steam gear clattered, stopped, clattered again; and the helmsman's eyeballs seemed to project out of a hungry face as if the compass card behind the binnacle glass had been meat. God knows how long he had been left there to steer, as if forgotten by all his shipmates. The bells had not been struck; there had been no reliefs; the ship's routine had gone down wind; but he was trying to keep her head north-north-east. The rudder might have been gone for all he knew, the fires out, the engines broken down, the ship ready to roll over like a corpse. He was anxious not to get muddled and lose control of her head, because the compass card swung far both ways, wriggling on the pivot, and sometimes seemed to whirl right round. He suffered from mental stress. He was horribly afraid, also, of the wheel-house going. Mountains of water kept on tumbling against it. When the ship took one of her desperate dives the corners of his lips twitched.

Captain MacWhirr looked up at the wheel-house clock. Screwed to the bulkhead, it had a white face on which the black hands appeared to stand quite still. It was half-past one in the morning.

'Another day,' he muttered to himself.

The second mate heard him, and lifting his head as one grieving amongst ruins, 'You won't see it break,' he exclaimed. His wrists and knees could be seen to shake violently. 'No, by God! You won't . . .'

He took his face again between his fists.

The body of the helmsman had moved slightly, but his head didn't budge on his neck, – like a stone head fixed to look one way from a column. During a roll that all but took his booted legs from under him, and in the very stagger to save himself, Captain MacWhirr said austerely, 'Don't you pay any attention to what that man says.' And then, with an indefinable change of tone, very grave, he added, 'He isn't on duty.'

The sailor said nothing.

The hurricane boomed, shaking the little place, which seemed air-tight; and the light of the binnacle flickered all the time.

'You haven't been relieved,' Captain MacWhirr went on, looking down. 'I want you to stick to the helm, though, as long as you can. You've got the hang of her. Another man coming here might make a mess of it. Wouldn't do. No child's play. And the hands are probably busy with a job down below. . . . Think you can?'

The steering-gear leaped into an abrupt short clatter, stopped, smouldering like an ember; and the still man, with a motionless gaze, burst out, as if all the passion in him had gone into his lips: 'By Heavens, sir! I can steer for ever if nobody talks to me.'

'Oh! aye! All right. . . .' The Captain lifted his eyes for the first time to the man. '. . . Hackett.'

And he seemed to dismiss this matter from his mind. He stooped to the engine-room speaking-tube, blew in, and bent his head. Mr. Rout below answered, and at once Captain MacWhirr put his lips to the mouthpiece.

With the uproar of the gale around him he applied alternately his lips and his ear, and the engineer's voice mounted to him, harsh and as if out of the heat of an engagement. One of the stokers was disabled, the others had given in, the second engineer and the donkey-man were firing-up. The third engineer was standing by the steam-valve. The engines were being tended by hand. How was it above?

'Bad enough. It mostly rests with you,' said Captain MacWhirr. Was the mate down there yet? No? Well, he would be presently. Would Mr. Rout let him talk through the speaking-tube? – through the deck speaking-tube, because he – the Captain – was going out again on the bridge directly. There was some trouble amongst the Chinamen. They were fighting, it seemed. Couldn't allow fighting anyhow. . . .

Mr. Rout had gone away, and Captain MacWhirr could feel against his ear the pulsation of the engines, like the beat of the ship's heart. Mr. Rout's voice down there shouted something distantly. The ship pitched headlong, the pulsation leaped with a hissing tumult, and stopped dead. Captain MacWhirr's face was impassive, and his eyes were fixed aimlessly on the crouching shape of the second mate. Again Mr. Rout's voice cried out in the depths, and the pulsating beats recommenced, with slow strokes – growing swifter.

Mr. Rout had returned to the tube. 'It don't matter much what they do,' he said hastily; and then, with irritation, 'She takes these dives as if she never meant to come up again.'

'Awful sea,' said the Captain's voice from above.

'Don't let me drive her under,' barked Solomon Rout up the pipe.

'Dark and rain. Can't see what's coming,' uttered the voice. 'Must – keep – her – moving – enough to steer – and chance it,' it went on to state distinctly.

'I am doing as much as I dare.'

'We are – getting – smashed up – a good deal up here,' proceeded the voice mildly. 'Doing – fairly well – though. Of course, if the wheel-house should go . . .'

Mr. Rout, bending an attentive ear, muttered peevishly something under his breath.

But the deliberate voice up there became animated to ask: 'Jukes turned up yet?' Then, after a short wait, 'I wish he would bear a hand. I want him to be done and come up here in case of anything. To look after the ship. I am all alone. The second mate's lost. . . .'

'What?' shouted Mr. Rout into the engine-room, taking his head away. Then up the tube he cried, 'Gone overboard?' and clapped his ear to.

'Lost his nerve,' the voice from above continued in a matter-of-fact tone. 'Damned awkward circumstance.'

Mr. Rout, listening with bowed neck, opened his eyes wide at this. However, he heard something like the sounds of a scuffle and broken exclamations coming down to him. He strained his hearing; and all the time Beale, the third engineer, with his arms uplifted, held between the palms of his hands the rim of a little black wheel projecting at the side of a big copper pipe. He seemed to be poising it above his head, as though it were a correct attitude in some sort of game.

To steady himself, he pressed his shoulder against the white bulkhead, one knee bent, and a sweat-rag tucked in his belt hanging on his hip. His smooth cheek was begrimed and flushed, and the coal dust on his eyelids, like the black pencilling of a make-up, enhanced the liquid brilliance of the whites, giving to his youthful face something of a feminine, exotic and fascinating aspect. When the ship pitched he would with hasty movements of his hands screw hard at the little wheel.

'Gone crazy,' began the Captain's voice suddenly in the tube. 'Rushed at me. . . . Just now. Had to knock him down. . . . This minute. You heard, Mr. Rout?'

'The devil!' muttered Mr. Rout. 'Look out, Beale!'

His shout rang out like the blast of a warning trumpet, between the iron walls of the engine-room. Painted white, they rose high into the dusk of the skylight, sloping like a roof; and the whole lofty space resembled the interior of a monument, divided by floors of iron grating, with lights flickering at different levels, and a mass of gloom lingering in the middle, within the columnar stir of machinery under the motionless swelling of the cylinders. A loud and wild resonance, made up of all the noises of the hurricane, dwelt in the still warmth of the air. There was in it the smell of hot metal, of oil, and a slight mist of steam. The blows of the sea seemed to traverse it in an unringing, stunning shock, from side to side.

Gleams, like pale long flames, trembled upon the polish of metal; from the flooring below the enormous crank-heads emerged in their turns with a flash of brass and steel – going over; while the connecting-rods, big-jointed, like skeleton limbs, seemed to thrust them down and pull them up again with an irresistible precision. And deep in the half-light other rods dodged deliberately to and fro, crossheads nodded, discs of metal rubbed smoothly against each other, slow and gentle, in a commingling of shadows and gleams.

Sometimes all those powerful and unerring movements would slow down simultaneously, as if they had been the functions of a living organism, stricken suddenly by the blight of langour; and Mr. Rout's eyes would blaze darker in his long sallow face. He was fighting this fight in a pair of carpet slippers. A short shiny jacket barely covered his loins, and his white wrists protruded far out of the tight sleeves, as though the emergency had added to his stature, had lengthened his limbs, augmented his pallor, hollowed his eyes.

He moved, climbing high up, disappearing low down, with a restless, purposeful industry, and when he stood still, holding the guard-rail in front of the starting-gear, he would keep glancing to the right at the steam-gauge, at the water-gauge, fixed upon the white wall in the light of a swaying lamp. The mouths of two speaking-tubes gaped stupidly at his elbow, and the dial of the engine-room telegraph resembled a clock of large diameter, bearing on its face curt words instead of figures. The grouped letters stood out heavily black, around the pivot-head of the indicator, emphatically symbolic of loud exclamations: AHEAD, ASTERN, SLOW, HALF, STAND BY; and the fat black hand pointed downwards to the word FULL, which, thus singled out, captured the eye as a sharp cry secures attention.

The wood-encased bulk of the low-pressure cylinder, frowning portly from above, emitted a faint wheeze at every thrust, and except for that low hiss the engines worked their steel limbs headlong or slow with a silent, determined smoothness. And all this, the white walls, the moving steel, the floor plates under Solomon Rout's feet, the floors of iron grating above his head, the dusk and the gleams, uprose and sank continuously, with one accord, upon the harsh wash of the waves against the ship's side. The whole loftiness of the place, booming hollow to the great voice of the wind, swayed at the top like a tree, would go over bodily, as if borne down this way and that by the tremendous blasts.

'You've got to hurry up,' shouted Mr. Rout, as soon as he saw Jukes appear in the stokehold doorway.

Jukes' glance was wandering and tipsy; his red face was puffy, as though he had overslept himself. He had had an arduous road, and had travelled over it with immense vivacity, the agitation of his mind corresponding to the exertions of his body. He had rushed up out of the bunker, stumbling in the dark alleyway amongst a lot of bewildered men who, trod upon, asked 'What's up, sir?' in awed mutters all round him; – down the stokehold ladder, missing many iron rungs in his hurry, down into a place deep as a well, black as Tophet, tipping over back and forth like a see-saw. The water in the bilges thundered at each roll, and lumps of coal skipped to and fro, from end to end, rattling like an avalanche of pebbles on a slope of iron.

Somebody in there moaned with pain, and somebody else could be seen crouching over what seemed the prone body of a dead man; a lusty voice blasphemed; and the glow under each fire-door was like a pool of flaming blood radiating quietly in a velvety blackness.

A gust of wind struck upon the nape of Jukes' neck, and next moment he felt it streaming about his wet ankles. The stokehold ventilators hummed: in front of the six fire-doors two wild figures, stripped to the waist, staggered and stooped, wrestling with two shovels.

'Hallo! Plenty of draught now,' yelled the second engineer at once, as though he had been all the time looking out for Jukes. The donkey-man, a dapper little chap with a dazzling fair skin and a tiny, gingery moustache, worked in a sort of mute transport. They were keeping a full head of steam, and a profound rumbling, as of an empty furniture van trotting over a bridge, made a sustained bass to all the other noises of the place.

'Blowing off all the time,' went on yelling the second. With a sound as of a hundred scoured saucepans, the orifice of a ventilator spat upon his shoulder a sudden gush of salt water, and he volleyed a stream of curses upon all things on earth including his own soul, ripping and raving, and all the time attending to his business. With a sharp clash of metal the ardent pale glare of the fire opened upon his bullet head, showing his spluttering lips, his insolent face, and with another clang closed like the white-hot wink of an iron eye.

'Where's the blooming ship? Can you tell me? blast my eyes! Under water – or what? It's coming down here in tons. Are the condemned cowls gone to Hades? Hey? Don't you know anything – you jolly sailor-man you . . .?'

Jukes, after a bewildered moment, had been helped by a roll to dart through; and as soon as his eyes took in the comparative vastness, peace and brilliance of the engine-room, the ship, setting her stern heavily in the water, sent him charging head down upon Mr. Rout.

The chief's arm, long like a tentacle, and straightening as if worked by a spring, went out to meet him, and deflected his rush into a spin towards the speaking-tubes. At the same time Mr. Rout repeated earnestly: 'You've got to hurry up, whatever it is.'

Jukes yelled 'Are you there, sir?' and listened. Nothing. Suddenly the roar of the wind fell straight into his ear, but presently a small voice shoved aside the shouting hurricane quietly.

'You, Jukes? – Well?'

Jukes was ready to talk: it was only time that seemed to be wanting. It was easy enough to account for everything. He could perfectly imagine the coolies battened down in the reeking 'tween-deck, lying sick and scared between the rows of chests. Then one of these chests – or perhaps several at once – breaking loose in a roll, knocking out others, sides splitting, lids flying open, and all these clumsy Chinamen rising up in a body to save their property. Afterwards every fling of the ship would hurl that tramping, yelling mob here and there, from side to side, in a whirl of smashed wood, torn clothing, rolling dollars. A struggle once started, they would be unable to stop themselves. Nothing could stop them now except main force. It was a disaster. He had seen it, and that was all he could say. Some of them must be dead, he believed. The rest would go on fighting. . . .

He sent up his words, tripping over each other, crowding the narrow tube. They mounted as if into a silence of an enlightened comprehension dwelling alone up there with a storm. And Jukes wanted to be dismissed from the face of that odious trouble intruding on the great need of the ship.

V

HE waited. Before his eyes the engines turned with slow labour, that in the moment of going off into a mad fling would stop dead at Mr. Rout's shout, 'Look out, Beale!' They paused in an intelligent immobility, stilled in mid-stroke, a heavy crank arrested on the cant, as if conscious of danger and the passage of time. Then, with a 'Now, then!' from the chief, and the sound of a breath expelled through clenched teeth, they would accomplish the interrupted revolution and begin another.

There was the prudent sagacity of wisdom and the deliberation of enormous strength in their movements. This was their work – this patient coaxing of a distracted ship over the fury of the waves and into the very eye of the wind. At times Mr. Rout's chin would sink on his breast, and he watched them with knitted eyebrows as if lost in thought.

The voice that kept the hurricane out of Jukes' ear began: 'Take the hands with you . . .' and left off unexpectedly.

'What could I do with them, sir?'

A harsh, abrupt, imperious clang exploded suddenly. The three pairs of eyes flew up to the telegraph dial to see the hand jump from FULL to STOP, as if snatched by a devil. And then these three men in the engine-room had the intimate sensation of a check upon the ship, of a strange shrinking, as if she had gathered herself for a desperate leap.

'Stop her!' bellowed Mr. Rout.

Nobody – not even Captain MacWhirr, who alone on deck had caught sight of a white line of foam coming on at such a height that he couldn't believe his eyes – nobody was to know the steepness of that sea and the awful depth of the hollow the hurricane had scooped out behind the running wall of water.

It raced to meet the ship, and, with a pause, as of girding the loins, the *Nan-Shan* lifted her bows and leaped. The flames in all the lamps sank, darkening the engine-room. One went out. With a tearing crash and a swirling, raving tumult, tons of water fell upon the deck, as though the ship had darted under the foot of a cataract.

Down there they looked at each other, stunned.

'Swept from end to end, by God!' bawled Jukes.

She dipped into the hollow straight down, as if going over the edge of the world. The engine-room toppled forward menacingly, like the inside of a tower nodding in an earthquake. An awful racket, of iron things falling, came from the stokehold. She hung on this appalling slant long enough for Beale to drop on his hands and knees and begin to crawl as if he meant to fly on all fours out of the engine-room, and for Mr. Rout to turn his head slowly, rigid, cavernous, with the lower jaw dropping. Jukes had shut his eyes, and his face in a moment became hopelessly blank and gentle, like the face of a blind man.

At last she rose slowly, staggering, as if she had to lift a mountain with her bows.

Mr. Rout shut his mouth; Jukes blinked; and little Beale stood up hastily.

'Another one like this, and that's the last of her,' cried the chief.

He and Jukes looked at each other, and the same thought came into their heads. The Captain! Everything must have been swept away. Steering-gear gone – ship like a log. All over directly.

'Rush!' ejaculated Mr. Rout thickly, glaring with enlarged, doubtful eyes at Jukes, who answered him by an irresolute glance.

The clang of the telegraph gong soothed them instantly. The black hand dropped in a flash from STOP to FULL.

'Now then, Beale!' cried Mr. Rout.

The steam hissed low. The piston-rods slid in and out. Jukes put his ear to the tube. The voice was ready for him. It said: 'Pick up all the money. Bear a hand now. I'll want you up here.' And that was all.

'Sir?' called up Jukes. There was no answer.

He staggered away like a defeated man from the field of battle. He had got, in some way or other, a cut above his left eyebrow – a cut to the bone. He was not aware of it in the least: quantities of the China Sea, large enough to break his neck for him, had gone over his head, had cleaned, washed, and salted that wound. It did not bleed, but only gaped red; and this gash over the eye, his dishevelled hair, the disorder of his clothes, gave him the aspect of a man worsted in a fight with fists.

'Got to pick up the dollars.' He appealed to Mr. Rout, smiling pitifully at random.

'What's that?' asked Mr. Rout wildly. 'Pick up . . . ? I don't care. . . .' Then, quivering in every muscle, but with an exaggeration of paternal tone, 'Go away now, for God's sake. You deck people'll drive me silly. There's that second mate been going for the old man. Don't you know? You fellows are going wrong for want of something to do. . . .'

At these words Jukes discovered in himself the beginnings of anger. Want of something to do – indeed. . . . Full of hot scorn against the chief, he turned to go the way he had come. In the stokehold the plump donkey-man toiled with his shovel mutely, as if his tongue had been cut out; but the second was carrying on like a noisy, undaunted maniac, who had preserved his skill in the art of stoking under a marine boiler.

'Hallo, you wandering officer! Hey! Can't you get some of your slush-slingers to wind up a few of them ashes? I am getting choked with them here. Curse it! Hallo! Hey! Remember the articles: *Sailors and firemen to assist each other*. Hey! D'ye hear?'

Jukes was climbing out frantically, and the other, lifting up his face after him, howled, 'Can't you speak? What are you poking about here for? What's your game, anyhow?'

A frenzy possessed Jukes. By the time he was back amongst the men in the darkness of the alleyway, he felt ready to wring all their necks at the slightest sign of hanging back. The very thought of it exasperated him. *He* couldn't hang back. They shouldn't.

The impetuosity with which he came amongst them carried them along. They had already been excited and startled at all his comings and goings – by the fierceness and rapidity of his movements; and more felt than seen in his rushes, he appeared formidable – busied with matters of life and death that brooked no delay. At his first word he heard them drop into the bunker one after another obediently, with heavy thumps.

They were not clear as to what would have to be done. 'What is it? What is it?' they were asking each other. The boatswain tried to explain; the sounds of a great scuffle surprised them: and the mighty shocks, reverberating awfully in the black bunker, kept them in mind of their danger. When the boatswain threw open the door it seemed that an eddy of the hurricane, stealing through the iron sides of the ship, had set all these bodies whirling like dust: there came to them a confused uproar, a tempestuous tumult, a fierce mutter, gusts of screams dying away, and the tramping of feet mingling with the blows of the sea.

For a moment they glared amazed, blocking the doorway. Jukes pushed through them brutally. He said nothing, and simply darted in. Another lot of coolies on the ladder, struggling suicidally to break through the battened hatch to a swamped deck, fell off as before, and he disappeared under them like a man overtaken by a landslide.

The boatswain yelled excitedly: 'Come along. Get the mate out. He'll be trampled to death. Come on.'

They charged in, stamping on breasts, on fingers, on faces, catching their feet in heaps of clothing, kicking broken wood; but before they could get hold of him Jukes emerged waist-deep in a multitude of clawing hands. In the instant he had been lost to view, all the buttons of his jacket had gone, its back had got split up to the collar, his waistcoat had been torn open. The central struggling mass of Chinamen went over to the roll, dark, indistinct, helpless, with a wild gleam of many eyes in the dim light of the lamps.

'Leave me alone – damn you. I am all right,' screeched Jukes. 'Drive them forward. Watch your chance when she pitches. Forward with 'em. Drive them against the bulkhead. Jam 'em up.'

The rush of the sailors into the seething 'tween-deck was like a splash of cold water into a boiling cauldron. The commotion sank for a moment.

The bulk of Chinamen were locked in such a compact scrimmage that, linking their arms and aided by an appalling dive of the ship, the seamen sent it forward in one great shove, like a solid block. Behind their backs small clusters and loose bodies tumbled from side to side.

The boatswain performed prodigious feats of strength. With his long arms open, and each great paw clutching at a stanchion, he stopped the rush of seven entwined Chinamen rolling like a boulder. His joints cracked; he said, 'Ha!' and they flew apart. But the carpenter showed the greater intelligence. Without saying a word to anybody he went back into the alleyway to fetch several coils of cargo gear he had seen there – chain and rope. With these life-lines were rigged.

There was really no resistance. The struggle, however it began, had turned into a scramble of blind panic. If the coolies had started up after their scattered dollars they were by that time fighting only for their footing. They took each other by the throat merely to save themselves from being hurled about. Whoever got a hold anywhere would kick at the others who caught at his legs and hung on, till a roll sent them flying together across the deck.

The coming of the white devils was a terror. Had they come to kill? The individuals torn out of the ruck became very limp in the seamen's hands: some, dragged aside by the heels, were passive, like dead bodies, with open, fixed eyes. Here and there a coolie would fall on his knees as if begging for mercy; several, whom the excess of fear made unruly, were hit with hard fists between the eyes, and cowered; while those who were hurt submitted to rough handling, blinking rapidly without a plaint. Faces streamed with blood; there were raw places on the shaven heads, scratches, bruises, torn wounds, gashes. The broken porcelain out of the chests was mostly responsible for the latter. Here and there a Chinaman, wild-eyed, with his tail unplaited, nursed a bleeding sole.

They had been ranged closely, after having been shaken into submission, cuffed a little to allay excitement, addressed in gruff words of encouragement that sounded like promises of evil. They sat on the deck in ghastly, drooping rows, and at the end the carpenter, with two hands to help him, moved busily from place to place, setting taut and hitching the life-lines. The boatswain, with one leg and one arm embracing a stanchion, struggled with a lamp pressed to his breast, trying to get a light, and growling all the time like an industrious gorilla. The figures of seamen stooped repeatedly, with the movements of gleaners, and everything was being flung into the bunker: clothing, smashed wood, broken china, and the dollars too, gathered up in men's jackets. Now and then a sailor would stagger towards the doorway with his arms full of rubbish; and dolorous, slanting eyes followed his movements.

With every roll of the ship the long rows of sitting Celestials would sway forward brokenly, and her headlong dives knocked together the line of shaven polls from end to end. When the wash of water rolling on the deck died away for a moment, it seemed to Jukes, yet quivering from his exertions, that in his mad struggle down there he had overcome the wind somehow: that a silence had fallen upon the ship, a silence in which the sea struck thunderously at her sides.

Everything had been cleared out of the 'tween-deck – all the wreckage, as the men said. They stood erect and tottering above the level of heads and drooping shoulders. Here and there a coolie sobbed for his breath. Where the high light fell, Jukes could see the salient ribs of one, the yellow, wistful face of another, bowed necks; or would meet a dull stare directed at his face. He was amazed that there had been no corpses; but the lot of them seemed at their last gasp, and they appeared to him more pitiful than if they had been all dead.

Suddenly one of the coolies began to speak. The light came and went on his lean, straining face; he threw his head up like a baying hound. From the bunker came the sounds of knocking and the tinkle of some dollars rolling loose; he stretched out his arm, his mouth yawned black, and the incomprehensible guttural hooting sounds, that did not seem to belong to a human language, penetrated Jukes with a strange emotion as if a brute had tried to be eloquent.

Two more started mouthing what seemed to Jukes fierce denunciations; the others stirred with grunts and growls. Jukes ordered the hands out of the 'tween-decks hurriedly. He left last himself, backing through the door, while the grunts rose to a loud murmur and hands were extended after him as after a malefactor. The boatswain shot the bolt, and remarked uneasily, 'Seems as if the wind had dropped, sir.'

The seamen were glad to get back into the alleyway. Secretly each of them thought that at the last moment he could rush out on deck – and that was a comfort. There is something horribly repugnant in the idea of being drowned under a deck. Now they had done with the Chinamen, they again became conscious of the ship's position.

Jukes on coming out of the alleyway found himself up to the neck in the noisy water. He gained the bridge, and discovered he

could detect obscure shapes as if his sight had become pre-
ternaturally acute. He saw faint outlines. They recalled not the
familiar aspect of the *Nan-Shan*, but something remembered – an
old dismantled steamer he had seen years ago rotting on a mud-
bank. She recalled that wreck.

There was no wind, not a breath, except the faint currents
created by the lurches of the ship. The smoke tossed out of the
funnel was settling down upon her deck. He breathed it as he
passed forward. He felt the deliberate throb of the engines, and
heard small sounds that seemed to have survived the great uproar:
the knocking of broken fittings, the rapid tumbling of some piece of
wreckage on the bridge. He perceived dimly the squat shape of his
captain holding on to a twisted bridge-rail, motionless and swaying
as if rooted to the planks. The unexpected stillness of the air
oppressed Jukes.

'We have done it, sir,' he gasped.

'Thought you would,' said Captain MacWhirr.

'Did you?' murmured Jukes to himself.

'Wind fell all at once,' went on the Captain.

Jukes burst out: 'If you think it was an easy job —'

But his captain, clinging to the rail, paid no attention. 'According
to the books the worst is not over yet.'

'If most of them hadn't been half dead with sea-sickness and
fright, not one of us would have come out of that 'tween-deck
alive,' said Jukes.

'Had to do what's fair by them,' mumbled MacWhirr stolidly.
'You don't find everything in books.'

'Why, I believe they would have risen on us if I hadn't ordered
the hands out of that pretty quick,' continued Jukes with warmth.

After the whisper of their shouts, their ordinary tones, so distinct,
rang out very loud to their ears in the amazing stillness of the air.
It seemed to them they were talking in a dark and echoing vault.

Through a jagged aperture in the dome of clouds the light of a
few stars fell upon the black sea, rising and falling confusedly.
Sometimes the head of a watery cone would topple on board and
mingle with the rolling flurry of foam on the swamped deck; and
the *Nan-Shan* wallowed heavily at the bottom of a circular cistern
of clouds. This ring of dense vapours, gyrating madly round the
calm of the centre, encompassed the ship like a motionless and

unbroken wall of an aspect inconceivably sinister. Within, the sea, as if agitated by an internal commotion, leaped in peaked mounds that jostled each other, slapping heavily against her sides; and a low moaning sound, the infinite plaint of the storm's fury, came from beyond the limits of the menacing calm. Captain MacWhirr remained silent, and Jukes' ready ear caught suddenly the faint, long-drawn roar of some immense wave rushing unseen under that thick blackness, which made the appalling boundary of his vision.

'Of course,' he started resentfully, 'they thought we had caught at the chance to plunder them. Of course! You said – pick up the money. Easier said than done. They couldn't tell what was in our heads. We came in, smash – right into the middle of them. Had to do it by a rush.'

'As long as it's done . . .,' mumbled the Captain, without attempting to look at Jukes. 'Had to do what's fair.'

'We shall find yet there's the devil to pay when this is over,' said Jukes, feeling very sore. 'Let them only recover a bit, and you'll see. They will fly at our throats, sir. Don't forget, sir, she isn't a British ship now. These brutes know it well, too. The damn'd Siamese flag.'

'We are on board, all the same,' remarked Captain MacWhirr.

'The trouble's not over yet,' insisted Jukes prophetically, reeling and catching on. 'She's a wreck,' he added faintly.

'The trouble's not over yet,' assented Captain MacWhirr, half aloud. . . . 'Look out for her a minute.'

'Are you going off the deck, sir?' asked Jukes hurriedly, as if the storm were sure to pounce upon him as soon as he had been left alone with the ship.

He watched her, battered and solitary, labouring heavily in a wild scene of mountainous black waters lit by the gleams of distant worlds. She moved slowly, breathing into the still core of the hurricane the excess of her strength in a white cloud of steam – and the deep-toned vibration of the escape was like the defiant trumpeting of a living creature of the sea impatient for the renewal of the contest. It ceased suddenly. The still air moaned. Above Jukes' head a few stars shone into the pit of black vapours. The inky edge of the cloud-disc frowned upon the ship under the patch of glittering sky. The stars too seemed to look at her intently, as if for the last time, and the cluster of their splendour sat like a diadem on a lowering brow.

Captain MacWhirr had gone into the chart-room. There was no light there; but he could feel the disorder of that place where he used to live tidily. His armchair was upset. The books had tumbled out on the floor: he scrunched a piece of glass under his boot. He groped for the matches, and found a box on a shelf with a deep ledge. He struck one, and puckering the corners of his eyes, held out the little flame towards the barometer whose glittering top of glass and metals nodded at him continuously.

It stood very low – incredibly low, so low that Captain MacWhirr grunted. The match went out, and hurriedly he extracted another, with thick, stiff fingers.

Again a little flame flared up before the nodding glass and metal of the top. His eyes looked at it, narrowed with attention, as if expecting an imperceptible sign. With his grave face he resembled a booted and misshapen pagan burning incense before the oracle of a Joss. There was no mistake. It was the lowest reading he had ever seen in his life.

Captain MacWhirr emitted a low whistle. He forgot himself till the flame diminished to a blue spark, burnt his fingers and vanished. Perhaps something had gone wrong with the thing!

There was an aneroid glass screwed above the couch. He turned that way, struck another match, and discovered the white face of the other instrument looking at him from the bulkhead, meaningly, not to be gainsaid, as though the wisdom of men were made unerring by the indifference of matter. There was no room for doubt now. Captain MacWhirr pshawed at it, and threw the match down.

The worst was to come, then – and if the books were right this worst would be very bad. The experience of the last six hours had enlarged his conception of what heavy weather could be like. 'It'll be terrific,' he pronounced mentally. He had not consciously looked at anything by the light of the matches except at the barometer; and yet somehow he had seen that his water-bottle and the two tumblers had been flung out of their stand. It seemed to give him a more intimate knowledge of the tossing the ship had gone through. 'I wouldn't have believed it,' he thought. And his table had been cleared too; his rulers, his pencils, the inkstand – all the things that had their safe appointed places – they were gone, as if a mischievous hand had plucked them out one by one and flung them on the wet floor. The hurricane had broken in upon the orderly arrangements of his privacy. This had never happened before, and the feeling of dismay reached the very seat of his composure. And the worst was to come yet! He was glad the trouble in the 'tween-deck had been discovered in time. If the ship had to go after all, then, at least, she wouldn't be going to the bottom with a lot of people in her fighting teeth and claw. That would have been odious. And in that feeling there was a humane intention and a vague sense of the fitness of things.

These instantaneous thoughts were yet in their essence heavy and slow, partaking of the nature of the man. He extended his hand to put back the matchbox in its corner of the shelf. There were always matches there – by his order. The steward had his instructions impressed upon him long before. 'A box . . . just there, see? Not so very full . . . where I can put my hand on it, steward. Might want a light in a hurry. Can't tell on board ship *what* you might want in a hurry. Mind, now.'

And of course on his side he would be careful to put it back in its place scrupulously. He did so now, but before he removed his hand it occurred to him that perhaps he would never have occasion to use that box any more. The vividness of the thought checked him, and for an infinitesimal fraction of a second his fingers closed again on the small object as though it had been the symbol of all these little habits that chain us to the weary round of life. He released it at last, and letting himself fall on the settee, listened for the first sounds of returning wind.

Not yet. He heard only the wash of water, the heavy splashes, the dull shocks of the confused seas boarding the ship from all sides. She would never have a chance to clear her decks.

But the quietude of the air was startlingly tense and unsafe, like a slender hair holding a sword suspended over his head. By this awful pause the storm penetrated the defences of the man and unsealed his lips. He spoke out in the solitude and the pitch darkness of the cabin, as if addressing another being awakened within his breast.

'I shouldn't like to lose her,' he said half aloud.

He sat unseen, apart from the sea, from his ship, isolated, as if withdrawn from the very current of his own existence, where such freaks as talking to himself surely had no place. His palms reposed on his knees, he bowed his short neck and puffed heavily, surrendering to a strange sensation of weariness he was not enlightened enough to recognize for the fatigue of mental stress.

From where he sat he could reach the door of a washstand locker. There should have been a towel there. There was. Good. . . . He took it out, wiped his face, and afterwards went on rubbing his wet head. He towelled himself with energy in the dark, and then remained motionless with the towel on his knees. A moment passed of a stillness so profound that no one could have guessed there was a man sitting in that cabin. Then a murmur arose.

'She may come out of it yet.'

When Captain MacWhirr came out on deck, which he did brusquely, as though he had suddenly become conscious of having stayed away too long, the calm had lasted already more than fifteen minutes – long enough to make itself intolerable even to his imagination. Jukes, motionless on the forepart of the bridge, began to speak at once. His voice, blank and forced as though he were talking through hard-set teeth, seemed to flow away on all sides into the darkness, deepening again upon the sea.

'I had the wheel relieved. Hackett began to sing out that he was done. He's lying in there alongside the steering-gear with a face like death. At first I couldn't get anybody to crawl out and relieve the poor devil. That boss'n's worse than no good, I always said. Thought I would have had to go myself and haul out one of them by the neck.'

'Ah, well,' muttered the Captain. He stood watchful by Jukes' side.

'The second mate's in there too, holding his head. Is he hurt, sir?'

'No – crazy,' said Captain MacWhirr, curtly.

'Looks as if he had a tumble, though.'

'I had to give him a push,' explained the Captain.

Jukes gave an impatient sigh.

'It will come very sudden,' said Captain MacWhirr, 'and from over there, I fancy. God only knows, though. These books are only good to muddle your head and make you jumpy. It will be bad, and there's an end. If we only can steam her round in time to meet it. . . .'

A minute passed. Some of the stars winked rapidly and vanished.

'You left them pretty safe?' began the Captain abruptly, as though the silence were unbearable.

'Are you thinking of the coolies, sir? I rigged life-lines all ways across that 'tween-deck.'

'Did you? Good idea, Mr. Jukes.'

'I didn't ... think you cared to ... know,' said Jukes – the lurching of the ship cut his speech as though somebody had been jerking him around while he talked – 'how I got on with ... that infernal job. We did it. And it may not matter in the end.'

'Had to do what's fair, for all – they are only Chinamen. Give them the same chance with ourselves – hang it all. She isn't lost yet. Bad enough to be shut up below in a gale —'

'That's what I thought when you gave me the job, sir,' interjected Jukes moodily.

'— without being battered to pieces,' pursued Captain MacWhirr with rising vehemence. 'Couldn't let that go on in my ship, if I knew she hadn't five minutes to live. Couldn't bear it, Mr. Jukes.'

A hollow echoing noise, like that of a shout rolling in a rocky chasm, approached the ship and went away again. The last star, blurred, enlarged, as if returning to the fiery mist of its beginning, struggled with the colossal depth of blackness hanging over the ship – and went out.

'Now for it!' muttered Captain MacWhirr. 'Mr. Jukes.'

'Here, sir.'

The two men were growing indistinct to each other.

'We must trust her to go through it and come out on the other side. That's plain and straight. There's no room for Captain Wilson's storm-strategy here.'

'No, sir.'

'She will be smothered and swept again for hours,' mumbled the Captain. 'There's not much left by this time above deck for the sea to take away – unless you or me.'

'Both, sir,' whispered Jukes breathlessly.

'You are always meeting trouble half-way, Jukes,' Captain MacWhirr remonstrated quaintly. 'Though it's a fact that the second mate is no good. D'ye hear, Mr. Jukes? You would be left alone if ...'

Captain MacWhirr interrupted himself, and Jukes, glancing on all sides, remained silent.

'Don't you be put out by anything,' the Captain continued, mumbling rather fast. 'Keep her facing it. They may say what they like, but the heaviest seas run with the wind. Facing it – always facing it – that's the way to get through. You are a young sailor. Face it. That's enough for any man. Keep a cool head.'

'Yes, sir,' said Jukes, with a flutter of the heart.

In the next few seconds the Captain spoke to the engine-room and got an answer.

For some reason Jukes experienced an access of confidence, a sensation that came from outside like a warm breath, and made him feel equal to every demand. The distant muttering of the darkness stole into his ears. He noted it unmoved, out of that sudden belief in himself, as a man safe in a shirt of mail would watch a point.

The ship laboured without intermission amongst the black hills of water, paying with this hard tumbling the price of her life. She rumbled in her depths, shaking a white plummet of steam into the night, and Jukes' thought skimmed like a bird through the engine-room, where Mr. Rout – good man – was ready. When the rumbling ceased it seemed to him that there was a pause of every sound, a dead pause in which Captain MacWhirr's voice rang out startlingly.

'What's that? A puff of wind?' – it spoke much louder than Jukes had ever heard it before – 'On the bow. That's right. She may come out of it yet.'

The mutter of the winds drew near apace. In the forefront could be distinguished a drowsy waking plaint passing on, and far off the growth of a multiple clamour, marching and expanding. There was the throb as of many drums in it, a vicious rushing note, and like the chant of a tramping multitude.

Jukes could no longer see his captain distinctly. The darkness was absolutely piling itself upon the ship. At most he made out movements, a hint of elbows spread out, of a head thrown up.

Captain MacWhirr was trying to do up the top button of his oilskin coat with unwonted haste. The hurricane, with its power to madden the seas, to sink ships, to uproot trees, to overturn strong walls and dash the very birds of the air to the ground, had found this taciturn man in its path, and, doing its utmost, had managed to wring out a few words. Before the renewed wrath of winds swooped on his ship, Captain MacWhirr was moved to declare, in a tone of vexation, as it were: 'I wouldn't like to lose her.'

He was spared that annoyance.

VI

On a bright sunshiny day, with the breeze chasing her smoke far ahead, the *Nan-Shan* came into Fu-Chau. Her arrival was at once noticed on shore, and the seamen in harbour said: 'Look! Look at that steamer. What's that? Siamese – isn't she? Just look at her!'

She seemed, indeed, to have been used as a running target for the secondary batteries of a cruiser. A hail of minor shells could not have given her upper works a more broken, torn, and devastated aspect: and she had about her the worn, weary air of ships coming from the far ends of the world – and indeed with truth, for in her short passage she had been very far; sighting, verily, even the coast of the Great Beyond, whence no ship ever returns to give up her crew to the dust of the earth. She was incrusted and grey with salt to the trucks of her masts and to the top of her funnel as though (as some facetious seaman said) 'the crowd on board had fished her out somewhere from the bottom of the sea and brought her in here for salvage'. And further, excited by the felicity of his own wit, he offered to give five pounds for her – 'as she stands'.

Before she had been quite an hour at rest, a meagre little man, with a red-tipped nose and a face cast in an angry mould, landed from a sampan on the quay of the Foreign Concession, and incontinently turned to shake his fist at her.

A tall individual, with legs much too thin for a rotund stomach, and with watery eyes, strolled up and remarked, 'Just left her – eh? Quick work.'

He wore a soiled suit of blue flannel with a pair of dirty cricketing shoes; a dingy grey moustache dropped from his lip, and daylight could be seen in two places between the rim and the crown of his hat.

'Hallo! what are you doing here?' asked the ex-second-mate of the *Nan-Shan*, shaking hands hurriedly.

'Standing by for a job – chance worth taking – got a quiet hint,' explained the man with the broken hat, in jerky, apathetic wheezes.

The second shook his fist again at the *Nan-Shan*. 'There's a fellow there that ain't fit to have the command of a scow,' he declared, quivering with passion, while the other looked about listlessly.

'Is there?'

But he caught sight on the quay of a heavy seaman's chest, painted brown under a fringed sailcloth cover, and lashed with new manila line. He eyed it with awakened interest.

'I would talk and raise trouble if it wasn't for that damned Siamese flag. Nobody to go to – or I would make it hot for him. The fraud! Told his chief engineer – that's another fraud for you – I had lost my nerve. The greatest lot of ignorant fools that ever sailed the seas. No! you can't think . . .'

'Got your money all right?' inquired his seedy acquaintance suddenly.

'Yes. Paid me off on board,' raged the second mate. ' "Get your breakfast on shore," says he.'

'Mean skunk!' commented the tall man vaguely, and passed his tongue on his lips. 'What about having a drink of some sort?'

'He struck me,' hissed the second mate.

'No! Struck! You don't say?' The man in blue began to bustle about sympathetically. 'Can't possibly talk here. I want to know all about it. Struck – eh? Let's get a fellow to carry your chest. I know a quiet place where they have some bottled beer. . . .'

Mr. Jukes, who had been scanning the shore through a pair of glasses, informed the chief engineer afterwards that 'our late second mate hasn't been long in finding a friend. A chap looking uncommonly like a bummer. I saw them walk away together from the quay.'

The hammering and banging of the needful repairs did not disturb Captain MacWhirr. The steward found in the letter he wrote, in a tidy chart-room, passages of such absorbing interest that twice he was nearly caught in the act. But Mrs. MacWhirr, in the drawing-room of the forty-pound house, stifled a yawn – perhaps out of self-respect – for she was alone.

She reclined in a plush-bottomed and gilt hammock-chair near a tiled fireplace, with Japanese fans on the mantel and a glow of coals in the grate. Lifting her hands, she glanced wearily here and there into the many pages. It was not her fault they were so prosy, so completely uninteresting – from 'My darling wife' at the beginning, to 'Your loving husband' at the end. She couldn't be really expected to understand all these ship affairs. She was glad of course, to hear from him, but she had never asked herself why, precisely.

'. . . They are called typhoons . . . The mate did not seem to like it . . . Not in books . . . Couldn't think of letting it go on. . . .'

The paper rustled sharply. '. . . A calm that lasted over twenty minutes,' she read perfunctorily; and the next words her thoughtless eyes caught, on the top of another page, were: 'see you and the children again. . . .' She had a movement of impatience. He was always thinking of coming home. He had never had such a good salary before. What was the matter now!

It did not occur to her to turn back overleaf to look. She would have found it recorded there that between 4 and 6 A.M. on December 25th, Captain MacWhirr did actually think that his ship could not possibly live another hour in such a sea, and that he would never see his wife and children again. Nobody was to know this (his letters got mislaid so quickly) – nobody whatever but the steward, who had been greatly impressed by that disclosure. So much so, that he tried to give the cook some idea of the 'narrow squeak we all had' by saying solemnly, 'The old man himself had a dam' poor opinion of our chance.'

'How do you know?' asked contemptuously the cook, an old soldier, 'He hasn't told you, maybe?'

'Well, he did give me a hint to that effect,' the steward brazened it out.

'Get along with you! He will be coming to tell *me* next,' jeered the old cook over his shoulder.

Mrs. MacWhirr glanced farther, on the alert. '. . . Do what's fair. . . . Miserable objects. . . . Only three, with a broken leg each, and one . . . Thought had better keep the matter quiet . . . hope to have done the fair thing. . . .'

She let fall her hands. No: there was nothing more about coming home. Must have been merely expressing a pious wish. Mrs. MacWhirr's mind was set at ease, and a black marble clock, priced by the local jeweller at £3 18s. 6d., had a discreet stealthy tick.

The door flew open, and a girl in the long-legged, short-frocked period of existence, flung into the room. A lot of colourless, rather lanky hair was scattered over her shoulders. Seeing her mother, she stood still, and directed her pale prying eyes upon the letter.

'From father,' murmured Mrs. MacWhirr. 'What have you done with your ribbon?'

The girl put her hands up to her head and pouted.

'He's well,' continued Mrs. MacWhirr languidly. 'At least I think so. He never says.' She had a little laugh. The girl's face expressed a wandering indifference, and Mrs. MacWhirr surveyed her with fond pride.

'Go and get your hat,' she said after a while. 'I am going out to do some shopping. There is a sale at Linom's.'

'Oh, how jolly!' uttered the child impressively, in unexpectedly grave vibrating tones, and bounded out of the room.

It was a fine afternoon, with a grey sky and dry sidewalks. Out side the draper's Mrs. MacWhirr smiled upon a woman in a black mantle of generous proportions, armoured in jet and crowned with flowers[22] blooming falsely above a bilious matronly countenance. They broke into a swift little babble of greetings and exclamations both together, very hurried, as if the street were ready to yawn open and swallow all that pleasure before it could be expressed.

Behind them the high glass doors were kept on the swing. People couldn't pass, men stood aside waiting patiently, and Lydia was absorbed in poking the end of her parasol between the stone flags. Mrs. MacWhirr talked rapidly.

'Thank you very much. He's not coming home yet. Of course it's very sad to have him away, but it's such a comfort to know he keeps so well.' Mrs. MacWhirr drew breath. 'The climate there agrees with him,' she added beamingly, as if poor MacWhirr had been away touring in China for the sake of his health.

Neither was the chief engineer coming home yet. Mr. Rout knew too well the value of a good billet.

'Solomon says wonders will never cease,' cried Mrs. Rout joyously at the old lady in her armchair by the fire. Mr. Rout's mother moved slightly, her withered hands lying in black half-mittens on her lap.

The eyes of the engineer's wife fairly danced on the paper. 'That captain of the ship he is in – a rather simple man, you remember, mother? – has done something rather clever, Solomon says.'

'Yes, my dear,' said the old woman meekly, sitting with bowed silvery head, and that air of inward stillness characteristic of very old people who seem lost in watching the last flickers of life. 'I think I remember.'

Solomon Rout, Old Sol, Father Sol, The Chief, 'Rout, good man' – Mr. Rout, the condescending and paternal friend of youth, had been the baby of her many children – all dead by this time. And she remembered him best as a boy of ten – long before he went away to serve his apprenticeship in some great engineering works in the North. She had seen so little of him since, she had gone through so many years, that she had now to retrace her steps very far back to recognise him plainly in the mist of time. Sometimes it seemed that her daughter-in-law was talking of some strange man.

Mrs. Rout junior was disappointed. 'H'm. H'm.' She turned the page. 'How provoking! He doesn't say what it is. Says I couldn't understand how much there was in it. Fancy! What could it be so very clever? What a wretched man not to tell us!'

She read on without further remark soberly, and at last sat looking into the fire. The chief wrote just a word or two of the typhoon; but something had moved him to express an increased longing for the companionship of the jolly woman. 'If it hadn't been that mother must be looked after, I would send you your passage-money to-day. You could set up a small house out here. I would have a chance to see you sometimes then. We are not growing younger. . . .'

'He's well, mother,' sighed Mrs. Rout, rousing herself.

'He always was a strong healthy boy,' said the old woman placidly.

But Mr. Jukes' account was really animated and very full. His friend in the Western Ocean trade imparted it freely to the other officers of his liner. 'A chap I know writes to me about an extra-ordinary affair that happened on board his ship in that typhoon – you know – that we read of in the papers two months ago. It's the funniest thing! Just see for yourself what he says. I'll show you his letter.'

There were phrases in it calculated to give the impression of light-hearted, indomitable resolution. Jukes had written them in good faith, for he felt thus when he wrote. He described with lurid effect the scenes in the 'tween-deck. '. . . It struck me in a flash that those confounded Chinamen couldn't tell we weren't a desperate kind of robbers. 'Tisn't good to part the Chinaman from his money if he is the stronger party. We need have been desperate indeed to go thieving in such weather, but what could these beggars know of us? So, without thinking of it twice, I got the hands away in a jiffy. Our work was done – that the old man had set his heart on. We cleared out without staying to inquire how they felt. I am convinced that if they had not been so unmercifully shaken, and afraid – each individual one of them – to stand up, we would have been torn to pieces. Oh! It was pretty complete, I can tell you; and you may run to and fro across the Pond to the end of time before you find yourself with such a job on your hands.'

After this he alluded professionally to the damage done to the ship, and went on thus:

'It was when the weather quieted down that the situation became confoundedly delicate. It wasn't made any better by us having been lately transferred to the Siamese flag; though the skipper can't see that it makes any difference – "as long as we are on board" – he says. There are feelings that this man simply hasn't got – and there's an end of it. You might just as well try to make a bedpost understand. But apart from this it is an infernally lonely state for a ship to be going about the China seas with no proper consuls, not even a gunboat of her own anywhere, nor a body to go to in case of some trouble.

'My notion was to keep these Johnnies under hatches for another fifteen hours or so; as we weren't much farther than that from Fu-chau. We would find there, most likely, some sort of man-of-war, and once under her guns we were safe enough; for surely any skipper of a man-of-war – English, French or Dutch – would see white men through as far as row on board goes. We could get rid of them and their money afterwards by delivering them to their Mandarin or Taotai, or whatever they call these chaps in goggles you see being carried about in sedan-chairs through their stinking streets.

'The old man wouldn't see it somehow. He wanted to keep the matter quiet. He got that notion into his head, and a steam windlass couldn't drag it out of him. He wanted as little fuss made as possible, for the sake of the ship's name and for the sake of the owners – "for the sake of all concerned," says he, looking at me very hard. It made me angry hot. Of course you couldn't keep a thing like that quiet; but the chests had been secured in the usual manner and were safe enough for any earthly gale, while this had been an altogether fiendish business I couldn't give you even an idea of.

'Meantime, I could hardly keep on my feet. None of us had a spell of any sort for nearly thirty hours, and there the old man sat rubbing his chin, rubbing the top of his head, and so bothered he didn't even think of pulling his long boots off.

'"I hope, sir," says I, "you won't be letting them out on deck before we make ready for them in some shape or other." Not, mind you, that I felt very sanguine about controlling these beggars if they meant to take charge. A trouble with a cargo of Chinamen is no child's play. I was dam' tired too. "I wish," said I, "you would let us throw the whole lot of these dollars down to them and leave them to fight it out amongst themselves, while we get a rest."

'"Now you talk wild, Jukes," says he, looking up in his slow way that makes you ache all over, somehow. "We must plan out something that would be fair to all parties."

'I had no end of work on hand, as you may imagine, so I set the hands going, and then I thought I would turn in a bit. I hadn't been asleep in my bunk ten minutes when in rushes the steward and begins to pull at my leg.

'"For God's sake, Mr. Jukes, come out! Come on deck quick, sir. Oh, do come out!"

'The fellow scared all the sense out of me. I didn't know what had happened: another hurricane – or what. Could hear no wind.

'"The Captain's letting them out. Oh, he is letting them out! Jump on deck, sir, and save us. The chief engineer has just run below for his revolver."

'That's what I understood the fool to say. However, Father Rout swears he went in there only to get a clean pocket-handkerchief. Anyhow, I made one jump into my trousers and flew on deck aft. There was certainly a good deal of noise going on forward of the bridge. Four of the hands with the boss'n were at work abaft. I passed up to them some of the rifles all the ships on the China coast carry in the cabin, and led them on the bridge. On the way I ran against Old Sol, looking startled and sucking at an unlighted cigar.

'"Come along," I shouted to him.

'We charged, the seven of us, up to the chart-room. All was over. There stood the old man with his sea-boots still drawn up to the hips and in shirt-sleeves – got warm thinking it out, I suppose. Bun-hin's dandy clerk at his elbow, as dirty as a sweep, was still green in the face. I could see directly I was in for something.

'"What the devil are these monkey tricks, Mr. Jukes?" asks the old man, as angry as ever he could be. I tell you frankly it made me lose my tongue. "For God's sake, Mr. Jukes," says he, "do take these rifles from the men. Somebody's sure to get hurt before long if you don't. Damme, if this ship isn't worse than Bedlam! Look sharp now. I want you up here to help me and Bun-hin's Chinaman to count that money. You wouldn't mind lending a hand too, Mr. Rout, now you are here. The more of us the better."

'He had settled it all in his mind while I was having a snooze. Had we been an English ship, or only going to land our cargo of coolies in an English port, like Hong Kong, for instance, there would have been no end of inquiries and bother, claims for damages and so on. But these Chinamen know their officials better than we do.

'The hatches had been taken off already, and they were all on deck after a night and a day down below. It made you feel queer to see so many gaunt, wild faces together. The beggars stared about at the sky, at the sea, at the ship, as though they had expected the whole thing to have been blown to pieces. And no wonder! They had had a doing that would have shaken the soul out of a white man. But then they say a Chinaman has no soul. He has, though, something about him that is deuced tough. There was a fellow (amongst others of the badly hurt) who had had his eye all but knocked out. It stood out of his head the size of half a hen's egg. This would have laid out a white man on his back for a month: and yet there was that chap elbowing here and there in the crowd and talking to the others as if nothing had been the matter. They made a great hubbub amongst themselves, and whenever the old man showed his bald head on the foreside of the bridge, they would all leave off jawing and look at him from below.

'It seems that after he had done his thinking he made that Bun-hin's fellow go down and explain to them the only way they could get their money back. He told me afterwards that, all the coolies having worked in the same place and for the same length of time, he reckoned he would be doing the fair thing by them as near as possible if he shared all the cash we had picked up equally among the lot. You couldn't tell one man's dollars from another's, he said, and if you asked each man how much money he brought on board he was afraid they would lie, and he would find himself a long way short. I think he was right there. As to giving up the money to any Chinese official he could scare up in Fu-chau, he said he might just as well put the lot in his own pocket at once for all the good it would be to them. I suppose they thought so too.

'We finished the distribution before dark. It was rather a sight: the sea running high, the ship a wreck to look at, these Chinamen staggering up on the bridge one by one for their share, and the old man still booted, and in his shirt-sleeves, busy paying out at the chart-room door, perspiring like anything, and now and then coming down sharp on myself or Father Rout about one thing or another not quite to his mind. He took the share of those who were disabled himself to them on the No. 2 hatch. There were three dollars left over, and these went to the three most damaged coolies, one to each. We turned-to afterwards, and shovelled out on deck heaps of wet rags, all sorts of fragments of things without shape, and that you couldn't give a name to, and let them settle the ownership themselves.

'This certainly is coming as near as can be to keeping the thing quiet for the benefit of all concerned. What's your opinion, you pampered mail-boat swell? The old chief says that this was plainly the only thing that could be done. The skipper remarked to me the other day, "There are things you find nothing about in books." I think that he got out of it very well for such a stupid man.'

AMY FOSTER

AMY FOSTER

KENNEDY is a country doctor, and lives in Colebrook, on the shores of Eastbay. The high ground rising abruptly behind the red roofs of the little town crowds the quaint High Street against the wall which defends it from the sea. Beyond the sea-wall there curves for miles in a vast and regular sweep the barren beach of shingle, with the village of Brenzett standing out darkly across the water, a spire in a clump of trees; and still further out the perpendicular column of a lighthouse, looking in the distance no bigger than a lead-pencil, marks the vanishing-point of the land. The country at the back of Brenzett is low and flat; but the bay is fairly well sheltered from the seas, and occasionally a big ship, windbound or through stress of weather, makes use of the anchoring ground a mile and a half due north from you as you stand at the back door of the Ship Inn in Brenzett. A dilapidated windmill near by, lifting its shattered arms from a mound no loftier than a rubbish-heap, and a Martello tower squatting at the water's edge half a mile to the south of the Coastguard cottages, are familiar to the skippers of small craft. These are the official seamarks for the patch of trustworthy bottom represented on the Admiralty charts by an irregular oval of dots enclosing several figures six, with a tiny anchor engraved among them, and the legend 'mud and shells' over all.

The brow of the upland overtops the square tower of the Colebrook Church. The slope is green and looped by a white road. Ascending along this road, you open a valley broad and shallow, a wide green trough of pastures and hedges merging inland into a vista of purple tints and flowing lines closing the view.

In this valley down to Brenzett and Colebrook and up to Darnford,[23] the market town fourteen miles away, lies the practice of my friend Kennedy. He had begun life as surgeon in the Navy, and afterwards had been the companion of a famous traveller, in the days when there were continents with unexplored interiors. His papers on the fauna and flora made him known to scientific societies. And now he had come to a country practice – from choice. The penetrating power of his mind, acting like a corrosive fluid, had destroyed his ambition, I fancy. His intelligence is of a scientific order, of an investigating habit, and of that unappeasable curiosity which believes that there is a particle of a general truth in every mystery.

A good many years ago now, on my return from abroad, he invited me to stay with him. I came readily enough, and as he could not neglect his patients to keep me company, he took me on his rounds – thirty miles or so of an afternoon, sometimes. I waited for him on the roads; the horse reached after the leafy twigs, and, sitting high in the dogcart, I could hear Kennedy's laugh through the half-open door of some cottage. He had a big, hearty laugh that would have fitted a man twice his size, a brisk manner, a bronzed face, and a pair of grey, profoundly attentive eyes. He had the talent of making people talk to him freely, and an inexhaustible patience in listening to their tales.

One day, as we trotted out of a large village into a shady bit of road, I saw on our left hand a low, brick cottage, with diamond panes in the windows, a creeper on the end wall, a roof of shingle, and some roses climbing on the rickety trellis-work of the tiny porch. Kennedy pulled up to a walk. A woman, in full sunlight, was throwing a dripping blanket over a line stretched between two old apple-trees. And as the bobtailed, long-necked chestnut, trying to get his head, jerked the left hand, covered by a thick dogskin glove, the doctor raised his voice over the hedge: 'How's your child, Amy?'

I had the time to see her dull face, red, not with a mantling blush, but as if her flat cheeks had been vigorously slapped, and to take in the squat figure, the scanty, dusty brown hair drawn into a tight knot at the back of the head. She looked quite young. With a distinct catch in her breath, her voice sounded low and timid.

'He's well, thank you.'

We trotted again. 'A young patient of yours,' I said; and the doctor, flicking the chestnut absently, muttered, 'Her husband used to be.'

'She seems a dull creature,' I remarked listlessly.

'Precisely,' said Kennedy. 'She is very passive. It's enough to look at the red hands hanging at the end of those short arms, at those slow, prominent brown eyes, to know the inertness of her mind – an inertness that one would think made it everlastingly safe from all the surprises of imagination. And yet which of us is safe? At any rate, such as you see her, she had enough imagination to fall in love. She's the daughter of one Isaac Foster, who from a small farmer has sunk into a shepherd, the beginning of his misfortunes dating from his runaway marriage with the cook of his widowed father – a well-to-do, apoplectic grazier, who passionately struck his name off his will, and had been heard to utter threats against his life. But this old affair, scandalous enough to serve as a motive for a Greek tragedy, arose from the similarity of their characters. There are other tragedies, less scandalous and of a subtler poignancy, arising from irreconcilable differences and from that fear of the Incomprehensible that hangs over all our heads – over all our heads. . . .'

The tired chestnut dropped into a walk; and the rim of the sun, all red in a speckless sky, touched familiarly the smooth top of a ploughed rise near the road as I had seen it times innumerable touch the distant horizon of the sea.[24] The uniform brownness of the harrowed field glowed with a rosy tinge, as though the powdered clods had sweated out in minute pearls of blood the toil of uncounted ploughmen. From the edge of a copse a waggon with two horses was rolling gently along the ridge. Raised above our heads upon the sky-line, it loomed up against the red sun, triumphantly big, enormous, like a chariot of giants drawn by two slow-stepping steeds of legendary proportions. And the clumsy figure of the man plodding at the head of the leading horse projected itself on the background of the Infinite with a heroic uncouthness. The end of his carter's whip quivered high up in the blue. Kennedy discoursed.

'She's the eldest of a large family. At the age of fifteen they put her out to service at the New Barns Farm. I attended Mrs. Smith, the tenant's wife, and saw that girl there for the first time. Mrs. Smith, a genteel person with a sharp nose, made her put on a black dress every afternoon. I don't know what induced me to notice her at all. There are faces that call your attention by a curious want of definiteness in their whole aspect, as, walking in a mist, you peer attentively at a vague shape which, after all, may be nothing more curious or strange than a signpost. The only peculiarity I perceived in her was a slight hesitation in her utterance: a sort of preliminary stammer which passes away with the first word. When sharply spoken to, she was apt to lose her head at once, but her heart was of the kindest. She had never been heard to express a dislike for a single human being, and she was tender to every living creature. She was devoted to Mrs. Smith, to Mr. Smith, to their dogs, cats, canaries; and as to Mrs. Smith's grey parrot, its peculiarities exercised upon her a positive fascination. Nevertheless, when that outlandish bird, attacked by the cat, shrieked for help in human accents, she ran out into the yard stopping her ears, and did not prevent the crime. For Mrs. Smith this was another evidence of her stupidity; on the other hand, her want of charm, in view of Smith's well-known frivolousness, was a great recommendation. Her short-sighted eyes would swim with pity for a poor mouse in a trap, and she had been seen once by some boys on her knees in the wet grass helping a toad in difficulties. If it's true, as some German fellow[25] has said, that without phosphorous there is no thought, it is still more true that there is no kindness of heart without a certain amount of imagination. She had some. She had even more than is necessary to understand suffering and to be moved by pity. She fell in love under circumstances that leave no room for doubt in the matter; for you need imagination to form a notion of beauty at all, and still more to discover your ideal in an unfamiliar shape.

'How this aptitude came to her, what it did feed upon, is an inscrutable mystery. She was born in the village, and had never been further away from it than Colebrook or perhaps Darnford. She lived for four years with the Smiths. New Barns is an isolated farmhouse a mile away from the road, and she was content to look day after day at the same fields, hollows, rises; at the trees and the hedgerows; at the faces of the four men about the farm, always the same – day after day, month after month, year after year. She never showed a desire for conversation, and, as it seemed to me, she did not know how to smile. Sometimes of a fine Sunday afternoon she would put on her best dress, a pair of stout boots, a large grey hat trimmed with a black feather (I've seen her in that finery), seize an absurdly slender parasol, climb over two stiles, tramp over three fields and along two hundred yards of road – never further. There stood Foster's cottage. She would help her mother to give their tea to the younger children, wash up the crockery, kiss the little ones, and go back to the farm. That was all. All the rest, all the change, all the relaxation. She never seemed to wish for anything more. And then she fell in love. She fell in love silently, obstinately – perhaps helplessly. It came slowly, but when it came it worked like a powerful spell; it was love as the Ancients understood it: an irresistible and fateful impulse – a possession! Yes, it was in her to become haunted and possessed by a face, by a presence, fatally, as though she had been a pagan worshipper of form under a joyous sky – and to be awakened at last from that mysteriousness forgetfulness of self, from that enchantment, from that transport, by a fear resembling the unaccountable terror of a brute. . . .'

With the sun hanging low on its western limit, the expanse of the grass-lands framed in the counterscarps of the rising ground took on a gorgeous and sombre aspect. A sense of penetrating sadness, like that inspired by a grave strain of music, disengaged itself from the silence of the fields. The men we met walked past, slow, unsmiling, with downcast eyes, as if the melancholy of an overburdened earth had weighted their feet, bowed their shoulders, borne down their glances.

'Yes,' said the doctor to my remark, 'one would think the earth is under a curse, since of all her children these that cling to her the closest are uncouth in body and as leaden of gait as if their very hearts were loaded with chains. But here on this same road you might have seen amongst these heavy men a being lithe, supple and long-limbed, straight like a pine, with something striving upwards in his appearance as though the heart within him had been buoyant. Perhaps it was only the force of the contrast, but when he was passing one of these villagers here, the soles of his feet did not seem to me to touch the dust of the road. He vaulted over the stiles, paced these slopes with a long elastic stride that made him noticeable at a great distance, and had lustrous black eyes. He was so different from the mankind around that, with his freedom of movement, his soft – a little startled – glance, his olive complexion and graceful bearing, his humanity suggested to me the nature of a woodland creature. He came from there.'

The doctor pointed with his whip, and from the summit of the descent seen over the rolling tops of the trees in a park by the side of the road, appeared the level sea far below us, like the floor of an immense edifice inlaid with bands of dark ripple, with still trails of glitter, ending in a belt of glassy water at the foot of the sky. The light blur of smoke, from an invisible steamer, faded on the great clearness of the horizon like the mist of a breath on a mirror; and, inshore, the white sails of a coaster, with the appearance of disentangling themselves slowly from under the branches, floated clear of the foliage of the trees.

'Shipwrecked in the bay?' I said.

'Yes; he was a castaway. A poor emigrant from Central Europe bound to America and washed ashore here in a storm. And for him, who knew nothing of the earth, England was an undiscovered country. It was some time before he learned its name; and for all I know he might have expected to find wild beasts or wild men here, when, crawling in the dark over the sea-wall, he rolled down the other side into a dyke, where it was another miracle he didn't get drowned. But he struggled instinctively like an animal under a net, and this blind struggle threw him out into a field. He must have been, indeed, of a tougher fibre than he looked to withstand without expiring such buffetings, the violence of his exertions, and so much fear. Later on, in his broken English that resembled curiously the speech of a young child, he told me himself that he put his trust in God, believing he was no longer in this world. And truly – he would add – how was he to know? He fought his way against the rain and the gale on all fours, and crawled at last among some sheep huddled close under the lee of a hedge. They ran off in all directions, bleating in the darkness, and he welcomed the first familiar sound he heard on these shores. It must have been two in the morning then. And this is all we know of the manner of his landing, though he did not arrive unattended by any means. Only his grisly company did not begin to come ashore till much later in the day. . . .'

The doctor gathered the reins, clicked his tongue; we trotted down the hill. Then turning, almost directly, a sharp corner into the High Street, we rattled over the stones and were home.

Late in the evening Kennedy, breaking a spell of moodiness that had come over him, returned to the story. Smoking his pipe, he paced the long room from end to end. A reading-lamp concentrated all its light upon the papers on his desk; and, sitting by the open window, I saw, after the windless, scorching day, the frigid splendour of a hazy sea lying motionless under the moon. Not a whisper, not a splash, not a stir of the shingle, not a footstep, not a sigh came up from the earth below – never a sign of life but the scent of climbing jasmine: and Kennedy's voice, speaking behind me, passed through the wide casement, to vanish outside in a chill and sumptuous stillness.

'. . . . The relations of shipwrecks in the olden time tell us of much suffering. Often the castaways were only saved from drowning to die miserably from starvation on a barren coast; others suffered violent death or else slavery, passing through years of precarious existence with people to whom their strangeness was an object of suspicion, dislike or fear. We read about these things, and they are very pitiful. It is indeed hard upon a man to find himself a lost stranger,[26] helpless, incomprehensible, and of a mysterious origin, in some obscure corner of the earth. Yet amongst all the adventurers shipwrecked in all the wild parts of the world, there is not one, it seems to me, that ever had to suffer a fate so simply tragic as the man I am speaking of, the most innocent of adventurers cast out by the sea in the bight of this bay, almost within sight from this very window.

'He did not know the name of his ship. Indeed, in the course of time we discovered he did not even know that ships had names – "like Christian people"; and when, one day, from the top of the Talfourd Hill, he beheld the sea lying open to his view, his eyes roamed afar, lost in an air of wild surprise, as though he had never seen such a sight before. And probably he had not. As far as I could make out, he had been hustled together with many others on board an emigrant ship lying at the mouth of the Elbe, too bewildered to take note of his surroundings, too weary to see anything, too anxious to care. They were driven below into the 'tween-deck and battened down from the very start. It was a low timber dwelling – he would say – with wooden beams overhead, like the houses in his country, but you went into it down a ladder. It was very large, very cold, damp and sombre, with places in the manner of wooden boxes where people had to sleep one above another, and it kept on rocking all ways at once all the time. He

141

crept into one of these boxes and lay down there in the clothes in which he had left his home many days before, keeping his bundle and his stick by his side. People groaned, children cried, water dripped, the lights went out, the walls of the place creaked, and everything was being shaken so that in one's little box one dared not lift one's head. He had lost touch with his only companion (a young man from the same valley, he said), and all the time a great noise of wind went on outside and heavy blows fell – boom! boom! An awful sickness overcame him, even to the point of making him neglect his prayers. Besides, one could not tell whether it was morning or evening. It seemed always to be night in that place.

'Before that he had been travelling a long, long time on the iron track. He looked out of the window, which had a wonderfully clear glass in it, and the trees, the houses, the fields, and the long roads seemed to fly round and round about him till his head swam. He gave me to understand that he had on his passage beheld un-counted multitudes of people – whole nations – all dressed in such clothes as the rich wear. Once he was made to get out of the carriage, and slept through a night on a bench in a house of bricks with his bundle under his head; and once for many hours he had to sit on a floor of flat stones dozing, with his knees up and with his bundle between his feet. There was a roof over him, which seemed made of glass, and was so high that the tallest mountain-pine he had ever seen would have had room to grow under it. Steam-machines rolled in at one end and out at the other. People swarmed more than you can see on a feast-day round the miraculous Holy Image in the yard of the Carmelite Convent down in the plains where, before he left his home, he drove his mother in a wooden cart: – a pious old woman who wanted to offer prayers and make a vow for his safety. He could not give me an idea of how large and lofty and full of noise and smoke and gloom, and clang of iron, the place was, but some one had told him it was called Berlin. Then they rang a bell, and another steam-machine came in, and again he was taken on and on through a land that wearied his eyes by its flatness without a single bit of a hill to be seen anywhere. One more night he spent shut up in a building like a good stable with a litter of straw on the floor, guarding his bundle amongst a lot of men, of whom not one could understand a single word he said. In the morning they were all led down to the stony shores of an

extremely broad muddy river, flowing not between hills but between houses that seemed immense. There was a steam-machine
that went on the water, and they all stood upon it packed tight,
only now there were with them many women and children who
made much noise. A cold rain fell, the wind blew in his face; he
was wet through, and his teeth chattered. He and the young man
from the same valley took each other by the hand.

'They thought they were being taken to America straight away,
but suddenly the steam-machine bumped against the side of a
thing like a great house on the water. The walls were smooth and
black, and there uprose, growing from the roof as it were, bare
trees in the shape of crosses, extremely high. That's how it appeared
to him then, for he had never seen a ship before. This was the ship
that was going to swim all the way to America. Voices shouted,
everything swayed; there was a ladder dipping up and down. He
went up on his hands and knees in mortal fear of falling into the
water below, which made a great splashing. He got separated from
his companion, and when he descended into the bottom of that
ship his heart seemed to melt suddenly within him.

'It was then also, as he told me, that he lost contact for good and
all with one of those three men who the summer before had been
going about through all the little towns in the foothills of his
country. They would arrive on market-days driving in a peasant's
cart, and would set up an office in an inn or some other Jew's
house. There were three of them, of whom one with a long beard
looked venerable; and they had red cloth collars round their necks
and gold lace on their sleeves like Government officials. They sat
proudly behind a long table; and in the next room, so that the
common people shouldn't hear, they kept a cunning telegraph
machine, through which they could talk to the Emperor of America. The fathers hung about the door, but the young men of the
mountains would crowd up to the table asking many questions,
for there was work to be got all the year round at three dollars a
day in America, and no military service to do.

'But the American Kaiser would not take everybody. Oh no! He
himself had a great difficulty in getting accepted, and the venerable
man in uniform had to go out of the room several times to work
the telegraph on his behalf. The American Kaiser engaged him at
last at three dollars, he being young and strong. However, many

able young men backed out, afraid of the great distance; besides, those only who had some money could be taken. There were some who sold their huts and their land because it cost a lot of money to get to America; but then, once there, you had three dollars a day, and if you were clever you could find places where true gold could be picked up on the ground. His father's house was getting over-full. Two of his brothers were married and had children. He promised to send money home from America by post twice a year. His father sold an old cow, a pair of piebald mountain ponies of his own raising, and a cleared plot of fair pasture land on the sunny slope of a pine-clad pass to a Jew inn-keeper, in order to pay the people of the ship that took men to America to get rich in a short time.

'He must have been a real adventurer at heart, for how many of the greatest enterprises in the conquest of the earth had for their beginning just such a bargaining away of the paternal cow for the mirage of true gold far away! I have been telling you more or less in my own words what I learned fragmentarily in the course of two or three years, during which I seldom missed an opportunity of a friendly chat with him. He told me this story of his adventure with many flashes of white teeth and lively glances of black eyes, at first in a sort of anxious baby-talk, then, as he acquired the language, with great fluency, but always with that singing, soft, and at the same time vibrating intonation that instilled a strangely penetrating power into the sound of the most familiar English words, as if they had been the words of an unearthly language. And he always would come to an end, with many emphatic shakes of his head, upon that awful sensation of his heart melting within him directly he set foot on board that ship. Afterwards there seemed to come for him a period of blank ignorance, at any rate as to facts. No doubt he must have been abominably seasick and abominably unhappy – this soft and passionate adventurer, taken thus out of his knowledge, and feeling bitterly as he lay in his emigrant bunk his utter loneliness; for his was a highly sensitive nature. The next think we know of him for certain is that he had been hiding in Hammond's pig-pound by the side of the road to Norton, six miles, as the crow flies, from the sea. Of these experiences he was unwilling to speak; they seemed to have seared into his soul a sombre sort of wonder and indignation. Through the rumours of the countryside, which lasted for a good many days after his arrival, we know that the fishermen of West Colebrook had been disturbed and startled by heavy knocks against the walls of weatherboard cottages, and by a voice crying piercingly strange words in the night. Several of them turned out even, but, no doubt, he had fled in sudden alarm at their rough angry tones hailing each other in the darkness. A sort of frenzy must have helped him up the steep Norton hill. It was he, no doubt, who early the following morning had been seen lying (in a swoon, I should say) on the roadside grass by the Brenzett carrier, who actually got down to have a nearer look, but drew back, intimidated by the perfect immobility, and by something queer in the aspect of that tramp, sleeping so still under the showers. As the day advanced, some children came dashing into school at Norton in such a fright that the schoolmistress went out and spoke indignantly to a "horrid-looking man" on the road. He edged away, hanging his head, for a few steps, and then suddenly ran off with extraordinary fleetness. The driver of Mr. Bradley's milk-cart made no secret of it that he had lashed with his whip at a hairy sort of gipsy fellow who, jumping up at a turn of the road by the Vents, made a snatch at the pony's bridle. And he caught him a good one too, right over the face, he said, that made him drop down in the mud a jolly sight quicker than he had jumped up; but it was a good half mile before he could stop the pony. Maybe that in his desperate endeavours to get help, and in his need to get in touch with some one, the poor devil had tried to stop the cart. Also three boys confessed afterwards to throwing stones at a funny tramp, knocking about all wet and muddy, and, it seemed, very drunk, in the narrow deep lane by the limekilns. All this was the talk of three villages for days; but we have Mrs. Finn's (the wife of Smith's waggoner) unimpeachable testimony that she saw him get over the low wall of Hammond's pig-pound and lurch straight at her, babbling aloud in a voice that was enough to make one die of fright. Having the baby with her in a perambulator, Mrs. Finn called out to him to go away, and as he persisted in coming nearer, she hit him courageously with her umbrella over the head, and, without once looking back, ran like the wind with the perambulator as far as the first house in the village. She stopped then, out of breath, and spoke to old Lewis, hammering there at a heap of stones; and the old chap, taking off his immense black wire goggles, got up on his shaky legs to look where she pointed. Together they followed with their eyes the figure of the man running over a field; they saw him fall down, pick himself up, and run on again, staggering and waving his long arms above his head, in the direction of the New Barns Farm. From that moment he is plainly in the toils of his obscure and touching destiny. There is no doubt after this of what happened to him. All is certain now: Mrs. Smith's intense terror; Amy Foster's stolid conviction held against the other's nervous attack, that the man "meant no harm"; Smith's exasperation (on his return from Darnford Market) at finding the dog barking himself into a fit, the back door locked, his wife in hysterics; and all for an unfortunate dirty tramp, supposed to be even then lurking in his stackyard. Was he? He would teach him to frighten women.

'Smith is notoriously hot-tempered, but the sight of some non-descript and miry creature sitting cross-legged amongst a lot of loose straw, and swinging itself to and fro like a bear in a cage, made him pause. Then this tramp stood up silently before him, one mass of mud and filth from head to foot. Smith, alone amongst his stacks with this apparition, in the stormy twilight ringing with the infuriated barking of the dog, felt the dread of an inexplicable strangeness. But when that being, parting with his black hands the long matted locks that hung before his face, as you part the two halves of a curtain, looked out at him with glistening, wild, black-and-white eyes, the weirdness of this silent encounter fairly staggered him. He has admitted since (for the story has been a legitimate subject of conversation about here for years) that he made more than one step backwards. Then a sudden burst of rapid, senseless speech persuaded him at once that he had to do with an escaped lunatic. In fact, that impression never wore off completely. Smith has not in his heart given up his secret conviction of the man's essential insanity to this very day.

'As the creature approached him, jabbering in a most discomposing manner, Smith (unaware that he was being addressed as "gracious lord", and adjured in God's name to afford food and shelter) kept on speaking firmly but gently to it, and retreating all the time into the other yard. At last, watching his chance, by a sudden charge he bundled him headlong into the wood-lodge, and instantly shot the bolt. Thereupon he wiped his brow, though the day was cold. He had done his duty to the community by shutting up a wandering and probably dangerous maniac. Smith isn't a hard man at all, but he had room in his brain only for that one idea of lunacy. He was not imaginative enough to ask himself whether the man might not be perishing with cold and hunger. Meantime, at first, the maniac made a great deal of noise in the lodge. Mrs. Smith was screaming upstairs, where she had locked herself in her bedroom; but Amy Foster sobbed piteously at the kitchen-door, wringing her hands and muttering "Don't! don't!" I daresay Smith had a rough time of it that evening with one noise and another, and this insane, disturbing voice crying obstinately through the door only added to his irritation. He couldn't possibly have connected this troublesome lunatic with the sinking of a ship in Eastbay, of which there had been a rumour in the Darnford market-place. And I daresay the man inside had been very near to insanity on that night. Before his excitement collapsed and he became unconscious he was throwing himself violently about in the dark, rolling on some dirty sacks, and biting his fists with rage, cold, hunger, amazement, and despair.

'He was a mountaineer of the eastern range of the Carpathians, and the vessel sunk the night before in Eastbay was the Hamburg emigrant ship *Herzogin Sophia–Dorothea*, of appalling memory.

'A few months later we could read in the papers the accounts of the bogus "Emigration Agencies" among the Sclavonian peasantry in the more remote provinces of Austria. The object of these scoundrels was to get hold of the poor ignorant people's home-steads, and they were in league with the local usurers. They exported their victims through Hamburg mostly. As to the ship, I had watched her out of this very window, reaching close-hauled under short canvas into the bay on a dark, threatening afternoon. She came to an anchor, correctly by the chart, off the Brenzett Coastguard station. I remember before the night fell looking out again at the outlines of her spars and rigging that stood out dark and pointed on a background of ragged, slaty clouds like another and a slighter spire to the left of the Brenzett church-tower. In the evening the wind rose. At midnight I could hear in my bed the terrific gusts and the sounds of a driving deluge.

'About that time the Coastguardmen thought they saw the lights of a steamer over the anchoring-ground. In a moment they vanished; but it is clear that another vessel of some sort had tried for shelter in the bay on that awful, blind night, had rammed the German ship amidships (a breach – as one of the divers told me afterwards – "that you could sail a Thames barge through"), and then had gone out either scathless or damaged, who shall say; but had gone out, unknown, unseen, and fatal, to perish mysteriously at sea. Of her nothing ever came to light, and yet the hue and cry that was raised all over the world would have found her out if she had been in existence anywhere on the face of the waters.

'A completeness without a clue, and a stealthy silence as of a neatly executed crime, characterise this murderous disaster, which, as you may remember, had its gruesome celebrity. The wind would have prevented the loudest outcries from reaching the shore; there had been evidently no time for signals of distress. It was death without any sort of fuss. The Hamburg ship, filling all at once, capsized as she sank, and at daylight there was not even the end of a spar to be seen above water. She was missed, of course, and at first the Coastguardmen surmised that she had either dragged her anchor or parted her cable some time during the night, and had been blown out to sea. Then, after the tide turned, the wreck must have shifted a little and released some of the bodies, because a child – a little fair-haired child in a red frock – came ashore abreast of the Martello tower. By the afternoon you could see along three miles of beach dark figures with bare legs dashing in and out of the tumbling foam, and rough-looking men, women with hard faces, children, mostly fair-haired, were being carried, stiff and dripping, on stretchers, on wattles, on ladders, in a long procession past the door of the Ship Inn, to be laid out in a row under the north wall of the Brenzett Church.

'Officially, the body of the little girl in the red frock is the first thing that came ashore from that ship. But I have patients among the seafaring population of West Colebrook, and, unofficially, I am informed that very early that morning two brothers, who went down to look after their cobble hauled up on the beach, found, a good way from Brenzett, an ordinary ship's hencoop lying high and dry on the shore, with eleven drowned ducks inside. Their families ate the birds, and the hencoop was split into firewood with a hatchet. It is possible that a man (supposing he happened to be on deck at the time of the accident) might have floated ashore on that hencoop. He might. I admit it is improbable, but there was the man – and for days, nay, for weeks – it didn't enter our heads that we had amongst us the only living soul that had escaped from that disaster. The man himself, even when he learned to speak intelligibly, could tell us very little. He remembered he had felt better (after the ship had anchored, I suppose), and that the darkness, the wind, and the rain took his breath away. This looks as if he had been on deck some time during that night. But we mustn't forget he had been taken out of his knowledge, that he had been sea-sick and battened down below for four days, that he had no general notion of a ship or of the sea, and therefore could have no definite idea of what was happening to him. The rain, the wind, the darkness he knew; he understood the bleating of the sheep, and he remembered the pain of his wretchedness and misery, his heartbroken astonishment that it was neither seen nor understood, his dismay at finding all the men angry and all the women fierce. He had approached them as a beggar, it is true, he said; but in his country, even if they gave nothing, they spoke gently to beggars. The children in his country were not taught to throw stones at those who asked for compassion. Smith's strategy overcame him completely. The wood-lodge presented the horrible aspect of a dungeon. What would be done to him next? ... No wonder that Amy Foster appeared to his eyes with the aureole of an angel of light. The girl had not been able to sleep for thinking of the poor man, and in the morning, before the Smiths were up, she slipped out across the back yard. Holding the door of the wood-lodge ajar, she looked in and extended to him half a loaf of white bread – "such bread as the rich eat in my country", he used to say.

'At this he got up slowly from amongst all sorts of rubbish, stiff, hungry, trembling, miserable, and doubtful. "Can you eat this?" she asked in her soft and timid voice. He must have taken her for a "gracious lady". He devoured ferociously, and tears were falling on the crust. Suddenly he dropped the bread, seized her wrist, and imprinted a kiss on her hand. She was not frightened. Through his forlorn condition she had observed that he was good-looking. She shut the door and walked back slowly to the kitchen. Much later on, she told Mrs. Smith, who shuddered at the bare idea of being touched by that creature.

'Through this act of impulsive pity he was brought back again within the pale of human relations with his new surroundings. He never forgot it – never.

'That very same morning old Mr. Swaffer[27] (Smith's nearest neighbour) came over to give his advice, and ended by carrying him off. He stood, unsteady on his legs, meek, and caked over in half-dried mud, while the two men talked around him in an incomprehensible tongue. Mrs. Smith had refused to come downstairs till the madman was off the premises; Amy Foster, far from within the dark kitchen, watched through the open back door; and he obeyed the signs that were made to him to the best of his ability. But Smith was full of mistrust. "Mind, sir! It may be all his cunning," he cried repeatedly in a tone of warning. When Mr. Swaffer started the mare, the deplorable being sitting humbly by his side, through weakness, nearly fell out over the back of the high two-wheeled cart. Swaffer took him straight home. And it is then that I come upon the scene.

'I was called in by the simple process of the old man beckoning to me with his forefinger over the gate of his house as I happened to be driving past. I got down, of course.

'"I've got something here," he mumbled, leading the way to an outhouse at a little distance from his other farm-buildings.

'It was there that I saw him first, in a long low room taken upon the space of that sort of coach-house. It was bare and whitewashed, with a small square aperture glazed with one cracked, dusty pane at its further end. He was lying on his back upon a straw pallet; they had given him a couple of horse-blankets, and he seemed to have spent the remainder of his strength in the exertion of cleaning himself. He was almost speechless; his quick breathing under the blankets pulled up to his chin, his glittering, restless black eyes reminded me of a wild bird caught in a snare. While I was examining him, old Swaffer stood silently by the door, passing the tips of his fingers along his shaven upper lip. I gave some directions, promised to send a bottle of medicine, and naturally made some inquiries.

'"Smith caught him in the stackyard at New Barns," said the old chap in his deliberate, unmoved manner, and as if the other had been indeed a sort of wild animal. "That's how I came by him. Quite a curiosity, isn't he? Now tell me, doctor – you've been all over the world – don't you think that's a bit of a Hindoo we've got hold of here."

'I was greatly surprised. His long black hair scattered over the straw bolster contrasted with the olive pallor of his face. It occurred to me he might be a Basque. It didn't necessarily follow that he should understand Spanish; but I tried him with the few words I know, and also with some French. The whispered sounds I caught by bending my ear to his lips puzzled me utterly. That afternoon the young ladies from the Rectory (one of them read Goethe with a dictionary, and the other had struggled with Dante for years), coming to see Miss Swaffer, tried their German and Italian on him from the doorway. They retreated, just the least bit scared by the flood of passionate speech which, turning on his pallet, he let out at them. They admitted that the sound was pleasant, soft, musical – but, in conjunction with his looks perhaps, it was startling – so excitable, so utterly unlike anything one had ever heard. The village boys climbed up the bank to have a peep through the little square aperture. Everybody was wondering what Mr. Swaffer would do with him.

'He simply kept him.

'Swaffer would be called eccentric were he not so much respected. They will tell you that Mr. Swaffer sits up as late as ten o'clock at night to read books, and they will tell you also that he can write a cheque for two hundred pounds without thinking twice about it. He himself would tell you that the Swaffers had owned land between this and Darnford for these three hundred years. He must be eighty-five to-day, but he does not look a bit older than when I first came here. He is a great breeder of sheep, and deals extensively in cattle. He attends market days for miles around in every sort of weather, and drives sitting bowed low over the reins, his lank grey hair curling over the collar of his warm coat, and with a green plaid rug round his legs. The calmness of advanced age gives a solemnity to his manner. He is clean-shaved; his lips are thin and sensitive; something rigid and monarchal in the set of his features lends a certain elevation to the character of his face. He has been known to drive miles in the rain to see a new kind of rose in somebody's garden, or a monstrous cabbage grown by a cottager. He loves to hear tell of or to be shown something what he calls "outlandish". Perhaps it was just that outlandishness of the man which influenced old Swaffer. Perhaps it was only an inexplicable caprice. All I know is that at the end of three weeks I caught sight of Smith's lunatic digging in Swaffer's kitchen garden. They had found out he could use a spade. He dug barefooted.

'His black hair flowed over his shoulders. I suppose it was Swaffer who had given him the striped old cotton shirt; but he wore still the national brown cloth trousers (in which he had been washed ashore) fitting to the leg almost like tights; was belted with a broad leathern belt studded with little brass discs; and had never yet ventured into the village. The land he looked upon seemed to him kept neatly, like the grounds round a landowner's house; the size of the cart-horses struck him with astonishment; the roads resembled garden walks, and the aspect of the people, especially on Sundays, spoke of opulence. He wondered what made them so hard-hearted and their children so bold. He got his food at the back door, carried it in both hands, carefully, to his outhouse, and, sitting alone on his pallet, would make the sign of the cross before he began. Beside the same pallet, kneeling in the early darkness of the short days, he recited aloud the Lord's Prayer before he slept. Whenever he saw old Swaffer he would bow with veneration from the waist, and stand erect while the old man, with his fingers over his upper lip, surveyed him silently. He bowed also to Miss Swaffer, who kept house frugally for her father – a broad-shouldered, big-boned woman of forty-five, with the pocket of her dress full of keys, and a grey, steady eye. She was Church – as people said (while her father was one of the trustees of the Baptist²⁸ Chapel) – and wore a little steel cross at her waist. She dressed severely in black, in memory of one of the innumerable Bradleys of the neighbourhood, to whom she had been engaged some twenty-five years ago – a young farmer who broke his neck out hunting on the eve of the wedding-day. She had the unmoved countenance of the deaf, spoke very seldom, and her lips, thin like her father's, astonished one some-times by a mysteriously ironic curl.

'These were the people to whom he owed allegiance, and an overwhelming loneliness seemed to fall from the leaden sky of that winter without sunshine. All the faces were sad. He could talk to no one, and had no hope of ever understanding anybody. It was as if these had been the faces of people from the other world – dead people – he used to tell me years afterwards. Upon my word, I wonder he did not go mad. He didn't know where he was. Somewhere very far from his mountains – somewhere over the water. Was this America, he wondered?

'If it hadn't been for the steel cross at Miss Swaffer's belt he would not, he confessed, have known whether he was in a Christian country at all. He used to cast stealthy glances at it, and feel comforted. There was nothing here the same as in his country! The earth and the water were different; there were no images of the Redeemer by the roadside. The very grass was different, and the trees. All the trees but the three old Norway pines on the bit of lawn before Swaffer's house, and these reminded him of his country. He had been detected once, after dusk, with his forehead against the trunk of one of them, sobbing, and talking to himself. They had been like brothers to him at that time, he affirmed. Everything else was strange. Conceive you the kind of an existence overshadowed, oppressed, by the everyday material appearances, as if by the visions of a nightmare. At night, when he could not sleep, he kept on thinking of the girl who gave him the first piece of bread he had eaten in this foreign land. She had been neither fierce nor angry, nor frightened. Her face he remembered as the only comprehensible face amongst all these faces that were as closed, as mysterious, and as mute as the faces of the dead who are possessed of a knowledge beyond the comprehension of the living. I wonder whether the memory of her compassion prevented him from cutting his throat. But there! I suppose I am an old sentimentalist, and forget the instinctive love of life which it takes all the strength of an uncommon despair to overcome.

'He did the work which was given him with an intelligence which surprised old Swaffer. By-and-by it was discovered that he could help at the ploughing, could milk the cows, feed the bullocks in the cattle-yard, and was of some use with the sheep. He began to pick up words, too, very fast; and suddenly, one fine morning in spring, he rescued from an untimely death a grandchild of old Swaffer.

'Swaffer's younger daughter is married to Willcox, a solicitor and the Town Clerk of Colebrook. Regularly twice a year they come to stay with the old man for a few days. Their only child, a little girl not three years old at the time, ran out of the house alone in her little white pinafore, and, toddling across the grass of a terraced garden, pitched herself over a low wall head first into the horse-pond in the yard below.

'Our man was out with the waggoner and the plough in the field nearest to the house, and as he was leading the team round to begin a fresh furrow, he saw, through the gap of a gate, what for anybody else would have been a mere flutter of something white. But he had straight-glancing, quick, far-reaching eyes, that only seemed to flinch and lose their amazing power before the immensity of the sea. He was barefooted, and looking as outlandish as the heart of Swaffer could desire. Leaving the horses on the turn, to the inexpressible disgust of the waggoner he bounded off, going over the ploughed ground in long leaps, and suddenly appeared before the mother, thrust the child into her arms, and strode away.

'The pond was not very deep; but still, if he had not had such good eyes, the child would have perished – miserably suffocated in the foot or so of sticky mud at the bottom. Old Swaffer walked out slowly into the field, waited till the plough came over to his side, had a good look at him, and without saying a word went back to the house. But from that time they laid out his meals on the kitchen table; and at first, Miss Swaffer, all in black and with an inscrutable face, would come and stand in the doorway of the living-room to see him make a big sign of the cross before he fell to. I believe that from that day, too, Swaffer began to pay him regular wages.

'I can't follow step by step his development. He cut his hair short, was seen in the village and along the road going to and fro to his work like any other man. Children ceased to shout after him. He became aware of social differences, but remained for a long time surprised at the bare poverty of the churches among so much wealth. He couldn't understand either why they were kept shut up on week-days. There was nothing to steal in them. Was it to keep people from praying too often? The rectory took much notice of him about that time, and I believe the young ladies attempted to prepare the ground for his conversion. They could not, however, break him of his habit of crossing himself, but he went so far as to take off the string with a couple of brass medals the size of a sixpence, a tiny metal cross, and a square sort of scapulary which he wore round his neck. He hung them on the wall by the side of his bed, and he was still to be heard every evening reciting the Lord's Prayer, in incomprehensible words and in a slow, fervent tone, as he had heard his old father do at the head of all the kneeling family, big and little, on every evening of his life. And though he wore corduroys at work, and a slop-made pepper-and-salt suit on Sundays, strangers would turn round to look after him on the road. His foreignness had a peculiar and indelible stamp. At last people became used to seeing him. But they never became used to him. His rapid, skimming walk; his swarthy complexion; his hat cocked on the left ear; his habit, on warm evenings, of wearing his coat over one shoulder, like a hussar's dolman; his manner of leaping over the stiles, not as a feat of agility, but in the ordinary course of progression – all these peculiarities were, as one may say, so many causes of scorn and offence to the inhabitants of the village. *They* wouldn't in their dinner hour lie flat on their backs on the grass to stare at the sky. Neither did they go about the fields screaming dismal tunes. Many times have I heard his high-pitched voice from behind the ridge of some sloping sheep-walk, a voice light and soaring, like a lark's, but with a melancholy human note, over our fields that hear only the song of birds.[29] And I would be startled myself. Ah! He was different: innocent of heart, and full of good will, which nobody wanted, this castaway, that, like a man transplanted into another planet, was separated by an immense space from his past and by an immense ignorance from his future. His quick, fervent utterance positively shocked everybody. "An excitable devil" they called him. One evening, in the tap-room of the Coach and Horses, (having drunk some whisky), he upset them all by singing a love-song of his country. They hooted him down, and he was pained; but Preble, the lame wheelwright, and Vincent, the fat blacksmith, and the other notables too, wanted to drink their evening beer in peace. On another occasion he tried to show them how to dance. The dust rose in clouds from the sanded floor; he leaped straight up amongst the deal tables, struck his heels together, squatted on one heel in front of old Preble, shooting out the other leg, uttered wild and exulting cries, jumped up to whirl on one foot, snapping his fingers above his head – and a strange carter who was having a drink in there began to swear, and cleared out with his half-pint in his hand into the bar. But when suddenly he sprang upon a table and continued to dance among the glasses, the landlord interfered. He didn't want any "acrobat tricks in the tap-room". They laid their hands on him. Having had a glass or two, Mr. Swaffer's foreigner tried to expostulate; was ejected forcibly; got a black eye.

'I believe he felt the hostility of his human surroundings. But he was tough – tough in spirit, too, as well as in body. Only the memory of the sea frightened him, with that vague terror that is left by a bad dream. His home was far away; and he did not want now to go to America. I had often explained to him that there is no place on earth where true gold can be found lying ready and to be got for the trouble of the picking up. How then, he asked, could he ever return home with empty hands when there had been sold a cow, two ponies, and a bit of land to pay for his going? His eyes would fill with tears, and, averting them from the immense shimmer of the sea, he would throw himself face down on the grass. But sometimes, cocking his hat with a little conquering air, he would defy my wisdom. He had found his bit of true gold. That was Amy Foster's heart, which was "a golden heart, and soft to people's misery", he would say in the accents of overwhelming conviction.

'He was called Yanko. He had explained that this meant Little John; but as he would also repeat very often that he was a mountaineer (some word sounding in the dialect of his country like Goorall) he got it for his surname. And this is the only trace of him that the succeeding ages may find in the marriage register of the parish. There it stands – Yanko Goorall[30] – in the rector's handwriting. The crooked cross made by the castaway, a cross whose tracing no doubt seemed to him the most solemn part of the whole ceremony, is all that remains now to perpetuate the memory of his name.

'His courtship had lasted some time – ever since he got his precarious footing in the community. It began by his buying for Amy Foster a green satin ribbon in Darnford. This was what you did in his country. You bought a ribbon at a Jew's stall on a fair-day. I don't suppose the girl knew what to do with it, but he seemed to think that his honourable intentions could not be mistaken.

'It was only when he declared his purpose to get married that I fully understood how, for a hundred futile and inappreciable reasons, how – shall I say odious? – he was to all the countryside. Every old woman in the village was up in arms. Smith, coming upon him near the farm, promised to break his head for him if he found him about again. But he twisted his little black moustache with such a bellicose air and rolled such big, black fierce eyes at

Smith that this promise came to nothing. Smith, however, told the girl that she must be mad to take up with a man who was surely wrong in his head. All the same, when she heard him in the gloaming whistle from beyond the orchard a couple of bars of a weird and mournful tune, she would drop whatever she had in her hand – she would leave Mrs. Smith in the middle of a sentence – and she would run out to his call. Mrs. Smith called her a shameless hussy. She answered nothing. She said nothing at all to anybody, and went on her way as if she had been deaf. She and I alone in all the land, I fancy, could see his very real beauty. He was very good-looking, and most graceful in his bearing, with that something wild as of a woodland creature in his aspect. Her mother moaned over her dismally whenever the girl came to see her on her day out. The father was surly, but pretended not to know; and Mrs. Finn once told her plainly that "this man, my dear, will do you some harm some day yet." And so it went on. They could be seen on the roads, she tramping stolidly in her finery – grey dress, black feather, stout boots, prominent white cotton gloves that caught your eye a hundred yards away; and he, his coat slung pic-turesquely over one shoulder, pacing by her side, gallant of bearing and casting tender glances upon the girl with the golden heart. I wonder whether he saw how plain she was. Perhaps among types so different from what he had ever seen, he had not the power to judge; or perhaps he was seduced by the divine quality of her pity.

'Yanko was in great trouble meantime. In his country you get an old man for an ambassador in marriage affairs. He did not know how to proceed. However, one day in the midst of sheep in a field (he was now Swaffer's under-shepherd with Foster) he took off his hat to the father and declared himself humbly. "I daresay she's fool enough to marry you," was all Foster said. "And then", he used to relate, "he puts his hat on his head, looks black at me as if he wanted to cut my throat, whistles the dog, and off he goes, leaving me to do the work." The Fosters, of course, didn't like to lose the wages the girl earned: Amy used to give all her money to her mother. But there was in Foster a very genuine aversion to that match. He contended that the fellow was very good with sheep, but was not fit for any girl to marry. For one thing, he used to go along the hedges muttering to himself like a dam' fool; and then, these foreigners behave very queerly to women sometimes.

And perhaps he would want to carry her off somewhere – or run off himself. It was not safe. He preached it to his daughter that the fellow might ill-use her in some way. She made no answer. It was, they said in the village, as if the man had done something to her. People discussed the matter. It was quite an excitement, and the two went on "walking out" together in the face of opposition. Then something unexpected happened.

'I don't know whether old Swaffer ever understood how much he was regarded in the light of a father by his foreign retainer. Anyway the relation was curiously feudal. So when Yanko asked formally for an interview – "and the Miss too" (he called the severe, deaf Miss Swaffer simply *Miss*) – it was to obtain their permission to marry. Swaffer heard him unmoved, dismissed him by a nod, and then shouted the intelligence into Miss Swaffer's best ear. She showed no surprise, and only remarked grimly, in a veiled blank voice, "He certainly won't get any other girl to marry him."

'It is Miss Swaffer who has all the credit of the munificence: but in a very few days it came out that Mr. Swaffer had presented Yanko with a cottage (the cottage you've seen this morning) and something like an acre of ground – had made it over to him in absolute property. Willcox expedited the deed, and I remember him telling me he had a great pleasure in making it ready. It recited: "In consideration of saving the life of my beloved grandchild, Bertha Willcox."

'Of course, after that no power on earth could prevent them from getting married.

'Her infatuation endured. People saw her going out to meet him in the evening. She stared with unblinking, fascinated eyes up the road where he was expected to appear, walking freely, with a swing from the hip, and humming one of the love-tunes of his country. When the boy was born, he got elevated at the Coach and Horses, essayed again a song and a dance, and was again ejected. People expressed their commiseration for a woman married to that Jack-in-the-box. He didn't care. There was a man now (he told me boastfully) to whom he could sing and talk in the language of his country, and show how to dance by-and-by.

'But I don't know. To me he appeared to have grown less springy of step, heavier in body, less keen of eye. Imagination, no doubt; but it seems to me now as if the net of fate had been drawn closer round him already.

'One day I met him on the footpath over the Talfourd Hill. He told me that "women were funny". I had heard already of some domestic differences. People were saying that Amy Foster was beginning to find out what sort of man she had married. He looked upon the sea with indifferent, unseeing eyes. His wife had snatched the child out of his arms one day as he sat on the doorstep crooning to it a song such as the mothers sing to babies in his mountains. She seemed to think he was doing it some harm. Women are funny. And she had objected to him praying aloud in the evening. Why? He expected the boy to repeat the prayer aloud after him by-and-by, as he used to do after his old father when he was a child – in his own country. And I discovered he longed for their boy to grow up so that he could have a man to talk with in that language that to our ears sounded so disturbing, so passionate, and so bizarre. Why his wife should dislike the idea he couldn't tell. But that would pass, he said. And tilting his head knowingly, he tapped his breastbone to indicate that she had a good heart: not hard, not fierce, open to compassion, charitable to the poor!

'I walked away thoughtfully; I wondered whether his difference, his strangeness, were not penetrating with repulsion that dull nature they had begun by irresistibly attracting. I wondered. . . .'

The Doctor came to the window and looked out at the frigid splendour of the sea, immense in the haze, as if enclosing all the earth with all the hearts lost among the passions of love and fear.

'Physiologically, now,' he said, turning away abruptly, 'it was possible. It was possible.'

He remained silent. Then went on –

'At all events, the next time I saw him he was ill – lung trouble. He was tough, but I daresay he was not acclimatised as well as I had supposed. It was a bad winter; and, of course, these mountaineers do get fits of homesickness; and a state of depression would make him vulnerable. He was lying half-dressed on a couch downstairs.

'A table covered with a dark oilcloth took up all the middle of the little room. There was a wicker cradle on the floor, a kettle spouting steam on the hob, and some child's linen lay drying on the fender. The room was warm, but the door opens right into the garden, as you noticed perhaps.

'He was very feverish, and kept on muttering to himself. She sat on a chair and looked at him fixedly across the table with her brown, blurred eyes. "Why don't you have him upstairs?" I asked. With a start and a confused stammer she said, "Oh! ah! I couldn't sit with him upstairs, sir."

'I gave her certain directions; and going outside, I said again that he ought to be in bed upstairs. She wrung her hands. "I couldn't. I couldn't. He keeps on saying something – I don't know what." With the memory of all the talk against the man that had been dinned into her ears, I looked at her narrowly. I looked into her short-sighted eyes, at her dumb eyes that once in her life had seen an enticing shape, but seemed, staring at me, to see nothing at all now. But I saw she was uneasy.

'"What's the matter with him?" she asked in a sort of vacant trepidation. "He doesn't look very ill. I never did see anybody look like this before. . . ."

'"Do you think," I asked indignantly, "he is shamming?"

'"I can't help it, sir," she said stolidly. And suddenly she clapped her hands and looked right and left. "And there's the baby. I am so frightened. He wanted me just now to give him the baby. I can't understand what he says to it."

'"Can't you ask a neighbour to come in to-night?" I asked.

'"Please, sir, nobody seems to care to come," she muttered, dully resigned all at once.

'I impressed upon her the necessity of the greatest care, and then had to go. There was a good deal of sickness that winter. "Oh, I hope he won't talk!" she exclaimed softly just as I was going away.

'I don't know how it is I did not see – but I didn't. And yet, turning in my trap, I saw her lingering before the door, very still, and as if meditating a flight up the miry road.

'Towards the night his fever increased.

'He tossed, moaned, and now and then muttered a complaint. And she sat with the table between her and the couch, watching every movement and every sound, with the terror, the unreasonable terror, of that man she could not understand creeping over her. She had drawn the wicker cradle close to her feet. There was nothing in her now but the maternal instinct and that unaccountable fear.

'Suddenly coming to himself, parched, he demanded a drink of water. She did not move. She had not understood, though he may have thought he was speaking in English. He waited, looking at her, burning with fever, amazed at her silence and immobility, and then he shouted impatiently, "Water! Give me water!"

'She jumped to her feet, snatched up the child, and stood still. He spoke to her, and his passionate remonstrances only increased her fear of that strange man. I believe he spoke to her for a long time, entreating, wondering, pleading, ordering, I suppose. She says she bore it as long as she could. And then a gust of rage came over him.

'He sat up and called out terribly one word – some word.[31] Then he got up as though he hadn't been ill at all, she says. And as in fevered dismay, indignation, and wonder he tried to get to her round the table, she simply opened the door and ran out with the child in her arms. She heard him call twice after her down the road in a terrible voice – and fled. . . . Ah! but you should have seen stirring behind the dull, blurred glance of those eyes the spectre of the fear which had hunted her on that night three miles and a half to the door of Foster's cottage! I did the next day.

'And it was I who found him lying face down and his body in a puddle, just outside the little wicket-gate.

'I had been called out that night to an urgent case in the village, and on my way home at daybreak passed by the cottage. The door stood open. My man helped me to carry him in. We laid him on the couch. The lamp smoked, the fire was out, the chill of the stormy night oozed from the cheerless yellow paper on the wall. "Amy!" I called aloud, and my voice seemed to lose itself in the emptiness of this tiny house as if I had cried in a desert. He opened his eyes. "Gone!" he said distinctly. "I had only asked for water – only for a little water. . . ."

'He was muddy. I covered him up and stood waiting in silence, catching a painfully gasped word now and then. They were no longer in his own language. The fever had left him, taking with it the heat of life. And with his panting breast and lustrous eyes he reminded me again of a wild creature under the net; of a bird caught in a snare. She had left him. She had left him – sick – helpless – thirsty. The spear of the hunter had entered his very soul. "Why?" he cried in the penetrating and indignant voice of a man calling to a responsible Maker. A gust of wind and a swish of rain answered.

'And as I turned away to shut the door he pronounced the word "Merciful!" and expired.

'Eventually I certified heart-failure as the immediate cause of death. His heart must have indeed failed him, or else he might have stood this night of storm and exposure, too. I closed his eyes and drove away. Not very far from the cottage I met Foster walking sturdily between the dripping hedges with his collie at his heels.

'"Do you know where your daughter is?" I asked.

'"Don't I!" he cried. "I am going to talk to him a bit. Frightening a poor woman like this."

'"He won't frighten her any more," I said. "He is dead."

'He struck with his stick at the mud.

'"And there's the child."

'Then, after thinking deeply for a while –

'"I don't know that it isn't for the best."

'That's what he said. And she says nothing at all now. Not a word of him. Never. Is his image as utterly gone from her mind as his lithe and striding figure, his carolling voice are gone from our fields? He is no longer before her eyes to excite her imagination into a passion of love or fear; and his memory seems to have vanished from her dull brain as a shadow passes away upon a white screen. She lives in the cottage and works for Miss Swaffer. She is Amy Foster for everybody, and the child is "Amy Foster's boy". She calls him Johnny – which means Little John.

'It is impossible to say whether this name recalls anything to her. Does she ever think of the past? I have seen her hanging over the boy's cot in a very passion of maternal tenderness. The little fellow was lying on his back, a little frightened at me, but very still, with his big black eyes, with his fluttered air of a bird in a snare. And looking at him I seemed to see again the other one – the father, cast out mysteriously by the sea to perish in the supreme disaster of loneliness and despair.'

FALK
A REMINISCENCE

FALK

A REMINISCENCE

SEVERAL of us,[32] all more or less connected with the sea, were dining in a small river-hostelry not more than thirty miles from London, and less than twenty from that shallow and dangerous puddle to which our coasting men give the grandiose name of 'German Ocean'. And through the wide windows we had a view of the Thames; an enfilading view down the Lower Hope Reach. But the dinner was execrable, and all the feast was for the eyes.

That flavour of salt water which for so many of us had been the very water of life permeated our talk. He who hath known the bitterness of the Ocean shall have its taste for ever in his mouth. But one or two of us, pampered by the life of the land, complained of hunger. It was impossible to swallow any of that stuff. And indeed there was a strange mustiness in everything. The wooden dining-room stuck out over the mud of the shore like a lacustrine dwelling; the planks of the floor seemed rotten; a decrepit old waiter tottered pathetically to and fro before an antediluvian and worm-eaten sideboard; the chipped plates might have been disinterred from some kitchen midden near an inhabited lake; and the chops recalled times more ancient still. They brought forcibly to one's mind the night of ages when the primeval man, evolving the first rudiments of cookery from his dim consciousness, scorched lumps of flesh at a fire of sticks in the company of other good fellows; then, gorged and happy, sat him back among the gnawed bones to tell his artless tales of experience – the tales of hunger and hunt – and of women, perhaps!

But luckily the wine happened to be as old as the waiter. So, comparatively empty, but upon the whole fairly happy, we sat back and told our artless tales. We talked of the sea and all its works. The sea never changes; and its works, for all the talk of men, are wrapped in mystery. But we agreed that the times were changed. And we talked of old ships, of sea-accidents, of break-

165

downs, dismastings; and of a man who brought his ship safe to Liverpool all the way from the River Plate under a jury rudder. We talked of wrecks, of short rations and of heroism – or at least of what the newspapers would have called heroism at sea – a manifestation of virtues quite different from the heroism of primitive times. And now and then falling silent all together we gazed at the sights of the river.

A P. & O. boat passed bound down. 'One gets jolly good dinners on board these ships,' remarked one of our band. A man with sharp eyes read out the name on her bows: *Arcadia*. 'What a beautiful model of a ship!' murmured some of us. She was followed by a small cargo-steamer, and the flag they hauled down aboard while we were looking showed her to be a Norwegian. She made an awful lot of smoke; and before it had quite blown away, a high-sided, short wooden barque, in ballast and towed by a paddle-tug, appeared in front of the windows. All her hands forward were busy setting up the headgear; and aft a woman in a red hood, quite alone with the man at the wheel, paced the length of the poop back and forth, with the grey wool of some knitting work in her hands.

'German, I should think,' muttered one. 'The skipper has his wife on board,' remarked another; and the light of the crimson sunset all ablaze behind the London smoke, throwing a glow of Bengal light upon the barque's spars, faded away from the Hope Reach.

Then one of us, who had not spoken before, a man of over fifty that had commanded ships for a quarter of a century, looking after the barque now gliding far away, all black on the lustre of the river, said:

This reminds me of an absurd episode in my life, now many years ago, when I got first the command of an iron barque, loading then in a certain Eastern seaport.[33] It was also the capital of an Eastern kingdom, lying up a river as might be London lies up this old Thames of ours. No more need be said of the place; for this sort of thing might have happened anywhere where there are ships, skippers, tugboats, and orphan nieces of indescribable splendour. And the absurdity of the episode concerns only me, my enemy Falk, and my friend Hermann.[34]

There seemed to be something like peculiar emphasis on the

words 'My friend Hermann', which caused one of us (for we had just been speaking of heroism at sea) to say idly and nonchalantly:

'And was this Hermann a hero?'

Not at all, said our grizzled friend. No hero at all. He was a *Schiff-führer*: Ship-conductor. That's how they call a Master Mariner in Germany. I prefer our way. The alliteration is good, and there is something in the nomenclature that gives to us as a body the sense of corporate existence: Apprentice, Mate, Master, in the ancient and honourable craft of the sea. As to my friend Hermann, he might have been a consummate master of the honourable craft, but he was called officially *Schiff-führer*, and had the simple, heavy appearance of a well-to-do farmer, combined with the good-natured shrewdness of a small shopkeeper. With his shaven chin, round limbs, and heavy eyelids he did not look like a toiler, and even less like an adventurer of the sea. Still, he toiled upon the seas, in his own way, much as a shopkeeper works behind his counter. And his ship was the means by which he maintained his growing family.

She was a heavy, strong, blunt-bowed affair, awakening the ideas of primitive solidity, like the wooden plough of our forefathers. And there were, about her, other suggestions of a rustic and homely nature. The extraordinary timber projections which I have seen in no other vessel made her square stern resemble the tail end of a miller's waggon. But the four stern ports of her cabin, glazed with six little greenish panes each, and framed in wooden sashes painted brown, might have been the windows of a cottage in the country. The tiny white curtains and the greenery of flower-pots behind the glass completed the resemblance. On one or two occasions when passing under her stern I had detected from my boat a round arm in the act of tilting a watering-pot, and the bowed sleek head of a maiden whom I shall always call Hermann's niece,[35] because as a matter of fact I've never heard her name, for all my intimacy with the family.

This, however, sprang up later on. Meantime in common with the rest of the shipping in that Eastern port, I was left in no doubt as to Hermann's notions of hygienic clothing. Evidently he believed in wearing good stout flannel next his skin. On most days little frocks and pinafores could be seen drying in the mizzen rigging of his ship, or a tiny row of socks fluttering on the signal halyards;

but once a fortnight the family washing was exhibited in force. It covered the poop entirely. The afternoon breeze would incite to a weird and flabby activity all that crowded mass of clothing, with its vague suggestions of drowned, mutilated and flattened humanity. Trunks without heads waved at you arms without hands; legs without feet kicked fantastically with collapsible flourishes; and there were long white garments that, taking the wind fairly through their neck openings edged with lace, became for a moment violently distended as by the passage of obese and invisible bodies. On these days you could make out that ship at a great distance by the multi-coloured grotesque riot going on abaft her mizzen-mast.

She had her berth just ahead of me, and her name was *Diana*, – Diana not of Ephesus[36] but of Bremen. This was proclaimed in white letters a foot long spaced widely across the stern (somewhat like the lettering of a shop-sign) under the cottage windows. This ridiculously unsuitable name struck one as an impertinence towards the memory of the most charming of goddesses; for, apart from the fact that the old craft was physically incapable of engaging in any sort of chase, there was a gang of four children belonging to her. They peeped over the rail at passing boats and occasionally dropped various objects into them. Thus, sometime before I knew Hermann to speak to, I received on my hat a horrid rag-doll belonging to Hermann's eldest daughter. However, these youngsters were upon the whole well-behaved. They had fair heads, round eyes, round little knobby noses, and they resembled their father a good deal.

This *Diana* of Bremen was a most innocent old ship, and seemed to know nothing of the wicked sea, as there are on shore households that know nothing of the corrupt world. And the sentiments she suggested were unexceptionable and mainly of a domestic order. She was a home. All these dear children had learned to walk on her roomy quarter-deck. In such thoughts there is something pretty, even touching. Their teeth, I should judge, they had cut on the ends of her running gear. I have many times observed the baby Hermann (Nicholas) engaged in gnawing the whipping of the fore-royal brace. Nicholas' favourite place of residence was under the main fife-rail. Directly he was let loose he would crawl off there, and the first seaman who came along would bring him, carefully held aloft in tarry hands, back to the cabin door. I fancy there must have been a standing order to that effect. In the course of these transportations the baby, who was the only peppery person in the ship, tried to smite these stalwart young German sailors on the face.

Mrs. Hermann, an engaging, stout housewife, wore on board baggy blue dresses with white dots. When, as happened once or twice, I caught her at an elegant little wash-tub rubbing hard on white collars, baby's socks, and Hermann's summer neck-ties, she would blush in girlish confusion, and raising her wet hands greet me from afar with many friendly nods. Her sleeves would be rolled up to the elbows, and the gold hoop of her wedding ring glittered among the soap-suds. Her voice was pleasant, she had a serene brow, smooth bands of very fair hair, and a good-humoured expression of the eyes. She was motherly and moderately talkative. When this simple matron smiled, youthful dimples broke out on her fresh broad cheeks. Hermann's niece, on the other hand, an orphan and very silent, I never saw attempt a smile. This, however, was not gloom on her part but the restraint of youthful gravity.

They had carried her about with them for the last three years, to help with the children and be company for Mrs. Hermann, as Hermann mentioned once to me. It had been very necessary while they were all little, he had added in a vexed manner. It was her arm and her sleek head that I had glimpsed one morning, through the stern-windows of the cabin, hovering over the pots of fuchsias and mignonette; but the first time I beheld her full length I surrendered to her proportions. They fix her in my mind, as great beauty, great intelligence, quickness of wit or kindness of heart might have made some other woman equally memorable.

With her it was form and size. It was her physical personality that had this imposing charm. She might have been witty, intelligent, and kind to an exceptional degree. I don't know, and this is not to the point. All I know is that she was built on a magnificent scale. Built is the only word. She was constructed, she was erected, as it were, with a regal lavishness. It staggered you to see this reckless expenditure of material upon a chit of a girl. She was youthful and also perfectly mature, as though she had been some fortunate immortal. She was heavy too, perhaps, but that's nothing. It only added to that notion of permanence. She was barely nineteen. But such shoulders! Such round arms! Such a shadowing forth of mighty limbs when with three long strides she pounced across the deck upon the overturned Nicholas – it's perfectly indescribable! She seemed a good, quiet girl, vigilant as to Lena's needs, Gustav's tumbles, the state of Carl's dear little nose – conscientious, hardworking, and all that. But what magnificent hair she had! Abundant, long, thick, of a tawny colour. It had the sheen of precious metals. She wore it plaited tightly into one single tress hanging girlishly down her back; and its end reached down to her waist. The massiveness of it surprised you. On my word it reminded one of a club. Her face was big, comely, of an unruffled expression. She had a good complexion, and her blue eyes were so pale that she appeared to look at the world with the empty white candour of a statue. You could not call her good-looking. It was something much more impressive. The simplicity of her apparel, the opulence of her form, her imposing stature, and the extraordinary sense of vigorous life that seemed to emanate from her like a perfume exhaled by a flower, made her beautiful with a beauty of a rustic and olympian order. To watch her reaching up to the clothes-line with both arms raised high above her head caused you to fall a-musing in a strain of pagan piety. Excellent Mrs. Hermann's baggy cotton gowns had some sort of rudimentary frills at neck and bottom, but this girl's print frocks hadn't even a wrinkle; nothing but a few straight folds in the skirt falling to her feet, and these, when she stood still, had a severe and statuesque quality. She was inclined naturally to be still whether sitting or standing. However, I don't mean to say she was statuesque. She was too generously alive; but she could have stood for an allegoric statue of the Earth. I don't mean the worn-out earth of our possession, but a young Earth, a virginal planet undisturbed by the vision of a future teeming with the monstrous forms of life and death, clamorous with the cruel battles of hunger and thought.

The worthy Hermann himself was not very entertaining, though his English was fairly comprehensible. Mrs. Hermann, who always let off one speech at least at me in an hospitable, cordial tone (and in Platt-Deutsch I suppose) I could not understand. As to their niece, however satisfactory to look upon (and she inspired you somehow with a hopeful view as to the prospects of mankind) she was a modest and silent presence, mostly engaged in sewing, only now and then, as I observed, falling over that work into a state of maidenly meditation. Her aunt sat opposite her, sewing also, with her feet propped on a wooden footstool. On the other side of the deck Hermann and I would get a couple of chairs out of the cabin and settle down to a smoking match, accompanied at long intervals by the pacific exchange of a few words. I came nearly every evening. Hermann I would find in his shirt-sleeves. As soon as he returned from the shore on board his ship he commenced operations by taking off his coat; then he put on his head an embroidered round cap with a tassel, and changed his boots for a pair of cloth slippers. Afterwards he smoked at the cabin door, looking at his children with an air of civic virtue, till they got caught one after another and put to bed in various staterooms. Lastly, we would drink some beer in the cabin, which was furnished with a wooden table on cross legs, and with black straight-backed chairs – more like a farm kitchen than a ship's cuddy. The sea and all nautical affairs seemed very far removed from the hospitality of this exemplary family.

And I liked this because I had a rather worrying time on board my own ship. I had been appointed *ex-officio* by the British Consul to take charge of her after a man who had died suddenly,[37] leaving for the guidance of his successor some suspiciously unreceipted bills, a few dry-dock estimates hinting at bribery, and a quantity of vouchers for three years' extravagant expenditure; all these mixed up together in a dusty old violin-case lined with ruby velvet. I found besides a large account-book, which, when opened hopefully, turned out to my infinite consternation to be filled with verses – page after page of rhymed doggerel of a jovial and improper character, written in the neatest minute hand I ever did see. In the same fiddle-case a photograph of my predecessor, taken lately in Saigon, represented in front of a garden view, and in company of a female in strange draperies, an elderly, squat rugged man of stern aspect in a clumsy suit of black broadcloth, and with the hair brushed forward above the temples in a manner reminding one of a boar's tusks. Of a fiddle, however, the only trace on board was the case, its empty husk as it were; but of the two last freights the ship had indubitably earned of late, there were not even the husks left. It was impossible to say where all that money had gone to. It wasn't on board. It had not been remitted home; for a letter from the owners, preserved in a desk evidently by the merest accident, complained mildly enough that they had not been favoured by a scratch of the pen[38] for the last eighteen months. There were next to no stores on board, not an inch of spare rope or a yard of canvas. The ship had been run bare, and I foresaw no end of difficulties before I could get her ready for sea.

As I was young then – not thirty yet – I took myself and my troubles very seriously. The old mate, who had acted as chief mourner at the captain's funeral, was not particularly pleased at my coming. But the fact is the fellow was not legally qualified for command, and the Consul was bound, if at all possible, to put a properly certificated man on board. As to the second mate, all I can say is his name was Tottersen,[39] or something like that. His practice was to wear on his head, in that tropical climate, a mangy fur cap. He was, without exception, the stupidest man I had ever seen on board ship. And he looked it, too. He looked so confoundedly stupid that it was a matter of surprise for me when he answered to his name.

I drew no great comfort from their company, to say the least of it; while the prospect of making a long sea passage with those two fellows was depressing. And my other thoughts in solitude could not be of a gay complexion. The crew was sickly, the cargo was coming very slow; I foresaw I would have lots of trouble with the charterers, and doubted whether they would advance me enough money for the ship's expenses. Their attitude towards me was unfriendly. Altogether I was not getting on. I would discover at odd times (generally about midnight) that I was totally inexperienced, greatly ignorant of business, and hopelessly unfit for any sort of command; and when the steward had to be taken to the hospital ill with choleraic symptoms I felt bereaved of the only decent person at the after end of the ship. He was fully expected to recover, but in the meantime had to be replaced by some sort of servant. And on the recommendation of a certain Schomberg,[40] the proprietor of the smaller of the two hotels in the place, I engaged a Chinaman. Schomberg, a brawny, hairy Alsatian, and an awful gossip, assured me that it was all right. 'First-class boy that. Came in the suite of his Excellency Tseng the Commissioner – you know. His Excellency Tseng lodged with me here for three weeks.'

He mouthed the Chinese Excellency at me with great unction,

though the specimen of the 'suite' did not seem very promising. At the time, however, I did not know what an untrustworthy humbug Schomberg was. The 'boy' might have been forty or a hundred and forty for all you could tell – one of those Chinamen of the death's-head type of face and completely inscrutable. Before the end of the third day he had revealed himself as a confirmed opium-smoker, a gambler, a most audacious thief,[41] and a first-class sprinter. When he departed at the top of his speed with thirty-two golden sovereigns of my own hard-earned savings it was the last straw. I had reserved that money in case my difficulties came to the worst. Now it was gone I felt as poor and naked as a fakir. I clung to my ship, for all the bother she caused me, but what I could not bear were the long lonely evenings in her cuddy, where the atmosphere, made smelly by a leaky lamp, was agitated by the snoring of the mate. That fellow shut himself up in his stuffy cabin punctually at eight, and made gross and revolting noises like a water-logged trombone. It was odious not to be able to worry oneself in comfort on board one's own ship. Everything in this world, I reflected, even the command of a nice little barque, may be made a delusion and a snare for the unwary spirit of pride in man.

From such reflections I was glad to make my escape on board that Bremen *Diana*. There apparently no whisper of the world's iniquities had ever penetrated. And yet she lived upon the wide sea: and the sea tragic and comic, the sea with its horrors and its peculiar scandals, the sea peopled by men and ruled by iron necessity is indubitably a part of the world. But that patriarchal old tub, like some saintly retreat, echoed nothing of it. She was world-proof. Her venerable innocence apparently had put a restraint on the roaring lusts of the sea. And yet I have known the sea too long to believe in its respect for decency. An elemental force is ruthlessly frank. It may, of course, have been Hermann's skilful seamanship, but to me it looked as if the allied oceans had refrained from smashing these high bulwarks, unshipping the lumpy rudder, frightening the children, and generally opening this family's eyes out of sheer reticence. It looked like reticence. The ruthless disclosure was, in the end, left for a man to make; a man strong and elemental enough and driven to unveil some secrets of the sea by the power of a simple and elemental desire.

This, however, occurred much later, and meantime I took sanctuary in that serene old ship early every evening. The only person on board that seemed to be in trouble was little Lena, and in due course I perceived that the health of the rag-doll was more than delicate. This object led a sort of *in extremis* existence in a wooden box placed against the starboard mooring-bitts, tended and nursed with the greatest sympathy and care by all the children, who greatly enjoyed pulling long faces and moving with hushed footsteps. Only the baby – Nicholas – looked on with a cold, ruffianly leer, as if he had belonged to another tribe altogether. Lena perpetually sorrowed over the box, and all of them were in deadly earnest. It was wonderful the way these children would work up their compassion for that bedraggled thing I wouldn't have touched with a pair of tongs. I suppose they were exercising and developing their racial sentimentalism by the means of that dummy. I was only surprised that Mrs. Hermann let Lena cherish and hug that bundle of rags to that extent, it was so disreputably and completely unclean. But Mrs. Hermann would raise her fine womanly eyes from her needlework to look on with amused sympathy, and did not seem to see it, somehow, that this object of affection was a disgrace to the ship's purity. Purity, not cleanliness, is the word. It was pushed so far that I seemed to detect in this too a sentimental excess, as if dirt had been removed in very love. It is impossible to give you an idea of such a meticulous neatness. It was as if every morning that ship had been arduously explored with – with toothbrushes. Her very bowsprit three times a week had its toilette made with a cake of soap and a piece of soft flannel. Arrayed – I *must* say arrayed – arrayed artlessly in dazzling white paint as to wood and dark green as to ironwork, the simple-minded distribution of these colours evoked the images of simple-minded peace, of arcadian felicity; and the childish comedy of disease and sorrow struck me sometimes as an abominably real blot upon that ideal state.

I enjoyed it greatly, and on my part I brought a little mild excitement into it. Our intimacy arose from the pursuit of that thief. It was in the evening, and Hermann, who, contrary to his habits, had stayed on shore late that day, was extricating himself backwards out of a little gharry on the river bank, opposite his ship, when the hunt passed. Realising the situation as though he had eyes in his shoulder-blades, he joined us with a leap and took

174

the lead. The Chinaman fled silent like a rapid shadow on the dust of an extremely oriental road. I followed. A long way in the rear my mate whooped like a savage. A young moon threw a bashful light on a plain like a monstrous waste ground: the architectural mass of a Buddhist temple far away projected itself in dead black on the sky. We lost the thief of course; but in my disappointment I had to admire Hermann's presence of mind. The velocity that stodgy man developed in the interests of a complete stranger earned my warm gratitude – there was something truly cordial in his exertions.

He seemed as vexed as myself at our failure, and would hardly listen to my thanks. He said it was 'nothings', and invited me on the spot to come on board his ship and drink a glass of beer with him. We poked sceptically for a while amongst the bushes, peered without conviction into a ditch or two. There was not a sound: patches of slime glimmered feebly amongst the reeds. Slowly we trudged back, drooping under the thin sickle of the moon, and I heard him mutter to himself, '*Himmel! Zwei und dreissig Pfund!*' He was impressed by the figure of my loss. For a long time we had ceased to hear the mate's whoops and yells.

Then he said to me, 'Everybody has his troubles', and as we went on remarked that he would never have known anything of mine hadn't he by an extraordinary chance been detained on shore by Captain Falk. He didn't like to stay late ashore – he added with a sigh. The something doleful in his tone I put to his sympathy with my misfortune, of course.

On board the *Diana* Mrs. Hermann's fine eyes expressed much interest and commiseration. We had found the two women sewing face to face under the open skylight in the strong glare of the lamp. Hermann walked in first, starting in the very doorway to pull off his coat, and encouraging me with loud, hospitable ejaculations: 'Come in! This way! Come in, captain!' At once, coat in hand, he began to tell his wife all about it. Mrs. Hermann put the palms of her plump hands together; I smiled and bowed with a heavy heart: the niece got up from her sewing to bring Hermann's slippers and his embroidered calotte, which he assumed pontifically, talking (about me) all the time. Billows of white stuff lay between the chairs on the cabin floor; I caught the words '*Zwei und dreissig Pfund*' repeated several times, and presently came the beer, which seemed delicious to my throat, parched with running and the emotions of the chase.

I didn't get away till well past midnight, long after the women had retired. Hermann had been trading in the East for three years or more, carrying freights of rice and timber mostly. His ship was well known in all the ports from Vladivostok to Singapore. She was his own property. The profits had been moderate, but the trade answered well enough while the children were small yet. In another year or so he hoped he would be able to sell the old *Diana* to a firm in Japan for a fair price. He intended to return home, to Bremen, by mail boat, second class, with Mrs. Hermann and the children. He told me all this stolidly, with slow puffs at his pipe. I was sorry when knocking the ashes out he began to rub his eyes. I would have sat with him till morning. What had I to hurry on board my own ship for? To face the broken rifled drawer in my stateroom. Ugh! The very thought made me feel unwell.

I became their daily guest, as you know. I think that Mrs. Hermann from the first looked upon me as a romantic person. I did not, of course, tear my hair *coram populo* over my loss, and she took it for lordly indifference. Afterwards, I daresay, I did tell them some of my adventures – such as they were – and they marvelled greatly at the extent of my experience. Hermann would translate what he thought the most striking passages. Getting upon his legs, and as if delivering a lecture on a phenomenon, he addressed himself, with gestures, to the two women, who would let their sewing sink slowly on their laps. Meantime I sat before a glass of Hermann's beer, trying to look modest. Mrs. Hermann would glance at me quickly, emit slight '*Ach*'s!' The girl never made a sound. Never. But she too would sometimes raise her pale eyes to look at me in her unseeing, gentle way. Her glance was by no means stupid; it beamed out soft and diffuse as the moon beams upon a landscape – quite differently from the scrutinizing inspection of the stars. You were drowned in it, and imagined yourself to appear blurred. And yet this same glance when turned upon Christian Falk must have been as efficient as the searchlight of a battleship.

Falk was the other assiduous visitor on board, but from his behaviour he might have been coming to see the quarter-deck capstan. He certainly used to stare at it a good deal when keeping us company outside the cabin door, with one muscular arm thrown over the back of the chair, and his big, shapely legs, in very tight white trousers, extended far out and ending in a pair of black shoes as roomy as punts. On arrival he would shake Hermann's hand with a mutter, bow to the women, and take up his careless and misanthropic attitude by our side. He departed abruptly, with a jump, going through the performance of grunts, handshakes, bow, as if in a panic. Sometimes, with a sort of discreet and convulsive effort, he approached the women and exchanged a few low words with them, half a dozen at most. On these occasions Hermann's usual stare became positively glassy and Mrs. Hermann's kind countenance would colour up. The girl herself never turned a hair.

Falk was a Dane or perhaps a Norwegian, I can't tell now. At all events he was a Scandinavian of some sort, and a bloated monopolist to boot. It is possible he was unacquainted with the word, but he had a clear perception of the thing itself. His tariff of charges for towing ships in and out was the most brutally inconsiderate document of the sort I had ever seen. He was the commander and owner of the only tugboat on the river, a very trim white craft of 150 tons or more, as elegantly neat as a yacht, with a round wheel-house rising like a glazed turret high above her sharp bows, and with one slender varnished pole mast forward. I daresay there are yet a few shipmasters afloat who remember Falk and his tug very well. He extracted his pound and a half of flesh from each of us merchant-skippers with an inflexible sort of indifference which made him detested and even feared. Schomberg used to remark: 'I won't talk about the fellow. I don't think he has six drinks from year's end to year's end in my place. But my advice is, gentlemen, don't you have anything to do with him, if you can help it.'

This advice, apart from unavoidable business relations, was easy to follow because Falk intruded upon no one. It seems absurd to compare a tugboat skipper to a centaur: but he reminded me somehow of an engraving in a little book I had as a boy, which represented centaurs at a stream, and there was one especially, in the foreground, prancing bow and arrows in hand, with regular severe features and an immense curled wavy beard, flowing down his breast. Falk's face reminded me of that centaur. Besides, he was a composite creature. Not a man-horse, it is true, but a man-boat.

He lived on board his tug, which was always dashing up and down the river from early morn till dewy eve. In the last rays of the setting sun you could pick out, far away down the reach, his beard borne high up on the white structure, foaming up stream to anchor for the night. There was the white-clad man's body, and the rich brown patch of the hair, and nothing below the waist but the 'thwart-ship white lines of the bridge-screens, that led the eye to the sharp white lines of the bows cleaving the muddy water of the river.

Separated from his boat, to me at least he seemed incomplete. The tug herself without his head and torso on the bridge looked mutilated as it were. But he left her very seldom. All the time I remained in harbour I saw him only twice on shore. On the first occasion it was at my charterers, where he came in misanthropically to get paid for towing out a French barque the day before. The second time I could hardly believe my eyes, for I beheld him reclining under his beard in a cane-bottomed chair in the billiard-room of Schomberg's hotel.

It was very funny to see Schomberg ignoring him pointedly. The artificiality of it contrasted strongly with Falk's natural unconcern. The big Alsatian talked loudly with his other customers, going from one little table to the other, and passing Falk's place of repose with his eyes fixed straight ahead. Falk sat there with an untouched glass at his elbow. He must have known by sight and name every white man in the room, but he never addressed a word to anybody. He acknowledged my presence by a drop of his eyelids, and that was all. Sprawling there in the chair, he would, now and again, draw the palms of both his hands down his face, giving at the same time a slight, almost imperceptible, shudder.

It was a habit he had, and of course I was perfectly familiar with it, since you could not remain an hour in his company without being made to wonder at such a movement breaking some long period of stillness. It was a passionate and inexplicable gesture. He used to make it at all sorts of times; as likely as not after he had been listening to little Lena's chatter about the suffering doll, for instance. The Hermann children always besieged him about his legs closely, though, in a gentle way, he shrank from them a little. He seemed, however, to feel a great affection for the whole family. For Hermann himself especially. He sought his company. In this case, for instance, he must have been waiting for him, because as soon as he appeared Falk rose hastily, and they went out together. Then Schomberg expounded in my hearing to three or four people his theory that Falk was after Captain Hermann's niece, and asserted confidently that nothing would come of it. It was the same last year when Captain Hermann was loading here, he said.

Naturally, I did not believe Schomberg, but I own that for a time I observed closely what went on. All I discovered was some impatience on Hermann's part. At the sight of Falk, stepping over the gangway, the excellent man would begin to mumble and chew between his teeth something that sounded like German swearwords. However, as I've said, I'm not familiar with the language, and Hermann's soft, round-eyed countenance remained unchanged. Staring stolidly ahead he greeted him with, *'Wie geht's?'* or in English, 'How are you?' with a throaty enunciation. The girl would look up for an instant and move her lips slightly: Mrs. Hermann let her hands rest on her lap to talk volubly to him for a minute or so in her pleasant voice before she went on with her sewing again. Falk would throw himself into a chair, stretch his big legs, as like as not draw his hands down his face passionately. As to myself, he was not pointedly impertinent: it was rather as though he could not be bothered with such trifles as my existence; and the truth is that being a monopolist he was under no necessity to be amiable. He was sure to get his own extortionate terms out of me for towage whether he frowned or smiled. As a matter of fact, he did neither: but before many days elapsed he managed to astonish me not a little and to set Schomberg's tongue clacking more than ever.

It came about in this way. There was a shallow bar at the mouth of the river which ought to have been kept down, but the authorities of the State were piously busy gilding afresh the great Buddhist Pagoda just then, and I suppose had no money to spare for dredging operations. I don't know how it may be now, but at the time I speak of that sandbank was a great nuisance to the shipping. One of its consequences was that vessels of a certain draught of water, like Hermann's or mine, could not complete their loading in the river. After taking in as much as possible of their cargo, they had to go outside to fill up. The whole procedure was an unmitigated bore. When you thought you had as much on board as your ship could carry safely over the bar, you went and gave notice to your agents. They, in their turn, notified Falk that so-and-so was ready to go out. Then Falk (ostensibly when it fitted in with his other work, but, if the truth were known, simply when his arbitrary spirit moved him), after ascertaining carefully in the office that there was enough money to meet his bill, would come along unsympathetically, glaring at you with his yellow eyes from the bridge, and would drag you out dishevelled as to rigging, lumbered as to the decks, with unfeeling haste, as if to execution. And he would force you, too, to take the end of his own wire hawser, for the use of which there was of course an extra charge. To your shouted remonstrances against this extortion this towering trunk with one hand on the engine-room telegraph only shook its bearded head above the splash, the racket and the clouds of smoke, in which the tug, backing and filling in the smother of churning paddle-wheels, behaved like a ferocious and impatient creature. He had her manned by the cheekiest gang of lascars I ever did see, whom he allowed to bawl at you insolently, and, once fast, he plucked you out of your berth as if he did not care what he smashed. Eighteen miles down the river you had to go behind him, and then three more along the coast to where a group of unin-habited rocky islets enclosed a sheltered anchorage. There you would have to lie at single anchor with your naked spars showing to seaward over these barren fragments of land scattered upon a very intensely blue sea. There was nothing to look at besides but a bare coast, the muddy edge of the brown plain with the sinuosities of the river you had left, traced in dull green, and the Great Pagoda uprising lonely and massive with shining curves and pinnacles like the gorgeous and stony efflorescence of tropical rocks. You had nothing to do but to wait fretfully for the balance of your cargo, which was sent out of the river with the greatest irregularity. And it was open to you to console yourself with the thought that, after all, this stage of bother meant that your departure from these shores was indeed approaching at last.

We both had to go through that stage, Hermann and I, and there was a sort of tacit emulation between the ships as to which should be ready first. We kept on neck and neck almost to the finish, when I won the race by going personally to give notice in the forenoon; whereas Hermann, who was very slow in making up his mind to go ashore, did not get to the agents' office till late in the day. They told him there that my ship was first on turn for next morning, and I believe he told them he was in no hurry. It suited him better to go the day after.

That evening, on board the *Diana*, he sat with his plump knees well apart, staring and puffing at the curved mouthpiece of his pipe. Presently he spoke with some impatience to his niece about putting the children to bed. Mrs. Hermann, who was talking to Falk, stopped short and looked at her husband uneasily, but the girl got up at once and drove the children before her into the cabin. In a little while Mrs. Hermann had to leave us to quell what, from the sounds inside, must have been a dangerous mutiny. At this Hermann grumbled to himself. For half an hour longer Falk, left alone with us, fidgeted on his chair, sighed lightly, then at last, after drawing his hands down his face, got up and, as if renouncing the hope of making himself understood (he hadn't opened his mouth once), said in English: 'Well ... Good night, Captain Hermann.' He stopped for a moment before my chair and looked down fixedly; I may even say he glared: and he went so far as to make a deep noise in his throat. There was in all this something so marked that for the first time in our limited inter-course of nods and grunts he excited in me something like interest. But next moment he disappointed me – for he strode away hastily without a nod even.

His manner was usually odd, it is true, and I certainly did not pay much attention to it; but that sort of obscure intention, which seemed to lurk in his nonchalance like a wary old carp in a pond, had never before come so near the surface. He had distinctly aroused my expectations. I would have been unable to say what it was I expected, but at all events I did not expect the absurd developments he sprung upon me no later than the break of the very next day.

I remember only that there was, on that evening, enough point in his behaviour to make me, after he had fled, wonder audibly what he might mean. To this Hermann, crossing his legs with a swing and settling himself viciously away from me in his chair, said: 'That fellow don't know himself what he means.'

There might have been some insight in such a remark. I said nothing, and, still averted, he added: 'When I was here last year he

181

was just the same.' An eruption of tobacco smoke enveloped his head as if his temper had exploded like gunpowder.

I had half a mind to ask him point blank whether he, at least, didn't know why Falk, a notoriously unsociable man, had taken to visiting his ship with such assiduity. After all, I reflected suddenly, it was a most remarkable thing. I wonder now what Hermann would have said. As it turned out he didn't let me ask. Forgetting all about Falk, apparently, he started a monologue on his plans for the future: the selling of the ship, the going home; and falling into a reflective and calculating mood he mumbled between regular jets of smoke about the expense. The necessity of disbursing passage-money for all his tribe seemed to disturb him in a manner that was the more striking because otherwise he gave no signs of a miserly disposition. And yet he fussed over the prospect of that voyage home in a mail-boat like a sedentary grocer who has made up his mind to see the world. He was racially thrifty I suppose, and for him there must have been a great novelty in finding himself obliged to pay for travelling – for sea travelling, which was the normal state of life for the family – from the very cradle for most of them. I could see he grudged prospectively every single shilling which must be spent so absurdly. It was rather funny. He would become doleful over it, and then again, with a fretful sigh, he would suppose there was nothing for it now but to take three second-class tickets – and there were the four children to pay for besides. A lot of money that, to spend at once. A big lot of money.

I sat with him listening (not for the first time) to these heart-searchings till I grew thoroughly sleepy, and then I left him and turned in on board my ship. At daylight I was awakened by a yelping of shrill voices, accompanied by a great commotion in the water, and the short, bullying blasts of a steam-whistle. Falk with his tug had come for me.

I began to dress. It was remarkable that the answering noise on board my ship together with the patter of feet above my head ceased suddenly. But I heard more remote guttural cries which seemed to express surprise and annoyance. Then the voice of my mate reached me howling expostulations to somebody at a distance. Other voices joined, apparently indignant; a chorus of something that sounded like abuse replied. Now and then the steam-whistle screeched.

Altogether that unnecessary uproar was distracting, but down there in my cabin I took it calmly. In another moment, I thought, I should be going down that wretched river, and in another week at the most I should be totally quit of the odious place and all the odious people in it.

Greatly cheered by the idea, I seized the hairbrushes and looking at myself in the glass began to use them. Suddenly a hush fell upon the noise outside, and I heard (the ports of my cabin were thrown open) – I heard a deep calm voice, not on board my ship, however, hailing resolutely in English, but with a strong foreign twang, 'Go ahead!'

There may be tides in the affairs of men which, taken at the flood . . . and so on.[42] Personally I am still on the look-out for that important turn. I am, however, afraid that most of us are fated to flounder for ever in the dead water of a pool whose shores are arid indeed. But I know that there are often in men's affairs unexpectedly – even irrationally – illuminating moments when an otherwise insignificant sound, perhaps only some perfectly commonplace gesture, suffices to reveal to us all the unreason, all the fatuous unreason, of our complacency. 'Go ahead' are not particularly striking words, even when pronounced with a foreign accent; yet they petrified me in the very act of smiling at myself in the glass. And then, refusing to believe my ears, but already boiling with indignation, I ran out of the cabin and up on deck.

It was incredibly true. It was perfectly true. I had no eyes for anything but the *Diana*. It was she that was being taken away. She was already out of her berth and shooting athwart the river. 'The way this loonatic plucked that ship out is a caution,' said the awed voice of my mate close to my ear. 'Hey! Hallo! Falk! Hermann! What's this infernal trick?' I yelled in a fury.

Nobody heard me. Falk certainly could not hear me. His tug was turning at full speed away under the other bank. The wire hawser between her and the *Diana*, stretched as taut as a harpstring, vibrated alarmingly.

The high black craft careened over to the awful strain. A loud crack came out of her, followed by the tearing and splintering of wood. 'There!' said the awed voice in my ear. 'He's carried away their towing chock.' And then, with enthusiasm, 'Oh! Look! Look, sir! Look at them Dutchmen skipping out of the way on the forecastle. I hope to goodness he'll break a few of their shins before he's done with 'em.'

I yelled my vain protests. The rays of the rising sun coursing level along the plain warmed my back, but I was hot enough with rage. I could not have believed that a simple towing operation could suggest so plainly the idea of abduction, of rape. Falk was simply running off with the *Diana*.

The white tug careered out into the middle of the river. The red floats of her paddle-wheels revolving with mad rapidity tore up the whole reach into foam. The *Diana* in mid-stream waltzed round with as much grace as an old barn, and flew after her ravisher. Through the ragged fog of smoke driving headlong upon the water I had a glimpse of Falk's square motionless shoulders under a white hat as big as a cart-wheel, of his red face, his yellow staring eyes, his great beard. Instead of keeping a look-out ahead, he was deliberately turning his back on the river to glare at his tow. The tall heavy craft, never so used before in her life, seemed to have lost her senses; she took a wild sheer against her helm, and for a moment came straight at us, menacing and clumsy, like a runaway mountain. She piled up a streaming, hissing, boiling wave half-way up her blunt stern, my crew let out one great howl, – and then we held our breaths. It was a near thing. But Falk had her! He had her in his clutch. I fancied I could hear the steel hawser ping as it surged across the *Diana*'s forecastle, with the hands on board of her bolting away from it in all directions. It was a near thing. Hermann, with his hair rumpled, in a snuffy flannel shirt and a pair of mustard-coloured trousers, had rushed to help with the wheel. I saw his terrified round face; I saw his very teeth uncovered by a sort of ghastly fixed grin; and in a great leaping tumult of water between the two ships the *Diana* whisked past so close that I could have flung a hairbrush at his head, for, it seems, I had kept them in my hands all the time. Meanwhile Mrs. Hermann sat placidly on the skylight, with a woollen shawl on her shoulders. The excellent woman in response to my indignant gesticulations fluttered a handkerchief, nodding and smiling in the kindest way imaginable. The boys, only half-dressed, were jumping about the poop in great glee, displaying their gaudy braces; and Lena in a short scarlet petticoat, with peaked elbows and thin bare arms, nursed the rag-doll with devotion. The whole family passed before my sight as if dragged across a scene of unparalleled violence. The last I saw was Hermann's niece with the baby Hermann in her arms standing apart from the others. Magnificent in her close-fitting print frock, she displayed something so commanding in the manifest perfection of her figure that the sun seemed to be rising for her alone. The flood of light brought out the opulence of her form and the vigour of her youth in a glorifying way. She went by perfectly motionless and as if lost in meditation; only the hem of her skirt stirred in the draught; the sun-rays broke on her sleek tawny hair; that bald-headed ruffian, Nicholas, was whacking her on the shoulder. I saw his tiny fat arm rise and fall in a workmanlike manner. And then the four cottage windows of the *Diana* came into view retreating swiftly down the river. The sashes were up, and one of the white calico curtains fluttered straight out like a streamer above the agitated water of the wake.

To be thus tricked out of one's turn was an unheard-of occurrence. In my agent's office, where I went to complain at once, they protested with apologies they couldn't understand how the mistake arose; but Schomberg, when I dropped in later to get some tiffin, though surprised to see me, was perfectly ready with an explanation. I found him seated at the end of a long narrow table, facing his wife – a scraggy little woman, with long ringlets and a blue tooth, who smiled abroad stupidly and looked frightened when you spoke to her. Between them a waggling punkah fanned twenty vacant cane-bottomed chairs and two rows of shiny plates. Three Chinamen in white jackets loafed with napkins in their hands around that desolation. Schomberg's pet *table d'hôte* was not much of a success that day. He was feeding himself furiously and seemed to overflow with bitterness.

He began by ordering in a brutal voice the chops to be brought back for me, and turning in his chair: 'Mistake they told you? Not a bit of it! Don't you believe it for a moment, captain! Falk isn't a man to make mistakes unless on purpose.' His firm conviction was that Falk had been trying all along to curry favour on the cheap with Hermann. 'On the cheap – mind you! It doesn't cost him a cent to put that insult upon you, and Captain Hermann gets in a day ahead of your ship. Time's money! Eh? You are very friendly with Captain Hermann I believe, but a man is bound to be pleased at any little advantage he may get. Captain Hermann is a good business man, and there's no such thing as a friend in business. Is there?' He leaned forward and began to cast stealthy glances as usual. 'But Falk is, and always was, a miserable fellow. I would despise him.'

I muttered, grumpily, that I had no particular respect for Falk.

'I would despise him,' he insisted, with an appearance of anxiety which would have amused me if I had not been fathoms deep in discontent. To a young man fairly conscientious and as well-meaning as only the young can be, the current ill-usage of life comes with peculiar cruelty. Youth that is fresh enough to believe in guilt, in innocence, and in itself, will always doubt whether it have not perchance deserved its fate. Sombre of mind and without appetite, I struggled with the chop while Mrs. Schomberg sat with her everlasting stupid grin and Schomberg's talk gathered way like a slide of rubbish.

'Let me tell you. It's all about that girl. I don't know what Captain Hermann expects, but if he asked me I could tell him something about Falk. He's a miserable fellow. That man is a perfect slave. That's what I call him. A slave. Last year I started this *table d'hôte*, and sent cards out – you know. You think he had one meal in the house? Give the thing a trial? Not once. He has got hold now of a Madras cook – a blamed fraud that I hunted out of my cookhouse with a rattan. He was not fit to cook for white men. No, not for the white men's dogs either; but, see, any damned native that can boil a pot of rice is good enough for Mr. Falk. Rice and a little fish he buys for a few cents from the fishing-boats outside is what he lives on. You would hardly credit it – eh? A white man, too. . . .'

He wiped his lips, using the napkin with indignation, and looking at me. It flashed through my mind in the midst of my depression that if all the meat in the town was like these *table-d'hôte* chops, Falk wasn't so far wrong. I was on the point of saying this, but Schomberg's stare was intimidating. 'He's a vegetarian, perhaps,' I murmured instead.

'He's a miser. A miserable miser,' affirmed the hotel-keeper with great force. 'The meat here is not so good as at home – of course. And dear, too. But look at me. I only charge a dollar for the tiffin, and one dollar and fifty cents for the dinner. Show me anything cheaper. Why am I doing it? There's little profit in this game. Falk wouldn't look at it. I do it for the sake of a lot of young white fellows here that hadn't a place where they could get a decent meal and eat it decently in good company. There's first-rate company always at my table.'

The convinced way he surveyed the empty chairs made me feel as if I had intruded upon a tiffin of ghostly Presences.

'A white man should eat like a white man, dash it all,' he burst out impetuously. 'Ought to eat meat, must eat meat. I manage to get meat for my patrons all the year round. Don't I? I am not catering for a dam' lot of coolies: Have another chop, captain.... No? You, boy – take away!'

He threw himself back and waited grimly for the curry. The half-closed jalousies darkened the room pervaded by the smell of fresh whitewash: a swarm of flies buzzed and settled in turns, and poor Mrs. Schomberg's smile seemed to express the quintessence of all the imbecility that had ever spoken, had ever breathed, had ever been fed on infamous buffalo meat within these bare walls. Schomberg did not open his lips till he was ready to thrust therein a spoonful of greasy rice. He rolled his eyes ridiculously before he swallowed the hot stuff, and only then broke out afresh.

'It is the most degrading thing. They take the dish up to the wheel-house for him with a cover on it, and he shuts both the doors before he begins to eat. Fact! Must be ashamed of himself. Ask the engineer. He can't do without an engineer – don't you see – and as no respectable man can be expected to put up with such a table, he allows them fifteen dollars a month extra mess money. I assure you it is so! You just ask Mr. Ferdinand da Costa. That's the engineer he has now. You may have seen him about my place, a delicate dark young man, with very fine eyes and a little moustache. He arrived here a year ago from Calcutta. Between you and me, I guess the money-lenders there must have been after him. He rushes here for a meal every chance he can get, for just please tell me what satisfaction is that for a well-educated young fellow to feed all alone in his cabin – like a wild beast? That's what Falk expects his engineers to put up with for fifteen dollars extra. And the rows on board every time a little smell of cooking gets about on deck! You wouldn't believe! The other day da Costa got the cook to fry a steak for him – a turtle steak it was too, not beef at all – and the fat caught or something. Young da Costa himself was telling me of it here in this room. 'Mr. Schomberg' – says he – 'if I had let a cylinder cover blow off through the skylight by my negligence Captain Falk couldn't have been more savage. He frightened the cook so that he won't put anything on the fire for me now.' Poor da Costa had tears in his eyes. Only try to put yourself in his place, captain: a sensitive, gentlemanly young fellow. Is he expected to eat his food raw? But that's your Falk all over. Ask anyone you like. I suppose the fifteen dollars extra he has to give keep on rankling – in there.'

And Schomberg tapped his manly breast. I sat half stunned by his irrelevant babble. Suddenly he gripped my forearm in an impressive and cautious manner, as if to lead me into a very cavern of confidence.

'It's nothing but enviousness,' he said in a lowered tone, which had a stimulating effect upon my wearied hearing. 'I don't suppose there is one person in this town that he isn't envious of. I tell you he's dangerous. Even I myself am not safe from him. I know for certain he tried to poison. . . . '

'Oh, come now,' I cried, revolted.

'But I know for certain. The people themselves came and told me of it. He went about saying everywhere I was a worse pest to this town than the cholera. He had been talking against me ever since I opened this hotel. And he poisoned Captain Hermann's mind too. Last time the *Diana* was loading here Captain Hermann used to come in every day for a drink or a cigar. This time he hasn't been here twice in a week. How do you account for that?'

He squeezed my arm till he extorted from me some sort of mumble.

'He makes ten times the money I do. I've another hotel to fight against, and there is no other tug on the river. I am not in his way, am I? He wouldn't be fit to run an hotel if he tried. But that's just his nature. He can't bear to think I am making a living. I only hope it makes him properly wretched. He's like that in everything. He would like to keep a decent table well enough. But no – for the sake of a few cents. Can't do it. It's too much for him. That's what I call being a slave to it. But he's mean enough to kick up a row when his nose gets tickled a bit. See that? That just paints him. Miserly and envious. You can't account for it any other way. Can you? I have been studying him these three years.'

He was anxious I should assent to his theory. And indeed on thinking it over it would have been plausible enough if there hadn't been always the essential falseness of irresponsibility in Schomberg's chatter. However, I was not disposed to investigate the psychology of Falk. I was engaged just then in eating despondently a piece of stale Dutch cheese, being too much crushed to care what I swallowed myself, let alone bothering my head about Falk's ideas of gastronomy. I could expect from their study no clue to his conduct in matters of business, which seemed to me totally unrestrained by morality or even by the commonest sort of decency. How insignificant and contemptible I must appear, for the fellow to dare treat me like this – I reflected suddenly, writhing in silent agony. And I consigned Falk and all his peculiarities to the devil with so much mental fervour as to forget Schomberg's existence, till he grabbed my arm urgently. 'Well, you may think and think till every hair of your head falls off, captain; but you can't explain it in any other way.'

For the sake of peace and quietness I admitted hurriedly that I couldn't; persuaded that now he would leave off. But the only result was to make his moist face shine with the pride of cunning. He removed his hand for a moment to scare a black mass of flies off the sugar-basin, and caught hold of my arm again.

'To be sure. And in the same way everybody is aware he would like to get married. Only he can't. Let me quote you an instance. Well, two years ago a Miss Vanlo, a very ladylike girl, came from home to keep house for her brother, Fred, who had an engineering shop for small repairs by the waterside. Suddenly Falk takes to going up to their bungalow after dinner and sitting for hours in the verandah saying nothing. The poor girl couldn't tell for the life of her what to do with such a man, so she would keep on playing the piano and singing to him evening after evening till she was ready to drop. And it wasn't as if she had been a strong young woman either. She was thirty, and the climate had been playing the deuce with her. Then – don't you know – Fred had to sit up with them for propriety, and during whole weeks on end never got a single chance to get to bed before midnight. That was not pleasant for a tired man – was it? And besides Fred had worries then because his shop didn't pay and he was dropping money fast. He just longed to get away from here and try his luck somewhere else, but for the sake of his sister he hung on and on till he ran himself into debt over his ears – I can tell you. I, myself, could show a handful of his chits for meals and drinks in my drawer. I could never find out tho' where he found all the money at last. Can't be but he must have got something out of that brother of his, a coal merchant in Port Said. Anyhow he paid everybody before he left, but the girl nearly broke her heart. Disappointment, of course, and at her age, don't you know. . . . Mrs. Schomberg here was very friendly with her, and she could tell you. Awful despair. Fainting fits. It was a scandal. A notorious scandal. To that extent that old Mr. Siegers[43] – not your present charterer, but Mr. Siegers the father, the old gentleman who retired from business on a fortune and got buried at sea going home, *he* had to interview Falk in his private office. He was a man who could speak like a Dutch Uncle, and, besides, Messrs. Siegers had been helping Falk with a good bit of money from the start. In fact you may say they made him as far as that goes. It so happened that just at the time he turned up here, their firm was chartering a lot of sailing-ships every year, and it suited their business that there should be good towing facilities on the river. See? . . . Well – there's always an ear at the keyhole – isn't there? In fact,' he lowered his tone confidentially, 'in this case it was a good friend of mine; a man you can see here any evening; only they conversed rather low. Anyhow my friend's certain that Falk was trying to make all sorts of excuses, and old Mr. Siegers was coughing a lot. And yet Falk wanted all the time to be married, too. Why! It's notorious the man has been longing for years to make a home for himself. Only he can't face the expense. When it comes to putting his hand in his pocket – it chokes him off. That's the truth and no other. I've always said so, and everybody agrees with me by this time. What do you think of that – eh?'

He appealed confidently to my indignation, but having a mind to annoy him I remarked that 'it seemed to me very pitiful – if true'.

He bounced in his chair as if I had run a pin into him. I don't know what he might have said, only at that moment we heard through the half-open door of the billiard-room the footsteps of two men entering from the verandah, a murmur of two voices; at the sharp tapping of a coin on a table Mrs. Schomberg half rose irresolutely. 'Sit still,' he hissed at her, and then, in an hospitable, jovial tone, contrasting amazingly with the angry glance that had made his wife sink in her chair, he cried very loud: 'Tiffin still going on in here, gentlemen.'

There was no answer, but the voices dropped suddenly. The head Chinaman went out. We heard the clink of ice in the glasses, pouring sounds, the shuffling of feet, the scraping of chairs. Schomberg, after wondering in a low mutter who the devil could be there at this time of day, got up napkin in hand to peep through the doorway cautiously. He retreated rapidly on tip-toe, and whispering behind his hand informed me that it was Falk, Falk himself who was in there, and, what's more, he had Captain Hermann with him.

The return of the tug from the outer Roads was unexpected but possible, for Falk had taken away the *Diana* at half-past five, and it was now two o'clock. Schomberg wished me to observe that neither of these men would spend a dollar on a tiffin, which they must have wanted. But by the time I was ready to leave the dining-room Falk had gone. I heard the last of his big boots on the planks of the verandah. Hermann was sitting quite alone in the large, wooden room with the two lifeless billiard tables shrouded in striped covers, mopping his face diligently. He wore his best go-ashore clothes, a stiff collar, black coat, large white waistcoat, grey trousers. A white cotton sunshade with a cane handle reposed between his legs, his side whiskers were neatly brushed, his chin had been freshly shaved; and he only distantly resembled the dishevelled and terrified man in a snuffy night-shirt and ignoble old trousers I had seen in the morning hanging on to the wheel of the *Diana*.

He gave a start at my entrance, and addressed me at once in some confusion, but with genuine eagerness. He was anxious to make it clear he had nothing to do with what he called the 'tam pizness' of the morning. It was most inconvenient. He had reckoned upon another day up in town to settle his bills and sign certain papers. There were also some few stores to come, and sundry pieces of 'my ironwork', as he called it quaintly, landed for repairs, had been left behind. Now he would have to hire a native boat to take all this out to the ship. It would cost five or six dollars perhaps. He had had no warning from Falk. Nothing. . . . He hit the table with his dumpy fist. . . . *Der verfluchte Kerl* came in the morning like a 'tam' ropper', making a great noise, and took him away. His mate was not prepared, his ship was moored fast – he protested it was shameful to come upon a man in that way. Shameful! Yet such was the power Falk had on the river that when I suggested in a chilling tone that he might have simply refused to have his ship moved, Hermann was quite startled at the idea. I never realised so well before that this is an age of steam. The exclusive possession of a marine boiler had given Falk the whip hand of us all. Hermann, recovering, put it to me appealingly that I knew very well how unsafe it was to contradict that fellow. At this I only smiled distantly.

'*Der Kerl!*' he cried. He was sorry he had not refused. He was indeed. The damage! The damage! What for all that damage! There was no occasion for damage. Did I know how much damage he had done? It gave me a certain satisfaction to tell him that I had heard his old waggon of a ship crack fore and aft as she went by. 'You passed close enough to me,' I added significantly.

He threw both his hands up to heaven at the recollection. One of them grasped by the middle the white parasol, and he resembled curiously a caricature of a shopkeeping citizen in one of his own German comic papers. '*Ach!* That was dangerous,' he cried. I was amused. But directly he added with an appearance of simplicity, 'The side of your iron ship would have been crushed in like – like this matchbox.'

'Would it?' I growled, much less amused now; but by the time I had decided that this remark was not meant for a dig at me he had worked himself into a high state of resentfulness against Falk. The inconvenience, the damage, the expense! Gottferdam! Devil take the fellow. Behind the bar Schomberg, with a cigar in his teeth, pretended to be writing with a pencil on a large sheet of paper; and as Hermann's excitement increased it made me comfortably aware of my own calmness and superiority. But it occurred to me while I listened to his revilings, that after all the good man had come up in the tug. There perhaps – since he must come to town – he had no option. But evidently he had had a drink with Falk, either accepted or offered. How was that? So I checked him by saying loftily that I hoped he would make Falk pay for every penny of the damage.

'That's it! That's it! Go for him,' called out Schomberg from the bar, flinging his pencil down and rubbing his hands.

We ignored his noise. But Hermann's excitement suddenly went off the boil as when you remove a saucepan from the fire. I urged on his consideration that he had done now with Falk and Falk's confounded tug. He, Hermann, would not, perhaps, turn up again in this part of the world for years to come, since he was going to sell the *Diana* at the end of this very trip ('Go home passenger in a mail boat,' he murmured mechanically). He was therefore safe from Falk's malice. All he had to do was to race off to his consignees and stop payment of the towage bill before Falk had the time to get in and lift the money.

Nothing could have been less in the spirit of my advice than the thoughtful way in which he set about making his parasol stay propped against the edge of the table.

While I watched his concentrated efforts with astonishment he threw at me one or two perplexed, half-shy glances. Then he sat down. 'That's all very well,' he said reflectively.

It cannot be doubted that the man had been thrown off his balance by being hauled out of the harbour against his wish. His stolidity had been profoundly stirred, else he would never have made up his mind to ask me unexpectedly whether I had not remarked that Falk had been casting eyes upon his niece. 'No more than myself,' I answered with literal truth. The girl was of the sort one necessarily casts eyes at in a sense. She made no noise, but she filled most satisfactorily a good bit of space.

'But you, captain, are not the same kind of man,' observed Hermann.

I was not, I am happy to say, in a position to deny this. 'What about the lady?' I could not help asking. At this he gazed for a time into my face, earnestly, and made as if to change the subject. I heard him beginning to mutter something unexpected, about his children growing old enough to require schooling. He would have to leave them ashore with their grandmother when he took up that new command he expected to get in Germany.

This constant harping on his domestic arrangements was funny. I suppose it must have been like the prospect of a complete alteration in his life. An epoch. He was going, too, to part with the *Diana*! He had served in her for years. He had inherited her. From an uncle, if I remember rightly. And the future loomed big before him, occupying his thought exclusively with all its aspects as on the eve of a venturesome enterprise. He sat there frowning and biting his lip, and suddenly he began to fume and fret.

I discovered to my momentary amusement that he seemed to imagine I could, should or ought, have caused Falk in some way to pronounce himself. Such a hope was incomprehensible, but funny. Then the contact with all this foolishness irritated me. I said crossly that I had seen no symptoms, but if there were any – since he, Hermann, was so sure – then it was still worse. What pleasure Falk found in humbugging people in just that way I couldn't say. It was, however, my solemn duty to warn him. It had lately, I said, come to my knowledge that there was a man (not a very long time ago either) who had been taken in just like this.

All this passed in undertones, and at this point Schomberg, exasperated at our secrecy, went out of the room slamming the door with a crash that positively lifted us in our chairs. This, or else what I had said, huffed my Hermann. He supposed, with a contemptuous toss of his head towards the door which trembled yet, that I had got hold of some of that man's silly tales. It looked, indeed, as though his mind had been thoroughly poisoned against Schomberg. 'His tales were – they were' he repeated, seeking for the word, 'trash!' They were trash, he reiterated, and moreover I was young yet. . . .

This horrid aspersion (I regret I am no longer exposed to that sort of insult) made me huffy too. I felt ready in my own mind to back up every assertion of Schomberg's and on any subject. In a moment, devil only knows why, Hermann and I were looking at each other most inimically. He caught up his hat without more ado and I gave myself the pleasure of calling after him:

'Take my advice and make Falk pay for breaking up your ship. You aren't likely to get anything else out of him.'

When I got on board my ship later on, the old mate, who was very full of the events of the morning, remarked:

'I saw the tug coming back from the outer Roads just before two P.M.' (He never by any chance used the words morning or afternoon. Always P.M. or A.M., log-book style.) 'Smart work that. Man's always in a state of hurry. He's a regular chucker-out, ain't he, sir? There's a few pubs I know of in the East-end of London that would be all the better for one of his sort around the bar.' He chuckled at his joke. 'A regular chucker-out. Now he has fired out that Dutchman head over heels, I suppose our turn's coming to-morrow morning.'

We were all on deck at break of day (even the sick – poor devils – had crawled out) ready to cast off in the twinkling of an eye. Nothing came. Falk did not come. At last, when I began to think that probably something had gone wrong in his engine-room, we perceived the tug going by, full pelt, down the river, as if we hadn't existed. For a moment I entertained the wild notion that he was going to turn round in the next reach. Afterwards I watched his smoke appear above the plain, now here, now there, according to the windings of the river. It disappeared. Then without a word I went down to breakfast. I just simply went down to breakfast.

Not one of us uttered a sound till the mate, after imbibing – by means of suction out of a saucer – his second cup of tea, exclaimed: 'Where the devil is the man gone to?'

'Courting!' I shouted, with such a fiendish laugh that the old chap didn't venture to open his lips any more.

I started to the office perfectly calm. Calm with excessive rage. Evidently they knew all about it already, and they treated me to a show of consternation. The manager, a soft-footed, immensely obese man, breathing short, got up to meet me, while all round the room the young clerks, bending over the papers on their desks, cast upward glances in my direction. The fat man, without waiting for my complaint, wheezing heavily and in a tone as if he himself were incredulous, conveyed to me the news that Falk – Captain Falk – had declined – had absolutely declined – to tow my ship – to have anything to do with my ship – this day or any other day. Never!

I did my best to preserve a cool appearance, but, all the same, I must have shown how much taken aback I was. We were talking in the middle of the room. Suddenly behind my back some ass blew his nose with great force, and at the same time another quill-driver jumped up and went out on the landing hastily. It occurred to me I was cutting a foolish figure there. I demanded angrily to see the principal in his private room.

The skin of Mr. Siegers' head showed dead white between the iron-grey streaks of hair lying plastered cross-wise from ear to ear over the top of his skull in the manner of a bandage. His narrow sunken face was of a uniform and permanent terra-cotta colour, like a piece of pottery. He was sickly, thin, and short, with wrists like a boy of ten. But from that debile body there issued a bullying voice, tremendously loud, harsh and resonant, as if produced by some powerful mechanical contrivance in the nature of a fog-horn. I do not know what he did with it in the private life of his home, but in the larger sphere of business it presented the advantage of overcoming arguments without the slightest mental effort, by the mere volume of sound. We had several passages of arms. It took me all I knew to guard the interests of my owners – whom, *nota bene*, I had never seen – while Siegers (who had made their acquaintance some years before, during a business tour in Australia) pretended to the knowledge of their innermost minds, and, in the character of 'our very good friends', threw them perpetually at my head.

He looked at me with a jaundiced eye (there was no love lost between us), and declared at once that it was strange, very strange. His pronunciation of English was so extravagant that I can't even attempt to reproduce it. For instance, he said 'Fferie strantch'. Combined with the bellowing intonation it made the language of one's childhood sound weirdly startling, and even if considered purely as a kind of unmeaning noise it filled you with astonishment at first. 'They had', he continued, 'been acquainted with Captain Falk for many years, and never had any reason . . .'

'That's why I come to you, of course,' I interrupted. 'I've the right to know the meaning of this infernal nonsense.' In the half-light of the room, which was greenish, because of the tree-tops screening the window, I saw him writhe his meagre shoulders. It came into my head, as disconnected ideas will come at all sorts of times into one's head, that this, most likely, was the very room where, if the tale were true, Falk had been lectured by Mr. Siegers, the father. Mr. Siegers' (the son's) overwhelming voice, in brassy blasts, as though he had been trying to articulate his words through a trombone, was expressing his great regret at conduct characterised by a very marked want of discretion . . . As I lived, I was being lectured too! His deafening gibberish was difficult to follow, but it was *my* conduct – mine! – that . . . Damn! I wasn't going to stand this.

'What on earth are you driving at?' I asked in a passion. I put my hat on my head (he never offered a seat to anybody), and as he seemed for the moment struck dumb by my irreverence, I turned my back on him and marched out. His vocal arrangements blared after me a few threats of coming down on the ship for the demurrage of the lighters, and all the other expenses consequent upon the delays arising from my frivolity.

Once outside in the sunshine my head swam. It was no longer a question of mere delay. I perceived myself involved in hopeless and humiliating absurdities that were leading me to something very like a disaster. 'Let us be calm,' I muttered to myself, and ran into the shade of a leprous wall. From that short side-street I could see the broad main thoroughfare, ruinous and gay, running away, away between stretches of decaying masonry, bamboo fences, ranges of arcades of brick and plaster, hovels of lath and mud, lofty temple gates of carved timber, huts of rotten mats – an immensely wide thoroughfare, loosely packed as far as the eye could reach with a barefooted and brown multitude paddling ankle-deep in the dust. For a moment I felt myself about to go out of my mind with worry and desperation.

Some allowance must be made for the feelings of a young man new to responsibility. I thought of my crew. Half of them were ill, and I really began to think that some of them would end by dying on board if I couldn't get them out to sea soon. Obviously I should have to take my ship down the river, either working under canvas or dredging with the anchor down; operations which, in common with many modern sailors, I only knew theoretically. And I almost shrank from undertaking them shorthanded and without local knowledge of the river bed, which is so necessary for the confident handling of the ship. There were no pilots, no beacons, no buoys of any sort; but there was a very devil of a current for anybody to see, no end of shoal places, and at least two obviously awkward turns of the channel between me and the sea. But how dangerous these turns were I could not tell. I didn't even know what my ship was capable of! I had never handled her in my life. A misunderstanding between a man and his ship, in a difficult river with no room to make it up, is bound to end in trouble for the man. On the other hand, it must be owned I had not much reason to count upon a general run of good luck. And suppose I had the misfortune to pile her up high and dry on some beastly shoal? That would have been the final undoing of that voyage. It was plain that if Falk refused to tow me out he would also refuse to pull me off. This meant – what? A day lost at the very best; but more likely a whole fortnight of frizzling on some pestilential mudflat, of desperate work, of discharging cargo; more than likely it meant borrowing money at an exorbitant rate of interest – from the Siegers' gang too at that. They were a power in the port. And that elderly seaman of mine, Gambril, had looked pretty ghastly when I went forward to dose him with quinine[44] that morning. *He* would certainly die – not to speak of two or three others that seemed nearly as bad, and of the rest of them just ready to catch any tropical disease going. Horror, ruin and everlasting remorse. And no help. None. I had fallen amongst a lot of unfriendly lunatics!

At any rate, if I must take my ship down myself it was my duty to procure if possible some local knowledge. But that was not easy. The only person I could think of for that service was a certain Johnson, formerly captain of a country ship, but now spliced to a country wife and gone utterly to the bad. I had only heard of him in the vaguest way, as living concealed in the thick of two hundred thousand natives, and only emerging into the light of day for the purpose of hunting up some brandy. I had a notion that if I could lay my hands on him I would sober him on board my ship and use him for a pilot. Better than nothing. Once a sailor always a sailor – and he had known the river for years. But in our Consulate (where I arrived dripping after a sharp walk) they could tell me nothing. The excellent young men on the staff, though willing to help me, belonged to a sphere of the white colony for which that sort of Johnson does not exist. Their suggestion was that I should hunt the man up myself with the help of the Consulate's constable – an ex-sergeant-major of a regiment of hussars.

This man, whose usual duty apparently consisted in sitting behind a little table in an outer room of Consular offices, when ordered to assist me in my search for Johnson displayed lots of energy and a marvellous amount of local knowledge of a sort. But he did not conceal an immense and sceptical contempt for the whole business. We explored together on that afternoon an infinity of infamous grog shops, gambling dens, opium dens. We walked up narrow lanes where our gharry – a tiny box of a thing on wheels, attached to a jibbing Burmah pony – could by no means have passed. The constable seemed to be on terms of scornful intimacy with Maltese, with Eurasians, with Chinamen, with Klings, and with the sweepers attached to a temple, with whom he talked at the gate. We interviewed also through a grating in a mud wall closing a blind alley an immensely corpulent Italian, who, the ex-sergeant-major remarked to me perfunctorily, had 'killed another man last year'. Thereupon he addressed him as 'Antonio' and 'Old Buck', though that bloated carcase, apparently more than half filling the sort of cell wherein it sat, recalled rather a fat pig in a stye. Familiar and never unbending, the sergeant chucked – absolutely chucked – under the chin a horribly wrinkled and shrivelled old hag propped on a stick, who had volunteered some sort of information: and with the same stolid face he kept up an animated conversation with the groups of swathed brown women who sat smoking cheroots on the doorsteps of a long range of clay hovels. We got out of the gharry and clambered into dwellings airy like packing crates, or descended into places sinister like cellars. We got in, we drove on, we got out again for the sole purpose, as it seemed, of looking behind a heap of rubble. The sun declined; my companion was curt and sardonic in his answers, but it appears we were just missing Johnson all along. At last our conveyance stopped once more with a jerk; and the driver, jumping down, opened the door.

A black mudhole blocked the lane. A mound of garbage crowned with the dead body of a dog arrested us not. An empty Australian beef-tin bounded cheerily before the toe of my boot. Suddenly we clambered through a gap in a prickly fence. . . .

It was a very clean native compound: and the big native woman, with bare brown legs as thick as bedposts, pursuing on all fours a silver dollar that came rolling out from somewhere, was Mrs. Johnson herself. 'Your man's at home,' said the ex-sergeant, and stepped aside in complete and marked indifference to anything that might follow. Johnson – at home – stood with his back to a native house built on posts and with its walls made of mats. In his left hand he held a banana. Out of the right he dealt another dollar into space. The woman captured this one on the wing, and there and then plumped down on the ground to look at us with greater comfort.

'My man' was sallow of face, grizzled, unshaven, muddy on elbows and back; where the seams of his serge coat yawned you could see his white nakedness. The vestiges of a paper collar encircled his neck. He looked at us with a grave, swaying surprise. 'Where do you come from?' he asked. My heart sank. How could I have been stupid enough to waste energy and time for this?

But having already gone so far I approached a little nearer and declared the purpose of my visit. He would have to come at once with me, sleep on board my ship, and to-morrow, with the first of the ebb, he would give me his assistance in getting my ship down to the sea, without steam. A six-hundred-ton barque, drawing nine feet aft. I proposed to give him eighteen dollars for his local knowledge; and all the time I was speaking he kept on considering attentively the various aspects of the banana, holding first one side up to his eye, then the other.

'You've forgotten to apologise,' he said at last with extreme precision. 'Not being a gentleman yourself, you don't know apparently when you intrude upon a gentleman. I am one. I wish you to understand that when I am in funds I don't work, and now . . .'

I would have pronounced him perfectly sober had he not paused in great concern to try and brush a hole off the knee of his trousers.

'I have money – and friends. Every gentleman has. Perhaps you would like to know my friend? His name is Falk. You could borrow some money. Try to remember. F-A-L-K. Falk.' Abruptly his tone changed. 'A noble heart,' he said muzzily.

'Has Falk been giving you some money?' I asked, appalled by the detailed finish of the dark plot.

'Lent me, my good man, not given me,' he corrected suavely. 'Met me taking the air last evening, and being as usual anxious to oblige — Hadn't you better go to the devil out of my compound?'

And upon this, without other warning, he let fly with the banana, which missed my head and took the constable just under the left eye. He rushed at the miserable Johnson, stammering with fury. They fell. . . . But why dwell on the wretchedness, the breathlessness, the degradation, the senselessness, the weariness, the ridicule and humiliation and – and – the perspiration, of these moments? I dragged the ex-hussar off. He was like a wild beast. It seems he had been greatly annoyed at losing his free afternoon on my account. The garden of his bungalow required his personal attention, and at the slight blow of the banana the brute in him had broken loose. We left Johnson on his back still black in the face, but beginning to kick feebly. Meantime, the big woman had remained sitting on the ground, apparently paralysed with extreme terror.

For half an hour we jolted inside our rolling box, side by side, in profound silence. The ex-sergeant was busy staunching the blood of a long scratch on his cheek. 'I hope you're satisfied,' he said suddenly. 'That's what comes of all that tomfool business. If you hadn't quarrelled with that tugboat skipper over some girl or other, all this wouldn't have happened.'

'You heard *that* story?' I said.

'Of course I heard. And I shouldn't wonder if the Consul-General himself doesn't come to hear of it. How am I to go before him to-morrow with that thing on my cheek – I want to know. It's *you* who ought to have got this!'

After that, till the gharry stopped and he jumped out without leave-taking, he swore to himself steadily, horribly; muttering great, purposeful, trooper oaths, to which the worst a sailor can do is like the prattle of a child. For my part I had just the strength to crawl into Schomberg's coffee-room, where I wrote at a little table a note to the mate instructing him to get everything ready for dropping down the river next day. I couldn't face my ship. Well! she had a clever sort of skipper and no mistake – poor thing! What a horrid mess! I took my head between my hands. At times the obviousness of my innocence would reduce me to despair. What had I done? If I had done something to bring about the situation I should at least have learned not to do it again. But I felt guiltless to the point of imbecility. The room was empty yet; only Schomberg prowled round me goggle-eyed and with a sort of awed respectful curiosity. No doubt he had set the story going himself; but he was a good-hearted chap, and I am really persuaded he participated in all my troubles. He did what he could for me. He ranged aside the heavy matchstand, set a chair straight, pushed a spittoon slightly with his foot – as you show small attentions to a friend under a great sorrow – sighed, and at last, unable to hold his tongue:

'Well! I warned you, captain. That's what comes of running your head against Mr. Falk. Man'll stick at nothing.'

I sat without stirring, and after surveying me with a sort of commiseration in his eyes, he burst out in a hoarse whisper: 'But for a fine lump of a girl, she's a fine lump of a girl.' He made a loud smacking noise with his thick lips. 'The finest lump of a girl that I ever . . .' he was going on with great unction, but for some reason or other broke off. I fancied myself throwing something at his head. 'I don't blame you, captain. Hang me if I do,' he said with a patronising air.

'Thank you,' I said resignedly. It was no use fighting against this false fate. I don't know even if I was sure myself where the truth of the matter began. The conviction that it would end disastrously had been driven into me by all the successive shocks my sense of security had received. I began to ascribe an extraordinary potency to agents in themselves powerless. It was as if Schomberg's baseless gossip had the power to bring about the thing itself or the abstract enmity of Falk could put my ship ashore.

I have already explained how fatal this last would have been. For my further action, my youth, my inexperience, my very real concern for the health of my crew must be my excuse. The action itself, when it came, was purely impulsive. It was set in movement quite undiplomatically and simply by Falk's appearance in the doorway of the coffee-room.

The room was full by then and buzzing with voices. I had been looked at with curiosity by every one, but how am I to describe the sensation produced by the appearance of Falk himself blocking the doorway? The tension of expectation could be measured by the profundity of the silence that fell upon the very click of the billiard balls. As to Schomberg, he looked extremely frightened; he hated mortally any sort of row ('fracas' he called it) in his establishment. 'Fracas' was bad for business, he affirmed; but, in truth, this specimen of portly, middle-aged manhood was of a timid disposition. I don't know what, considering my presence in the place, they all hoped would come of it. A sort of stag fight, perhaps. Or they may have supposed Falk had come in only to annihilate me completely. As a matter of fact, Falk had come in because Hermann had asked him to inquire after the precious white cotton parasol which, in the worry and excitement of the previous day, he had forgotten at the table where we had held our little discussion.

It was this that gave me my opportunity. I don't think I would have gone to seek Falk out. No. I don't think so. There are limits. But there was an opportunity and I seized it – I have already tried to explain why. Now I will merely state that, in my opinion, to get his sickly crew into the sea air and secure a quick despatch for his ship a skipper would be justified in going to any length, short of absolute crime. He should put his pride in his pocket; he may accept confidences; he must explain his innocence as if it were a sin; he may take advantage of misconceptions, of desires and of weaknesses; he ought to conceal his horror and other emotions, and, if the fate of a human being, and that human being a magnificent young girl, is strangely involved – why, he should contemplate that fate (whatever it might seem to be) without turning a hair. And all these things I have done; the explaining, the listening, the pretending – even to the discretion – and nobody, not even Hermann's niece, I believe, need throw stones at me now. Schomberg at all events needn't, since from first to last, I am happy to say, there was not the slightest 'fracas'.

Overcoming a nervous contraction of the windpipe, I had managed to exclaim 'Captain Falk!' His start of surprise was perfectly genuine, but afterwards he neither smiled nor scowled. He simply waited. Then, when I had said, 'I must have a talk with you,' and had pointed to a chair at my table, he moved up to me, though he didn't sit down. Schomberg, however, with a long tumbler in his hand, was making towards us prudently, and I discovered then the only sign of weakness in Falk. He had for Schomberg a repulsion resembling that sort of physical fear some people experience at the sight of a toad. Perhaps to a man so essentially and silently concentrated upon himself (though he could talk well enough, as I was to find out presently) the other's irrepressible loquacity, embracing every human being within range of the tongue, might have appeared unnatural, disgusting, and monstrous. He suddenly gave signs of restiveness – positively like a horse about to rear, and, muttering hurriedly as if in great pain, 'No. I can't stand that fellow,' seemed ready to bolt. This weakness of his gave me the advantage at the very start. 'Verandah,' I suggested, as if rendering him a service, and walked him out by the arm. We stumbled over a few chairs; we had the feeling of open space before us, and felt the fresh breath of the river – fresh, but tainted. The Chinese theatres across the water made, in the sparsely twinkling masses of gloom an Eastern town presents at night, blazing centres of light, and of a distant and howling uproar. I felt him become suddenly tractable again like an animal, like a good-tempered horse when the object that scares him is removed. Yes. I felt in the darkness there how tractable he was, without my conviction of his inflexibility – tenacity, rather, perhaps – being in the least weakened. His very arm abandoning itself to my grasp was as hard as marble – like a limb of iron. But I heard a tumultuous scuffling of boot-soles within. The unspeakable idiots inside were crowding to the windows, climbing over each other's backs behind the blinds, billiard cues and all. Somebody broke a window-pane, and with the sound of falling glass, so suggestive of riot and devastation, Schomberg reeled out after us in a state of funk which had prevented his parting with his brandy and soda. He must have trembled like an aspen leaf. The piece of ice in the long tumbler he held in his hand tinkled with an effect of chattering teeth. 'I beg you, gentlemen,' he expostulated thickly. 'Come! Really, now, I must insist . . .'

How proud I am of my presence of mind! 'Hallo,' I said instantly in a loud and naïve tone, 'somebody's breaking your windows, Schomberg. Would you please tell one of your boys to bring out here a pack of cards and a couple of lights? And two long drinks. Will you?'

To receive an order soothed him at once. It was business. 'Certainly,' he said in an immensely relieved tone. The night was rainy, with wandering gusts of wind, and while we waited for the candles Falk said, as if to justify his panic, 'I don't interfere in anybody's business. I don't give any occasion for talk. I am a respectable man. But this fellow is always making out something wrong, and can never rest till he gets somebody to believe him.'

This was the first of my knowledge of Falk. This desire of respectability, of being like everybody else, was the only recognition he vouchsafed to the organisation of mankind. For the rest he might have been a member of a herd, not of a society. Self-preservation was his only concern. Not selfishness, but mere self-preservation. Selfishness presupposes consciousness, choice, the presence of other men; but his instinct acted as though he were the last of mankind nursing that law like the only spark of a sacred fire. I don't mean to say that living naked in a cavern would have satisfied him. Obviously he was the creature of the conditions to which he was born. No doubt self-preservation meant also the preservation of these conditions. But essentially it meant something much more simple, natural and powerful. How shall I express it? It meant the preservation of the five senses of his body – let us say – taking it in its narrowest as well as in its widest meaning. I think you will admit before long the justice of this judgment. However, as we stood there together in the dark verandah I had judged nothing as yet – and I had no desire to judge – which is an idle practice anyhow. The light was long in coming.

'Of course,' I said in a tone of mutual understanding, 'it isn't exactly a game of cards I want with you.'

I saw him draw his hands down his face – the vague stir of the passionate and meaningless gesture; but he waited in silent patience. It was only when the lights had been brought out that he opened his lips. I understood his mumble to mean that he 'didn't know any game'.

'Like this, Schomberg and all the other fools will have to keep off,' I said, tearing open the pack. 'Have you heard that we are universally supposed to be quarrelling about a girl? You know who – of course. I am really ashamed to ask, but is it possible that you do me the honour to think me dangerous?'

As I said these words I felt how absurd it was and also I felt flattered – for, really, what else could it be? His answer, spoken in his usual dispassionate undertone, made it clear that it was so, but not precisely as flattering as I supposed. He thought me dangerous with Hermann, more than with the girl herself; but, as to quarrelling, I saw at once how inappropriate the word was. We had no quarrel. Natural forces are not quarrelsome. You can't quarrel with the wind that inconveniences and humiliates you by blowing off your hat in a street full of people. He had no quarrel with me. Neither would a boulder, falling on my head, have had. He fell upon me in accordance with the law by which he was moved – not of gravitation, like a detached stone, but of self-preservation.[45] Of course this is giving it a rather wide interpretation. Strictly speaking, he had existed and could have existed without being married. Yet he told me that he had found it more and more difficult to live alone. Yes. He told me this in his low, careless voice; to such a pitch of confidence had we arrived at the end of half an hour.

It took me just about that time to convince him that I had never dreamed of marrying Hermann's niece. Could any necessity have been more extravagant? And the difficulty was the greater because he was so hard hit that he couldn't imagine anybody being able to remain in a state of indifference. Any man with eyes in his head, he seemed to think, could not help coveting so much bodily magnificence. This profound belief was conveyed by the manner he listened sitting sideways to the table and playing absently with a few cards I had dealt to him at random. And the more I saw into him the more I saw of him. The wind swayed the lights so that his sunburnt face, whiskered to the eyes, seemed to successively flicker crimson at me and to go out. I saw the extraordinary breadth of the high cheek-bones, the perpendicular style of the features, the massive forehead, steep like a cliff, denuded at the top, largely uncovered at the temples. The fact is I had never before seen him without his hat; but now, as if my fervour had made him hot, he had taken it off and laid it gently on the floor. Something peculiar in the shape and setting of his yellow eyes gave them the provoking silent intensity which characterised his glance. But the face was thin, furrowed, worn; I discovered that through the bush of his hair, as you may detect the gnarled shape of a tree trunk lost in a dense undergrowth. These overgrown cheeks were sunken. It was an anchorite's bony head fitted with a Capuchin's beard and adjusted to a herculean body. I don't mean athletic. Hercules, I take it, was not an athlete. He was a strong man, susceptible to female charms, and not afraid of dirt. And thus with Falk, who was a strong man. He was extremely strong, just as the girl (since I must think of them together) was magnificently attractive by the masterful power of flesh and blood, expressed in shape, in size, in attitude – that is, by a straight appeal to the senses. His mind, meantime, preoccupied with respectability, quailed before Schomberg's tongue and seemed absolutely impervious to my protestations; and I went so far as to protest that I would just as soon think of marrying my mother's (dear old lady!) faithful female cook as Hermann's niece. Sooner, I protested, in my desperation, much sooner; but it did not appear that he saw anything outrageous in the proposition, and in his sceptical immobility he seemed to nurse the argument that at all events the cook was very, very far away. It must be said that, just before, I had gone wrong by appealing to the evidence of my manner whenever I called on board the *Diana*. I had never attempted to approach the girl, or to speak to her, or even to look at her in any marked way. Nothing could be clearer. But, as his own idea of – let us say – courting seemed to consist precisely in sitting silently for hours in the vicinity of the beloved object, that line of argument inspired him with distrust. Staring down his extended legs he let out a grunt – as much as to say, 'That's all very fine, but you can't throw dust in *my* eyes.'

At last I was exasperated into saying, 'Why don't you put the matter at rest by talking to Hermann?' and I added sneeringly: 'You don't expect me perhaps to speak for you?'

To this he said, very loud for him, 'Would you?'

And for the first time he lifted his head to look at me with wonder and incredulity. He lifted his head so sharply that there could be no mistake. I had touched a spring. I saw the whole extent of my opportunity, and could hardly believe in it.

'Why. Speak to . . . Well, of course,' I proceeded very slowly, watching him with great attention, for, on my word, I feared a joke. 'Not, perhaps, to the young lady herself. I can't speak German, you know. But . . .'

He interrupted me with the earnest assurance that Hermann had the highest opinion of me; and at once I felt the need for the greatest possible diplomacy at this juncture. So I demurred just enough to draw him on. Falk sat up, but except for a very noticeable enlargement of the pupils, till the irises of his eyes were reduced to two narrow yellow rings, his face, I should judge, was incapable of expressing excitement. 'Oh, yes! Hermann did have the greatest . . .'

'Take up your cards. Here's Schomberg peeping at us through the blind!' I said.

We went through the motions of what might have been a game of écarté. Presently the intolerable scandalmonger withdrew, probably to inform the people in the billiard-room that we two were gambling on the verandah like mad.

We were not gambling, but it was a game; a game in which I felt I held the winning cards. The stake, roughly speaking, was the success of the voyage – for me; and he, I apprehended, had nothing to lose. Our intimacy matured rapidly, and before many words had been exchanged I perceived that the excellent Hermann had been making use of me. That simple and astute Teuton had been, it seems, holding me up to Falk in the light of a rival. I was young enough to be shocked at so much duplicity. 'Did he tell you that in so many words?' I asked with indignation.

Hermann had not. He had given hints only; and of course it had not taken very much to alarm Falk; but, instead of declaring himself, he had taken steps to remove the family from under my influence. He was perfectly straightforward about it – as straightforward as a tile falling on your head. There was no duplicity in that man; and when I congratulated him on the perfection of his arrangements – even to the bribing of the wretched Johnson against me – he had a genuine movement of protest. Never bribed. He knew the man wouldn't work as long as he had a few cents in his pocket to get drunk on, and, naturally, (he said – '*naturally*') he let him have a dollar or two. He was himself a sailor, he said, and anticipated the view another sailor, like myself, was bound to take. On the other hand, he was sure that I should have to come to grief. He hadn't been knocking about for the last seven years up and down that river for nothing. It would have been no disgrace to me – but he asserted confidently I would have had my ship very awkwardly ashore at a spot two miles below the Great Pagoda. . . .

And with all that he had no ill-will. That was evident. This was a crisis in which his only object had been to gain time – I fancy. And presently he mentioned that he had written for some jewellery, real good jewellery – had written to Hong Kong for it. It would arrive in a day or two.

'Well, then,' I said cheerily, 'everything is all right. All you've got to do is to present it to the lady together with your heart, and live happy ever after.'

Upon the whole he seemed to accept that view as far as the girl was concerned, but his eyelids drooped. There was still something in the way. For one thing Hermann disliked him so much. As to me, on the contrary, it seemed as though he could not praise me enough. Mrs. Hermann too. He didn't know why they disliked him so. It made everything most difficult.

I listened impassive, feeling more and more diplomatic. His speech was not transparently clear. He was one of those men who seem to live, feel, suffer in a sort of mental twilight. But as to being fascinated by the girl and possessed by the desire of home life with her – it was as clear as daylight. So much being at stake, he was afraid of putting it to the hazard of the declaration. Besides, there was something else. And with Hermann being so set against him . . .

'I see,' I said thoughtfully, while my heart beat fast with the excitement of my diplomacy. 'I don't mind sounding Hermann. In fact, to show you how mistaken you were, I am ready to do all I can for you in that way.'

A light sigh escaped him. He drew his hands down his face, and it emerged, bony, unchanged of expression, as if all the tissues had been ossified. All the passion was in those big brown hands. He was satisfied. Then there was that other matter. If there were anybody on earth it was I who could persuade Hermann to take a reasonable view! I had a knowledge of the world and lots of experience. Hermann admitted this himself. And then I was a sailor, too. Falk thought that a sailor would be able to understand certain things best. . . .

He talked as if the Hermanns had been living all their life in a rural hamlet, and I alone had been capable, with my practice in life, of a large and indulgent view of certain occurrences. That was what my diplomacy was leading me to. I began suddenly to dislike it.

'I say, Falk,' I asked quite brusquely, 'you haven't already a wife put away somewhere?'

The pain and disgust of his denial were very striking. Couldn't I understand that he was as respectable as any white man here-abouts; earning his living honestly. He was suffering from my suspicion, and the low undertone of his voice made his prot-estations sound very pathetic. For a moment he shamed me, but, my diplomacy notwithstanding, I seemed to develop a conscience, as if in very truth it were in my power to decide the success of this matrimonial enterprise. By pretending hard enough we come to believe anything – anything to our advantage. And I had been pretending very hard, because I meant yet to be towed safely down the river. But, through conscience or stupidity, I couldn't help alluding to the Vanlo affair. 'You acted rather badly there. Didn't you?' was what I ventured actually to say – for the logic of our conduct is always at the mercy of obscure and unforeseen impulses.

His dilated pupils swerved from my face, glancing at the window with a sort of scared fury. We heard behind the blinds the continuous and sudden clicking of ivory, a jovial murmur of many voices, and Schomberg's deep manly laugh.

'That confounded old woman of a hotel-keeper then would never, never let it rest!' Falk exclaimed. Well, yes! It had happened two years ago. When it came to the point he owned he couldn't make up his mind to trust Fred Vanlo – no sailor, a bit of a fool too. He could not trust him, but, to stop his row, he had lent him enough money to pay all his debts before he left. I was greatly surprised to hear this. Then Falk could not be such a miser after all. So much the better for the girl. For a time he sat silent; then he picked up a card, and while looking at it he said:

'You need not think of anything bad. It was an accident. I've been unfortunate once.'

'Then in heaven's name say nothing about it.'

As soon as these words were out of my mouth I fancied I had said something immoral. He shook his head negatively. It had to be told. He considered it proper that the relations of the lady should know. No doubt – I thought to myself – had Miss Vanlo not been thirty and damaged by the climate he would have found it possible to entrust Fred Vanlo with this confidence. And then the figure of Hermann's niece appeared before my mind's eye, with the wealth of her opulent form, her rich youth, her lavish strength. With that powerful and immaculate vitality, her girlish form must have shouted aloud of life to that man, whereas poor Miss Vanlo could only sing sentimental songs to the strumming of a piano.

'And that Hermann hates me, I know it!' he cried in his undertone, with a sudden recrudescence of anxiety. 'I must tell them. It is proper that they should know. You would say so yourself.'

He then murmured an utterly mysterious allusion to the necessity for peculiar domestic arrangements. Though my curiosity was excited I did not want to hear any of his confidences. I feared he might give me a piece of information that would make my assumed *rôle* of a match-maker odious – however unreal it was. I was aware that he could have the girl for the asking; and keeping down a desire to laugh in his face, I expressed a confident belief in my ability to argue away Hermann's dislike for him. 'I am sure I can make it all right,' I said. He looked very pleased.

And when we rose not a word had been said about towage! Not

a word! The game was won and the honour was safe. Oh! blessed white cotton umbrella! We shook hands, and I was holding myself with difficulty from breaking into a step-dance of joy when he came back, striding all the length of the verandah, and said doubtfully:

'I say, captain, I have your word? You – you – won't turn round?'

Heavens! The fright he gave me. Behind his tone of doubt there was something desperate and menacing. The infatuated ass. But I was equal to the situation.

'My dear Falk,' I said, beginning to lie with a glibness and effrontery that amazed me even at the time – 'confidence for confidence.' (He had made no confidences.) 'I will tell you that I am already engaged to an extremely charming girl at home, and so you understand . . .'

He caught my hand and wrung it in a crushing grip.

'Pardon me. I feel it every day more difficult to live alone . . .'

'On rice and fish,' I interrupted smartly, giggling with the sheer nervousness of a danger escaped.

He dropped my hand as if it had become suddenly red-hot. A moment of profound silence ensued, as though something extraordinary had happened.

'I promise you to obtain Hermann's consent,' I faltered out at last, and it seemed to me that he could not help seeing through that humbugging promise. 'If there's anything else to get over I shall endeavour to stand by you,' I conceded further, feeling somehow defeated and overborne; 'but you must do your best yourself.'

'I have been unfortunate once,' he muttered unemotionally, and turning his back on me he went away, thumping slowly the plank floor as if his feet had been shod with iron.

Next morning, however, he was lively enough as man-boat, a combination of splashing and shouting; of the insolent commotion below with the steady overbearing glare of the silent head-piece above. He turned us out most unnecessarily at an ungodly hour, but it was nearly eleven in the morning before he brought me up a cable's length from Hermann's ship. And he did it very badly too, in a hurry, and nearly contriving to miss altogether the patch of good holding ground, because, forsooth, he had caught sight of

Hermann's niece on the poop. And so did I; and probably as soon as he had seen her himself. I saw the modest, sleek glory of the tawny head, and the full, grey shape of the girlish print frock she filled so perfectly, so satisfactorily, with the seduction of unfaltering curves – a very nymph of Diana the Huntress. And *Diana* the ship sat, high-walled and as solid as an institution, on the smooth level of the water, the most uninspiring and respectable craft upon the seas, useful and ugly, devoted to the support of domestic virtues like any grocer's shop on shore. At once Falk steamed away; for there was some work for him to do. He would return in the evening.

He ranged close by us, passing out dead slow, without a hail. The beat of the paddle-wheels reverberating amongst the stony islets, as if from the ruined walls of a vast arena, filled the anchorage confusedly with the clapping sounds of a mighty and leisurely applause. Abreast of Hermann's ship he stopped the engines; and a profound silence reigned over the rocks, the shore and the sea, for the time it took him to raise his hat aloft before the nymph of the grey print frock. I had snatched up my binoculars, and I can answer for it she didn't stir a limb, standing by the rail shapely and erect, with one of her hands grasping a rope at the height of her head, while the way of the tug carried slowly past her the lingering and profound homage of the man. There was for me an enormous significance in the scene, the sense of having witnessed a solemn declaration. The die was cast. After such a manifestation he couldn't back out. And I reflected that it was nothing whatever to me now. With a rush of black smoke belching suddenly out of the funnel, and a mad swirl of paddle-wheels provoking a burst of weird and precipitated clapping, the tug shot out of the desolate arena. The rocky islets lay on the sea like the heaps of a cyclopean ruin on a plain; the centipedes and scorpions lurked under the stones; there was not a single blade of grass in sight anywhere, not a single lizard sunning himself on a boulder by the shore. When I looked again at Hermann's ship the girl had disappeared. I could not detect the smallest dot of a bird on the immense sky, and the flatness of the land continued the flatness of the sea to the naked line of the horizon.

This is the setting now inseparably connected with my knowledge of Falk's misfortune. My diplomacy had brought me there, and now I had only to wait the time for taking up the *rôle* of an ambassador. My diplomacy was a success; my ship was safe; old Gambril would probably live; a feeble sound of a tapping hammer came intermittently from the *Diana*. During the afternoon I had looked at times at the old homely ship, the faithful nurse of Hermann's progeny, or yawned towards the distant temple of Buddha, like a lonely hillock on the plain, where shaven priests cherish the thoughts of that Annihilation which is the worthy reward of us all. Unfortunate! He had been unfortunate once. Well, that was not so bad as life goes. And what the devil could be the nature of that misfortune? I remembered that I had known a man before who had declared himself to have fallen, years ago, a victim to misfortune; but this misfortune, whose effects appeared permanent (he looked desperately hard up) when considered dispassionately, seemed indistinguishable from a breach of trust. Could it be something of that nature? Apart, however, from the utter improbability that he would offer to talk of it even to his future uncle-in-law I had a strange feeling that Falk's physique unfitted him for that sort of delinquency. As the person of Hermann's niece exhaled the profound physical charm of feminine form, so her adorer's big frame embodied to my senses the hard, straight masculinity that would conceivably kill but would not condescend to cheat. The thing was obvious. I might just as well have suspected the girl of a curvature of the spine. And I perceived that the sun was about to set.

The smoke of Falk's tug hove in sight, far away at the mouth of the river. It was time for me to assume the character of an ambassador, and the negotiation would not be difficult except in the matter of keeping my countenance. It was all too extravagantly nonsensical, and I conceived that it would be best to compose for myself a grave demeanour. I practised this in my boat as I went along, but the bashfulness that came secretly upon me the moment I stepped on the deck of the *Diana* is inexplicable. As soon as we had exchanged greetings Hermann asked me eagerly if I knew whether Falk had found his white parasol.

'He's going to bring it to you himself directly,' I said with great solemnity. 'Meantime I am charged with an important message for which he begs your favourable consideration. He is in love with your niece. . . .'

'*Ach so!*' he hissed with an animosity that made my assumed gravity change into the most genuine concern. What meant this tone? And I hurried on.

'He wishes, with your consent of course, to ask her to marry him at once – before you leave here, that is. He would speak to the Consul.'

Hermann sat down and smoked violently. Five minutes passed in that furious meditation, and then, taking the long pipe out of his mouth, he burst into a hot diatribe against Falk – against his cupidity, his stupidity (a fellow that can hardly be got to say 'yes' or 'no' to the simplest question) – against his outrageous treatment of the shipping in port (because he saw they were at his mercy) – and against his manner of walking, which to his (Hermann's) mind showed a conceit positively unbearable. The damage to the old *Diana* was not forgotten, of course, and there was nothing of any nature said or done by Falk (even to the last offer of refreshment in the hotel) that did not seem to have been a cause of offence. 'Had the cheek' to drag him (Hermann) into that coffee room; as though a drink from him could make up for forty-seven dollars and fifty cents of damage in the cost of wood alone – not counting two days' work for the carpenter. Of course he would not stand in the girl's way. He was going home to Germany. There were plenty of poor girls walking about in Germany.

'He's very much in love,' was all I found to say.

'Yes,' he cried. 'And it is time, too, after making himself and me talked about ashore that last voyage I was here, and then now again; coming on board every evening unsettling the girl's mind, and saying nothing. What sort of conduct is that?'

The seven thousand dollars the fellow was always talking about did not, in his opinion, justify such behaviour. Moreover, nobody had seen them. He (Hermann) seriously doubted if there were seven thousand cents, and the tug, no doubt, was mortgaged up to the top of the funnel to the firm of Siegers. But let that pass. He wouldn't stand in the girl's way. Her head was so turned that she had become no good to them of late. Quite unable even to put the children to bed without her aunt. It was bad for the children; they got unruly; and yesterday he actually had to give Gustav a thrashing.

For that, too, Falk was made responsible apparently. And looking at my Hermann's heavy, puffy, good-natured face, I knew he would not exert himself till greatly exasperated, and, therefore, would thrash very hard, and being fat would resent the necessity. How Falk had managed to turn the girl's head was more difficult to understand. I supposed Hermann would know. And then hadn't there been Miss Vanlo? It could not be his silvery tongue, or the subtle seduction of his manner; he had no more of what is called 'manner' than an animal – which, however, on the other hand is never, and can never be called, vulgar. Therefore it must have been his bodily appearance, exhibiting a virility of nature as exaggerated as his beard, and resembling a sort of constant ruthlessness. It was seen in the very manner he lolled in the chair. He meant no offence, but his intercourse was characterised by that sort of frank disregard of susceptibilities a man of seven-foot six, living in a world of dwarfs, would naturally assume, without in the least wishing to be unkind. But amongst men of his own stature, or nearly, this frank use of his advantages, in such matters as the awful towage bills for instance, caused much impotent gnashing of teeth. When attentively considered it seemed appalling at times. He was a strange beast. But maybe women liked it. Seen in that light he was well worth taming, and I suppose every woman at the bottom of her heart considers herself as a tamer of strange beasts. But Hermann arose with precipitation to carry the news to his wife. I had barely the time, as he made for the cabin door, to grab him by the seat of his inexpressibles. I begged him to wait till Falk in person had spoken with him. There remained some small matter to talk over, as I understood.

He sat down again at once, full of suspicion.

'What matter?' he said surlily. 'I have had enough of his nonsense. There's no matter at all, as he knows very well; the girl has nothing in the world. She came to us in one thin dress when my brother died, and I have a growing family.'

'It can't be anything of that kind,' I opined. 'He's desperately enamoured of your niece. I don't know why he did not say so before. Upon my word, I believe it is because he was afraid to lose, perhaps, the felicity of sitting near her on your quarter deck.'

I intimated my conviction that his love was so great as to be in a sense cowardly. The effects of a great passion are unaccountable. It has been known to make a man timid. But Hermann looked at me as if I had foolishly raved; and the twilight was dying out rapidly.

'You don't believe in passion, do you, Hermann?' I said cheerily. 'The passion of fear will make a cornered rat courageous. Falk's in a corner. He will take her off your hands in one thin frock just as she came to you. And after ten years' service it isn't a bad bargain,' I added.

Far from taking offence, he resumed his air of civic virtue. The sudden night came upon him while he stared placidly along the deck, bringing in contact with his thick lips, and taking away again after a jet of smoke, the curved mouthpiece fitted to the stem of his pipe. The night came upon him and buried in haste his whiskers, his globular eyes, his puffy pale face, his fat knees and the vast flat slippers on his fatherly feet. Only his short arms in respectable white shirt-sleeves remained very visible, propped up like the flippers of a seal reposing upon the strand.

'Falk wouldn't settle anything about repairs. Told me to find out first how much wood I should require and he would see,' he remarked; and after he had spat peacefully in the dusk we heard over the water the beat of the tug's floats. There is, on a calm night, nothing more suggestive of fierce and headlong haste than the rapid sound made by the paddle-wheels of a boat threshing her way through a quiet sea; and the approach of Falk towards his fate seemed to be urged by an impatient and passionate desire. The engines must have been driven to the very utmost of their revolutions. We heard them slow down at last, and, vaguely, the white hull of the tug appeared moving against the black islets, whilst a slow and rhythmical clapping as of thousands of hands rose on all sides. It ceased all at once, just before Falk brought her up. A single brusque splash was followed by the long-drawn rumbling of iron links running through the hawse pipe. Then a solemn silence fell upon the Roadstead.

'He will soon be here,' I murmured, and after that we waited for him without a word. Meantime, raising my eyes, I beheld the glitter of a lofty sky above the *Diana*'s mastheads. The multitude of stars gathered into clusters, in rows, in lines, in masses, in groups, shone all together, unanimously – and the few isolated ones, blazing by themselves in the midst of dark patches, seemed to be of a superior kind and of an inextinguishable nature. But long striding footsteps were heard hastening along the deck; the high bulwarks of the *Diana* made a deeper darkness. We rose from our chairs quickly, and Falk, appearing before us, all in white, stood still.

Nobody spoke at first, as though we had been covered with confusion. His arrival was fiery, but his white bulk, of indefinite shape and without features, made him loom up like a man of snow.

'The captain here has been telling me . . .' Hermann began in a homely and amicable voice; and Falk had a low, nervous laugh. His cool, negligent undertone had no inflexions, but the strength of a powerful emotion made him ramble in his speech. He had always desired a home. It was difficult to live alone, though he was not answerable. He was domestic; there had been difficulties; but since he had seen Hermann's niece he found that it had become at last impossible to live by himself. 'I mean – impossible,' he repeated with no sort of emphasis and only with the slightest of pauses, but the word fell into my mind with the force of a new idea.

'I have not said anything to her yet,' Hermann observed quietly. And Falk dismissed this by a 'That's all right. Certainly. Very proper.' There was necessity for perfect frankness – in marrying, especially. Hermann seemed attentive, but he seized the first opportunity to ask us into the cabin. 'And by-the-by, Falk,' he said innocently, as we passed in, 'the timber came to no less than forty-seven dollars and fifty cents.'

Falk, uncovering his head, lingered in the passage. 'Some other time,' he said; and Hermann nudged me angrily – I don't know why. The girl alone in the cabin sat sewing at some distance from the table. Falk stopped short in the doorway. Without a word, without a sign, without the slightest inclination of his bony head, by the silent intensity of his look alone, he seemed to lay his herculean frame at her feet. Her hands sank slowly on her lap, and raising her clear eyes, she let her soft, beaming glance enfold him from head to foot like a slow and pale caress. He was very hot when he sat down; she, with bowed head, went on with her sewing; her neck was very white under the light of the lamp; but Falk, hiding his face in the palms of his hands, shuddered faintly. He drew them down, even to his beard, and his uncovered eyes astonished me by their tense and irrational expression – as though he had just swallowed a heavy gulp of alcohol. It passed away while he was binding us to secrecy. Not that he cared, but he did not like to be spoken about; and I looked at the girl's marvellous, at her wonderful, at her regal hair, plaited tight into that one astonishing and maidenly tress. Whenever she moved her well-shaped head it would stir stiffly to and fro on her back. The thin cotton sleeve fitted the irreproachable roundness of her arm like a skin; and her very dress, stretched on her bust, seemed to palpitate like a living tissue with the strength of vitality animating her body. How good her complexion was, the outline of her soft cheek and the small convoluted conch of her rosy ear! To pull her needle she kept the little finger apart from the others; it seemed a waste of power to see her sewing – eternally sewing – with that industrious and precise movement of her arm, going on eternally upon all the oceans, under all the skies, in innumerable harbours. And suddenly I heard Falk's voice declare that he could not marry a woman unless she knew of something in his life that had happened ten years ago. It was an accident. An unfortunate accident. It would affect the domestic arrangements of their home, but, once told, it need not be alluded to again for the rest of their lives. 'I should want my wife to feel for me,' he said. 'It has made me unhappy.' And how could he keep the knowledge of it to himself – he asked us – perhaps through years and years of companionship? What sort of companionship would that be? He had thought it over. A wife must know. Then why not at once? He counted on Hermann's kindness for presenting the affair in the best possible light. And Hermann's countenance, mystified before, became very sour. He stole an inquisitive glance at me. I shook my head blankly. Some people thought, Falk went on, that such an experience changed a man for the rest of his life. He couldn't say. It was hard, awful, and not to be forgotten, but he did not think himself a worse man than before. Only he talked in his sleep now, he believed. . . . At last I began to think he had accidentally killed someone; perhaps a friend – his own father maybe; when he went on to say that probably we were aware he never touched meat. Throughout he spoke English, of course, on my account.

He swayed forward heavily.

The girl, with her hands raised before her pale eyes, was threading her needle. He glanced at her, and his mighty trunk over-shadowed the table, bringing nearer to us the breadth of his shoulders, the thickness of his neck, and that incongruous, anchorite head, burnt in the desert, hollowed and lean as if by excesses of vigils and fasting. His beard flowed imposingly downwards, out of sight, between the two brown hands gripping the edge of the table, and his persistent glance made sombre by the wide dilations of the pupils, fascinated.

'Imagine to yourself,' he said in his ordinary voice, 'that I have eaten man.'[46]

I could only ejaculate a faint 'Ah!' of complete enlightenment. But Hermann, dazed by the excessive shock, actually murmured, '*Himmel!* What for?'

'It was my terrible misfortune to do so,' said Falk in a measured undertone. The girl, unconscious, sewed on. Mrs. Hermann was absent in one of the staterooms, sitting up with Lena, who was feverish; but Hermann suddenly put both his hands up with a jerk. The embroidered calotte fell, and, in the twinkling of an eye, he had rumpled his hair all ends up in a most extravagant manner. In this state he strove to speak; with every effort his eyes seemed to start further out of their sockets; his head looked like a mop. He choked, gasped, swallowed, and managed to shriek out the one word, 'Beast!'

From that moment till Falk went out of the cabin the girl, with her hands folded on the work lying in her lap, never took her eyes off him. His own, in the blindness of his heart, darted all over the cabin, only seeking to avoid the sight of Hermann's raving. It was ridiculous, and was made almost terrible by the stillness of every other person present. It was contemptible, and was made appalling by the man's overmastering horror of this awful sincerity, coming to him suddenly, with the confession of such a fact. He walked with great strides; he gasped. He wanted to know from Falk how dared he to come and tell him this? Did he think himself a proper person to be sitting in this cabin where his wife and children lived? Tell his niece! Expected him to tell his niece! His own brother's daughter! Shameless! Did I ever hear tell of such impudence! – he appealed to me. 'This man here ought to have gone and hidden himself out of sight instead of . . .'

'But it's a great misfortune for me. But it's a great misfortune for me,' Falk would ejaculate from time to time.

However, Hermann kept on running frequently against the

corners of the table. At last he lost a slipper, and crossing his arms on his breast, walked up with one stocking foot very close to Falk, in order to ask him whether he did think there was anywhere on earth a woman abandoned enough to mate with such a monster. 'Did he? Did he? Did he?' I tried to restrain him. He tore himself out of my hands; he found his slipper, and, endeavouring to put it on, stormed standing on one leg – and Falk, with a face unmoved and averted eyes, grasped all his mighty beard in one vast palm.

'Was it right then for me to die myself?' he asked thoughtfully. I laid my hand on his shoulder.

'Go away,' I whispered imperiously, without any clear reason for this advice, except that I wished to put an end to Hermann's odious noise. 'Go away.'

He looked searchingly for a moment at Hermann before he made a move. I left the cabin too to see him out of the ship. But he hung about the quarter-deck.

'It is my misfortune,' he said in a steady voice.

'You were stupid to blurt it out in such a manner. After all, we don't hear such confidences every day.'

'What does the man mean?' he mused in deep undertones. 'Somebody had to die – but why me?'

He remained still for a time in the dark – silent; almost invisible. All at once he pinned my elbows to my sides. I felt utterly powerless in his grip, and his voice, whispering in my ear, vibrated.

'It's worse than hunger. Captain, do you know what that means? And I could kill then – or be killed. I wish the crowbar had smashed my skull ten years ago. And I've got to live now. Without her. Do you understand? Perhaps many years. But how? What can be done? If I had allowed myself to look at her once I would have carried her off before that man in my hands – like this.'

I felt myself snatched off the deck, then suddenly dropped – and I staggered backwards, feeling bewildered and bruised. What a man! All was still; he was gone. I heard Hermann's voice declaiming in the cabin, and I went in.

I could not at first make out a single word, but Mrs. Hermann, who, attracted, by the noise, had come in some time before, with an expression of surprise and mild disapproval depicted broadly on her face, was giving now all the signs of profound, helpless agitation. Her husband shot a string of guttural words at her, and instantly putting out one hand to the bulkhead as if to save herself from falling, she clutched the loose bosom of her dress with the other. He harangued the two women extraordinarily, with much of his shirt hanging out of his waistbelt, stamping his foot, turning from one to the other, sometimes throwing both his arms together, straight up above his rumpled hair, and keeping them in that position while he uttered a passage of loud denunciation; at others folding them tight across his breast – and then he hissed with indignation, elevating his shoulders and protruding his head. The girl was crying.

She had not changed her attitude. From her steady eyes that, following Falk in his retreat, had remained fixed wistfully on the cabin door, the tears fell rapid, thick, on her hands, on the work in her lap, warm and gentle like a shower in spring. She wept without grimacing, without noise – very touching, very quiet, with something more of pity than of pain in her face, as one weeps in compassion rather than in grief – and Hermann, before her, declaimed. I caught several times the word *'Mensch'*, man; and also *'Fressen'*, which last I looked up afterwards in my dictionary. It means 'Devour'. Hermann seemed to be requesting an answer of some sort from her; his whole body swayed. She remained mute and perfectly still; at last his agitation gained her; she put the palms of her hands together, her full lips parted, no sound came. His voice scolded shrilly, his arms went like a windmill – suddenly he shook a thick fist at her. She burst out into loud sobs. He seemed stupefied.

Mrs. Hermann rushed forward babbling rapidly. The two women fell on each other's necks, and, with an arm round her niece's waist, she led her away. Her own eyes were simply streaming, her face was flooded. She shook her head back at me negatively, I wonder why to this day. The girl's head dropped heavily on her shoulder. They disappeared together.

Then Hermann sat down and stared at the cabin floor.

'We don't know all the circumstances,' I ventured to break the silence. He retorted tartly that he didn't want to know of any. According to his ideas no circumstances could excuse a crime – and certainly not such a crime. This was the opinion generally received. The duty of a human being was to starve. Falk therefore was a beast, an animal; base, low, vile, despicable, shameless, and deceitful. He had been deceiving him since last year. He was, however, inclined to think that Falk must have gone mad quite recently; for no sane person, without necessity, uselessly, for no earthly reason, and regardless of another's self-respect and peace of mind, would own to having devoured human flesh. 'Why tell?' he cried. 'Who was asking him?' It showed Falk's brutality because after all he had selfishly caused him (Hermann) much pain. He would have preferred not to know that such an unclean creature had been in the habit of caressing his children. He hoped I would say nothing of all this ashore, though. He wouldn't like it to get about that he had been intimate with an eater of men – a common cannibal. As to the scene he had made (which I judged quite unnecessary) he was not going to inconvenience and restrain himself for a fellow that went about courting and upsetting girls' heads, while he knew all the time that no decent housewifely girl could think of marrying him. At least he (Hermann) could not conceive how any girl could. 'Fancy Lena! . . . No, it was impossible. The thoughts that would come into their heads every time they sat down to a meal. Horrible! Horrible!'

'You are too squeamish, Hermann,' I said.

He seemed to think it was eminently proper to be squeamish if the word meant disgust at Falk's conduct; and turning up his eyes sentimentally he drew my attention to the horrible fate of the victims – the victims of that Falk. I said that I knew nothing about them. He seemed surprised. Could not anybody imagine without knowing? He – for instance – felt he would like to avenge them. But what if – said I – there had not been any? They might have died as it were, naturally – of starvation. He shuddered. But to be eaten – after death! To be devoured! He gave another deep shudder, and asked suddenly, 'Do you think it is true?'

His indignation and his personality together would have been enough to spoil the reality of the most authentic thing. When I looked at him I doubted the story – but the remembrance of Falk's words, looks, gestures, invested it not only with an air of reality but with the absolute truth of primitive passion.

'It is true just as much as you are able to make it; and exactly in the way you like to make it. For my part, when I hear you clamouring about it, I don't believe it is true at all.'

And I left him pondering. The men in my boat, lying at the foot of the *Diana*'s side-ladder, told me that the captain of the tug had gone away in his gig some time ago.

I let my fellows pull an easy stroke; because of the heavy dew the clear sparkle of the stars seemed to fall on me cold and wetting. There was a sense of lurking gruesome horror somewhere in my mind, and it was mingled with clear and grotesque images. Schomberg's gastronomic tittle-tattle was responsible for these; and I half hoped I should never see Falk again. But the first thing my anchorwatchman told me was that the captain of the tug was on board. He had sent his boat away and was now waiting for me in the cuddy.

He was lying full length on the stern settee, his face buried in the cushions. I had expected to see it discomposed, contorted, despairing. It was nothing of the kind; it was just as I had seen it twenty times, steady and glaring from the bridge of the tug. It was immovably set and hungry, dominated like the whole man by the singleness of one instinct.

He wanted to live. He had always wanted to live. So we all do – but in us the instinct serves a complex conception, and in him this instinct existed alone. There is in such simple development a gigantic force, and like the pathos of a child's naïve and uncontrolled desire. He wanted that girl, and the utmost that can be said for him was that he wanted that particular girl alone. I think I saw then the obscure beginning, the seed germinating in the soil of an unconscious need, the first shoot of that tree bearing now for a mature mankind the flower and the fruit, the infinite gradation in shades and in flavour of our discriminating love. He was a child. He was as frank as a child too. He was hungry for the girl, terribly hungry, as he had been terribly hungry for food.

Don't be shocked if I declare that in my belief it was the same need, the same pain, the same torture. We are in his case allowed to contemplate the foundation of all the emotions – that one joy which is to live, and the one sadness at the root of the innumerable torments. It was made plain by the way he talked. He had never suffered so. It was gnawing, it was fire; it was there, like this! And after pointing below his breastbone, he made a hard wringing motion with his hands. And I assure you that, seen as I saw it with my bodily eyes, it was anything but laughable. And again, as he was presently to tell me (alluding to an early incident of the disastrous voyage when some damaged meat had been flung overboard), he said that a time soon came when his heart ached (that was the expression he used), and he was ready to tear his hair out at the thought of all that rotten beef thrown away.

I had heard all this; I witnessed his physical struggles, seeing the working of the rack and hearing the true voice of pain. I witnessed it all patiently, because the moment I came into the cuddy he had called upon me to stand by him – and this, it seems, I had diplomatically promised.

His agitation was impressive and alarming in the little cabin, like the floundering of a great whale driven into a shallow cove in a coast. He stood up; he flung himself down headlong; he tried to tear the cushion with his teeth; and again hugging it fiercely to his face he let himself fall on the couch. The whole ship seemed to feel the shock of his despair; and I contemplated with wonder the lofty forehead, the noble touch of time on the uncovered temples, the unchanged hungry character of the face – so strangely ascetic and so incapable of portraying emotion.

What should he do? He had lived by being near her. He had sat – in the evening – I knew? – all his life! She sewed. Her head was bent – so. Her head – like this – and her arms. Ah! Had I seen? Like this.

He dropped on a stool, bowed his powerful neck whose nape was red, and with his hands stitched the air, ludicrous, sublimely imbecile and comprehensible.

And now he couldn't have her? No! That was too much. After thinking too that . . . What had he done? What was my advice? Take her by force? No? Mustn't he? Who was there then to kill him? For the first time I saw one of his features move; a fighting teeth-baring curl of the lip. . . . 'Not Hermann, perhaps.' He lost himself in thought as though he had fallen out of the world.

I may note that the idea of suicide apparently did not enter his head for a single moment. It occurred to me to ask:

'Where was it that this shipwreck of yours took place?'

'Down south,' he said vaguely with a start.

'You are not down south now,' I said. 'Violence won't do. They would take her away from you in no time. And what was the name of the ship?'

'*Borgmester Dahl*,' he said. 'It was no shipwreck.'

He seemed to be waking up by degrees from that trance, and waking up calmed.

'Not a shipwreck? What was it?'

'Break-down,' he answered, looking more like himself every moment. By this only I learned that it was a steamer. I had till then supposed they had been starving in boats or on a raft – or perhaps on a barren rock.

'She did not sink, then?' I asked in surprise. He nodded. 'We sighted the southern ice,' he pronounced dreamily.

'And you alone survived?'

He sat down. 'Yes. It was a terrible misfortune for me. Everything went wrong. All the men went wrong. I survived.'

Remembering the things one reads of it was difficult to realise the true meaning of his answers. I ought to have seen at once – but I did not; so difficult is it for our minds, remembering so much, instructed so much, informed of so much, to get in touch with the real actuality at our elbow. And with my head full of preconceived notions as to how a case of 'cannibalism and suffering at sea' should be managed I said – 'You were then so lucky in the drawing of lots?'

'Drawing of lots?' he said. 'What lots? Do you think I would have allowed my life to go for the drawing of lots?'

Not if he could help it, I perceived, no matter what other life went.

'It was a great misfortune. Terrible. Awful,' he said. 'Many heads went wrong, but the best men would live.'

'The toughest, you mean,' I said. He considered the word. Perhaps it was strange to him, though his English was so good.

'Yes,' he asserted at last. 'The best. It was everybody for himself at last and the ship open to all.'

Thus from question to question I got the whole story. I fancy it was the only way I could that night have stood by him. Outwardly at least he was himself again; the first sign of it was the return of that incongruous trick he had of drawing both his hands down his face – and it had its meaning now, with that slight shudder of the frame, and the passionate anguish of these hands uncovering a hungry immovable face, the wide pupils of the intent, silent, fascinating eyes.

It was an iron steamer of a most respectable origin. The burgomaster of Falk's native town had built her. She was the first steamer ever launched there. The burgomaster's daughter had christened her. Country people drove in carts from miles around to see her. He told me all this. He got the berth as what we should call a chief mate. He seemed to think it had been a feather in his cap; and, in his own corner of the world, this lover of life was of good parentage.

The burgomaster had advanced ideas in the ship-owning line. At that time not everyone would have known enough to think of despatching a cargo steamer to the Pacific. But he loaded her with pitch-pine deals and sent her off to hunt for her luck. Wellington was to be the first port, I fancy. It doesn't matter, because in latitude 44° south and somewhere halfway between Good Hope and New Zealand the tail-shaft broke and the propeller dropped off.

They were steaming then with a fresh gale on the quarter and all their canvas set, to help the engines. But by itself the sail power was not enough to keep way on her. When the propeller went the ship broached-to at once, and the masts got whipped overboard.

The disadvantage of being dismasted consisted in this, that they had nothing to hoist flags on to make themselves visible at a distance. In the course of the first few days several ships failed to sight them; and the gale was drifting them out of the usual track. The voyage had been, from the first, neither very successful nor very harmonious. They had been quarrels on board. The captain was a clever, melancholic man, who had no unusual grip on his crew. The ship had been amply provisioned for the passage, but, somehow or other, several barrels of meat were found spoiled on opening, and had been thrown overboard soon after leaving home, as a sanitary measure. Afterwards the crew of the *Borgmester Dahl* thought of that rotten carrion with tears of regret, covetousness and despair.

She drove south. To begin with, there had been an appearance of organisation, but soon the bonds of discipline became relaxed. A sombre idleness succeeded. They looked with sullen eyes at the horizon. The gales increased: she lay in the trough, the seas made a clean breach over her. On one frightful night, when they expected their hulk to turn over with them every moment, a heavy sea broke on board, deluged the store-rooms and spoiled the best part of the remaining provisions. It seems the hatch had not been properly secured. This instance of neglect is characteristic of utter discouragement. Falk tried to inspire some energy in his captain, but failed. From that time he retired more into himself, always trying to do his utmost in the situation. It grew worse. Gale succeeded gale, with black mountains of water hurling themselves on the *Borgmester Dahl*. Some of the men never left their bunks; many became quarrelsome. The chief engineer, an old man, refused to speak at all to anybody. Others shut themselves up in their berths to cry. On calm days the inert steamer rolled on a leaden sea under a murky sky, or showed, in sunshine, the squalor of sea waifs: the dried white salt, the rust, the jagged broken places. Then the gales came again. They kept body and soul together on short rations. Once, an English ship, scudding in a storm, tried to stand by them, heaving-to pluckily under their lee. The seas swept her decks; the men in oilskins clinging to her rigging looked at them, and they made desperate signs over their shattered bulwarks. Suddenly her main-topsail went, yard and all, in a terrific squall; she had to bear up under bare poles and disappeared.

Other ships had spoken them before, but at first they had refused to be taken off, expecting the assistance of some steamer. There were very few steamers in those latitudes then; and when they desired to leave this dead and drifting carcase, no ship came in sight. They had drifted south out of men's knowledge. They failed to attract the attention of a lonely whaler: and very soon the edge of the polar ice-cap rose from the sea and closed the southern horizon like a wall. One morning they were alarmed by finding themselves floating amongst detached pieces of ice. But the fear of sinking passed away like their vigour, like their hopes; the shocks of the floes knocking against the ship's side could not rouse them from their apathy; and the *Borgmester Dahl* drifted out again, unharmed, into open water. They hardly noticed the change.

The funnel had gone overboard in one of the heavy rolls; two of their three boats had disappeared, washed away in bad weather, and the davits swung to and fro, unsecured, with chafed ropes' ends waggling to the roll. Nothing was done on board, and Falk told me how he had often listened to the water washing about the dark engine-room where the engines, stilled for ever, were decaying slowly into a mass of rust, as the stilled heart decays within the lifeless body. At first, after the loss of the motive power, the tiller had been thoroughly secured by lashings. But in course of time these had rotted, chafed, rusted, parting one by one: and the rudder, freed, banged heavily to and fro night and day, sending dull shocks through the whole frame of the vessel. This was dangerous. Nobody cared enough to lift a little finger. He told me that even now sometimes waking up at night, he fancied he could hear the dull vibrating thuds. The pintles carried away, and it dropped off at last.

The final catastrophe came with the sending off of their one remaining boat. It was Falk who had managed to preserve her intact, and now it was agreed that some of the hands should sail away into the track of the shipping to procure assistance. She was provisioned with all the food they could spare for the six who were to go. They waited for a fine day. It was long in coming. At last one morning they lowered her into the water.

Directly, in that demoralised crowd, trouble broke out. Two men who had no business there had jumped into the boat under the pretence of unhooking the tackles, while some sort of squabble arose on the deck amongst these weak, tottering spectres of a ship's company. The captain, who had been for days living secluded and unapproachable in the chart-room, came to the rail. He ordered the two men to come up on board and menaced them with his revolver. They pretended to obey, but suddenly cutting the boat's painter, gave a shove against the ship's side and made ready to hoist the sail.

'Shoot, sir! Shoot them down!' cried Falk – 'and I will jump overboard to regain the boat.' But the captain, after taking aim with an irresolute arm, turned suddenly away.

A howl of rage arose. Falk dashed into his cabin for his own pistol. When he returned it was too late. Two more men had leaped into the water, but the fellows in the boat beat them off with the oars, hoisted the boat's lug and sailed away. They were never heard of again.

Consternation and despair possessed the remaining ship's company, till the apathy of utter hopelessness reasserted its sway. That day a fireman committed suicide, running up on deck with his throat cut from ear to ear, to the horror of all hands. He was thrown overboard. The captain had locked himself in the chart-room and Falk, knocking vainly for admittance, heard him reciting over and over again the names of his wife and children, not as if calling upon them or commending them to God, but in a mechanical voice like an exercise of memory. Next day the doors of the chart-room were swinging open to the roll of the ship, and the captain had disappeared. He must during the night have jumped into the sea. Falk locked both the doors and kept the keys.

The organised life of the ship had come to an end. The solidarity of the men had gone. They become indifferent to each other. It was Falk who took in hand the distribution of such food as remained. They boiled their boots for soup to eke out the rations, which only made their hunger more intolerable. Sometimes whispers of hate were heard passing between the languid skeletons that drifted endlessly to and fro, north and south, east and west, upon that carcase of a ship.

And in this lies the grotesque horror of this sombre story. The last extremity of sailors, overtaking a small boat or a frail craft, seems easier to bear, because of the direct danger of the seas. The confined space, the close contact, the imminent menace of the waves, seem to draw men together, in spite of madness, suffering and despair. But there was a ship – safe, convenient, roomy: a ship with beds, bedding, knives, forks, comfortable cabins, glass and china, and a complete cook's gallery, pervaded, ruled and possessed by the pitiless spectre of starvation. The lamp oil had been drunk, the wicks cut up for food, the candles eaten. At night she floated dark in all her recesses, and full of fears. One day Falk came upon a man gnawing a splinter of pine wood. Suddenly he threw the piece of wood away, tottered to the rail, and fell over. Falk, too late to prevent the act, saw him claw the ship's side desperately before he went down. Next day another man did the same thing, after uttering horrible imprecations. But this one somehow managed to get hold of the broken rudder chains and hung on there, silently. Falk set about trying to save him, and all the time the man, holding with both hands, looked at him anxiously with his sunken eyes. Then, just as Falk was ready to put his hand on him, the man let go his hold and sank like a stone. Falk reflected on these sights. His heart revolted against the horror of death, and he said to himself that he would struggle for every precious minute of his life.

One afternoon – as the survivors lay about on the after-deck –

the carpenter, a tall man with a black beard, spoke of the last sacrifice. There was nothing eatable left on board. Nobody said a word to this; but that company separated quickly, these listless feeble spectres slunk off one by one to hide in fear of each other. Falk and the carpenter remained on deck together. Falk liked the big carpenter. He had been the best man of the lot, helpful and ready as long as there was anything to do, the longest hopeful, and had preserved to the last some vigour and decision of mind.

They did not speak to each other. Henceforth no voices were to be heard conversing sadly on board that ship. After a time the carpenter tottered away forward; but later on Falk, going to drink at the fresh-water pump, had the inspiration to turn his head. The carpenter had stolen upon him from behind, and, summoning all his strength, was aiming with a crowbar a blow at the back of his skull.

Dodging just in time, Falk made his escape and ran into his cabin. While he was loading his revolver there, he heard the sound of heavy blows struck upon the bridge. The locks of the chart-room doors were slight, they flew open, and the carpenter, possessing himself of the captain's revolver, fired a shot of defiance.

Falk was about to go on deck and have it out at once, when he remarked that one of the ports of his cabin commanded the approaches to the fresh-water pump. Instead of going out he remained in and secured the door. 'The best man shall survive,' he said to himself – and the other, he reasoned, must at some time or other come there to drink. These starving men would drink often to cheat the pangs of their hunger. But the carpenter too must have noticed the position of the port. They were the two best men in the ship, and the game was with them. All the rest of the day Falk saw no one and heard no sound. At night he strained his eyes. It was dark – he heard a rustling noise once, but he was certain that no one could have come near the pump. It was to the left of his deck port, and he could not have failed to see a man, for the night was clear and starry. He saw nothing; towards morning another faint noise made him suspicious. Deliberately and quietly he unlocked his door. He had not slept, and had not given way to the horror of the situation. He wanted to live.

But during the night the carpenter, without at all trying to approach the pump, had managed to creep quietly along the starboard bulwark, and, unseen, had crouched down right under Falk's deck port. When daylight came he rose up suddenly, looked in, and putting his arm through the round brass-framed opening, fired at Falk within a foot. He missed – and Falk, instead of attempting to seize the arm holding the weapon, opened the door unexpectedly, and with the muzzle of his long revolver nearly touching the other's side shot him dead.

The best man had survived. Both of them had at the beginning just strength enough to stand on their feet, and both had displayed pitiless resolution, endurance, cunning and courage – all the qualities of classic heroism. At once Falk threw overboard the captain's revolver. He was a born monopolist. Then after the report of the two shots, followed by a profound silence, there crept out into the cold, cruel dawn of Antarctic regions, from various hiding-places, over the deck of that dismantled corpse of a ship floating on a grey sea ruled by iron necessity and with a heart of ice – there crept into view one by one, cautious, slow, eager, glaring, and unclean, a band of hungry and livid skeletons. Falk faced them, the possessor of the only fire-arm on board, and the second-best man – the carpenter – was lying dead between him and them.

'He was eaten, of course,' I said.

He bent his head slowly, shuddered a little, drawing his hands over his face, and said, 'I had never any quarrel with that man. But there were our lives between him and me.'

Why continue the story of that ship, that story before which, with its fresh-water pump like a spring of death, its man with the weapon, the sea ruled by iron necessity, its spectral band swayed by terror and hope, its mute and unhearing heaven? – the fable of the *Flying Dutchman* with its convention of crime and its sentimental retribution [47] fades like a graceful wreath, like a wisp of white mist. What is there to say that every one of us cannot guess for himself? I believe Falk began by going through the ship, revolver in hand, to annex all the matches. Those starving wretches had plenty of matches! He had no mind to have the ship set on fire under his feet, either from hate or from despair. He lived in the open, camping on the bridge, commanding all the after-deck and the only approach to the pump. He lived! Some of the others lived too – concealed, anxious, coming out one by one from their hiding-places at the seductive sound of a shot. And he was not selfish. They shared, but only three of them all were alive when a whaler, returning from her cruising-ground, nearly ran over the water-logged hull of the *Borgmester Dahl*, which, it seems, in the end had in some way sprung a leak in both her holds, but being loaded with deals could not sink.

'They all died,' Falk said. 'These three too, afterwards. But I would not die. All died, all! under this terrible misfortune. But was I, too, to throw away my life? Could I? Tell me, captain? I was alone there, quite alone, just like the others. Each man was alone. Was I to give up my revolver? Who to? Or was I to throw it into the sea? What would have been the good? Only the best man would survive. It was a great, terrible, and cruel misfortune.'

He had survived! I saw him before me as though preserved for a witness to the mighty truth of an unerring and eternal principle. Great beads of perspiration stood on his forehead. And suddenly it struck the table with a heavy blow, as he fell forward throwing his hands out.

'And this is worse,' he cried. 'This is a worse pain! This is more terrible.'

He made my heart thump with the profound conviction of his cry. And after he had left me alone I called up before my mental eye the image of the girl weeping silently, abundantly, patiently, and as if irresistibly. I thought of her tawny hair. I thought how, if unplaited, it would have covered her all round as low as the hips, like the hair of a siren. And she had bewitched him. Fancy a man who would guard his own life with the inflexibility of a pitiless and immovable fate, being brought to lament that once a crowbar had missed his skull! The sirens sing and lure to death, but this one had been weeping silently as if for the pity of his life. She was the tender and voiceless siren of this appalling navigator. He evidently wanted to live his whole conception of life. Nothing else would do. And she too was a servant of that life that, in the midst of death, cries aloud to our senses. She was eminently fitted to interpret for him its feminine side. And in her own way, and with her own profusion of sensuous charms, she also seemed to illustrate the eternal truth of an unerring principle. I don't know though what sort of principle Hermann illustrated when he turned up early on board my ship with a most perplexed air. It struck me, however, that he too would do his best to survive. He seemed greatly calmed on the subject of Falk, but still very full of it.

'What is it you said I was last night? You know,' he asked after some preliminary talk. 'Too – too – I don't know. A very funny word.'

'Squeamish?' I suggested.

'Yes. What does it mean?'

'That you exaggerate things – to yourself. Without inquiry, and so on.'

He seemed to turn it over in his mind. We went on talking. This Falk was the plague of his life. Upsetting everybody like this! Mrs. Hermann was unwell rather this morning. His niece was crying still. There was nobody to look after the children. He struck his umbrella on the deck. She would be like that for months. Fancy carrying all the way home, second class, a perfectly useless girl who is crying all the time. It was bad for Lena too, he observed; but on what grounds I could not guess. Perhaps of the bad example. That child was already sorrowing and crying enough over the rag doll. Nicholas was really the least sentimental person of the family.

'Why does she weep?' I asked.

'From pity,' cried Hermann.

It was impossible to make out women. Mrs. Hermann was the only one he pretended to understand. She was very, very upset and doubtful.

'Doubtful about what?' I asked.

He averted his eyes and did not answer this. It was impossible to make them out. For instance, his niece was weeping for Falk. Now he (Hermann) would like to wring his neck – but then . . . He supposed he had too tender a heart. 'Frankly,' he asked at last, 'what do you think of what we heard last night, captain?'

'In all these tales,' I observed, 'there is always a good deal of exaggeration.'

And not letting him recover from his surprise I assured him that I knew all the details. He begged me not to repeat them. His heart was too tender. They made him feel unwell. Then, looking at his feet and speaking very slowly, he supposed that he need not see much of them after they were married. For, indeed, he could not bear the sight of Falk. On the other hand it was ridiculous to take home a girl with her head turned. A girl that weeps all the time and is of no help to her aunt.

'Now you will be able to do with one cabin only on your passage home,' I said.

'Yes, I had thought of that,' he said brightly, almost. Yes! Himself, his wife, four children – one cabin might do. Whereas if his niece went . . .

'And what does Mrs. Hermann say to it?' I inquired.

Mrs. Hermann did not know whether a man of that sort could make a girl happy – she had been greatly deceived in Captain Falk. She had been very upset last night.

Those good people did not seem to be able to retain an impression for a whole twelve hours. I assured him on my own personal knowledge that Falk possessed in himself all the qualities to make his niece's future prosperous. He said he was glad to hear this, and that he would tell his wife. Then the object of the visit came out. He wished me to help him to resume relations with Falk. His niece, he said, had expressed the hope I would do so in my kindness. He was evidently anxious that I should, for though he seemed to have forgotten nine-tenths of his last night's opinions and the whole of his indignation, yet he evidently feared to be sent to the right-about. 'You told me he was very much in love,' he concluded slyly, and leered in a sort of bucolic way.

As soon as he had left my ship I called Falk on board by signal – the tug still lying at the anchorage. He took the news with calm gravity, as though he had all along expected the stars to fight for him in their courses.

I saw them once more together, and only once – on the quarter-deck of the *Diana*. Hermann sat smoking with a shirt-sleeved elbow hooked over the back of his chair. Mrs. Hermann was sewing alone. As Falk stepped over the gangway, Hermann's niece, with a slight swish of the skirt and a swift friendly nod to me, glided past my chair.

They met in sunshine abreast of the mainmast. He held her hands and looked down at them, and she looked up at him with her candid and unseeing glance. It seemed to me they had come together as if attracted, drawn and guided to each other by a mysterious influence. They were a complete couple. In her grey frock, palpitating with life, generous of form, olympian and simple, she was indeed the siren to fascinate that dark navigator, this ruthless lover of the five senses. From afar I seemed to feel the masculine strength with which he grasped those hands she had extended to him with a womanly swiftness. Lena, a little pale, nursing her beloved lump of dirty rags, ran towards her big friend; and then in the drowsy silence of the good old ship Mrs. Hermann's voice rang out so changed that it made me spin round in my chair to see what was the matter.

'Lena, come here!' she screamed. And this good-natured matron gave me a wavering glance, dark and full of fearsome distrust. The child ran back, surprised, to her knee. But the two, standing before each other in sunlight with clasped hands, had heard nothing, had seen nothing and no one. Three feet away from them in the shade a seaman sat on a spar, very busy splicing a strop, and dipping his fingers into a tar-pot, as if utterly unaware of their existence.

When I returned in command of another ship, some five years afterwards, Mr. and Mrs. Falk had left the place. I should not wonder if Schomberg's tongue had succeeded at last in scaring Falk away for good; and, indubitably, there was a tale still going about the town of a certain Falk, owner of a tug, who had won his wife at cards from the captain of an English ship.

TO-MORROW

TO-MORROW[48]

WHAT was known of Captain Hagberd in the little seaport of Colebrook was not exactly in his favour. He did not belong to the place. He had come to settle there under circumstances not at all mysterious – he used to be very communicative about them at the time – but extremely morbid and unreasonable. He was possessed of some little money evidently, because he bought a plot of ground, and had a pair of ugly yellow brick cottages run up very cheaply. He occupied one of them himself and let the other to Josiah Carvil – blind Carvil, the retired boat-builder – a man of evil repute as a domestic tyrant.

These cottages had one wall in common, shared in a line of iron railing dividing their front gardens; a wooden fence separated their back gardens. Miss Bessie Carvil was allowed, as it were of right, to throw over it the tea-cloths, blue rags, or an apron that wanted drying.

'It rots the wood, Bessie my girl,' the captain would remark mildly, from his side of the fence, each time he saw her exercising that privilege.

She was a tall girl; the fence was low, and she could spread her elbows on the top. Her hands would be red with the bit of washing she had done, but her forearms were white and shapely, and she would look at her father's landlord in silence – in an informed silence which had an air of knowledge, expectation and desire.

'It rots the wood,' reported Captain Hagberd. 'It is the only unthrifty, careless habit I know in you. Why don't you have a clothes-line out in your back yard?'

Miss Carvil would say nothing to this – she only shook her head negatively. The tiny back yard on her side had a few stone-bordered little beds of black earth, in which the simple flowers she found time to cultivate appeared somehow extravagantly overgrown, as if belonging to an exotic clime; and Captain Hagberd's upright,

239

hale person, clad in No. 1 sailcloth from head to foot, would be emerging knee-deep out of rank grass and the tall weeds on his side of the fence. He appeared, with the colour and uncouth stiffness of the extraordinary material in which he chose to clothe himself – 'for the time being', would be his mumbled remark to any observation on the subject – like a man roughened out of granite, standing in a wilderness not big enough for a decent billiard-room. A heavy figure of a man of stone, with a red handsome face, a blue wandering eye, and a great white beard flowing to his waist and never trimmed as far as Colebrook knew.

Seven years before, he had seriously answered 'Next month, I think' to the chaffing attempt to secure his custom made by that distinguished local wit, the Colebrook barber, who happened to be sitting insolently in the tap-room of the New Inn near the harbour, where the captain had entered to buy an ounce of tobacco. After paying for his purchase with three half-pence extracted from the corner of a handkerchief which he carried in the cuff of his sleeve, Captain Hagberd went out. As soon as the door was shut the barber laughed. 'The old one and the young one will be strolling arm in arm to get shaved in my place presently. The tailor shall be set to work, and the barber, and the candlestick maker. High old times are coming for Colebrook; they are coming, to be sure. It used to be "next week", now it has come to "next month", and so on – soon it will be "next spring", for all I know.'

Noticing a stranger listening to him with a vacant grin, he explained, stretching out his legs cynically, that this queer old Hagberd, a retired coasting-skipper, was waiting for the return of a son of his. The boy had been driven away from home, he shouldn't wonder; had run away to sea and had never been heard of since. Put to rest in Davy Jones's locker this many a day, as likely as not. That old man came flying to Colebrook three years ago all in black broadcloth (had lost his wife lately then), getting out of a third-class smoker as if the devil had been at his heels; and the only thing that brought him down was a letter – a hoax probably. Some joker had written to him about a seafaring man with some such name who was supposed to be hanging about some girl or other, either in Colebrook or in the neighbourhood. 'Funny, ain't it?' The old chap had been advertising in the London papers for Harry Hagberd, and offering rewards for any sort of likely information.

And the barber would go on to describe with sardonic gusto how that stranger in mourning had been seen exploring the country, in carts, on foot, taking everybody into his confidence, visiting all the inns and alehouses for miles around, stopping people on the road with his questions, looking into the very ditches almost; first in the greatest excitement, then with a plodding sort of perseverance, growing slower and slower; and he could not even tell you plainly how his son looked. The sailor was supposed to be one of two that had left a timber ship, and to have been seen dangling after some girl; but the old man described a boy of fourteen or so – 'a clever-looking, high-spirited boy'. And when people only smiled at this he would rub his forehead in a confused sort of way before he slunk off, looking offended. He found nobody, of course; not a trace of anybody – never heard of anything worth belief, at any rate; but he had not been able, somehow, to tear himself away from Colebrook.

'It was the shock of this disappointment, perhaps, coming soon after the loss of his wife, that had driven him crazy on that point,' the barber suggested, with an air of great psychological insight. After a time the old man abandoned the active search. His son had evidently gone away; but he settled himself to wait. His son had been once at least in Colebrook in preference to his native place. There must have been some reason for it, he seemed to think, some very powerful inducement, that would bring him back to Colebrook again.

'Ha, ha, ha! Why, of course, Colebrook. Where else? That's the only place in the United Kingdom for your long-lost sons. So he sold up his old home in Colchester, and down he comes here. Well, it's a craze, like any other. Wouldn't catch me going crazy over any of my youngsters clearing out. I've got eight of them at home.' The barber was showing off his strength of mind in the midst of a laughter that shook the tap-room.

Strange though, that sort of thing, he would confess with the frankness of a superior intelligence, seemed to be catching. His establishment, for instance, was near the harbour, and whenever a sailorman came in for a hair-cut or a shave – if it was a strange face he couldn't help thinking directly, 'Suppose he's the son of old Hagberd!' He laughed at himself for it. It was a strong craze. He could remember the time when the whole town was full of it. But he had his hopes of the old chap yet. He would cure him by a course of judicious chaffing. He was watching the progress of the treatment. Next week – next month – next year! When the old skipper had put off the date of that return till next year, he would be well on his way to not saying any more about it. In other matters he was quite rational, so this, too, was bound to come. Such was the barber's firm opinion.

Nobody had ever contradicted him; his own hair had gone grey since that time, and Captain Hagberd's beard had turned quite white, and had acquired a majestic flow over the No. 1 canvas suit, which he had made for himself secretly with tarred twine, and had assumed suddenly, coming out in it one fine morning, whereas the evening before he had been seen going home in his mourning of broadcloth. It caused a sensation in the High Street – shopkeepers coming to their doors, people in the houses snatching up their hats to run out – a stir at which he seemed strangely surprised at first, and then scared; but his only answer to the wondering questions was that startled and evasive 'For the present'.

That sensation had been forgotten long ago; and Captain Hagberd himself, if not forgotten, had come to be disregarded – the penalty of dailiness – as the sun itself is disregarded unless it makes its power felt heavily. Captain Hagberd's movements showed no infirmity; he walked stiffly in his suit of canvas, a quaint and remarkable figure; only his eyes wandered more furtively perhaps than of yore. His manner abroad had lost its excitable watchfulness; it had become puzzled and diffident, as though he had suspected that there was somewhere about him something slightly compromising, some embarrassing oddity; and yet had remained unable to discover what on earth this something wrong could be.

He was unwilling now to talk with the townsfolk. He had earned for himself the reputation of an awful skinflint, of a miser in the matter of living. He mumbled regretfully in the shops, bought inferior scraps of meat after long hesitations; and discouraged all allusions to his costume. It was as the barber had foretold. For all one could tell, he had recovered already from the disease of hope; and only Miss Bessie Carvil knew that he said nothing about his son's return because with him it was no longer 'next week', 'next month', or even 'next year'. It was 'to-morrow'.

In their intimacy of back yard and front garden he talked with her paternally, reasonably, and dogmatically, with a touch of arbitrariness. They met on the ground of unreserved confidence, which was authenticated by an affectionate wink now and then. Miss Carvil had come to look forward rather to these winks. At first they had discomposed her: the poor fellow was mad. Afterwards she had learned to laugh at them: there was no harm in him. Now she was aware of an unacknowledged, pleasurable, incredulous emotion, expressed by a faint blush. He winked not in the least vulgarly; his thin red face with a well-modelled curved nose had a sort of distinction – the more so that when he talked to her he looked with a steadier and more intelligent glance. A handsome, hale, upright, capable man, with a white beard. You did not think of his age. His son, he affirmed, had resembled him amazingly from his earliest babyhood.

Harry would be one-and-thirty next July, he declared. Proper age to get married with a nice, sensible girl that could appreciate a good home. He was a very high-spirited boy. High-spirited husbands were the easiest to manage. These mean, soft chaps, that you would think butter wouldn't melt in their mouths, were the ones to make a woman thoroughly miserable. And there was nothing like home – a fireside – a good roof: no turning out of your warm bed in all sorts of weather. 'Eh, my dear?'

Captain Hagberd had been one of those sailors that pursue their calling within sight of land. One of the many children of a bankrupt farmer, he had been apprenticed hurriedly to a coasting-skipper, and had remained on the coast all his sea life. It must have been a hard one at first: he had never taken to it; his affection turned to the land, with its innumerable houses, with its quiet lives gathered round its firesides. Many sailors feel and profess a rational dislike for the sea, but his was a profound and emotional animosity – as if the love of the stabler element had been bred into him through many generations.

'People did not know what they let their boys in for when they let them go to sea,' he expounded to Bessie. 'As soon make convicts of them at once.' He did not believe you ever got used to it. The weariness of such a life got worse as you got older. What sort of trade was it in which more than half your time you did not put your foot inside your house? Directly you got out to sea you had no means of knowing what went on at home. One might have thought him weary of distant voyages; and the longest he had ever made had lasted a fortnight, of which the most part had been spent at anchor, sheltering from the weather. As soon as his wife had inherited a house and enough to live on (from a bachelor uncle who had made some money in the coal business) he threw up his command of an East-coast collier with a feeling as though he had escaped from the galleys. After all these years he might have counted on the fingers of his two hands all the days he had been out of sight of England. He had never known what it was to be out of soundings. 'I have never been further than eighty fathoms from the land' was one of his boasts.

Bessie Carvil heard all these things. In front of their cottage grew an undersized ash; and on summer afternoons she would bring out a chair on the grass-plot and sit down with her sewing. Captain Hagberd, in his canvas suit, leaned on a spade. He dug every day in his front plot. He turned it over and over several times every year, but was not going to plant anything 'just at present'.

To Bessie Carvil he would state more explicitly: 'Not till our Harry comes home to-morrow.' And she had heard this formula of hope so often that it only awakened the vaguest pity in her heart for that hopeful old man.

Everything was put off in that way, and everything was being prepared likewise for to-morrow. There was a boxful of packets of various flower-seeds to choose from, for the front garden. 'He will doubtless let you have your say about that, my dear,' Captain Hagberd intimated to her across the railing.

Miss Bessie's head remained bowed over her work. She had heard all this so many times. But now and then she would rise, lay down her sewing, and come slowly to the fence. There was a charm in these gentle ravings. He was determined that his son should not go away again for the want of a home all ready for him. He had been filling the other cottage with all sorts of furniture. She imagined it all new, fresh with varnish, piled up as in a warehouse. There would be tables wrapped up in sacking; rolls of carpets thick and vertical, like fragments of columns; the gleam of white marble tops in the dimness of the drawn blinds. Captain Hagberd always described his purchases to her, carefully, as to a person having a legitimate interest in them. The overgrown yard of his cottage could be laid over with concrete . . . after to-morrow.

'We may just as well do away with the fence. You could have your drying-line out, quite clear of your flowers.' He winked, and she would blush faintly.

This madness that had entered her life through the kind impulses of her heart had reasonable details. What if some day his son returned? But she could not even be quite sure that he ever had a son; and if he existed anywhere he had been too long away. When Captain Hagberd got excited in his talk she would steady him by a pretence of belief, laughing a little to salve her conscience.

Only once she had tried pityingly to throw some doubt on that hope doomed to disappointment, but the effect of her attempt had scared her very much. All at once over that man's face there came an expression of horror and incredulity, as though he had seen a crack open out in the firmament.

'You – you – you don't think he's drowned!'

For a moment he seemed to her ready to go out of his mind, for in his ordinary state she thought him more sane than people gave him credit for. On that occasion the violence of the emotion was followed by a most paternal and complacent recovery.

'Don't alarm yourself, my dear,' he said a little cunningly, 'the sea can't keep him. He does not belong to it. None of us Hagberds ever did belong to it. Look at me; I didn't get drowned. Moreover, he isn't a sailor at all; and if he is not a sailor he's bound to come back. There's nothing to prevent him coming back. . . .'

His eyes began to wander.

'To-morrow.'

She never tried again, for fear the man should go out of his mind on the spot. He depended on her. She seemed the only sensible person in the town; and he would congratulate himself frankly before her face on having secured such a level-headed wife for his son. The rest of the town, he confided to her once, in a fit of temper, was certainly queer. The way they looked at you – the way they talked to you! He had never got on with any one in the place. Didn't like the people. He would not have left his own country if it had not been clear that his son had taken a fancy to Colebrook.

She humoured him in silence, listening patiently by the fence; crocheting with downcast eyes. Blushes came with difficulty on her dead-white complexion, under the negligently twisted opulence of mahogany-coloured hair. Her father was frankly carroty.

She had a full figure; a tired, unrefreshed face. When Captain Hagberd vaunted the necessity and propriety of a home and the delights of one's own fireside, she smiled a little, with her lips only. Her home delights had been confined to the nursing of her father during the ten best years of her life.

A bestial roaring coming out of an upstairs window would interrupt their talk. She would begin at once to roll up her crochet-work or fold her sewing, without the slightest sign of haste. Meanwhile the howls and roars of her name would go on, making the fishermen strolling upon the sea-wall on the other side of the road turn their heads towards the cottages. She would go in slowly at the front door, and a moment afterwards there would fall a profound silence. Presently she would reappear, leading by the hand a man, gross and unwieldy like a hippopotamus, with a bad-tempered, surly face.

He was a widowed boat-builder, whom blindness had overtaken years before in the full flush of business. He behaved to his daughter as if she had been responsible for its incurable character. He had been heard to bellow at the top of his voice, as if to defy Heaven, that he did not care: he had made enough money to have ham and eggs for his breakfast every morning. He thanked God for it, in a fiendish tone as though he were cursing.

Captain Hagberd had been so unfavourably impressed by his tenant that once he told Miss Bessie, 'He is a very extravagant fellow, my dear.'

She was knitting that day, finishing a pair of socks for her father, who expected her to keep up the supply dutifully. She hated knitting, and, as she was just at the heel part, she had to keep her eyes on her needles.

'Of course it isn't as if he had a son to provide for,' Captain Hagberd went on a little vacantly. 'Girls, of course, don't require so much – h'm – h'm. They don't run away from home, my dear.'

'No,' said Miss Bessie, quietly.

Captain Hagberd, amongst the mounds of turned-up earth, chuckled. With his maritime rig, his weather-beaten face, his beard of Father Neptune, he resembled a deposed sea-god who had exchanged the trident for the spade.

'And he must look upon you as already provided for, in a

manner. That's the best of it with the girls. The husbands . . .' He winked. Miss Bessie, absorbed in her knitting, coloured faintly.

'Bessie! my hat!' old Carvil bellowed out suddenly. He had been sitting under the tree mute and motionless, like an idol of some remarkably monstrous superstition. He never opened his mouth but to howl for her, at her, sometimes about her; and then he did not moderate the terms of his abuse. Her system was never to answer him at all; and he kept up his shouting till he got attended to – till she shook him by the arm, or thrust the mouthpiece of his pipe between his teeth. He was one of the few blind people who smoke. When he felt the hat being put on his head he stopped his noise at once. Then he rose, and they passed together through the gate.

He weighed heavily on her arm. During their slow, toilful walks she appeared to be dragging with her for a penance the burden of that infirm bulk. Usually they crossed the road at once (the cottages stood in the fields near the harbour, two hundred yards away from the end of the street), and for a long, long time they would remain in view, ascending imperceptibly the flight of wooden steps that led to the top of the sea-wall. It ran on from east to west, shutting out the Channel like a neglected railway embankment, on which no train had ever rolled within memory of man. Groups of sturdy fishermen would emerge upon the sky, walk along for a bit, and sink without haste. Their brown nets, like the cobwebs of gigantic spiders, lay on the shabby grass of the slope; and, looking up from the end of the street, the people of the town would recognise the two Carvils, by the creeping slowness of their gait. Captain Hagberd, pottering aimlessly about his cottages, would raise his head to see how they got on in their promenade.

He advertised still in the Sunday papers for Harry Hagberd. These sheets were read in foreign parts to the end of the world, he informed Bessie. At the same time he seemed to think that his son was in England – so near to Colebrook that he would of course turn up 'to-morrow'. Bessie, without committing herself to that opinion in so many words, argued that in that case the expense of advertising was unnecessary; Captain Hagberd had better spend that weekly half-crown on himself. She declared she did not know what he lived on. Her argumentation would puzzle him and cast him down for a time. 'They all do it,' he pointed out. There was a whole column devoted to appeals after missing relatives. He would bring the newspaper to show her. He and his wife had advertised for years; only she was an impatient woman. The news from Colebrook had arrived the very day after her funeral; if she had not been so impatient she might have been here now, with no more than one day more to wait. 'You are not an impatient woman, my dear.'

'I've no patience with you, sometimes,' she would say.

If he still advertised for his son he did not offer rewards for information any more: for, with the muddled lucidity of a mental derangement, he had reasoned himself into a conviction as clear as daylight that he had already attained all that could be expected in that way. What more could he want? Colebrook was the place, and there was no need to ask for more. Miss Carvil praised him for his good sense, and he was soothed by the part she took in his hope, which had become his delusion; in that idea which blinded his mind to truth and probability, just as the other old man in the other cottage had been made blind, by another disease, to the light and beauty of the world.

But anything he could interpret as a doubt – any coldness of assent, or even a simple inattention to the development of his projects of a home with his returned son and his son's wife – would irritate him into flings and jerks and wicked side glances. He would dash his spade into the ground and walk to and fro before it. Miss Bessie called it his tantrums. She shook her finger at him. Then, when she came out again, after he had parted with her in anger, he would watch out of the corner of his eyes for the least sign of encouragement to approach the iron railings and resume his fatherly and patronising relations.

For all their intimacy, which had lasted some years now, they had never talked without a fence or a railing between them. He described to her all the splendours accumulated for the setting-up of their housekeeping, but had never invited her to an inspection. No human eye was to behold them till Harry had his first look. In fact, nobody had ever been inside his cottage; he did his own housework, and he guarded his son's privilege so jealously that the small objects of domestic use he bought sometimes in the town were smuggled rapidly across the front garden under his canvas coat. Then, coming out, he would remark apologetically, 'It was only a small kettle, my dear.'

And, if not too tired with her drudgery, or worried beyond endurance by her father, she would laugh at him with a blush, and say: 'That's all right, Captain Hagberd; I am not impatient.'

'Well, my dear, you haven't long to wait now,' he would answer with a sudden bashfulness, and looking about uneasily, as though he had suspected that there was something wrong somewhere.

Every Monday she paid him his rent over the railings. He clutched the shillings greedily. He grudged every penny he had to spend on his maintenance, and when he left her to make his purchases his bearing changed as soon as he got into the street. Away from the sanction of her pity, he felt himself exposed without defence. He brushed the walls with his shoulder. He mistrusted the queerness of the people; yet, by then, even the town children had left off calling after him, and the tradesmen served him without a word. The slightest allusion to his clothing had the power to puzzle and frighten especially, as if it were something utterly unwarranted and incomprehensible.

In the autumn, the driving rain drummed on his sailcloth suit saturated almost to the stiffness of sheet iron, with its surface flowing with water. When the weather was too bad, he retreated under the tiny porch, and, standing close against the door, looked at his spade left planted in the middle of the yard. The ground was so much dug up all over, that as the season advanced it turned to a quagmire. When it froze hard, he was disconsolate. What would Harry say? And as he could not have so much of Bessie's company at that time of year, the roars of old Carvil, that came muffled through the closed windows, calling her indoors, exasperated him greatly.

'Why don't that extravagant fellow get you a servant?' he asked impatiently one mild afternoon. She had thrown something over her head to run out for a while.

'I don't know,' said the pale Bessie, wearily, staring away with her heavy-lidded, grey, and unexpectant glance. There were always smudgy shadows under her eyes, and she did not seem able to see any change or any end to her life.

'You wait till you get married, my dear,' said her only friend, drawing closer to the fence. 'Harry will get you one.'

His hopeful craze seemed to mock her own want of hope with so bitter an aptness that in her nervous irritation she could have screamed at him outright. But she only said in self-mockery, and speaking to him as though he had been sane, 'Why, Captain Hagberd, your son may not even want to look at me.'

He flung his head back and laughed his throaty affected cackle of anger.

'What! That boy? Not want to look at the only sensible girl for miles around? What do you think I am here for, my dear – my dear – my dear? . . . What? You wait. You just wait. You'll see to-morrow. I'll soon —'

'Bessie! Bessie! Bessie!' howled old Carvil inside. 'Bessie! – my pipe!' That fat blind man had given himself up to a very lust of laziness. He would not lift his hand to reach for the things she took care to leave at his very elbow. He would not move a limb; he would not rise from his chair, he would not put one foot before another in that parlour (where he knew his way as well as if he had his sight) without calling her to his side and hanging all his atrocious weight on her shoulder. He would not eat one single mouthful of food without her close attendance. He had made himself helpless beyond his affliction, to enslave her better. She stood still for a moment, setting her teeth in the dusk, then turned and walked slowly indoors.

Captain Hagberd went back to his spade. The shouting in Carvil's cottage stopped, and after a while the window of the parlour downstairs was lit up. A man coming from the end of the street with a firm leisurely step passed on, but seemed to have caught sight of Captain Hagberd, because he turned back a pace or two. A cold white light lingered in the western sky. The man leaned over the gate in an interested manner.

'You must be Captain Hagberd,' he said, with easy assurance.

The old man spun round, pulling out his spade, startled by the strange voice.

'Yes, I am,' he answered nervously.

The other, smiling straight at him, uttered very slowly: 'You've been advertising for your son, I believe?'

'My son Harry,' mumbled Captain Hagberd, off his guard for once. 'He's coming home to-morrow.'

'The devil he is!' The stranger marvelled greatly, and then went on, with only a slight change of tone: 'You've grown a beard like Father Christmas himself.'

Captain Hagberd drew a little nearer, and leaned forward over his spade. 'Go your way,' he said, resentfully and timidly at the same time, because he was always afraid of being laughed at. Every mental state, even madness, has its equilibrium based upon self-esteem. Its disturbance causes unhappiness; and Captain Hagberd lived amongst a scheme of settled notions which it pained him to feel disturbed by people's grins. Yes, people's grins were awful. They hinted at something wrong: but what? He could not tell; and that stranger was obviously grinning – had come on purpose to grin. It was bad enough on the streets, but he had never before been outraged like this.

The stranger, unaware how near he was of having his head laid open with a spade, said seriously: 'I am not trespassing where I stand, am I? I fancy there's something wrong about your news. Suppose you let me come in.'

'*You* come in!' murmured old Hagberd, with inexpressible horror.

'I could give you some real information about your son – the very latest tip, if you care to hear.'

'No,' shouted Hagberd. He began to pace wildly to and fro, he shouldered his spade, he gesticulated with his other arm. 'Here's a fellow – a grinning fellow, who says there's something wrong. I've got more information than you're aware of. I've all the information I want. I've had it for years – for years – for years – enough to last me till to-morrow. Let you come in, indeed! What would Harry say?'

Bessie Carvil's figure appeared in black silhouette on the parlour window; then, with the sound of an opening door, flitted out before the other cottage, all black, but with something white over her head. These two voices beginning to talk suddenly outside (she had heard them indoors) had given her such an emotion that she could not utter a sound.

Captain Hagberd seemed to be trying to find his way out of a cage. His feet squelched in the puddles left by his industry. He stumbled in the holes of the ruined grass-plot. He ran blindly against the fence.

'Here, steady a bit!' said the man at the gate, gravely, stretching his arm over and catching him by the sleeve. 'Somebody's been trying to get at you. Hallo! what's this rig you've got on? Storm canvas, by George!' He had a big laugh. 'Well, you *are* a character!'

Captain Hagberd jerked himself free, and began to back away shrinkingly. 'For the present,' he muttered, in a crestfallen tone.

'What's the matter with him?' The stranger addressed Bessie with the utmost familiarity, in a deliberate, explanatory tone. 'I didn't want to startle the old man.' He lowered his voice as though he had known her for years. 'I dropped into a barber's on my way, to get a twopenny shave, and they told me there he was something of a character. The old man has been a character all his life.'

Captain Hagberd, daunted by the allusion to his clothing, had retreated inside, taking his spade with him; and the two at the gate, startled by the unexpected slamming of the door, heard the bolts being shot, the snapping of the lock, and the echo of an affected gurgling laugh within.

'I didn't want to upset him,' the man said, after a short silence. 'What's the meaning of all this? He isn't quite crazy?'

'He has been worrying a long time about his lost son,' said Bessie, in a low, apologetic tone.

'Well, I am his son.'

'Harry!' she cried – and was profoundly silent.

'Know my name? Friends with the old man, eh?'

'He's our landlord,' Bessie faltered out, catching hold of the iron railing.

'Owns both them rabbit-hutches, does he?' commented young Hagberd scornfully: 'just the thing he would be proud of. Can you tell me who's that chap coming to-morrow? You must know something of it. I tell you, it's a swindle on the old man – nothing else.'

She did not answer, helpless before an insurmountable difficulty, appalled before the necessity, the impossibility and the dread of an explanation in which she and madness seemed involved together.

'Oh – I am so sorry,' she murmured.

'What's the matter?' he said, with serenity. 'You needn't be afraid of upsetting me. It's the other fellow that'll be upset when he least expects it. I don't care a hang; but there will be some fun when he shows his mug to-morrow. I don't care *that* for the old man's pieces, but right is right. You shall see me put a head on that coon – whoever he is!'

He had come nearer, and towered above her on the other side of the railings. He glanced at her hands. He fancied she was trembling, and it occurred to him that she had her part perhaps in that little game that was to be sprung on his old man to-morrow. He had come just in time to spoil their sport. He was entertained by the idea – scornful of the baffled plot. But all his life he had been full of indulgence for all sorts of women's tricks; She really was trembling very much; her wrap had slipped off her head. 'Poor devil!' he thought. 'Never mind about that chap. I daresay he'll change his mind before to-morrow. But what about me? I can't loaf about the gate till the morning.'

She burst out: 'It is *you* – you yourself that he's waiting for. It is *you* who come to-morrow.'

He murmured: 'Oh! It's me!' blankly, and they seemed to become breathless together. Apparently he was pondering over what he had heard; then, without irritation, but evidently perplexed, he said: 'I don't understand. I hadn't written or anything. It's my chum who saw the paper and told me – this very morning. . . . Eh? what?'

He bent his ear; she whispered rapidly, and he listened for a while, muttering the words 'yes' and 'I see' at times. Then, 'But why won't to-day do?' he queried at last.

'You didn't understand me!' she exclaimed impatiently. The clear streak of light under the clouds died out in the west. Again he stooped slightly to hear better; and the deep night buried everything of the whispering woman and the attentive man, except the familiar contiguity of their faces, with its air of secrecy and caress.

He squared his shoulders; the broad-brimmed shadow of a hat sat cavalierly on his head. 'Awkward, this, eh?' he appealed to her. 'To-morrow? Well, well! Never heard tell of anything like this. It's all to-morrow, then, without any sort of to-day, as far as I can see.'

She remained still and mute.

'And you have been encouraging this funny notion,' he said.

'I never contradicted him.'

'Why didn't you?'

'What for should I?' she defended herself. 'It would only have made him miserable. He would have gone out of his mind.'

'His mind!' he muttered, and heard a short nervous laugh from her.

'Where was the harm? Was I to quarrel with the poor old man? It was easier to half believe it myself.'

'Aye, aye,' he meditated intelligently. 'I suppose the old chap got around you somehow with his soft talk. You are good-hearted.'

Her hands moved up in the dark nervously. 'And it might have been true. It was true. It has come. Here it is. This is the to-morrow we have been waiting for.'

She drew a breath, and he said good-humouredly: 'Aye, with the door shut. I wouldn't care if . . . And you think he could be brought round to recognise me . . . Eh? What? . . . You could do it? In a week you say? H'm, I daresay you could – but do you think I could hold out a week in this dead-alive place? Not me! I want either hard work, or an all-fired racket, or more space than there is in the whole of England. I have been in this place, though, once before, and for more than a week. The old man was advertising for me then, and a chum I had with me had a notion of getting a couple of quid out of him by writing a lot of silly nonsense in a letter. That lark did not come off, though. We had to clear out – and none too soon. But this time I've a chum waiting for me in London, and besides . . .'

Bessie Carvil was breathing quickly.

'What if I tried a knock at the door?' he suggested.

'Try,' she said.

Captain Hagberd's gate squeaked, and the shadow of his son moved on, then stopped with another deep laugh in the throat, like the father's, only soft and gentle, thrilling to the woman's heart, awakening to her ears.

'He isn't frisky – is he? I would be afraid to lay hold of him. The chaps are always telling me I don't know my own strength.'

'He's the most harmless creature that ever lived,' she interrupted.

'You wouldn't say so if you had seen him chasing me upstairs with a hard leather strap,' he said; 'I haven't forgotten it in sixteen years.'

She got warm from head to foot under another soft subdued laugh. At the rat-tat-tat of the knocker her heart flew into her mouth.

'Hey, dad! Let me in. I am Harry, I am. Straight! Come back home a day too soon.'

One of the windows upstairs ran up.

'A grinning information fellow,' said the voice of old Hagberd, up in the darkness. 'Don't you have anything to do with him. It will spoil everything.'

She heard Harry Hagberd say, 'Hallo, dad', then a clanging clatter. The window rumbled down, and he stood before her again.

'It's just like old times. Nearly walloped the life out of me to stop me going away, and now I come back he throws a confounded shovel at my head to keep me out. It grazed my shoulder.'

She shuddered.

'I wouldn't care,' he began, 'only I spent my last shillings on the railway fare and my last twopence on a shave – out of respect for the old man.'

'Are you really Harry Hagberd?' she asked swiftly. 'Can you prove it?'

'Can I prove it? Can any one else prove it?' he said jovially. 'Prove with what? What do I want to prove? There isn't a single corner in the world, barring England, perhaps, where you could not find some man, or more likely a woman, that would remember me for Harry Hagberd. I am more like Harry Hagberd than any man alive; and I can prove it to you in a minute, if you will let me step inside your gate.'

'Come in,' she said.

He entered then the front garden of the Carvils. His tall shadow strode with a swagger; she turned her back on the window and waited, watching the shape, of which the footfalls seemed the most material part. The light fell on a tilted hat; a powerful shoulder, that seemed to cleave the darkness; on a leg stepping out. He swung about and stood still, facing the illuminated parlour window at her back, turning his head from side to side, laughing softly to himself.

'Just fancy, for a minute, the old man's beard stuck on to my chin. Hey? Now say. I was the very spit of him from a boy.'

'It's true,' she murmured to herself.

'And that's about as far as it goes. He was always one of your domestic characters. Why, I remember how he used to go about looking very sick for three days before he had to leave home on one of his trips to South Shields for coal. He had a standing charter from the gas-works. You would think he was off on a whaling cruise – three years and a tail. Ha, ha! Not a bit of it. Ten days on the outside. The *Skimmer of the Seas*[49] was a smart craft. Fine name, wasn't it? Mother's uncle owned her. . . .'

He interrupted himself, and in a lowered voice, 'Did he ever tell you what mother died of?' he asked.

'Yes,' said Miss Bessie, bitterly. 'From impatience.'

He made no sound for a while; then brusquely: 'They were so afraid I would turn out badly that they fairly drove me away. Mother nagged at me for being idle, and the old man said he would cut my soul out of my body rather than let me go to sea. Well, it looked as if he would do it too – so I went. It looks to me sometimes as if I had been born to them by a mistake – in that other hutch of a house.'

'Where ought you to have been born by rights?' Bessie Carvil interrupted him defiantly.

'In the open, upon a beach, on a windy night,' he said, quick as lightning. Then he mused slowly. 'They were characters, both of them, by George; and the old man keeps it up well – don't he? A damned shovel on the — Hark! who's that making that row? "Bessie, Bessie." It's in your house.'

'It's for me,' she said with indifference.

He stepped aside, out of the streak of light. 'Your husband?' he inquired, with the tone of a man accustomed to unlawful trysts. 'Fine voice for a ship's deck in a thundering squall.'

'No; my father. I am not married.'

'You seem a fine girl, Miss Bessie dear,' he said at once.

She turned her face away.

'Oh, I say, – what's up? Who's murdering him?'

'He wants his tea.' She faced him, still and tall, with averted head, with her hands hanging clasped before her.

'Hadn't you better go in?' he suggested, after watching for a while the nape of her neck, a patch of dazzling white skin and soft shadow above the sombre line of her shoulders. Her wrap had slipped down to her elbows. 'You'll have all the town coming out presently. I'll wait here a bit.'

Her wrap fell to the ground, and he stooped to pick it up; she had vanished. He threw it over his arm, and approaching the window squarely he saw a monstrous form of a fat man in an armchair, an unshaded lamp, the yawning of an enormous mouth in a big flat face encircled by a ragged halo of hair, – Miss Bessie's head and bust. The shouting stopped; the blind ran down. He lost himself in thinking how awkward it was. Father mad; no getting into the house. No money to get back; a hungry chum in London who would begin to think he had been given the go-by. 'Damn!' he muttered. He could break the door in, certainly; but they would perhaps bundle him into chokey for that without asking questions – no great matter, only he was confoundedly afraid of being locked up, even in mistake. He turned cold at the thought. He stamped his feet on the sodden grass.

'What are you? – a sailor?' said an agitated voice.

She had flitted out, a shadow herself, attracted by the reckless shadow waiting under the wall of her home.

'Anything. Enough of a sailor to be worth my salt before the mast. Came home that way this time.'

'Where do you come from?' she asked.

'Right away from a jolly good spree,' he said, 'by the London train – see? Ough! I hate being shut up in a train. I don't mind a house so much.'

'Ah,' she said; 'that's lucky.'

'Because in a house you can at any time open the blamed door and walk away straight before you.'

'And never come back?'

'Not for sixteen years at least,' he laughed. 'To a rabbit hutch, and get a confounded old shovel . . .'

'A ship is not so very big,' she taunted.

'No, but the sea is great.'

She dropped her head, and as if her ears had been opened to the voices of the world, she heard beyond the rampart of sea-wall the swell of yesterday's gale breaking on the beach with monotonous and solemn vibrations, as if all the earth had been a tolling bell.

'And then, why, a ship's a ship. You love her and leave her; and a voyage isn't a marriage.' He quoted the sailor's saying lightly.

'It is not a marriage,' she whispered.

'I never took a false name, and I've never yet told a lie to a woman. What lie? Why, *the* lie —. Take me or leave me, I say: and if you take me, then it is . . .' He hummed a snatch very low, leaning against the wall.

> Oh, oh, ho! Rio! . . .
> And fare thee well,
> My bonnie young girl,
> We're bound to Rio . . . Grande.

'Capstan song,'[50] he explained. Her teeth chattered.

'You are cold,' he said. 'Here's that affair of yours I picked up.' She felt his hands about her, wrapping her closely. 'Hold the ends together in front,' he commanded.

'What did you come here for?' she asked, repressing a shudder.

'Five quid,' he answered promptly. 'We let our spree go on a little too long and got hard up.'

'You've been drinking?' she said.

'Blind three days; on purpose. I am not given that way – don't you think. There's nothing and nobody that can get over me unless I like. I can be as steady as a rock. My chum sees the paper this morning and says he to me: "Go on, Harry: loving parent. That's five quid sure." So we scraped all our pockets for the fare. Devil of a lark!'

'You have a hard heart, I am afraid,' she sighed.

'What for? For running away? Why! he wanted to make a lawyer's clerk of me – just to please himself. Master in his own house; and my poor mother egged him on – for my good, I suppose. Well, then – so long; and I went. No, I tell you: the day I cleared out, I was all black and blue from his great fondness for me. Ah! he was always a bit of a character. Look at that shovel, now. Off his chump? Not much. That's just exactly like my dad. He wants me here just to have somebody to order about. However, we two were hard up; and what's five quid to him – once in sixteen hard years?'

'Oh, but I am sorry for you. Did you never want to come back home?'

'Be a lawyer's clerk and rot here – in some such place as this?' he cried in contempt. 'What! if the old man set me up in a home to-day, I would kick it down about my ears – or else die there before the third day was out.'

'And where else is it that you hope to die?'

'In the bush somewhere; in the sea; on a blamed mountain-top for choice. At home? Yes! the world's my home; but I expect I'll die in a hospital some day. What of that? Any place is good enough, as long as I've lived; and I've been everything you can think of almost but a tailor or soldier. I've been a boundary rider; I've sheared sheep; and humped my swag; and harpooned a whale. I've rigged ships, and prospected for gold, and skinned dead bullocks, – and turned my back on more money than the old man would have scraped in his whole life. Ha, ha!'

He overwhelmed her. She pulled herself together and managed to utter, 'Time to rest now.'

He straightened himself up, away from the wall, and in a severe voice said, 'Time to go.'

But he did not move. He leaned back again, and hummed thoughtfully a bar or two of an outlandish tune.

She felt as if she were about to cry. 'That's another of your cruel songs,' she said.

'Learned it in Mexico – in Sonora.' He talked easily. 'It is the song of the Gambusinos. You don't know? The song of restless men. Nothing could hold them in one place – not even a woman. You used to meet one of them now and again, in the old days, on the edge of the gold country, away north there beyond the Rio Gila. I've seen it. A prospecting engineer in Mazatlán took me along with him to help look after the waggons. A sailor's a handy chap to have about you anyhow. It's all a desert: cracks in the earth that you can't see the bottom of; and mountains – sheer rocks standing up high like walls and church spires, only a hundred times bigger. The valleys are full of boulders and black stones. There's not a blade of grass to see; and the sun sets more red over that country than I have seen it anywhere – blood-red and angry. It *is* fine.'

'You do not want to go back there again?' she stammered out.

He laughed a little. 'No. That's the blamed gold country. It gave me the shivers sometimes to look at it – and we were a big lot of men together, mind; but these Gambusinos wandered alone. They knew that country before anybody had ever heard of it. They had a sort of gift for prospecting, and the fever of it was on them too; and they did not seem to want the gold very much. They would find some rich spot, and then turn their backs on it; pick up perhaps a little – enough for a spree – and then be off again, looking for more. They never stopped long where there were houses; they had no wife, no chick, no home, never a chum. You couldn't be friends with a Gambusino; they were too restless – here to-day, and gone, God knows where, to-morrow. They told no one of their finds, and there has never been a Gambusino well off. It was not for the gold they cared; it was the wandering about looking for it in the stony country that got into them and wouldn't let them rest: so that no woman yet born could hold a Gambusino for more than a week. That's what the song says. It's all about a pretty girl that tried hard to keep hold of a Gambusino lover, so that he should bring her lots of gold. No fear! Off he went, and she never saw him again.'

'What became of her?' she breathed out.

'The song don't tell. Cried a bit, I daresay. They were the fellows: kiss and go. But it's the looking for a thing – a something ... Sometimes I think I am a sort of Gambusino myself.'

'No woman can hold you, then,' she began in a brazen voice, which quavered suddenly before the end.

'No longer than a week,' he joked, playing upon her very heartstrings with the gay, tender note of his laugh; 'and yet I am fond of them all. Anything for a woman of the right sort. The scrapes they got me into, and the scrapes they got me out of! I love them at first sight. I've fallen in love with you already, Miss – Bessie's your name – eh?'

She backed away a little, and with a trembling laugh: 'You haven't seen my face yet.'

He bent forward gallantly. 'A little pale: it suits some. But you are a fine figure of a girl, Miss Bessie.'

She was all in a flutter. Nobody had ever said so much to her before.

His tone changed. 'I am getting middling hungry, though. Had no breakfast to-day. Couldn't you scare up some bread from that tea for me, or —'

She was gone already. He had been on the point of asking her to let him come inside. No matter. Anywhere would do. Devil of a fix! What would his chum think?

'I didn't ask you as a beggar,' he said jestingly, taking a piece of bread-and-butter from the plate she held before him. 'I asked as a friend. My dad is rich, you know.'

'He starves himself for your sake.'

'And I have starved for his whim,' he said, taking up another piece.

'All he has in the world is for you,' she pleaded.

'Yes, if I come here to sit on it like a dam' toad in a hole. Thank you; and what about the shovel, eh? He always had a queer way of showing his love.'

'I could bring him round in a week,' she suggested timidly.

He was too hungry to answer her; and, holding the plate submissively to his hand, she began to whisper up to him in a quick, panting voice. He listened, amazed, eating slower and slower, till at last his jaws stopped altogether. 'That's his game, is it?' he said, in a rising tone of scathing contempt. An ungovernable movement of his arm sent the plate flying out of her fingers. He shot out a violent curse.

She shrank from him, putting her hand against the wall.

'No!' he raged. 'He expects! Expects *me* – for his rotten money! ... Who wants his home? Mad – not he! Don't you think. He wants his own way. He wanted to turn me into a miserable lawyer's clerk, and now he wants to make of me a blamed tame rabbit in a cage. Of me! Of me!' His subdued angry laugh frightened her now.

'The whole world ain't a bit too big for me to spread my elbows in, I can tell you – what's your name – Bessie – let alone a dam' parlour in a hutch. Marry! He wants me to marry and settle! And as likely as not he has looked out the girl too – dash my soul! And do you know the Judy, may I ask?'

She shook all over with noiseless dry sobs; but he was fuming and fretting too much to notice her distress. He bit his thumb with rage at the mere idea. A window rattled up.

'A grinning, information fellow,' pronounced old Hagberd dogmatically, in measured tones. And the sound of his voice seemed to Bessie to make the night itself mad – to pour insanity and disaster on the earth. 'Now I know what's wrong with the people here, my dear. Why, of course! With this mad chap going about. Don't you have anything to do with him, Bessie. Bessie, I say!'

They stood as if dumb. The old man fidgeted and mumbled to himself at the window. Suddenly he cried piercingly: 'Bessie – I see you. I'll tell Harry.'

She made a movement as if to run away, but stopped and raised her hands to her temples. Young Hagberd, shadowy and big, stirred no more than a man of bronze. Over their heads the crazy night whimpered and scolded in an old man's voice.

'Send him away, my dear. He's only a vagabond. What you want is a good home of your own. That chap has no home – he's not like Harry. He can't be Harry. Harry is coming to-morrow. Do you hear? One day more,' he babbled more excitedly; 'never you fear – Harry shall marry you.'

His voice rose very shrill and mad against the regular deep soughing of the swell coiling heavily about the outer face of the sea-wall.

'He will have to. I shall make him, or if not' – he swore a great oath – 'I'll cut him off with a shilling to-morrow, and leave everything to you. I shall. To you. Let him starve.'

The window rattled down.

Harry drew a deep breath, and took one step towards Bessie. 'So it's you – the girl,' he said, in a lowered voice. She had not moved, and she remained half turned away from him, pressing her head in the palms of her hands. 'My word!' he continued, with an invisible half-smile on his lips. 'I have a great mind to stop . . .'

Her elbows were trembling violently.

'For a week,' he finished without a pause.

She clapped her hands to her face.

He came up quite close, and took hold of her wrists gently. She felt his breath on her ear.

'It's a scrape I am in – this, and it is you that must see me through.' He was trying to uncover her face. She resisted. He let her go then, and stepping back a little, 'Have you got any money?' he asked. 'I must be off now.'

She nodded quickly her shamefaced head, and he waited, looking away from her, while, trembling all over and bowing her neck, she tried to find the pocket of her dress.

'Here it is!' she whispered. 'Oh, go away! go away for God's sake! If I had more – more – I would give it all to forget – to make you forget.'

He extended his hand. 'No fear! I haven't forgotten a single one of you in the world. Some gave me more than money – but I am a beggar now – and you women always had to get me out of my scrapes.'

He swaggered up to the parlour window, and in the dim light filtering through the blind, looked at the coin lying in his palm. It was a half-sovereign. He slipped it into his pocket. She stood a little on one side, with her head drooping, as if wounded; with her arms hanging passive by her side, as if dead.

'You can't buy me in,' he said, 'and you can't buy yourself out.'

He set his hat firmly with a little tap, and next moment she felt herself lifted up in the powerful embrace of his arms. Her feet lost the ground; her head hung back; he showered kisses on her face with a silent and overmastering ardour, as if in haste to get at her very soul. He kissed her pale cheeks, her hard forehead, her heavy eyelids, her faded lips; and the measured blows and sighs of the rising tide accompanied the enfolding power of his arms, the overwhelming might of his caresses. It was as if the sea, breaking down the wall protecting all the homes of the town, had sent a wave over her head. It passed on; she staggered backwards, with her shoulders against the wall, exhausted, as if she had been stranded there after a storm and a shipwreck.

She opened her eyes after a while; and, listening to the firm, leisurely footsteps going away with their conquest, began to gather her skirts, staring all the time before her. Suddenly she darted through the open gate into the dark and deserted street.

'Stop!' she shouted. 'Don't go!'

And listening with an attentive poise of the head, she could not tell whether it was the beat of the swell or his fateful tread that seemed to fall cruelly upon her heart. Presently every sound grew fainter, as though she were slowly turning into stone. A fear of this awful silence came to her – worse than the fear of death. She called upon her ebbing strength for the final appeal:

'Harry!'

Not even the dying echo of a footstep. Nothing. The thundering of the surf, the voice of the restless sea itself, seemed stopped. There was not a sound – no whisper of life, as though she were alone, and lost in that stony country of which she had heard, where madmen go looking for gold and spurn the find.

Captain Hagberd, inside his dark house, had kept on the alert. A window ran up; and in the silence of the stony country a voice spoke above her head, high up in the black air – the voice of madness, lies and despair – the voice of inextinguishable hope. 'Is he gone yet – that information fellow? Do you hear him about, my dear?'

She burst into tears. 'No! no! no! I don't hear him any more,' she sobbed.

He began to chuckle up there triumphantly. 'You frightened him away. Good girl. Now we shall be all right. Don't you be impatient, my dear. One day more.'[51]

In the other house old Carvil, wallowing regally in his arm-chair, with a globe lamp burning by his side on the table, yelled for her in a fiendish voice: 'Bessie! Bessie! You, Bessie!'

She heard him at last, and, as if overcome by fate, began to totter silently back towards her stuffy little inferno of a cottage. It had no lofty portal, no terrific inscription of forfeited hopes – she did not understand wherein she had sinned.

Captain Hagberd had gradually worked himself into a state of noisy happiness up there.

'Go in! Keep quiet!' she turned upon him tearfully, from the doorstep below.

He rebelled against her authority in his great joy at having got rid at last of that 'something wrong'. It was as if all the hopeful madness of the world had broken out to bring terror upon her heart, with the voice of that old man shouting of his trust in an everlasting to-morrow.

APPENDIX
One Day More

APPENDIX
ONE DAY MORE

CONRAD completed the first version of his stage adaptation of
'To-morrow' in early February 1904 (*CLJC*, 3, pp. 110–12); John
Galsworthy, in his Introduction to *Laughing Anne & One Day More*
(London: John Castle, 1924, p. 6) testified that the writing was
done 'in my studio workroom on Campden Hill. Conrad worked at
one end of it, on *One Day More*, while, at the other end, I was
labouring at *The Man of Property*.' At this time Conrad was staying
in Kensington near his collaborator, Ford Madox Ford [pseudonym
of Ford Hermann Hueffer], and a legend has been growing that the
play was a full-fledged collaboration, or was even entirely written
by Ford, who allowed Conrad to claim sole credit. Arthur Mizener,
in *The Saddest Story: A Biography of Ford Madox Ford* (New York,
1971, pp. 107–9) quotes Ford's letter to Pinker early in 1905
saying that Granville-Barker had asked to see 'a play of mine' and
requesting Pinker to 'forward him that one I sent you – and would
you impress him with the idea that it's merely in a sketchy stage?
and that C. and I would work it up any amount if there were a
definite chance of production – but not otherwise?' (Ford had just
sent Pinker the 'play'; Mizener does not mention that this was a
year after Conrad spoke of having finished *One Day More*.) In his
next letter to Pinker, Ford took a different line: 'Certainly you can
say the play is by self and Conrad – C., that is, will do more to it if
there is a reasonable certainty of its being accepted – and for all I
sh'd care, he c'd call it quite his own.' Mizener concludes (p. 108):
'The suggestion of these letters that Ford had done the actual
dramatization of *One Day More* is borne out by the existence of
forty-three pages of manuscript of the play in Ford's hand.'

I have examined this manuscript (actually forty-one pages), and
far from bearing out the 'suggestion' it goes a long way towards
discrediting it. The manuscript roughly corresponds to the first

two scenes, about sixteen pages of the printed text. It breaks off, at the *top* of the last page, at the point where the play's real dramatic action begins: the entrance of Harry Hagberd. The dialogue differs markedly from that of the published play. Carvil says nothing about ham and eggs – his hallmark in the story – and one of the most chilling lines – the death of Hagberd's wife 'from impatience' – is also missing. On the other hand, Carvil accuses Bessie of having 'a screw loose' and claims to have read ten years before that Harry was hanged for murdering a woman in Liverpool. Exposition about Hagberd and Harry is largely entrusted to a fish-hawker, who occupies over a quarter of the fragment. (In the play he has disappeared.) Conrad apparently wrote to Ford in April 1905 asking if he wished his name associated with the play; instead of replying to Conrad, Ford wrote directly to Sidney Colvin, who was the moving force behind the Stage Society's production. Conrad then tried to set the record straight to Colvin (I have italicized the parts of Conrad's letter which Mizener omits when quoting it):

> The facts are that Hueffer *a good and dear friend* helped me by *spending a whole day in* taking out the dialogue of story [sic] in a typewritten extract *for my use and reference*. The play, *as can be shown by the MS*, has been written entirely in my own hand; *and I wrote it alone in a room lent me by an acquaintance to ensure perfect quiet for the six days it took me to achieve that very small feat. In such matters however one cannot be too scrupulous. I won't say any more. You'll understand a demi-mot* [You'll take the hint]. *And of course now Ford has written to you You'll allow me to show you the MS on my return.* Five minutes' perusal will show you *the exact value of the sample which caused me to refer to Hueffer at the last moment and the genuineness* of his disclaimer. *I've always looked upon the play as mine only till brought to terms – as it were – by the offer of the Stage Society for which – as for the very inception of the play I have to thank your unwearied interest.* (CLJC, 3, p. 236)

Mizener calls this letter 'curiously defensive'. I find it understandably diplomatic. In consulting Ford before signing a contract Conrad was being as considerate as he could to a man to whom he owed much, both as lenient landlord and literary collaborator; a man whom he regarded as a friend but who, he knew, given an inch would claim a mile (see Introduction, note 32).

Whether Ford wrote his preliminary sketch during or after a

session with Conrad, comparison of manuscript and published play leaves no doubt that Conrad adapted his own story. (Conrad's own manuscript – sixty-one pages – is now in the Berg Collection.) In the version Conrad sent to Beerbohm Tree in March 1904, incorporating Colvin's suggestions, the fish-hawker was 'cut down considerably, also old Carvil at the very beginning' (*CLJC*, 3, p. 124). In April 1905 Conrad told Colvin: 'I am ready to defer to the suggestions as to cutting out which our unique G. B. S. will favour me with. The artificiality of the abominable fish-hawker has ever been an offence to me.... It is a gross artifice I own – and I am glad to be shown I was mistaken' (*CLJC*, 3, p. 242). Whoever dreamt up the fish-hawker (who corresponds to the barber in the story), it seems that Bernard Shaw finally had more of a hand in the play than Ford Madox Ford.

One Day More ran for three evening performances and two matinees at the Royalty Theatre from 25 to 27 June 1905. Shaw thought Conrad should write another, and Max Beerbohm called the play 'terrible and haunting' and 'a powerful tragedy', although he confessed it had moved him less than the story. For his part, Conrad thought the play a failure, although in 1919 he pointed out to Pinker that it had been by then performed 'in three English towns, in Paris and also (for a week) in Chicago' (*LL*, II, p. 225). (One production was by the celebrated Birmingham Repertory Theatre on 12 September 1918.) In 1923, in a letter to Louise Burleigh, Conrad referred to an imminent production in the United States, pointing out that Hagberd's line about impatience was not meant to be comic. The play was performed by the Provincetown Players in New York in 1933, and most recently in 1988 by a theatre group from Kent University at conferences held respectively in London by the Joseph Conrad Society (UK) and in Lund, Sweden by the Scandinavian Joseph Conrad Society.

The weak point of the play is its forced exposition: Carvil's tyranny, Hagberd's madness and Harry's story need to be firmly established before any dramatic action can begin. However, Carvil's self-indulgent materialism in the first scene is well counterpointed by Hagberd's self-starving idea-worship in the second, and visually emphasized by the two men's contrasting physiques (Carvil's ponderousness and immobility as against Hagberd's nervous scurrying movements). A semi-expressionistic production might work: the scene between Bessie and Harry is in some respects a dramatic analogue of the Gentleman Caller scene in *The Glass Menagerie*. But the mood recalls O'Neill at his bleakest.

During Conrad's lifetime *One Day More* was published in the *English Review* (August 1913) and in limited editions in London (1917 and 1919) and New York (1920). It was last reprinted in 1955, by Eric Bentley in his anthology *The Modern Theatre* (New York: Doubleday, 1955, Vol. 3). The present text is based on the one introduced by Galsworthy (see above), published shortly after Conrad's death. I have made slight changes in punctuation, and two substantive changes from the typescript in the Lord Chamberlain's Play Collection: after Harry's sea-shanty Bessie asks 'What's that?' (p. 286), not 'What's this?' and Carvil says 'Seeing them', not 'Seeing him' (p. 272). I have also emended 'let their boys into' to 'let their boys in for' (p. 275), as in 'To-morrow', and 'everlasted' to 'everlasting' (p. 289), as in the 1919 limited edition.

ONE DAY MORE

CHARACTERS

CAPTAIN HAGBERD, *a retired coasting skipper.*
JOSIAH CARVIL, *formerly a shipbuilder – a widower – blind.*
HARRY HAGBERD, *son of* CAPTAIN HAGBERD, *who, as a boy, ran away from home.*
A LAMPLIGHTER
BESSIE CARVIL, *daughter of* JOSIAH CARVIL.

PLACE: *A small sea-port.*
TIME: *The present – early autumn, towards dusk.*
STAGE Represents: *To right – two yellow brick cottages belonging to* CAPTAIN HAGBERD, *one inhabited by himself, the other by the* CARVILS. *A lamp-post in front. The red roofs of the town in the background. A sea-wall to left.*

Note. – The division into scenes is made in a purely dramatic sense. It has nothing to do with the scenery. It relates only to the varied grouping of the characters with the consequent changes in the mental and emotional atmosphere of the situation.

SCENE 1

CURTAIN *rises disclosing* CARVIL *and* BESSIE *moving away from sea-wall.* BESSIE, *about twenty-five. Black dress; black straw hat. A lot of mahogany-coloured hair loosely done up. Pale face. Full figure. Very quiet.* CARVIL, *blind, unwieldy. Reddish whiskers; slow, deep voice produced without effort. Immovable, big face.*

CARVIL [*hanging heavily on* BESSIE's *arm*]: Careful! Go slow! [*Stops;* BESSIE *waits patiently.*] Want your poor blind father to break his neck? [*Shuffles on.*] In a hurry to get home and start that everlasting yarn with your chum the lunatic?

271

BESSIE: I am not in a hurry to get home, father.

CARVIL: Well, then, go steady with a poor blind man. Blind! Helpless! [*Strikes the ground with his stick.*] Never mind! I've had time to make enough money to have ham and eggs for breakfast every morning – thank God! And thank God, too, for it, girl. You haven't known a single hardship in all the days of your idle life. Unless you think that a blind, helpless father —

BESSIE: What is there for me to be in a hurry for?

CARVIL: What did you say?

BESSIE: I said there was nothing for me to hurry home for.

CARVIL: There is, tho'. To yarn with a lunatic. Anything to get away from your duty.

BESSIE: Captain Hagberd's talk never hurt you or anybody else.

CARVIL: Go on. Stick up for your only friend.

BESSIE: Is it my fault that I haven't another soul to speak to?

CARVIL [*snarls*]: It's mine, perhaps. Can I help being blind? You fret because you want to be gadding about – with a helpless man left all alone at home. Your own father, too.

BESSIE: I haven't been away from you half a day since mother died.

CARVIL [*viciously*]: He's a lunatic, our landlord is. That's what he is. Has been for years – long before those damned doctors destroyed my sight for me. [*Growls angrily, then sighs.*]

BESSIE: Perhaps Captain Hagberd is not so mad as the town takes him for.

CARVIL [*grimly*]: Don't everybody know how he came here from the North to wait till his missing son turns up – here – of all places in the world. His boy that ran away to sea sixteen years ago and never did give a sign of life since! Don't I remember seeing people dodge round corners out of his way when he came along High Street? Seeing them, I tell you. [*Groan*] He bothered everybody so with his silly talk of his son being sure to come back home – next year – next spring – next month —. What is it by this time, hey?

BESSIE: Why talk about it? He bothers no one now.

CARVIL: No. They've grown too fly. You've only to pass a remark on his sail-cloth coat to make him shut up. All the town knows it. But he's got you to listen to his crazy talk whenever he chooses. Don't I hear you two at it, jabber, jabber, mumble, mumble —

BESSIE: What is there so mad in keeping up hope?

CARVIL [*scathing scorn*]: Not mad! Starving himself to lay money by – for that son. Filling his house with furniture he won't let anyone see – for that son. Advertising in the papers every week, these sixteen years – for that son. Not mad! Boy, he calls him. Boy Harry. His boy Harry. His lost boy Harry. Yah! Let him lose his sight to know what real trouble means. And the boy – the man, I should say – must've been put away safe in Davy Jones's locker for many a year – drowned – food for fishes – dead. . . . Stands to reason, or he would have been here before, smelling around the old fool's money. [*Shakes* BESSIE's *arm slightly.*] Hey?

BESSIE: I don't know. Maybe.

CARVIL [*bursting out*]: Damme if I don't think he ever had a son.

BESSIE: Poor man. Perhaps he never had.

CARVIL: Ain't that mad enough for you? But I suppose you think it sensible.

BESSIE: What does it matter? His talk keeps him up.

CARVIL: Aye! And it pleases you. Anything to get away from your poor blind father . . . jabber, jabber – mumble, mumble – till I begin to think you must be as crazy as he is. What do you find to talk about, you two? What's your game?

[*During the scene* CARVIL *and* BESSIE *have crossed stage from L. to R. slowly with stoppages.*]

BESSIE: It's warm. Will you sit out for a while?

CARVIL [*viciously*]: Yes, I will sit out. [*Insistent.*] But what can be your game? What are you up to? [*They pass through garden gate.*] Because if it's his money you are after —

BESSIE: Father! How can you!

CARVIL [*disregarding her*]: – to make you independent of your poor blind father, then you are a fool. [*Drops heavily on seat.*] He's too much of a miser to ever make a will – even if he weren't mad.

BESSIE: Oh! It never entered my head. I swear it never did.

CARVIL: Never did. Hey! Then you are a still bigger fool. . . . I want to go to sleep!

273

[*Takes off his hat, drops it on the ground, and leans his head back against the wall.*]

BESSIE: And I have been a good daughter to you. Won't you say that for me?

CARVIL [*very distinctly*]: I want – to – go – to – sleep. I'm tired. [*Closes his eyes.*]

[*During the scene* CAPTAIN HAGBERD *has been seen hesitating at the back of stage then running quickly to the door of his cottage. He puts inside a tin kettle – from under his coat – and comes down to the railing between the two gardens stealthily.*]

SCENE 2

CARVIL *seated.* BESSIE. CAPTAIN HAGBERD [*white beard, sail-cloth jacket*].

BESSIE [*knitting*]: You've been out this afternoon for quite a long time, haven't you?

CAPT. HAGBERD [*eager*]: Yes, my dear. [*Slyly*] Of course you saw me come back.

BESSIE: Oh, yes. I did see you. You had something under your coat.

CAPT. H. [*anxiously*]: It was only a kettle, my dear. A tin water-kettle. I am glad I thought of it just in time. [*Winks, nods.*] When a husband gets back from his work he needs a lot of water for a wash. See? [*Dignified*] Not that Harry'll ever need to do a hand's turn after he comes home . . . [*Falters – casts stealthy glances on all sides*] . . . to-morrow.

BESSIE [*looks up, grave*]: Captain Hagberd, have you ever thought that perhaps your son will not . . .

CAPT. H. [*paternally*]: I've thought of everything, my dear – of everything a reasonable young couple may need for house-keeping. Why, I can hardly turn about in my room up there, the house is that full. [*Rubs his hands with satisfaction.*] For my son, Harry – when he comes home. One day more.

BESSIE [*flattering*]: Oh, you are a great one for bargains. [CAPT. H. *delighted*] But, Captain Hagberd – if – if – you don't know what may happen – if all that home you've got together were to be wasted – for nothing – after all. [*Aside*] Oh, I can't bring it out.

CAPT. H. [*agitated; flings arms up, stamps feet; stuttering*]: What? What d'ye mean? What's going to happen to the things?

BESSIE [*soothing*]: Nothing! Nothing! Dust – or moth – you know. Damp, perhaps. You never let anyone into the house . . .

CAPT. H.: Dust! Damp! [*Has a throaty, gurgling laugh.*] I light the fires and dust the things myself. [*Indignant*] Let anyone into the house, indeed! What would Harry say! [*Walks up and down his garden hastily with tosses, flings, and jerks of his whole body.*]

BESSIE [*with authority*]: Now, then, Captain Hagberd! You know I won't put up with your tantrums. [*Shakes finger at him.*]

CAPT. H. [*subdued, but still sulky, with his back to her*]: You want to see the things. That's what you're after. Well, no, not even you. Not till Harry has had his first look.

BESSIE: Oh, no! I don't. [*Relenting.*] Not till you're willing. [*Smiles at* CAPT. H., *who has turned half round already.*] You mustn't excite yourself. [*Knits.*]

CAPT. H. [*condescending*]: And you the only sensible girl for miles and miles around. Can't you trust me? I am a domestic man. Always was, my dear. I hated the sea. People don't know what they let their boys in for when they send them to sea. As soon make convicts of them at once. What sort of life is it? Most of your time you don't know what's going on at home [*Insinuating.*] There's nothing anywhere on earth as good as a home, my dear. [*Pause.*] With a good husband . . .

CARVIL [*heard from his seat fragmentarily*]: There they go . . . jabber, jabber . . . mumble, mumble. [*With a groaning effort.*] Helpless! [BESSIE *has glanced round at him.*]

CAPT. H. [*mutters*]: Extravagant ham-and-eggs fellow. [*Louder.*] Of course it isn't as if he had a son to make a home ready for. Girls are different, my dear. They don't run away, my dear, my dear. [*Agitated.*]

BESSIE [*drops her arms wearily*]: No, Captain Hagberd – they don't.

CAPT. H. [*slowly*]: I wouldn't let my own flesh and blood go to sea. Not I.

BESSIE: And the boy ran away.

CAPT. H. [*a little vacantly*]: Yes, my only son Harry. [*Rouses himself.*] Coming home, to-morrow.

BESSIE [*looks at him pityingly; speaks softly*]: Sometimes, Captain Hagberd, a hope turns out false.

CAPT. H. [*uneasy*]: What's that got to do with Harry's coming back?

BESSIE: It's good to hope for something. But suppose now — [*Feeling her way.*] Yours is not the only lost son that's never . . .

CAPT. H.: Never what! You don't believe he's drowned. [*Crouches, glaring and grasping the rails.*]

BESSIE [*frightened, drops knitting*]: Captain Hagberd – don't. [*Catches hold of his shoulders over the railings.*] Don't – my God! He's going out of his mind! [*Cries.*] I didn't mean it! I don't know.

CAPT. H. [*has backed away. An affected burst of laughter*]: What nonsense! None of us Hagberds belonged to the sea. All farmers for hundreds of years. [*Paternal and cunning.*] Don't alarm yourself, my dear. The sea can't get us. Look at me! I didn't get drowned. Moreover, Harry ain't a sailor at all. And if he isn't a sailor, he's bound to come back – to-morrow.

BESSIE [*has been facing him; murmurs*]: No. I give it up. He scares me. [*Aloud, sharply*] Then I would give up that advertising in the papers.

CAPT. H. [*surprised and puzzled*]: Why, my dear? Everybody does it. His poor mother and I have been advertising for years and years. But she was an impatient woman. She died.

BESSIE: If your son's coming, as – as you say – what's the good of that expense? You had better spend that half-crown on yourself. I believe you don't eat enough.

CAPT. H. [*confused*]: But it's the right thing to do. Look at the Sunday papers. Missing relatives on top page – all proper. [*Looks unhappy.*]

BESSIE [*tartly*]: Ah, well! I declare I don't know what you live on.

CAPT. H.: Are you getting impatient, my dear? Don't get impatient – like my poor wife. If she'd only been patient she'd be here. Waiting – only one day more. [*Pleadingly*] Don't be impatient, my dear.

BESSIE: I've no patience with you sometimes.

CAPT. H. [*flash of lucidity*]: Why? What's the matter? [*Sympathetic*] You're tired out, my dear that's what it is.

BESSIE: Yes, I am. Day after day. [*Stands listless, arms hanging down.*]

CAPT. H. [*timidly*]: House dull?

BESSIE [*apathetic*]: Yes.

CAPT. H. [*as before*]: H'm. Wash, cook, scrub. Hey?

BESSIE [*as before*]: Yes.

CAPT. H. [*pointing stealthily at the sleeping* CARVIL]: Heavy?

BESSIE [*in a dead voice*]: Like a millstone.

[*A silence.*]

CAPT. H. [*burst of indignation*]: Why don't that extravagant fellow get you a servant?

BESSIE: I don't know.

CAPT. H. [*cheerily*]: Wait till Harry comes home. He'll get you one.

BESSIE [*almost hysterical; laughs*]: Why, Captain Hagberd, perhaps your son won't even want to look at me – when he comes home.

CAPT. H. [*in a great voice*]: What! [*Quite low*] The boy wouldn't dare. [*Rising choler*] Wouldn't dare to refuse the only sensible girl for miles around. That stubborn jackanapes refuse to marry a girl like you! [*Walks about in a fury.*] You trust me, my dear, my dear, my dear. I'll make him. I'll – I'll — [*splutters.*] Cut him off with a shilling.

BESSIE: Hush! [*Severe*] You mustn't talk like that. What's this? More of your tantrums?

CAPT. H. [*quite humble*]: No, no – this isn't my tantrums – when I don't feel quite well in my head. Only I can't stand this. . . . I've grown as fond of you as if you'd been the wife of my Harry already. And to be told – [*Can't restrain himself; shouts.*] Jackanapes!

BESSIE: Sh —! Don't you worry! [*Wearily.*] I must give that up too, I suppose. [*Aloud*] I didn't mean it, Captain Hagberd.

CAPT. H.: It's as if I were to have two children to-morrow. My son Harry – and the only sensible girl — Why, my dear, I couldn't get on without you. We two are reasonable together. The rest of the people in this town are crazy. The way they stare at you. And the grins – they're all on the grin. It makes me dislike to go out. [*Bewildered*] It seems as if there was something wrong about – somewhere. My dear, is there anything wrong – you who are sensible . . .

BESSIE [*soothingly tender*]: No, no, Captain Hagberd. There is nothing wrong about you anywhere.

CARVIL [*lying back*]: Bessie! [*Sits up.*] Get my hat, Bessie. . . . Bessie, my hat. . . . Bessie . . . Bessie . . . [*At the first sound* BESSIE *picks up and puts away her knitting. She walks towards him, picks up his hat, puts it on his head.*] Bessie, my . . . [*Hat on head; shouting stops.*]

BESSIE [*quietly*]: Will you go in, now?

CARVIL: Help me up. Steady. I'm dizzy. It's the thundery weather. An autumn thunderstorm means a bad gale. Very fierce – and sudden. There will be shipwrecks tonight on our coast.

[*Exit* BESSIE *and* CARVIL *through door of their cottage. It has fallen dusk.*]

CAPT. H. [*picks up spade*]: Extravagant fellow! And all this town is mad – perfectly mad. I found them out years ago. Thank God they don't come this way staring and grinning. I can't bear them. I'll never go again into that High Street. [*Agitated*] Never, never, never. Won't need to after to-morrow. Never! [*Flings down spade in a passion.*]

[*While* HAGBERD *speaks, the bow window of the* CARVILS *is lit up, and* BESSIE *is seen settling her father in a big armchair. Pulls down blind. Enter* LAMPLIGHTER. CAPT. H. *picks up the spade and leans forward on it with both hands; very still, watching him light the lamp.*]

LAMPLIGHTER [*jocular*]: There! You will be able to dig by lamp-light if the fancy takes you.

[*Exit* LAMPLIGHTER *to back.*]

CAPT. H. [*disgusted*]: Ough! The people here . . . [*Shudders.*]

LAMPLIGHTER'S VOICE [*heard loudly beyond the cottages*]: Yes, that's the way.

[*Enter* HARRY *from back.*]

SCENE 3

CAPTAIN HAGBERD. HARRY. *Later* BESSIE.

HARRY HAGBERD [*Thirty-one, tall, broad shoulders, shaven face, small moustache. Blue serge suit. Coat open. Grey flannel shirt without collar and tie. No waistcoat. Belt with buckle. Black, soft felt hat, wide-brimmed, worn crushed in the crown and a little on one side. Good nature, recklessness, some swagger in the bearing. Assured, deliberate walk with a heavy tread. Slight roll in the gait. Walks down. Stops, hands in pockets. Looks about. Speaks*]: This must be it. Can't see anything beyond. There's somebody. [*Walks up to* CAPT. H.*'s gate.*] Can you tell me ... [*Manner changes. Leans elbow on gate.*] Why, you must be Captain Hagberd himself.

CAPT. H. [*in garden, both hands on spade, peering, startled*]: Yes, I am.

HARRY [*slowly*]: You've been advertising in the papers for your son, I believe.

CAPT. H. [*off his guard, nervous*]: Yes. My only boy Harry. He's coming home to-morrow. [*Mumbles.*] For a permanent stay.

HARRY [*surprised*]: The devil he is! [*Change of tone.*] My word! You've grown a beard like Father Christmas himself.

CAPT. H. [*impressively*]: Go your way. [*Waves one hand loftily.*] What's that to you. Go your way. [*Agitated*] Go your way.

HARRY: There, there. I am not trespassing in the street – where I stand – am I? Tell you what, I fancy there's something wrong about your nerves. Suppose you let me come in – for a quiet chat, you know.

CAPT. H. [*horrified*]: Let you – *you* come in!

HARRY [*persuasive*]: Because I could give you some real information about your son. The – very – latest – tip. If you care to hear.

CAPT. H. [*explodes*]: No! I don't care to hear. [*Begins to pace to and fro, spade on shoulder. Gesticulating with his other arm.*] Here's a fellow – a grinning town fellow, who says there's something wrong. [*Fiercely*] I have got more information than you're aware of. I have all the information I want. I have had it for years – for years – for years – enough to last me till to-morrow! Let you come in, indeed! What would Harry say?

[BESSIE CARVIL *enters at cottage door with a white wrap on her head and stands in her garden trying to see.*]

BESSIE: What's the matter?

CAPT. H. [*beside himself*]: An information fellow. [*Stumbles.*]

HARRY [*putting out arm to steady him, gravely*]: Here! Steady a bit! Seems to me somebody's been trying to get at you. [*Change of tone.*] Hullo! What's this rig you've got on? . . . Storm canvas coat, by George! [*He gives a big, throaty laugh.*] Well! You *are* a character!

CAPT. H. [*daunted by the allusion, looks at coat*]: I – I wear it for – for the time being. Till – till – to-morrow. [*Shrinks away, spade in hand, to door of his cottage.*]

BESSIE [*advancing*]: And what may you want, sir?

HARRY [*turns to* BESSIE *at once; easy manner*]: I'd like to know about this swindle that's going to be sprung on him. I didn't mean to startle the old man. You see, on my way here I dropped into a barber's to get a twopenny shave, and they told me there that he was something of a character. He has been a character all his life.

BESSIE [*very low, wondering*]: What swindle?

CAPT. H.: A grinning fellow! [*Makes sudden dash indoors with the spade. Door slams. Lock clicks. Affected gurgling laugh within.*]

SCENE 4

BESSIE *and* HARRY. *Later* CAPT. HAGBERD *from window.*

HARRY [*after short silence*]: What on earth's upset him so? What's the meaning of all this fuss? He isn't always like that, is he?

BESSIE: I don't know who you are; but I may tell you that his mind has been troubled for years about an only son who ran away from home – a long time ago. Everybody knows that here.

HARRY [*thoughtfully*]: Troubled – for years! [*Suddenly*] Well, I am the son.

BESSIE [*steps back*]: You! . . . Harry!

HARRY [*amused, dry tone*]: Got hold of my name, eh? Been making friends with the old man?

BESSIE [*distressed*]: Yes . . . I . . . sometimes . . . [*Rapidly*] He's our landlord.

HARRY [*scornfully*]: Owns both them rabbit hutches, does he? Just a thing he'd be proud of ... [*Earnest*] And now you had better tell me all about that chap who's coming to-morrow. Know anything of him? I reckon there's more than one in that little game. Come! Out with it! [*Chaffing*] I don't take no ... from women.

BESSIE [*bewildered*]: Oh! It's so difficult.... What had I better do?

HARRY [*good-humoured*]: Make a clean breast of it.

BESSIE [*wildly to herself*]: Impossible! [*Starts.*] You don't understand. I must think – see – try to – I, I must have time. Plenty of time.

HARRY: What for? Come. Two words. And don't be afraid for yourself. I ain't going to make it a police job. But it's the other fellow that'll get upset when he least expects it. There'll be some fun when he shows his mug here to-morrow. [*Snaps fingers.*] I don't care that for the old man's dollars, but right is right. You shall see me put a head on that coon, whoever he is.

BESSIE [*wrings hands slightly*]: What had I better do? [*Suddenly to* HARRY] It's you – you yourself that we – that he's waiting for. It's *you* who are to come to-morrow.

HARRY [*slowly*]: Oh! It's me [*Perplexed.*] There's something there I can't understand. I haven't written ahead or anything. It was my chum who showed me the advertisement with the old boy's address, this very morning – in London.

BESSIE [*anxious*]: How can I make it plain to you without ... [*Bites her lip, embarrassed.*] Sometimes he talks so strangely.

HARRY [*expectant*]: Does he? What about?

BESSIE: Only you. And he will stand no contradicting.

HARRY: Stubborn. Eh? The old man hasn't changed much from what I can remember. [*They stand looking at each other helplessly.*]

BESSIE: He's made up his mind you would come back ... to-morrow.

HARRY: I can't hang about here till morning. Got no money to get a bed. Not a cent. But why won't to-day do?

BESSIE: Because you've been too long away.

HARRY [*with force*]: Look here, they fairly drove me out. Poor mother nagged at me for being idle, and the old man said he would cut my soul out of my body rather than let me go to sea.

BESSIE [*murmurs*]: He can bear no contradicting.

HARRY [*continuing*]: Well, it looked as tho' he would do it, too. So I went. [*Moody.*] It seems to me sometimes I was born to them by a mistake . . . in that other rabbit hutch of a house.

BESSIE [*a little mocking*]: And where do you think you ought to have been born by rights?

HARRY: In the open – upon a beach – on a windy night.

BESSIE [*faintly*]: Ah!

HARRY: They were characters, both of them, by George! Shall I try the door.

BESSIE: Wait. I must explain to you why it is to-morrow.

HARRY: Aye. That you must, or . . .

[*Window in* HAGBERD'S *cottage runs up.*]

CAPT. H'S VOICE [*above*]: A – grinning – information – fellow coming to worry me in my own garden! What next?

[*Window rumbles down.*]

BESSIE: Yes. I must. [*Lays hand on* HARRY'S *sleeve.*] Let's get further off. Nobody ever comes this way after dark.

HARRY [*careless laugh*]: Aye. A good road for a walk with a girl.

[*They turn their backs on audience and move up the stage slowly. Close together.* HARRY *bends his head over* BESSIE.]

BESSIE'S VOICE [*beginning eagerly*]: People here somehow did not take kindly to him.

HARRY'S VOICE: Aye. Aye. I understand that.

[*They walk slowly back towards the front.*]

BESSIE: He was almost ready to starve himself for your sake.

HARRY: And I had to starve more than once for his whim.

BESSIE: I'm afraid you've a hard heart. [*Remains thoughtful.*]

HARRY: What for? For running away? [*Indignant*] Why, he wanted to make a blamed lawyer's clerk of me.

[*From here this scene goes on mainly near and about the street lamp.*]

BESSIE [*rousing herself*]: What are you? A sailor?

HARRY: Anything you like. [*Proudly.*] Sailor enough to be worth my salt on board any craft that swims the seas.

BESSIE: He will never, never believe it. He mustn't be contradicted.

HARRY: Always liked to have his own way. And you've been encouraging him.

BESSIE [*earnestly*]: No! – not in everything – not really!

HARRY [*vexed laugh*]: What about that pretty to-morrow notion? I've a hungry chum in London – waiting for me.

BESSIE [*defending herself*]: Why should I make the poor old friendless man miserable? I thought you were far away. I thought you were dead. I didn't know but you had never been born. I ... I ... [HARRY *turns to her. She desperately.*] It was easier to believe it myself. [*Carried away.*] And after all it's true. It's come to pass. This is the to-morrow we've been waiting for.

HARRY [*half perfunctorily*]: Aye. Anybody can see that your heart is as soft as your voice.

BESSIE [*as if unable to keep back the words*]: I didn't think you would have noticed my voice.

HARRY [*already inattentive*]: H'm! Dashed scrape. This is a queer to-morrow, without any sort of to-day, as far as I can see. [*Resolutely.*] I must try the door.

BESSIE: Well – try, then.

HARRY [*from gate looking over shoulder at* BESSIE]: He ain't likely to fly out at me, is he? I would be afraid of laying my hands on him. The chaps are always telling me I don't know my own strength.

BESSIE [*in front*]: He's the most harmless creature that ever ...

HARRY: You wouldn't say so if you had seen him walloping me with a hard leather strap. [*Walking up garden.*] I haven't forgotten it in sixteen long years. [*Rat-tat-tat twice.*] Hallo, Dad. [BESSIE *intensely expectant. Rat-tat-tat.*] Hullo, Dad – let me in. I am your own Harry. Straight. Your son Harry come back home – a day too soon.

[*Window above rumbles up.*]

CAPT. H. [*seen leaning out, aiming with spade*]: Aha!

BESSIE [*warningly*]: Look out, Harry! [*Spade falls.*] Are you hurt? [*Window rumbles down.*]

HARRY [*in the distance*]: Only grazed my hat.

BESSIE: Thank God! [*Intensely*] What'll he do now?

HARRY [*comes forward, slamming gate behind him*]: Just like old times. Nearly licked the life out of me for wanting to go away, and now I come back he shies a confounded old shovel at my head. [*Fumes. Laughs a little.*] I wouldn't care, only poor little Ginger – Ginger's my chum up in London – he will starve while I walk back all the way from here. [*Faces* BESSIE *blankly.*] I spent my last twopence on a shave . . . out of respect for the old man.

BESSIE: I think, if you let me, I could manage to talk him round in a week, maybe.

[*A muffled periodical bellowing has been heard faintly for some time.*]

HARRY [*on the alert*]: What's this? Who's making this row? Hark! Bessie, Bessie. It's in your house, I believe.

BESSIE [*without stirring, drearily*]: It's for me.

HARRY [*discreetly, whispering*]: Good voice for a ship's deck in a squall. Your husband? [*Steps out of lamplight.*]

BESSIE: No. My father. He's blind. [*Pause.*] I'm not married.

[*Bellowings grow louder.*]

HARRY: Oh, I say. What's up. Who's murdering him?

BESSIE [*calmly*]: I expect he's finished his tea.

[*Bellowing continues regularly.*]

HARRY: Hadn't you better see to it? You'll have the whole town coming out here presently. [BESSIE *moves off.*] I say! [BESSIE *stops.*] Couldn't you scare up some bread and butter for me from that tea? I'm hungry. Had no breakfast.

BESSIE [*starts off at the word 'hungry', dropping to the ground the white woollen shawl*]: I won't be a minute. Don't go away.

HARRY [*alone; picks up shawl absently, and, looking at it spread out in his hands, pronounces slowly*]: A – damn' – silly – scrape. [*Pause. Throws shawl on arm. Strolls up and down. Mutters.*] No money to get back. [*Louder*] Silly little Ginger'll think I've got hold of the pieces and given the old shipmate the go-by. One good shove – [*Makes motion of bursting in door with his shoulders*] – would burst that door in – I bet. [*Looks about.*] I wonder where the nearest bobby is! No. They would want to bundle me neck and crop into chokey. [*Shudders.*] Perhaps. It makes me dog-sick to think of being locked up. Haven't got the nerve. Not for prison. [*Leans against lamp-post.*] And not a cent for my fare. I wonder if that girl now . . .

BESSIE [*coming hastily forward, plate with bread and meat in hand*]: I didn't take time to get anything else. . . .

HARRY [*begins to eat*]: You're not standing treat to a beggar. My dad is a rich man – you know.

BESSIE [*plate in hand*]: You resemble your father.

HARRY: I was the very image of him in face from a boy – [*Eats*] – and that's about as far as it goes. He was always one of your domestic characters. He looked sick when he had to go to sea for a fortnight's trip. [*Laughs.*] He was all for house and home.

BESSIE: And you? Have you never wished for a home?

[*Goes off with empty plate and puts it down hastily on* CARVIL'S *bench – out of sight.*]

HARRY [*left in front*]: Home! If I found myself shut up in what the old man calls a home, I would kick it down about my ears on the third day – or else go to bed and die before the week was out. Die in a house – ough!

BESSIE [*returning; stops and speaks from garden railing*]: And where is it that you wish to die?

HARRY: In the bush, in the sea, on some blamed mountain-top for choice. No such luck, tho', I suppose.

BESSIE [*from distance*]: Would that be luck?

HARRY: Yes! For them that make the whole world their home.

BESSIE [*comes forward shyly*]: The world's a cold home – they say.

HARRY [*a little gloomy*]: So it is. When a man's done for.

BESSIE: You see! [*Taunting*] And a ship's not so very big after all.

HARRY: No. But the sea is great. And then what of the ship! You love her and leave her, Miss – Bessie's your name isn't it? . . . I like that name.

BESSIE: You like my name! I wonder you remembered it. . . . That's why, I suppose.

HARRY [*slight swagger in voice*]: What's the odds! As long as a fellow has lived. And a voyage isn't a marriage – as we sailors say.

BESSIE: So you're not married – [*Movement of* HARRY] – to any ship.

HARRY [*soft laugh*]: Ship! I've loved and left more of them than I can remember. I've been nearly everything you can think of but a tinker or a soldier; I've been a boundary rider; I've sheared sheep and humped my swag and harpooned a whale; I've rigged ships and skinned dead bullocks and prospected for gold – and turned my back on more money than the old man would have scraped together in his whole life.

BESSIE [*thoughtfully*]: I could talk him over in a week. . . .

HARRY [*negligently*]: I dare say you could. [*Joking*] I don't know but what I could make shift to wait if you only promise to talk to me now and then. I've grown quite fond of your voice. I like a right woman's voice.

BESSIE [*averted head*]: Quite fond. [*Sharply*] Talk! Nonsense! Much you'd care. [*Business-like*] Of course I would have to sometimes. . . . [*Thoughtful again*] Yes. In a week – if – if only I knew you would try to get on with him afterwards.

HARRY [*leaning against lamp-post; growls through his teeth*]: More humouring. Ah! well, no! [*Hums significantly.*]

> Oh, oh, oh, Rio, . . .
> And fare thee well
> My bonnie young girl,
> We're bound for Rio Grande.

BESSIE [*shivering*]: What's that?

HARRY: Why! The chorus of an up-anchor tune. Kiss and go. A deep-water ship's good-bye. . . . You are cold. Here's that thing of yours I've picked up and forgot there on my arm. Turn round a bit. So. [*Wraps her up – commanding.*] Hold the ends together in front.

BESSIE [*softly*]: A week is not so very long.

HARRY [*begins violently*]: You think that I — [*Stops with side-long look at her.*] I can't dodge about in ditches and live on air and water. Can I? I haven't any money – you know.

BESSIE: He's been scraping and saving up for years. All he has is for you, and perhaps . . .

HARRY [*interrupts*]: Yes. If I come to sit on it like a blamed toad in a hole. Thank you.

BESSIE [*angrily*]: What did you come for, then?

HARRY [*promptly*]: For five quid – [*Pause*] – after a jolly good spree.

BESSIE [*scathingly*]: You and that – that – chum of yours have been drinking.

HARRY [*laughs*]: Don't fly out, Miss Bessie – dear. Ginger's not a bad little chap. Can't take care of himself, tho'. Blind three days. [*Serious.*] Don't think I am given that way. Nothing and nobody can get over me unless I like. I can be as steady as a rock.

BESSIE [*murmurs*]: Oh! I don't think you are bad.

HARRY [*approvingly*]: You're right there. [*Impulsive*] Ask the girls all over — [*Checks himself.*] Ginger, he's long-headed, too, in his way – mind you. He sees the paper this morning and he says to me, 'Hallo! Look at that, Harry – loving parents – that's five quid, sure.' So we scraped all our pockets for the fare. . . .

BESSIE [*unbelieving*]: You came here for that.

HARRY [*surprised*]: What else would I want here? Five quid isn't much to ask for – once in sixteen years. [*Through his teeth with a sidelong look at* B.] And now I am ready to go – for my fare.

BESSIE [*clasping her hands*]: Whoever heard a man talk like this before! I can't believe you mean it?

HARRY: What? That I would go? You just try and see.

BESSIE [*disregarding him*]: Don't you care for anyone? Didn't you ever want anyone in the world to care for you?

HARRY: In the world! [*Boastful.*] There's hardly a place you can go in the world where you wouldn't find somebody that did care for Harry Hagberd. [*Pause*] I'm not the sort that go about skulking under false names.

BESSIE: Somebody – that means a woman.

HARRY: Well! And if it did?

BESSIE: [*unsteadily*]: Oh, I see how it is. You get round them with your soft speeches, your promises, and then . . .

HARRY [*violently*]: *Never!*

BESSIE [*startled, steps back*]: Ah – you never . . .

HARRY [*calm*]: Never yet told a lie to a woman.

BESSIE: What lie?

HARRY: Why, the lie that comes glib to a man's tongue. None of that for me. I leave the sneaking off to them soft-spoken chaps you're thinking of. No! If you love me you take me. And if you take me – why, then, the capstan-song of deep-water ships is sure to settle it all some fine day.

BESSIE [*after a short pause, with effort*]: It's like your ships, then.

HARRY [*amused*]: Exactly, up to now. Or else I wouldn't be here in a silly fix.

BESSIE [*assumed indifference*]: Perhaps it's because you've never yet met — [*Voice fails.*]

HARRY [*negligently*]: Maybe. And perhaps never shall. . . . What's the odds? It's the looking for a thing. . . . No matter, I love them all – ships and women. The scrapes they got me into, and the scrapes they got me out of – my word! I say, Miss Bessie, what are you thinking of?

BESSIE [*lifts her head*]: That you are supposed never to tell a lie.

HARRY: Never, eh? You wouldn't be that hard on a chap.

BESSIE [*recklessly*]: Never to a woman, I mean.

HARRY: Well, no. [*Serious.*] Never anything that matters. [*Aside*] I don't seem to get any nearer to my railway fare.

[*Leans wearily against the lamp-post with a far-off look.* BESSIE *to L. looks at him.*]

BESSIE: Now what are *you* thinking of?

HARRY [*turns his head; stares at* B.]: Well, I was thinking what a fine figure of a girl you are.

BESSIE [*looks away a moment*]: Is that true, or is it only one of them that don't matter?

HARRY [*laughing a little*]: No! no! That's true. Haven't you ever been told that before? The men . . .

BESSIE: I hardly speak to a soul from year's end to year's end. Father's blind. He don't like strangers, and he can't bear to think of me out of his call. Nobody comes near us much.

HARRY [*absent-minded*]: Blind – ah! of course.

BESSIE: For years and years . . .

HARRY [*commiserating*]: For years and years. In one of them hutches. You are a good daughter. [*Brightening up*] A fine girl

altogether. You seem the sort that makes a good chum to a man
in a fix. And there's not a man in this whole town who found
you out? I can hardly credit it, Miss Bessie. [B. *shakes her head.*]
Man I said! [*contemptuous*] A lot of tame rabbits in hutches I call
them. . . . [*Breaks off.*] I say, when's the last train up to London?
Can you tell me?

BESSIE [*gazes at him steadily*]: What for? You've no money.

HARRY: That's just it. [*Leans back against post again.*] Hard
luck. [*Insinuating*] But there was never a time in all my travels
that a woman of the right sort did not turn up to help me out of
a fix. I don't know why. It's perhaps because they know without
telling that I love them all. [*Playful*] I've almost fallen in love
with you, Miss Bessie.

BESSIE [*unsteady laugh*]: Why! How you talk! You haven't even seen
my face properly. [*One step towards* HARRY, *as if compelled.*]

HARRY [*bending forward gallantly*]: A little pale. It suits some.
[*Puts out his hand, catches hold of* B's *arm, draws her to him.*]
Let's see. . . . Yes, it suits *you.*

[*It's a moment before* B. *puts up her hands, palms out, and
turns away her head.*]

BESSIE [*whispering*]: Don't. [*Struggles a little. Released, stands
averted.*]

HARRY: No offence. [*Stands, back to audience, looking at* CAPT.
H's *cottage.*]

BESSIE [*alone in front; faces audience; whispers*] My voice – my
figure – my heart – my face. . . .

[*A silence.* B.'s *face gradually lights up. Directly* HARRY
speaks, expression of hopeful attention.]

HARRY [*from railings*]: The old man seems to have gone to
sleep waiting for that to-morrow of his.

BESSIE: Come away. He sleeps very little.

HARRY [*strolls down*]: He has taken an everlasting jamming
hitch round the whole business. [*Vexed*] Cast it loose who may.
[*Contemptuous exclamation*] To-morrow. Pooh! It'll be just another mad to-day.

BESSIE: It's the brooding over his hope that's done it. People
teased him so. It's his fondness for you that's troubled his mind.

289

HARRY: Aye. A confounded shovel on the head. The old man had always a queer way of showing his fondness for me.

BESSIE: A hopeful, troubled, expecting old man – left alone – all alone.

HARRY [*lower tone*]: Did he ever tell you what mother died of?

BESSIE: Yes. [*A little bitter*] From impatience.

HARRY [*makes a gesture with his arms; speaks vaguely but with feeling*]: I believe you have been very good to my old man. . . .

BESSIE [*tentative*]: Wouldn't you try to be a son to him?

HARRY [*angrily*]: No contradicting; is that it? You seem to know my dad pretty well. And so do I. He's dead nuts on having his own way – and I've been used to have my own too long. It's the deuce of a fix.

BESSIE: How could it hurt you not to contradict him for a while – and perhaps in time you would get used . . .

HARRY [*interrupts sulkily*]: I ain't accustomed to knuckle under. There's a pair of us. Hagberds both. I ought to be thinking of my train.

BESSIE [*earnestly*]: Why? There's no need. Let us get away up the road a little.

HARRY [*through his teeth*]: And no money for the fare. [*Looks up.*] Sky's come overcast. Black, too. It'll be a wild, windy night . . . to walk the high-road on. But I and wild nights are old friends wherever the free wind blows.

BESSIE [*entering*]: No need. No need. [*Looks apprehensively at* HAGBERD'S *cottage. Takes a couple of steps up as if to draw* HARRY *further off.* HARRY *follows. Both stop.*]

HARRY [*after waiting*]: What about this to-morrow whim?

BESSIE: Leave that to me. Of course all his fancies are not mad. They aren't. [*Pause.*] Most people in this town would think what he had set his mind on quite sensible. If he ever talks to you of it, don't contradict him. It would – it would be dangerous.

HARRY [*surprised*]: What would he do?

BESSIE: He would – I don't know – something rash.

HARRY [*startled*]: To himself?

BESSIE: No. It'd be against you – I fear.

HARRY [*sullen*]: Let him.

BESSIE: Never. Don't quarrel. But perhaps he won't even try

290

to talk to you of it. [*Thinking aloud*] Who knows what I can do with him in a week! I can, I can, I can – I must.

HARRY: Come – what's this sensible notion of his that I mustn't quarrel about?

BESSIE [*turns to* HARRY, *calm, forcible*]: If I make him once see that you've come back, he will be as sane as you or I. All his mad notions will be gone. But that other is quite sensible. And you mustn't quarrel over it.

[*Moves up to back of stage.* HARRY *follows a little behind, away from audience.*]

HARRY'S VOICE [*calm*]: Let's hear what it is.

[*Voices cease. Action visible as before.* HARRY *steps back and walks hastily down.* BESSIE *at his elbow, follows with her hands clasped.*]

[*Loud burst of voice.*]

HARRY [*raving to and fro*]: No! Expects me – a home. Who wants his home? ... What I want is hard work, or an all-fired racket, or more room than there is in the whole of England. Expects me! A man like me – for his rotten money – there ain't enough money in the world to turn me into a blamed tame rabbit in a hutch. [*He stops suddenly before* BESSIE, *arms crossed on breast. Violently*] Don't you see it?

BESSIE [*terrified, stammering faintly*]: Yes. Yes. Don't look at me like this. [*Sudden scream.*] Don't quarrel with him. He's mad!

HARRY [*headlong utterance*]: Mad! Not he. He likes his own way. Tie me up by the neck here. Here! Ha! Ha! Ha! [*Louder*] And the whole world is not a bit too big for me to spread my elbows in, I can tell you – what's your name – Bessie. [*Rising scorn*] Marry! Wants me to marry and settle.... [*Scathingly*] And as likely as not he has looked out the girl too – dash my soul. Talked to you about it – did he? And do you happen to know the Judy – may I ask?

[*Window in* CAPT. H.*'s cottage runs up. They start and stand still.*]

CAPT. H. [*above, begins slowly*]: A grinning information fellow from a crazy town. [*Voice changes.*] Bessie, I see you . . .

BESSIE [*shrilly*]: Captain Hagberd! Say nothing. You don't understand. For heaven's sake don't.

CAPT. H.: Send him away this minute, or I will tell Harry. They know nothing of Harry in this crazy town. Harry's coming home to-morrow. Do you hear? One day more!

[*Silence.*]

HARRY [*mutters*]: Well! – he *is* a character.

CAPT. H. [*chuckles softly*]: Never you fear! The boy shall marry you. [*Sudden anger*] He'll have to. I'll make him. Or, if not – [*Furious*] – I'll cut him off with a shilling, and leave everything to you. Jackanapes! Let him starve!

[*Window rumbles down.*]

HARRY [*slowly*]: So it's you – the girl. It's you! Now I begin to see. . . . By heavens, you have a heart as soft as your woman's voice.

BESSIE [*half averted, face in hands*]: You see! Don't come near me.

HARRY [*makes a step towards her*]: I must have another look at your pale face.

BESSIE [*turns unexpectedly and pushes him with both hands; HARRY staggers back and stands still; BESSIE, fiercely*]: Go away.

HARRY [*watching her*]: Directly. But women always had to get me out of my scrapes. I am a beggar now, and you must help me out of my scrape.

BESSIE [*who at the word 'beggar' had began fumbling in the pocket of her dress, speaks wildly*]: Here it is. Take it. Don't look at me. Don't speak to me!

HARRY [*swaggers up under the lamp; looks at a coin in his palm*]: Half a quid . . . my fare!

BESSIE [*hands clenched*]: Why are you still here?

HARRY: Well, you *are* a fine figure of a girl. My word! I've a good mind to stop – for a week.

BESSIE [*pain and shame*]: Oh! . . . What are you waiting for? If I had more money I would give it all, all. I would give everything

I have to make you go – to make you forget you had ever heard my voice and seen my face. [*Covers face with hands.*]

HARRY [*sombre, watches her*]: No fear! I haven't forgotten a single one of you in the world. Some've given me more than money. No matter. You can't buy me in – and you can't buy yourself out . . .

[*Strides towards her. Seizes her arms. Short struggle.* BESSIE *gives way. Hair falls loose.* HARRY *kisses her forehead, cheeks, lips, then releases her.* BESSIE *staggers against railings. Exit* HARRY; *measured walk without haste.*]

SCENE 5

BESSIE. CAPT. HAGBERD *at window.*

BESSIE [*staring eyes, hair loose, back against railings; calls out*]: Harry! [*Gathers up her skirts and runs a little way.*] Come back, Harry. [*Staggers forward against lamp-post.*] Harry! [*Much lower.*] Harry! [*In a whisper.*] Take me with you. [*Begins to laugh, at first faintly, then louder.*]

[*Window rumbles up, and* CAPT. H.'s *chuckle mingles with* BESSIE's *laughter, which abruptly stops.*]

CAPT. H. [*goes on chuckling; speaks cautiously*]: Is he gone yet, that information fellow? Do you see him anywhere, my dear?

BESSIE [*low and stammering*]: N-no, no! [*Totters away from lamp-post.*] I don't see him.

CAPT. H. [*anxious*]: A grinning vagabond, my dear. Good girl. It's you who drove him away. Good girl.

[*Stage gradually darkens.*]

BESSIE: Go in; be quiet! You have done harm enough.

CAPT. H. [*alarmed*]: Why? Do you hear him yet, my dear?

BESSIE [*sobs, drooping against the railings*]: No! No! I don't. I don't hear him any more.

CAPT. H. [*triumphant*]: Now we shall be all right, my dear, till our Harry comes home to-morrow. [*Affected gurgling laugh.*]

BESSIE [*distracted*]: Be quiet. Shut yourself in. You will make me mad. [*Losing control of herself, repeats with rising inflexion.*] You make me mad. [*With despair.*] There is no to-morrow! [*Sinks to ground near middle railings. Low sobs.*]

[*Stage darkens perceptibly.*]

CAPT. H. [*above, in a voice suddenly dismayed and shrill*]: What! What do you say, my dear? No to-morrow? [*Broken, very feebly*] No – to-morrow?

[*Window runs down.*]

CARVIL [*heard within, muffled bellowing*]: Bessie – Bessie – Bessie – Bessie —— [*At the first call* BESSIE *springs up and begins to stumble blindly towards the door. A faint flash of lightning, followed by a very low rumble of thunder.*] You! – Bessie!

CURTAIN

NOTES

1. Epigraph: *Endymion*, lines 866–8. It should read:

> *Far as the mariner on highest mast*
> *Can see all round upon the calmed vast,*
> *So wide was Neptune's hall . . .*

2. Dedication: Robert Bontine Cunninghame Graham (1852–1936) was a Scottish aristocrat who spent his youth among cattle-ranchers in South and Central America; later he prospected for gold in Spain, travelled in North Africa and wrote many books of essays, travel sketches and stories. An MP from 1886 to 1892, he was a passionate socialist, anti-imperialist and Scottish nationalist. (See *JCLCG*, pp. 3–42.) Perhaps it was the very fact that Conrad could not share Graham's hopes for humanity that made his lifelong friendship with Graham, begun in 1897, precious to him. There may be even deeper psychological affinities: the combination in Graham of an essentially aristocratic outlook and impulsive, warm-hearted sympathy for the underdog strikingly recalls the temperament of Conrad's own father, Apollo Korzeniowski, as described by Conrad's maternal uncle and beloved guardian Thaddeus Bobrowski (See Baines, p. 8). Conrad had originally planned to dedicate the volume *Youth* to Graham, but deferred to the wishes of William Blackwood, to whom Graham's socialism was anathema. Eventually Conrad dedicated *Youth* to his wife, with an appropriate epigraph; the Keats epigraph was transferred to *Typhoon* along with the dedication to Graham.

3. *Author's Note* (p. 49): This note was written for the Doubleday (Sun-Dial) collected edition. In August 1919 Conrad confessed to Pinker that he had 'a certain difficulty' in beginning it (*LL*, II, p. 227), a difficulty reflected in the inaccuracies and stumbling grammar of the opening lines; however, Conrad progressively warms to his subject.

4. *the order in which they appear in the book* (p. 49): The correct order of writing is 'Typhoon', 'Falk', 'Amy Foster' and 'To-morrow'.

5. *Blackwood's Magazine* (p. 49): *Blackwood's* serialized 'Youth', 'Heart of Darkness', 'The End of the Tether' and *Lord Jim*.

6. *I had just finished writing 'The End of the Tether'* (p. 49): Conrad did not begin writing 'The End of the Tether' until March 1902, after all the stories in *Typhoon* had been written.

7. *Captain MacWhirr* (p. 50): Conrad sailed from Amsterdam to Semerang (18 February to 20 June 1887) as first mate on the barque *Highland Forest* under Captain John McWhir (Najder, pp. 94–6). In *The Mirror of the Sea* Conrad remembers 'good Captain MacW—', a man of 'amiable character' who replied to his officers in a 'mild and friendly tone' when they reported to him through the door of his cabin, where he had his meals sent in. (MacWhirr has his sent up to the bridge.) Conrad recalls going about his duties with the flattering sense of being in command, but adds: 'Still, whatever the greatness of my illusion, the fact remains that the real commander was there, backing up my self-confidence, though invisible to my eyes behind a maplewood veneered cabin door with a white china handle' (Dent Collected Edition, pp. 5–6).

8. *storm-piece* (p. 50): The *Daily Mail* reviewer on 22 April 1903 called it 'the most elaborate storm piece that one can recall in English literature' (*CH*, p. 146).

9. *too profoundly moved to speak* (p. 51): The girl, Falk and MacWhirr all share the quality of taciturnity, and all three are in touch with deep truths. As the language-teacher observes on the first page of *Under Western Eyes*: 'Words . . . are the great foes of reality.'

10. *Nan-Shan* (p. 55): On three occasions that the *Vidar* was in Singapore while Conrad was her chief mate (August 1887 to January 1888), a ship called the *Nan-Shan* was also in port. She arrived on 30 September 1887 with 546 Chinese on board, just as the *Vidar* was leaving for Berau. (See *CEW*, p. 30 and N. Sherry, ed., *The Nigger of the 'Narcissus', Typhoon, Falk and Other Stories* (London: Dent, 1974), p. 289 n.)

11. *gamp* (p. 56): The term derives from Mrs Gamp's elegant but unwieldy umbrella in Dickens' *Martin Chuzzlewit*. During a coach ride in Chapter 29 it terrorizes the passengers and is moved so often that it 'seemed not one umbrella but fifty' (See Introduction, p. ix).

12. *Sigg* (p. 58): A firm of teak merchants in Bangkok called Jucker, Sigg and Co. were the charterers of Conrad's first command, the *Otago*; Conrad used the name 'Yucker' in *Lord Jim* and in the manuscript of 'Falk', afterwards changing it to 'Siegers' (*CEW*, pp. 238–9).

13. *the little straws . . .'* (p. 59): i.e., small details have great importance. Conrad may have remembered a version of the proverb from Byron's *Don Juan* (XIV, viii): 'You know, or don't know, that great Bacon saith,/ 'Fling up a straw 'twill show the way the wind blows.'

14. *expedient to transfer her to the Siamese flag* (p. 60): no doubt because of fiscal reasons or 'flag discrimination', i.e., preferential charges or facilities.

15. *the season of typhoons* (p. 68): According to Merrifield's *Treatise on Navigation* (London, 1883, p. 274), hurricanes in the northern hemisphere 'must occur from July to October' and typhoons 'are met with from May to

October'. Conrad here contradicts one of the authorities on navigation of the 1880s.

16. *blanked ... blank ... condemned ... decayed ... gory ... crimson* (pp. 70–71): humorous euphemisms, the first two perhaps for unprintable words, the others for 'damned', 'rotten', 'bloody', 'bleeding'.

17. *faint* (p. 71): either another euphemism or a transitive use meaning 'to make faint' (*Chambers Scots Dictionary*, Edinburgh 1984), in scornful allusion to the firemen 'going faint'.

18. *raging inwardly* (p. 74): The second mate recalls Donkin in *The Nigger of the 'Narcissus'*, who appears 'as if consumed slowly by an inward rage at the injustice of men and of fate' (London, Penguin Classics, 1988, p. 106). But instead of being, like Donkin, a demagogue stirring up revolt by 'hopeful doctrines' (*ibid.*, p. 76), he is, on the contrary, self-isolated: the only main character who writes no letters. His personal malevolence is not used to support tendentious social comment.

19. *the chapter on the storms* (p. 77): Merrifield, in his chapter on storms, gives the following advice (p. 276):

> As an example, suppose a ship to be in north latitude, the wind blowing heavily, and it has changed from SSE to SE and ESE: state how a person should act. First, by standing with his back to the wind, the left hand points out wsw., i.e. eight points to the right of the direction of the wind as the direction of the focus, and the ship is in the NE quadrant of the storm. The wind has changed to the left, hence the ship is in the left-hand semicircle, or to the left of the line of progression. To prove this, draw three concentric circles and place dots on the circumference of each, where the wind will be found blowing as in the example, beginning with the outermost circle. Join these dots by a straight line – this will give the direction the storm is travelling, in this case easterly; and hence the ship is in the most dangerous quadrant, and should go off to the northward, i.e. keep the wind on the starboard quarter. But if the wind is so heavy as to make it dangerous to sail, the ship must be hove-to, and this should be done on the port tack, because the vessel is in the left-hand semicircle. At first sight this would appear contrary to the law for avoiding the centre; but it must be borne in mind that when hove-to the ship makes but very little progress; and being hove-to on the port tack she always presents her bows to the sea, a necessary precaution when a heavy sea is running ...'

20. *eight points off the wind* (p. 78): Merrifield writes (p. 277): 'In the northern hemisphere allow eight points to the right of the wind ... : this will give the direction of the centre of the cyclone.'

21. *Melita* (p. 79): the name of the vessel on which Conrad left from Singapore on 19 December 1887 to take his first command, the *Otago*, in Bangkok (Najder p. 103).

22. *crowned with flowers* (p. 126): The New York *Critic* text reads 'ornate

with flowers'. Purdy (*op. cit.*, pp. 108–9) believes that Conrad changed it to echo the second mate's parasitic crony who has 'daylight . . . in two places between the rim and crown of his hat', thereby pointing the comic parallel between the two pavement scenes. (Similarly the 'bright sunshiny day' of the *Nan-Shan*'s arrival may be humorously paralleled by the weather in the 'northern suburb' of Britain: 'a fine afternoon, with a grey sky and dry sidewalks'.)

23. *Brenzett, Colebrook, Darnford* (p. 135): All place-names in the story are fictitious. 'Brenzett' (at first 'Skychurch' in the manuscript) does not refer to the inland town of Brenzett. The geographical focus of imagination probably lies on the coast between the seamen's graves at Winchelsea and the anecdotal shipwreck at Dungeness (see Introduction, p.).

24. *horizon of the sea* (p. 137): In *A Personal Record* (Dent Collected Edition, p. 22) Conrad describes being driven by the son of his grandmother's coachman on a visit to Bobrowski in the Ukraine in 1893: 'I saw again the sun setting on the plains as I saw it in the travels of my childhood. It set, clear and red, dipping into the snow in full view as if it were setting on the sea.' The echo may simply reflect a writer's embellishment of a personal memoir by a phrase that had already done service in fiction. On the other hand it may reveal an antecedent link between the world of 'Amy Foster' and the Ukraine, which Conrad visited as the child of parents sentenced to a penal colony in central Russia but, for health reasons, allowed a few months' leave on Bobrowski's estate. The latter possibility gains credence from a reminiscence by Irena Rakowska-Łuniewska of being taken by Conrad in 1924 to see a view in Kent which, he told her, 'strongly reminds me of the Ukraine' (*Conrad Under Familial Eyes*, ed. Z. Najder, Cambridge University Press, 1984, p. 270). The imaginative association (with the sea in both cases representing freedom) would account for the curiously pessimistic view of Kentish agriculture and confirm Juliet McLauchlan's detection of echoes from Conrad's childhood (see Introduction, note 31), as well as Bertrand Russell's claim that the story was a key to Conrad's character (see Baines, p. 267 n.).

25. *some German fellow* (p. 138): 'No phosphorous, no thought' was the phrase in which the Dutch philosopher and physiologist Jacob Moleschott (b. 1822, Hertogenbosch, Netherlands; d. 1893, Rome) summed up his doctrine of scientific materialism, in opposition to the official philosophy of German universities which claimed speculation about consciousness as the preserve of Church and State. Moleschott's *Lehre der Nahrungsmittel* (1850) and *Der Kreislauf des Lebens* (1852), gave considerable stimulus to nineteenth-century materialism, and the evocation of his name by Kennedy is thus appropriate to the theme of materialism in the story.

26. *a lost stranger* (p. 141): The manuscript (pp. 24–25) is more poignant

and personal: '. . . the lot of the castaway is a hard one – as you who have
been wrecked yourself ought to know. No matter how sure we may be of
kindness we feel profoundly our own strangeness – the strangeness of
creatures thrown out suddenly by the sea upon the mercy of another race,
perhaps whose tongue, thoughts, manners are a complete and momentous
mystery. The faces appear like masks, all the eyes are full of surprise and
wonder, your difference you feel creates a gulph – and there is no retreat.'

27. *Swaffer* (p. 150): MS and serial read 'Rigby'.

28. *Baptist* (p. 152): MS and serial read 'Wesleyan'.

29. *the song of birds* (p. 155): The serial has 'the heartless song of birds'. It
would be tempting to regard the omission of 'heartless' in the first edition
as a compositor's error that Conrad overlooked (as he did 'mirage or' for
'mirage of', 'wicker' for 'wicket' or 'black' for 'brick'). Not only does the
adjective nicely balance 'human'; it adds depth by suggesting a quality of
suffering specific to human consciousness and otherwise absent in nature,
making all of us castaways, as it were. (Hardy's 'The Darkling Thrush' had
been written only a few months before.)

30. *Yanko Goorall* (p. 156): 'Yanko' is a dialect form of 'Janek', the dim-
inutive of the Polish 'Jan' (John). 'Goorall' corresponds to the Polish '*Góral*',
or 'Highlander'. In the late nineteenth century there was a strong Polish
literary interest in the Highlanders of the Tatra Mountains, and Conrad
may have drawn on a stereotype of the *Góral* in Polish literature and oral
tradition (Busza, pp. 229–30).

31. *some word* (p. 161): The MS adds: 'wife – I suppose'.

32. *Several of us* (p. 165): The group of convives recalls those of 'Youth'
and 'Heart of Darkness'; the device of a narrator telling his story to a small
group of listeners, with a proleptic setting or prologue, was probably
derived most directly from Maupassant, whom Conrad had read avidly.
The 'small river hostelry' suggests the Bull Inn, Chatham or the Lobster
Arms, Hole Haven, where, according to G. F. W. Hope, he and Conrad
often stopped during their excursions on the Thames in Hope's yacht
Nellie, mentioned in 'Heart of Darkness' (Sherry, *op. cit.*, p. 296 n.).

33. *Eastern seaport* (p. 166): Bangkok, capital of Siam (now Thailand)
lying on the Meinam river (now Chao Praya). Bangkok also figures in 'The
Secret Sharer' and *The Shadow-Line*.

34. *my enemy Falk, and my friend Hermann* (p. 166): According to Sherry,
the name 'Falk' was taken from the firm of Falck and Beideck, which
existed in Bangkok in 1888; he also believes that Conrad had in mind a
German steamer in Bangkok called the *Hermann* when describing the *Diana*
and transferred the name Hermann to her fictional owner (*CEW*, p. 236).

35. *whom I shall always call Hermann's niece* (p. 167): The MS reads:
'whom I shall call Grätchen'.

36. *Diana not of Ephesus* (p. 168): Diana (or Artemis) of Ephesus differed from the Artemis worshipped in Arcadia and throughout Greece. The latter was usually represented as a young narrow-hipped virgin of rural aspect, wearing a short tunic. Diana of Ephesus, although the patroness of chastity, was a fertility goddess; she wore a tight robe covered with animal heads, exposing her bosom of multiple breasts.

37. *a man who had died suddenly* (p. 171): This account of the captain's predecessor is similar to that given by the narrator of *The Shadow-Line*, and was taken at face value by Conrad's first biographer, Jean-Aubry. However, Sherry has shown how Conrad altered facts to suit his fictional purpose. A. T. Saunders, who had corresponded with Conrad and known the previous captain of the *Otago*, John Snadden, wrote that because Conrad had depended on reports by his officers, the account of Captain Snadden in *The Shadow-Line* (and thus in 'Falk') was 'absurd'. (See *CEW*, pp. 211–27, 322.) 'Falk', for all its mosaic of facts, is fiction: the narrator returns to Bangkok five years later commanding another ship; Conrad never did.

38. *favoured by a scratch of the pen* (p. 172): Conrad took this phrase from a business letter he received from the co-owner of the *Otago* (*CEW*, p. 226).

39. *Tottersen* (p. 172): The MS reads 'Totterman', the name of the second mate of the *Otago* on her return from Mauritius (*CEW*, p. 249 n.)

40. *a certain Schomberg* (p. 172): He appears briefly in *Lord Jim* and, along with his wife, more actively in *Victory*. In a note to the first edition of that novel Conrad describes him as showing 'indubitably the psychology of a Teuton' (London: Methuen, 1915, p. viii). Sherry believes Conrad altered the curious name of a respected German broker in Singapore called 'Schombergk' (*CEW*, pp. 241–2).

41. *a most audacious thief* (p. 173): A *Bangkok Times* report shows that the original theft was from a member of Conrad's crew. Conrad, together with his mate, arrested the thief, who managed to get away (*CEW*, p. 234).

42. *tides in the affairs of men which, taken at the flood . . . and so on* (p. 183): This allusion to Shakespeare's *Julius Caesar* (IV. iii. 216–19) is similar to Byron's: ' "There is a tide in the affairs of men,/which, taken at the flood," –you know the rest' (*Don Juan*, VI, i).

43. *Mr. Siegers* (p. 190): See Note 12 above.

44. *Gambril . . . quinine* (p. 198): In *The Shadow-Line* Gambril and the entire crew except Ransome also come down with 'choleraic symptoms'. However, a comparison of the crew's illness in the two works is an object-lesson in subordination of material to artistic design. The quinine with which the captain treats Gambril in 'Falk' turns out precisely to be missing in *The Shadow-Line*, causing the captain to blame himself. When Cedric Watts writes that in *The Shadow-Line* 'the steward remains unaffected by the illness' (*'Typhoon' and Other Tales*, OUP World's Classics, 1986, p. 301), he is referring to Ransome; but in fact the narrator of *The Shadow-Line* states: 'The first member of the crew fairly knocked over was the steward — the first man to whom I had spoken on board. He was taken ashore (with choleraic symptoms), and died there at the end of a week' (Penguin Classics, 1986, p. 93). (Ransome is introduced a few paragraphs later as 'the cook'; he later doubles as steward.) In 'Falk', by contrast, no member of the crew dies or is finally likely to; the crew's illness is a simple harmonic of the captain's financial troubles ('The crew was sickly, the cargo was coming very slow; I foresaw I would have lots of trouble with the charterers, and doubted whether they would advance me enough money for the ship's expenses.') When the narrator's relations with Falk improve, so does the outlook for the crew: 'My diplomacy was a success; my ship was safe; old Gambril would probably live.'

45. *He fell upon me ... self-preservation* (p. 205): This may be an echo of Schopenhauer's aphorism: 'Spinoza ... says that if a stone which has been projected through the air had consciousness, it would believe that it was moving of its own free will. I add to this only that the stone would be right' (*The World as Will and Idea*, London, 1883–6, I, 164).

46. *I have eaten man* (p. 219): Jessie Conrad (p. 118) relates that 'Falk' was 'culled from a short paragraph in a newspaper which had some relation to an episode known to Conrad many years before, while he was at sea.' Conrad may have been reminded of the episode by a short paragraph referring to 'the arrest of Andersen and Thomassen, the Swedish survivors of the ship *Drot*, who are alleged to have committed acts of cannibalism on a raft after the wreck of that vessel' (*The Times*, 25 September 1899, p. 7). In 1884 two shipwrecked sailors convicted of murder for cannibalism were shown leniency on the grounds that they were justified in sacrificing the weakest survivor to save the others (see Watts, *op. cit.*, p. 303).

47. Flying Dutchman ... *retribution* (p. 231): Although Conrad probably used visual memories of Wagner's opera (see Note 41 to the Introduction), this account of the 'fable' tallies better with the version in *The Phantom Ship* (1839) by Frederick Marryat, one of Conrad's favourite boyhood authors. Here the Dutchman is guilty not just of blasphemous pride, as in Wagner's opera, but of having unintentionally killed the pilot who opposed his mad efforts to round the Cape of Good Hope. The dead pilot's spirit, the one-eyed Schriften, frustrates the Dutchman's son Philip in his efforts to find his father and lift the curse. Instead of the Wagnerian quest for faithful love, there is 'sentimental retribution': Philip loses his loving wife, as foretold by Schriften. He frees his father's spirit only when he is able to forgive his enemy, the man his father murdered. Conrad mentions Schriften's name, misspelling it, in his essay 'Tales of the Sea' (*Notes on Life and Letters*, London: Dent, 1921, p. 74).

48. *To-morrow* (p. 239): Conrad's first title for the story was 'The Son'. He wrote to Ford in early January 1902 that it was 'All *your* suggestion and absolutely *my* conception' (*CLJC*, 2, p. 372). 'Conception', however, was for Conrad the operative word. Six months earlier he had written to Ford that technique 'has importance only when the Conception of the whole has a significance of its own apart from the details that go to make it up' (*CLJC*, 2, p. 332). A possible hint of Ford's 'suggestion' appears in Conrad's preliminary account to Pinker of 'the story of a retired skipper who lives in a cottage and expects his long lost son to return every day. He even plans a marriage for him with the daughter of their neighbour – who is the girl of the story. At last a young man arrives. He is the son but his behaviour is so extremely unlike what the capt expected (in fact he runs off with the spoons) that the father comforts himself with the idea that the fellow is an impostor. But a shipmate comes upon the scene and the capt is convinced at last. The girl is his consolation' (*CLJC*, 2, pp. 366–7).

49. Skimmer of the Seas (p. 256): The second British ship on which Conrad served, from July to September 1878, was the *Skimmer of the Sea*, a coaster running between Lowestoft and Newcastle. Writing to Cunninghame Graham in February 1898 he referred to it as the *Skimmer of the Seas* (*CLJC*, 2, p. 35).

50. *'Capstan song,'* (p. 258): The 'Rio Grande' shanties were originally sung not about the Mexican Rio Grande del Nord but Rio Grande do Sul in Brazil after gold was discovered there. By the time gold was discovered in the Mexican Rio Grande district in the 1860s the shanty was well-known. The Scottish ballad beginning 'I've been a wanderer all my life' has similarities of melody. Rio Grande was an outward-bound song, always sung at the anchor-capstan, and was heard mainly on the decks of ships leaving the west coast of England. One of the innumerable versions went:

> *Hurrah you Rio!*
> *Rolling Rio!*
> *So fare-ye-well, you Liverpool gals*
> *For we're bound to Rio Grande.*

See Stan Hugill, *Shanties From the Seven Seas* (London: Routledge, 1961, pp. 87–9).

51. *One day more* (p. 264): These words eventually became the title of Conrad's stage adaptation of the story when it turned out that a play called *Tomorrow* was already touring the provinces (see Appendix).

GLOSSARY

abaft, aft, after-: behind; towards the stern of the ship.

anchor-watchman: man who keeps watch while the ship is at anchor.

aneroid glass: face of an aneroid barometer.

Arcadia: region of ancient Greece in the central Peloponnese celebrated as the abode of happiness and innocence.

articles: contract between the master and crew of a ship, setting out the conditions of employment and the duties of each member of the crew.

ashore (in 'put my ship ashore'): aground.

athwartship: running across the ship.

barque: three-masted ship with fore- and main-masts square-rigged and mizzen-mast fore-and-aft rigged.

battened: secured (under hatches) with battens (strips of wood).

Bedlam: Hospital of St Mary of Bethlehem founded in 1247 in Bishopsgate and used as a lunatic asylum.

Bengal light: firework with a steady light, used as a signal flare.

billet: job, berth.

binnacle: stand on which the compass bowl is supported. The upper part consists of a protective brass hood with a lamp illuminating the compass card.

black-squad: engine-room crew.

block: one or more grooved pulleys mounted in a shell fitted with a hook.

boatswain: the petty officer immediately in charge of all deck hands. He summons the crew to their duties and relieves the watch.

boss'n: abbreviation for boatswain.

boundary-rider: (Australian) a horseman who rides around the perimeter of a stock-farm and keeps its fences in good repair.

brace: rope controlling horizontal movement of the yards.

brass-bound: gold-braided, with a secondary sense of 'tradition-bound'.

bridge: platform amidships from which the captain navigates the ship.

broached-to: turned towards the wind by a sea striking the stern.

bulkhead: vertical partition separating compartments in a ship.

bulwark: side of a ship above deck.

bummer: lazy cadger.

bunker: compartment for storing fuel below decks.

bunting: worsted or cotton stuff used for flags.

burgomaster: mayor.

capstan: drum revolving on a vertical spindle, used for raising the anchor, etc. It is operated by steam or by pushing bars inserted in horizontal sockets round the top.

Capuchin: a Franciscan friar.

Celestial: a Chinaman (from the 'Celestial Empire').

chancery, in: held under an opponent's arm in wrestling (from the tenacity of the old Court of Chancery, as in *Bleak House*).

chocks: see *rolling*.

chokey: (Anglo-Indian) prison.

chronometer: time-keeper used for determining longitude and other exact observations at sea.

close-hauled under short canvas: with ropes hauled close so as to reduce the area of the sails and make headway as close to the wind as possible.

coal-trimmer: one who stows coal in loading a ship.

coamings: raised borders around deck openings to keep out water.

cobble: a sea fishing-boat with flat bottom, square stern and lug sail, used chiefly on the NE coast of England.

Colchester: town in Essex, SE England.

coming-to: coming to a stop by turning towards the wind.

companions: skylights or window-frames admitting light to a lower deck or cabin.

compass card: the circular card representing the plane of the horizon, attached to the needle of a magnetic compass.

coon: (US) derogatory slang for a Negro; (Australian) an Aboriginal.

coram populo: in public.

crank arrested on the cant: arm on a shaft stopped in a slanting position.

crosshead: bar at the end of the piston-rod of a steam-engine which communicates the motion to the connecting-rods.

cross swell: confused, undulating irregular sea running contrary to the wind, frequently caused by the shifting wind of a cyclonic storm.

cuddy: cabin or cookroom in the fore- or after-part of a small craft.

Damocles: flatterer of the tyrant Dionysius; when asked to assume the throne he so much admired he found a sword hanging above his head by a hair.

davits: small derricks used for hoisting boats, anchor, stores, etc.

deals: boards of standard size.

debile: weak (archaic, from the French *débile*).

demurrage: compensation made to a ship for earnings lost by detention beyond the stipulated time for receiving or discharging cargo.

Der verfluchte Kerl: the cursed fellow.

dodger: canvas screen on a ship's bridge for shelter in rough weather.

donkey-man: man in charge of a donkey-boiler (a small auxiliary engine).

drawing nine feet aft: needing nine feet of water at the stern.

draws over twenty feet: has a depth of over twenty feet in the water.

dredging with the anchor down: feeling one's way downstream by using a dropped anchor as a guide.

dry stick: uninteresting, unenterprising person.

Dumbarton: town on the Clyde, near Glasgow.

Dutchman: obsolete term for a German.

Dutch Uncle: one who lectures moralistically.

écarté: card game in which cards are discarded in exchange for others.

Elbe: river flowing through Germany into the North Sea at Hamburg.

enfilading: end-to-end.

fall: loose end of a rope to which power is applied for hoisting.

fiddle: steel grating fitted over the boiler-room hatch.

fife-rail: rail arranged in a semicircle at the foot of the main-mast, provided with holes for belaying pins (on which running-ropes are coiled).

Fo-kien (Fujian): province in SE China bordering on Taiwan Strait.

forebitts: posts for fastening cable at the foremast.

forecastle: forepart of the ship under the maindeck; the crew's quarters.

forefoot: foremost end of the keel, supporting the stem of the ship.

fore-royal brace: rope of the uppermost sail on the foremast.

friction winches: machines for hoisting by ropes, fitted with a foot-brake to prevent the cones of the drum being overhauled by the load when they are out of contact with the gear wheel.

Fu-chau (now Fuzhou): port on Minjuong River on Taiwan Strait.

Gambusino: gold prospector who looks for superficial deposits of gold that can be washed down; fortune-hunter.

gamp: large umbrella (after Mrs Sara Gamp in *Martin Chuzzlewit*).

gasket: small line or canvas strap used to secure a furled sail to a yard.

German Ocean: North Sea.

gharry: (Anglo-Indian) 'A horsed vehicle resembling a bathing machine' (The Shorter OED).

gimbals: a system of rings or hoops pivoted one within the other and arranged to allow any object suspended in their centre to remain in a horizontal position regardless of the ship's motion.

gins: hoisting pulleys.

Good Hope: southernmost tip of Africa.

gunny-bags: standard-sized bags made of strong jute fabric.

Hades: mythical underworld in ancient Greece; a euphemism for Hell.

halyards: ropes for hoisting or lowering a sail, yard or flag.

hawse pipe: a pipe situated near the stem of a vessel, through which the anchor-cable runs.

head-sheets: ropes attached to fore-and-aft sails in front of the fore-mast.

heaving to: causing the wind to act on the forward surface of the sails or the sails to counteract each other, thereby checking the forward movement of the ship or immobilizing it.

Herzogin: Duchess.

'Himmel! Zwei und dreissig Pfund!': 'Heavens! Thirty-two pounds!'

hooker: originally a one-masted fishing smack; hence a depreciative or fond term for any vessel.

humped my swag: (Australian slang) tramped about with all my belongings on my back; lived rough.

in extremis: at the last gasp.

jalousies: outside shutters with slats.

Joss: a Chinese idol.

jury rudder: temporary or makeshift rudder.

keelson (pronounced kelson): a centre-line timber girder running from stem to stern inside a ship parallel with the keel, to which it is bolted so as to fasten the floor-timbers and keel together.

Klings: Indians of Asian and Malaysian seaports.

lascar: East Indian sailor.

lead-line: a line attached to a deep-sea or drift lead sinker, used for taking soundings by hand.

leeward: in the direction towards which the wind blows.

life-lines: lines stretched fore and aft along the decks to protect the crew from being washed overboard in heavy weather.

lighters: open boats used in loading and unloading ships.

log; log-book: a ship's journal or tabulated summary of the performance of the vessel and other daily events.

Lower Hope Reach: stretch of the Thames between its mouth and East Tilbury.

lug: square sail bent on a yard that hangs obliquely from a mast.

manila line: rope made from Manila hemp.

Martello tower: circular fort built for coastal defence during the Napoleonic wars.

Mazatlán: Pacific coast port in Mexico.

mizzen-mast: hindmost mast in a three-masted ship.

mizzen rigging: ropes of the mizzen-mast.

mooring-bitts: large hollow cast-iron posts, placed in pairs, to which mooring lines are made fast.

nap: card-game resembling euchre.

nota bene: please observe.

off-shore tack: that part of a zigzag course heading away from shore.

Ordinary Seaman: a member of the deck crew who is subordinate to an able seaman but has learned part of the trade and does maintenance and repairs on board. On passing an examination after a specified time he is eligible to sign on as an able seaman.

P. & O.: Peninsular and Oriental Steamship Company.

painter: rope for fastening a boat.

pintles: heavy pins or bolts on the forward edge of the rudder frame by which the rudder is hinged to the stern or rudderpost.

Platt-Deutsch (plattdeutsch): Low German dialect.

point: one of the 32 divisions of the compass, containing 11°15′.

pole-masts: masts without yards or sails.

Pond: facetious term for the Atlantic Ocean.

ports: portholes.

punkah: large mechanical fan.

quarter: curved part of a ship on either side at the stern.

quarter-deck: part of the deck to the rear of the mainmast.

quid: slang for a pound (or pounds).

Rio Gila: river flowing through New Mexico and Arizona.

River Plate (Rio de la Plata): estuary of the Paraná and Uruguay rivers between Uruguay and Argentina.

Roads, Roadstead: anchoring place for ships near a shore.

rolling chocks on bilges (also, bilge keels): fins fitted to the hull on each side of a ship at the turn of the bilge (the broadest part of a ship's bottom) to reduce rolling.

rudder chains: chains secured to the rudder horn and leading to each quarter of the vessel, used to control the vessel in case of break-down.

running gear: ropes running through blocks, used to haul spars and sails.

sampan: flat-bottomed Oriental boat.

scow: flat-bottomed boat, used as a lighter.

slice: metal bar fitted with a blade, used for clearing furnaces of clinkers.

slop-made: cheap ready-made.

slush: refuse grease and fat from cooking.

Sonora: state in northern Mexico, south of the Arizona border.

South Shields: county borough on the mouth of the Tyne, NE England.

sou'-wester: waterproof hat with a broad brim at the back to protect the neck from rain and spray.

sovereign: gold coin formerly worth one pound.

spoken them: hailed them.

starboard: right side of the ship, facing forward.

steam gear: apparatus in which a steam-engine supplies the necessary power for moving a ship's rudder.

strop: short length of rope with ends spliced together to make a loop.

Table Bay: Cape Town harbour, Republic of South Africa.

table d'hôte: hotel meal served at a fixed time and fixed price.

tack: direction taken by ship following a zig-zag course.

Talcahuano: city and port in central Chile.

Taotai: Chinese provincial officer (before 1911).

Teddington: suburb of London, near Kingston-on-Thames.

telegraph: a signalling apparatus operated by bells, gongs or horns.

tiffin: (Indian) a light meal.

tinker's curse: worthless oath.

Tophet: ancient place of human sacrifice near Jerusalem; synonym for Hell.

towing chock: iron casting at the bow through which a hawser is run for towing the ship.

treaty port: harbour on the China coast where foreigners were allowed, by treaty, to trade.

trimming ... the stokehold ventilators: turning the ventilators towards the wind so as to increase the passage of air into the stokehold.

trucks: caps at the tops of a ship's masts.

trysails: quadrilateral fore-and-aft sails with boom and gaff, carried abaft the mainmast of a brig and hoisted on a small mast called the trysail mast or on the lower mast.

turned-to: set to work.

'tween-deck: any deck below the upper deck and above the lowest deck.

watch below: seaman's time off duty.

weather-cloths: protective tarpaulins on deck.

West Hartlepool: coastal town just north of the mouth of the Tees, NE England.

wheel-house: house built over the steering wheel on the bridge as a protection for the helmsman.

whipping of the fore-royal brace: binding of twine round the end of the rope of the fore-royal (uppermost foremast) sail.

whipping up: hoisting by means of a 'whip' – a rope rove through a single fixed block.

whip-saw: narrow saw for cutting timber, often worked by two persons.

windlass: special form of winch used to hoist the anchors and house them safely, fitted with a braking device for paying out cable.

yard: a long beam on a mast for spreading square sails.

FOR THE BEST IN PAPERBACKS, LOOK FOR THE

In every corner of the world, on every subject under the sun, Penguin represents quality and variety – the very best in publishing today.

For complete information about books available from Penguin – including Puffins, Penguin Classics and Arkana – and how to order them, write to us at the appropriate address below. Please note that for copyright reasons the selection of books varies from country to country.

In the United Kingdom: Please write to *Dept E.P., Penguin Books Ltd, Harmondsworth, Middlesex, UB7 0DA.*

If you have any difficulty in obtaining a title, please send your order with the correct money, plus ten per cent for postage and packaging, to *PO Box No 11, West Drayton, Middlesex*

In the United States: Please write to *Dept BA, Penguin, 299 Murray Hill Parkway, East Rutherford, New Jersey 07073*

In Canada: Please write to *Penguin Books Canada Ltd, 2801 John Street, Markham, Ontario L3R 1B4*

In Australia: Please write to the *Marketing Department, Penguin Books Australia Ltd, P.O. Box 257, Ringwood, Victoria 3134*

In New Zealand: Please write to the *Marketing Department, Penguin Books (NZ) Ltd, Private Bag, Takapuna, Auckland 9*

In India: Please write to *Penguin Overseas Ltd, 706 Eros Apartments, 56 Nehru Place, New Delhi, 110019*

In the Netherlands: Please write to *Penguin Books Netherlands B.V., Postbus 195, NL–1380AD Weesp*

In West Germany: Please write to *Penguin Books Ltd, Friedrichstrasse 10–12, D–6000 Frankfurt/Main 1*

In Spain: Please write to *Longman Penguin España, Calle San Nicolas 15, E–28013 Madrid*

In Italy: Please write to *Penguin Italia s.r.l., Via Como 4, I-20096 Pioltello (Milano)*

In France: Please write to *Penguin Books Ltd, 39 Rue de Montmorency, F-75003 Paris*

In Japan: Please write to *Longman Penguin Japan Co Ltd, Yamaguchi Building, 2–12–9 Kanda Jimbocho, Chiyoda-Ku, Tokyo 101*

CLASSICS OF THE TWENTIETH CENTURY

Thirst for Love Yukio Mishima

Before her husband's death Etsuko had already learnt that jealousy is useless unless it can be controlled. Love, hatred, and a new, secret passion – she can control them all as long as there is hope. But as that hope fades, her frustrated desire gathers a momentum that can be checked only by an unspeakable act of violence.

The Collected Dorothy Parker

Dorothy Parker, more than any of her contemporaries, captured in her writing the spirit of the Jazz Age. Here, in a single volume, is the definitive Dorothy Parker: poetry, prose, articles and reviews. 'A good, fat book … greatly to be welcomed' – Richard Ingrams

Remembrance of Things Past (3 volumes) Marcel Proust

'What an extraordinary world it is, the universe that Proust created! Like all great novels, À la Recherche has changed and enlarged our vision of the "real" world in which we live' – Peter Quennell. Terence Kilmartin's flawless translation is 'as near to the real Proust as we can hope for' – Angus Wilson

The Sword of Honour Trilogy Evelyn Waugh

A glorious fusion of comedy, satire and farcical despair, Waugh's magnificently funny trilogy is also a bitter attack on a world where chivalry and nobility were betrayed at every hand. 'Unquestionably the finest novels to have come out of the war' – Cyril Connolly

Buddenbrooks Thomas Mann

Published in 1902, Mann's 'immortal masterpiece' was already a classic before it was banned and burned by Hitler. 'The richness and complexity … the interplay of action and ideas … has never been surpassed in German fiction' – J. P. Stern

Sanctuary William Faulkner

Faulkner draws America's Deep South exactly as he saw it – seething with life and corruption. In Sanctuary he asserts a compulsive and unsparing vision of human nature.

FOR THE BEST IN PAPERBACKS, LOOK FOR THE 🐧

CLASSICS OF THE TWENTIETH CENTURY

The Outsider   Albert Camus

Meursault leads an apparently unremarkable bachelor life in Algiers, until his involvement in a violent incident calls into question the fundamental values of society. 'The protagonist of *The Outsider* is undoubtedly the best achieved of all the central figures of the existential novel' – *Listener*

Dark as the Grave wherein my Friend is Laid   Malcolm Lowry

A Dantesque descent into hell: into Lowry's infernal landscape of Mexico – the Mexico of his masterpiece, *Under the Volcano* – and into Lowry's own personal abyss, reverberating with mental terrors and spiritual chasms.

I'm Dying Laughing   Christina Stead

A dazzling novel set in the 1930s and 1940s when fashionable Hollywood Marxism was under threat from the savage repression of McCarthyism. 'The Cassandra of the modern novel in English … reading her seems like plunging into the mess of life itself' – Angela Carter

The Desert of Love   François Mauriac

Two men, father and son, share a passion for the same woman – attractive, intelligent and proud, but an outcast from respectable society because of her position as a 'kept woman'. 'He writes with an intense, almost tempestuous force about the life of the emotions' – Olivia Manning

The Expelled and Other Novellas   Samuel Beckett

Rich in verbal and situational humour, these four stories offer the reader a fascinating insight into Beckett's preoccupation with the helpless individual consciousness, a preoccupation which has remained constant throughout his work.

Chance Acquaintances and Julie de Carneilhan   Colette

Two contrasting works in one volume. Colette's last full-length novel, *Julie de Carneilhan* was 'as close a reckoning with the elements of her second marriage as she ever allowed herself'. In *Chance Acquaintances*, Colette visits a health resort, accompanied only by her cat.

FOR THE BEST IN PAPERBACKS, LOOK FOR THE 🐧

CLASSICS OF THE TWENTIETH CENTURY

Petersburg Andrei Bely

'The most important, most influential and most perfectly realized Russian novel written in the twentieth century' (*The New York Times Book Review*), *Petersburg* is an exhilarating search for the identity of the city, presaging Joyce's search for Dublin in *Ulysses*.

The Miracle of the Rose Jean Genet

Within a squalid prison lies a world of total freedom, in which chains become garlands of flowers – and a condemned prisoner is discovered to have in his heart a rose of monstrous size and beauty. Of this profoundly shocking novel Sartre wrote: 'Genet holds the mirror up to us: we must look at it and see ourselves.'

Labyrinths Jorge Luis Borges

Seven parables, ten essays and twenty-three stories, including Borges's classic 'Tlön, Uqbar; Orbis Tertius', a new world where external objects are whatever each person wants, and 'Pierre Menard', the man who rewrote *Don Quixote* word for word without ever reading the original.

The Vatican Cellars André Gide

Admired by the Dadaists, denounced as nihilist, defended by its author as a satirical farce: five interlocking books explore a fantastic conspiracy to kidnap the Pope and place a Freemason on his throne. *The Vatican Cellars* teases and subverts as only the finest satire can.

The Rescue Joseph Conrad

'The air is thick with romance like a thunderous sky...' 'It matters not how often Mr Conrad tells the story of the man and the brig. Out of the million stories that life offers the novelist, this one is founded upon truth. And it is only Mr Conrad who is able to tell it us' – Virginia Woolf

Southern Mail/Night Flight Antoine de Saint-Exupéry

Both novels in this volume are concerned with the pilot's solitary struggle with the elements, his sensation of insignificance amid the stars' timelessness and the sky's immensity. Flying and writing were inextricably linked in the author's life and he brought a unique sense of dedication to both.

CLASSICS OF THE TWENTIETH CENTURY

Victory Joseph Conrad

Victory is both a tale of rescue and adventure and a perceptive study of a complex relationship and the power of love. Its hero Axel Heyst was described by Jocelyn Baines as 'perhaps the most interesting and certainly the most complex' of Conrad's characters.

The Apes of God Wyndham Lewis

'It is so immense, I have no words for it,' commented T. S. Eliot on his blistering satire on twenties Bohemianism. Lewis's prose is as original and exciting as Joyce's, and the verbal savagery of his lampooning reads like a head-on collision between Swift and the Machine Age.

Bend Sinister Vladimir Nabokov

A satirical fantasy on the rise of a tyrant state run by the 'Average Man' Party, which – under the slogans of equality and happiness for all – destroys individualism and free intelligence. 'Nabakov remains ... profoundly of our time and one of its spokesmen' – George Steiner

The Rainbow D. H. Lawrence

Suppressed by outraged moralists within six weeks of publication, *The Rainbow* is today seen as a great work of the metaphysical imagination that, despite its meticulous attention to detail and local colour, is both visionary and prophetic.

Tales of the Pacific Jack London

Shattered by tropical disease, London spent the last months of his life writing in Hawaii. Springing from his desire to reconcile the dream of an unfallen world with the harsh reality of twentieth-century materialism, these stories combine the power of Hemingway with a mastery of the short story form equal to Conrad's.

Clayhanger Arnold Bennett

The first book in the Clayhanger trilogy is a vivid portrayal of English provincial life at the turn of the century, revealing Bennett's fascination with the romance of manufacturing industry and also its slovenly ugliness.